CROWN OF MY ENEMY

LOVELY ENEMIES SERIES

A QUEEN BOWS FOR NO MAN, NOT EVEN A KING.

BY T.A.BENTON

Crown Of My Enemy

LOVELY ENEMIES SERIES

T.A. BENTON

For my Favorite Humans, Thank you for making life worthwhile.

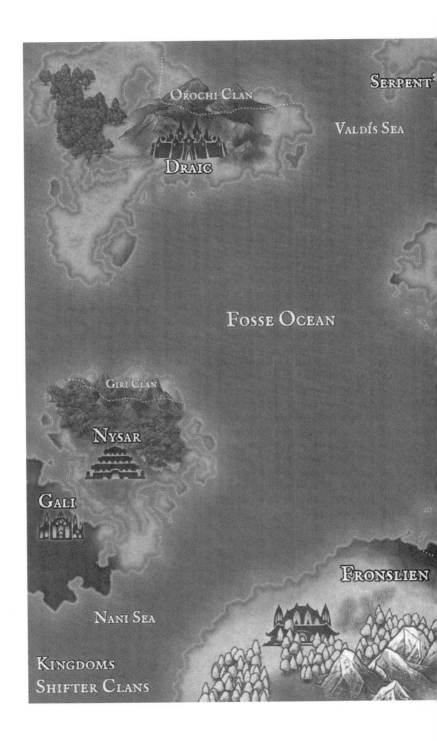

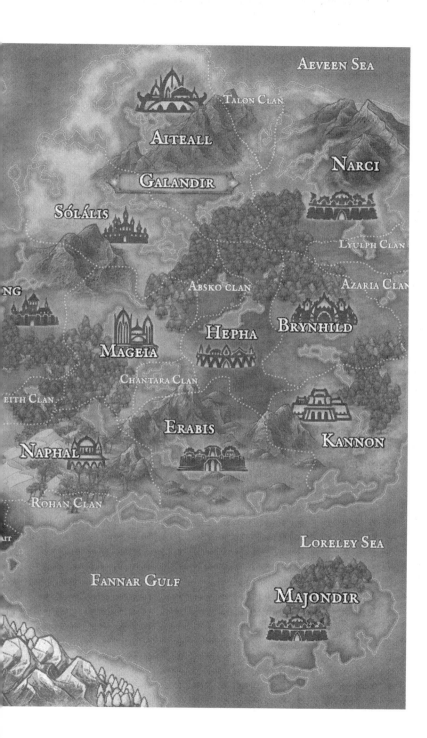

Prologue

OUR ENEMIES HAVE A WAY OF BREAKING US
OPEN AND BLEEDING US DRY.

DEVANY

It's early morning when I stumble into the kitchen for breakfast, mummy humming quietly to herself at the sink.

Her pale blonde hair is pulled back in one of those long, intricate braids that she loves so much, with soft curls framing her face. When she turns around, the sunlight streaming in from the window behind her makes her appear almost ethereal.

"Be sure to eat all your food if you wish to accompany your father to market," she states by way of greeting, a soft smile playing at her lips before turning back to finish the dishes.

I make my way to the table, and I can't suppress the groan when I see my plate—she knows I hate bacon. I'm not a big fan of meat in general, which is why she pushes the matter. Sighting something about wanting me to grow up strong. I'm strong enough for thirteen. I don't think bacon is going to make a difference. Quietly I pick up a slice, then slip my hand beneath the table to feed it to the dog.

"Don't even think about it, young lady." I jolt at the sound of my father's amused voice, catching me in the act with my fingertip's centimeters away from the dog's mouth. Juno's hot, damp breath washes over my hand as he waits patiently for his prize.

Daddy stands in the doorway, arms crossed, his red flannel shirt tucked into his plain brown pants. The heavy wool fabric pulled tight over his large chest with his suspenders hanging loose at his sides. His eyes dance with laughter even as he gives me a pointed look that has me placing the bacon back on my plate, though I have no intention of eating it.

I put on my best puppy dog eyes, ready to plead my case.

"Da—" I'm cut off by the sound of the back door ricocheting off the wall, the sound of it echoing down the long hall. Then the sound of pounding feet. My eyes go wide, and I suck in a surprised breath, twisting toward the back of the house. *What's going on?*

Before my mind fully comprehends the sound, Daddy yanks me from my chair, his fingertips digging into the sensitive skin under my arms. The chair scrapes along the wood floor before falling with a loud thump. The noise is almost deafening in the sudden silence. Several men crowd the wide doorway that leads into the kitchen from the back of the house. They don't move right away, their eyes moving over the three of us.

The calm before the storm.

The metallic taste of power coats my tongue as mom raises her hands. Water dances between her fingers and twists about her body—accumulating in the air before her, flowing in from the sink and flower vases, even the glasses on the table. Her silvery blonde hair breaks free of its braid, floating in a halo around her head.

Power pulses through the room, electrifying the small space as she pulls harder on the surrounding elements. The water now streams through the window behind her.

Her glamour falls away, leaving a terrifying beauty behind. Her skin shimmers iridescently in the light of the dawning sun. Her bright cerulean eyes pulse with power. But it's the finely pointed ears that give her away as *other*.

Our breath fogs, and the hair on my arms stands on end as the temperature plummets. The water freezes into spikes and with the flick of her wrist; they slice through the space, impaling the first man to step into the room. His blood and brain matter splatter the wall behind him.

I stand, unable to move, transfixed by the sight of the bright purplish blood sliding down the wall.

"Richard, get her out!" Mom's panicked voice brings me back to the present, my gaze swinging in her direction.

"What? Mum, no!" She looks to me, her eyes bright and vivid through unshed tears. It holds both an apology and a plea, begging me to go, but I can't leave her.

I can only manage to shake my head in response. When what I really want is to rage—to scream and cry at how unfair it all is. She looks over my shoulder to Daddy before her eyes slide back to the men in the doorway.

"We're leaving. Now!" Daddy says, grabbing my arm and dragging me away.

A heavy thud vibrates the front door, the hinges rattling from the force of it.

It's too late to escape now, they've cut us off.

"Come out, come out, wherever you are," A man taunts from the other side of the door, laughter soon following.

The door shakes violently again, testing the limits of the hinges until they ultimately fail and the door splinters inward. The men push their way through the doorway, climbing over the splintered remains. Their towering frames clad in finely tailored blue and gray uniforms.

They've trapped us, cutting us off from both exits. The normally open space feels far too small with the addition of our unwelcome guests, like the room no longer has enough air to sustain us all.

Their vacant eyes fall on me, and I take an unconscious step back. A fear-filled gasp falls from my lips. Daddy moves forward, blocking me from view with his large frame. But one still has me in his sights.

A shiver works its way up my spine at what I see in those dark eyes. That unconscious step. That single sign of fear has his eyes dancing in anticipation. His gaze trails down my body, a sadistic smile curling his lips. Fear clogs my throat, and my stomach threatens to revolt. My mum has always said 'the eyes don't lie,' I now understand what she meant. Their eyes are dull and lifeless, devoid of any emotion beyond malice.

Thick purple veins stand out against their unnaturally large muscles, and no matter the hue of their complexion, their skin seems leeched of color.

The heavy clink of steel and the following thud draws my attention away from the intruder. Daddy is sword to sword with one of them. Another's bleeding out on the ground.

I stare at the creep for so long I lost sight of the others. *Where is the third man?*

As if in answer to my question, someone wraps their hands around my neck from behind, shoving me to my knees. My eyes water, and it feels as if my ribs are crushing my lungs. My chest burns, frantic for even a single breath. I claw blindly at his wrist, digging my nails into the skin. Specks of bright light dance before my eyes, my head feeling weighty and dull. The edges of my vision blacken as the seconds tick by, and my hands slip away. Just as I'm about to lose consciousness, the pressure releases and with a desperate breath, I fill my lungs.

I collapse to my hands and knees as a body crumbles to the floor beside me, and I watch transfixed as water from the sink forces its way down my assailant's throat. Wet gurgling noises and distraught grunts leave his mouth.

I look up to find mummy standing in the middle of the room, with a fire raging behind her and smoke filling the space. She's walled off the men in the back hall with large blocks of ice. The look of hate that crosses my mum's lovely face is something I've never seen before. Her lips pull back from her teeth and her eyes are hard, like chips of ice.

She holds her hand out in his direction. The temperature drops once more. Ice skates across the floor to him, hoarfrost coating his neck. His throat swells and becomes bright red. As the water solidifies, the skin turns a blue so dark it's black. Like a deep bruise on a dead man. He thrashes on the floor, clawing at his skin, digging deep, bloody furrows into the flesh as if he can somehow clear his airway. It only takes seconds for him to stop moving, a thick layer of ice encasing his throat.

White noise fills my ears, as if I've been submerged in water. Numb and hollow, where do I go? I stagger to my feet, the small space filled with soldiers. *There's nowhere to hide.*

The whorl of bright color and blurry images overwhelm my vision as I fight to hold down the bile that threatens to escape.

I barely get my feet under me when I see another man pushing his way toward me. Frantically, I try to find somewhere to run or hide. But I have nowhere to go.

Backing away slowly, I trip over the deadman, landing on my back hard enough to force a painful breath from my lungs. The soldier reaches me before I can get to my feet, wrapping my hair around his meaty hand and dragging me to my knees. *Where are they all coming from?* My mind stops short when warm blood splatters on my face. The metallic scent of it stuck in my nose. I open my eyes and watch pull his sword back. *When had I closed my eyes? Coward!*

Mum screams out in agony, and the smell of burning flesh draws my attention to her. The soldiers have burned their way through the ice block and are now advancing.

Fire hovers in the hand of the soldier closest to mum, and an angry burn now covers most of her arm. The embers of fire dance behind her as the cabinets go up in flames. The soldier's sharply pointed ears tell me all I need to know. *They're Valore, elemental magic users. Just like Mum.*

Daddy jumps into the fray, rushing toward her. His sword cutting forward, piercing the chest of the man closest to her.

I fight to get back to my feet but only manage a step before my hair is pulled tight by my assailant before he spins me around and shoves me against the wall. A pained sound escapes my throat when he grinds my cheek against the worn wood, splinters digging into the soft flesh. The weight of his forearm sits heavy between my shoulder blades, pinning me in place. He kicks my legs apart and shoves his knee between them, his heavy weight making it impossible to move.

"You sure are pretty. Unfortunately, there won't be much of you left when we're done. Such a shame." The moist heat of his rancid breath coats my ear.

His warm, wet tongue licks along my jaw, and his teeth tease my earlobe. I try to turn away, but he roughly smashes my face against the wood once more in punishment before burying his nose in the crook of my neck. His fingers gather up the fabric of my skirt along my thighs.

I close my eyes firmly, trying to pretend I'm anywhere but here. Abruptly, the weight of his body is gone, followed by a heavy thump. When I open my eyes, his blood is pooling at my feet.

"Run, Devany!" The urgency in Daddy's voice is enough to wake me from my stupor. My feet move before I give his command conscious thought.

My hands are shaking, my movement jerky, making it difficult to get a hold of the fragmented pieces of the door. Each piece of wood far too heavy for me to move alone, leaving a small space close to the floor my only way out. Out of options, I have no other choice, but I get on my belly and crawl through the too small hole. Scraping my back and shoulders along the exposed wood. I turn back in time to see a sword pierce through Daddy's chest and the light go out in his brown eyes. His lifeless body crumples to the kitchen floor.

But I do as I'm told and run. Mom's screams follow me through the yard and into the woods.

My heartbeat rushes past my ears like a giant ocean crashing against the shore. I break through the trees; the branches tear at my skin and hair, leaving behind lines of fire that bring more tears to my eyes. My breath comes far too quickly, and my chest hurts so much—*Just keep going, that's all I have to do. Just a little further. If I can just make it to town, I can get help.*

Each panicked thought races through my mind. The unending flow of tears warps the world around me. A thin layer of sweat coats my skin, running down the back of my neck. My calves and thighs burn, and the heavy pounding of my bare feet against the ground feels too loud in the early morning quiet.

Rocks and twigs jam into the soft skin of my exposed feet, but I can't stop. I push harder, faster, to close the distance between me and the woods. Each ragged breath I take scorches my lungs. My throat is so dry it hurts to swallow. *Goddess, please don't let them follow me.*

Compelled by fear, I look over my shoulder just as I break through the underbrush and collide with something hard enough to knock me off my feet, sending me to the ground with a heavy thud. The impact knocks a painful breath from my chest as a horrible wailing sound escapes. *They've caught me.*

"Hey there, watch where you're going." The sound of his voice was loud in the quiet woods.

My muscles tense as I prepare to run. I keep my eyes on the ground like a coward, not wanting to see the strike coming.

"It's ok. You don't have to cry. Are you hurt?" His tone is gentle and much too close.

I look up and try to scoot away from the man kneeling in front of me. But he's not a man at all. He couldn't be much older than me. His warm brown hair hangs in waves just past his chin, sharply pointed ears cutting through the soft strands. *Another Valore.*

"There she is." A smile lights up his face, softening his sharp features. And for a moment, it feels like everything is going to be alright. But his questions bring it all back.

Slowly he raises his hand and wipes the tears from my cheek. "Are you alright?" he asks once again, but his hand freezes when he notices the rips in my clothes.

"What happened to you?" His eyes move over me, making note of every rip, stain, and bruise. "Who did this?" He goes perfectly still, his eyes darkening. His face clears of all emotions as he stares down at me.

"I'm not going to hurt you," he whispers, and I believe him. It makes absolutely no sense, but I do. "Just tell me what happened." Where there had been light in his voice, it was now something dark and frightening. His eyes bore into mine so intensely that I find myself compelled to answer.

"There were so many of them. They broke into our house— my ... my dad is dead—my mum... my mum..." I can't bring myself to say what they could be doing to her. The quiver in my voice distorts my words as I stutter around my sobs, but he understands just the same.

Goddess, my chest hurts. It feels like it's breaking open.

"Alright," he says as he gets to his feet, reaching down and pulling me to mine.

He places his warm hand on my lower back, and he leads me deeper into the woods, under the thick cover of the trees. I dig my heels in to stop us from going any further.

This isn't the way to town.

But he's stronger than me. Trying *once more* to stop us from moving, I turn around completely to face him. This time, he stops and looks at me. I hadn't realized how much taller he was than me, and I take an instinctive step back. His eyes soften when he sees the terror in my eyes.

"I have to get help, there's still a chance to save my mom!" Though I have no idea what this may do to her. *It's just... I can't lose her. She's all I have left in this world. What would I do without her?* Tears of frustration fall from my eyes. *It's not fair—none of this is fair.*

"Okay, Shhh. I've got you now... Just let me get you somewhere safe and I'll go check on your parents." He leads me toward a gigantic tree covered in twisted vines of ivy. With the flick of his wrist, the ivy parts, revealing an opening just big enough for me.

"In you go."

I take his hand in mine and squeeze. "No. No. I'm going with you... take me with you." I don't want to say it, but I'm scared. I look around nervously, shifting from foot to foot, spying on the shadows cast by the trees as the morning sun makes its way across the sky. *What if they find me?*

He kneels in front of me so that we're eye-to-eye, tucking a lock of hair behind my ear before cupping my face with his hands. His eyes move between mine as he talks. "Shhh, it's safer for you here. I'll be right back... promise." His soothing words calm some of my panic, but the adrenaline still courses through my veins. "Right back." He repeats the words and stands. The curtain of vines falls back, hiding me from the world.

Chapter One
TEN YEARS LATER

ASHER

Ansel sits across from me in my tent, his body strung tight, radiating tension. I stand at the foot of my pallets, contemplating which weapons to take with me on our ride into Erabis.

His fingers drum against the wood chest he's sitting on as he works hard not to raise his voice. I know my safety is his main concern, but I've been working toward this moment for the last ten years and I'm well aware of the dangers.

Ten years of planning and building an army. Carefully moving the game pieces around on the board to best suit my outcome, and now it's time to take what I came for.

Kól has asked for this face-to-face meeting to broker peace. Though peace has very little to do with it, I'm sure. He just wants to save his own ass and he'll do damn near anything to get me to move on from Erabis' border.

I'm going to walk straight into his kingdom and walk out with his most prized possession. A woman that I have thought about and coveted for more years than I care to admit.

I decide on easily concealed weapons; two daggers, one at my waist, the other in my boot. Methodically, I go through the motions of securing my weapons. To my forearm I strap a small but lethal three-blade Katar—a gift from a friend in Naphal.

Ansel's stare weighs heavily on my back while he evaluates whether it's in his best interest to speak his mind. Though I'm not entirely sure why; we both know he's going to say it, anyway.

He stands and begins pacing. "Are you sure this is a good idea?... I mean, you don't know how she may have turned out. All the rumors point to her being nothing more than a spoiled brat who cares only for herself, just like her father. Furthermore, there are no accounts of her having an ounce of power. She has none of the physical markers of a Valore."

It appears he has quite a few concerns... Ultimately; it changes nothing. But I understand his concerns. I turn around, giving him my full attention, wanting him to comprehend this is my final decision.

"Yes, this is a good idea. Hell, it's our only choice if we want to win this war. You know as well as I do that Minas won't be deterred. The enemy will be on our doorstep sooner than any of us are ready for. As far as how she turned out, it is what it is because the Goddess knows we need her. As far as power goes, she has it... Trust me. It may be latent, living within the warded walls of her father's kingdom. But more than likely she knows how to hide it, which would speak to the fact that she has no physical traits."

Ansel stops pacing with a long, low sigh leaving his throat. He stands at the foot of my bed, scrubbing a hand over his beard, as his gaze finally meets mine. I stare back at him and his shoulders slump in defeat, conceding I won't be dissuaded from my path.

The two of us have been together a long time. Each of us had been picked up and cared for by a caravan of thieves, mercenaries, and assassins as children. All of us trained to survive in a post-war world, where many live their lives with an every-man-for-himself mentality.

We each have a story of woe for how we got here after The Great War ended. Hell, everyone does at this point. But the past is irrelevant in the here and now.

There's not much I wouldn't do to keep those I care for safe. The Great War nearly destroyed the entire continent of Galandir. Many of the kingdoms are still recovering from the losses, and I have a feeling this time around we may not be so lucky.

This is the only course of action.

I grab my tunic from the small table in the corner and turn to find Ansel studying me. His dark brows drawn tight over his eyes and his nostrils flare with each breath he takes.

He's dressed in his fighting leathers. The crest of our kingdom emblazoned on his chest—two dragons in flight creating a circle, each eating the other's tail. His straight, auburn hair is braided away from his face, showing off his steeply pointed ears. His darker tan complexion is just enough of a hint that he's originally from the kingdom of Naphal.

We stare at each other, neither giving an inch.

When he says nothing, I pull on my tunic. The finest I brought with us on our march across Galandir with this meeting in mind. The fabric a blue so dark that it appears black until you step into the light, with the cuffs and collar adorned with gold embroidery.

I know this isn't easy for him... allowing me to walk into danger. Always playing the big brother, even knowing I can take care of myself.

But... as my second, he knows this is a sound plan.

If she is as Ansel fears, then I will use her for my own ends.

"Let's fetch my new bride, shall we?"

"What makes you so sure he's going to hand his daughter over to you? His only daughter, I might add." His copper eyes flash with concern and some amusement, his dark brows lift in question.

"Simple, old friend, I won't be giving him any other choice."

My voice is hard and unbending by the time the last word leaves my mouth.

There will be no other outcome. I may have only a small faction of my army with me, but it's still enough to cause a great deal of destruction.

She will be mine, just as she was meant to be.

Ansel and I walk through the rows of tents, greeting the people milling about. Each of them on high alert and cautiously optimistic of what's to come.

We're forty years removed from the end of The Great War, and we all feel the heavy breath of war on our necks once again. But with Devany's ties to the kingdoms of Aiteall and Erabis, we at least stand a chance.

I break off from the group, heading for the outer ring of tents, toward the temporary stables to retrieve Balius. The handsome beast waits patiently for me, a perfect specimen of a war horse. Standing tall enough to tower over me, his sleek charcoal coat is complemented beautifully by an onyx mane.

The stable master bows his head as he hands me the reins before retreating to retrieve Ansel's horse. I take the moment to center myself while my hands coast over Balius's thick mane. I send a silent prayer up to Cillian, the God of safe travel and protection.

The sun has barely crested the trees and the temperature is quickly rising. I swing up into my saddle, taking one last deep breath before directing Balius out of the stables, westward, towards the border Nephal shares with Erabis.

Toward my future.

The midday sun beats down on us as we crest the hills that lead to the city proper. Sweat drips between my shoulder blades, my cloak doing me no favors in the afternoon heat, outside of keeping my tunic clean.

We stand at the line of demarcation, where Naphal ends and Erabis begins. Lush land gives way to dead, cracked earth, with little to no vegetation. Beyond that, you can just make out the city of Achlys through the thin haze of dust. A great wall surrounds the whole of the capital city. The battlement stained with the blood of magic users.

Some may look at that wall and think it's protecting the people within from invasion, but they'd be mistaken. It's meant to keep them in. Hemmed in by nothing but barren land and skeletal trees as far as the eye can see, the air thick with filth and disease.

His people die inside a little more each year, and does Kól, that old fuck, care for his people's plight? The answer to that question is no... Not one fucking bit. These people work his lands, trying to get them to yield enough to not only pay their tithes, but feed their families.

No matter how hard they work, it will never produce enough because these lands are as barren as his cold, black heart.

A small wave of my hand signals my men to follow me toward the massive gate within the wall, one step closer to furthering my plan.

A step closer to her.

As we cross the boundary of the city, I feel the protection wards skate over my skin, recognizing me as different. When preparing for this mission, I made sure my men were aware of the likelihood of wards protecting the city. Although using the word *protecting* is a stretch because they can't actually keep us out, only make it uncomfortable to pass over, but rich humans enjoy lying to themselves. This is just another farce that couldn't be further from the truth. Even a weaker Valore can pass through wards, it just... hurts more. What has growing up behind these warded walls done to her powers? Or her, for that matter?

The conditions within the city proper aren't much better than the lands outside the wall. Filth and debris clutter the streets.

The foul stench of bodily waste assaults my senses. There are people unconscious in the alleyways. The buildings are old and in desperate need of repair. I don't hear the sounds of children in the streets. In fact, the streets are oppressively quiet. The people we pass keep their eyes on the ground in hopes we won't turn our attention toward them, no doubt living in a constant state of fear.

We reach a large well in the middle of the city. From here, we have a clear view of the palace just past the abandoned market square. It hides on a hill behind a wall almost as high as the main battlement, looking down on all those Kól finds unworthy.

A thick iron gate is the only thing that breaks up the dingy stone barrier. I make note of the fifteen guards patrolling the parapet, all of them furious they must allow me passage.

The palace itself is made up of the same drab stonework, lacking warmth of any kind. The upper floor windows, tall and thin, more than likely by design as a protection if the palace were ever attacked. I think Kól finds it to be a happy coincidence that the design limits sunlight from penetrating too deeply within the palace. Just one more way to further oppress his people.

There are no windows on the lower levels, and the small bricked-in courtyard is composed of wooden stables and cobblestone floors that are covered in dirt, clay, and grime.

What must it have been like for her to grow up here, surrounded by wards meant to keep Valore out?

We arrive at the palace gates far faster than I had anticipated, pulled from my thoughts by the loud *clank* of the iron gate.

The concerns of her powers will have to be a problem for another day. It's time to divest King Kól of his no-doubt lovely daughter, if her mother's looks were anything to go by. She had once been one of the most beautiful of women to grace this world according to most.

I make eye contact with each of my men, a look meant to remind them of the surrounding dangers.

"Look alive boys, we're bringing home my bride today." My

tone is jovial and unworried. The face of a carefree king, completely secure in his ability to walk away with what he came for.

Devany is mine!

"The fuck you are," one guard, in a sea of red uniforms, huffs under his breath as if he has any say in today's outcome. He's obviously ignorant of how good a Valore's hearing is.

My head swings toward the offending voice, pinning him in place with my stare. The smile vanishes from my face like the illusion it was, replaced by something cold and vicious.

"Care to place a wager?" I query.

"There's no way the king would hand over our princess to the likes of you." It seems the foolish oaf wishes to push his luck. Far be it from me to stop him if that's the way he wants to play it.

Dismounting, I hand my reins over to one of my men and move toward the offending male with slow, measured steps. Those around him hurry to remove themselves from my path. No one willing to stand with him in the face of my ire.

I stop within striking distance, looking down into his fearful dull gray eyes, his pasty face leeching of color. It seems he is no longer so brave now that the twenty-odd men that had been between us have gone.

"If a wager is what you wish, here are the terms. Should I leave here empty-handed with no agreement for her hand, I will give you twenty gold pieces." A grin lights up his greedy face, surely already counting his winnings before he's even gotten his hands on them.

"But should I win..." I pause to add a little more drama to the moment, looking over my shoulder at Ansel to see what he thinks of this. He just continues to stare back at me like I've lost my everloving mind. I throw him a wink, and he rolls his eyes. I'm sure he's wishing he could throttle me at this point. That look alone has me smirking at him, turning my smile just a little more real, flashing him one of my fangs. Slowly, I move my gaze back to the guard. I'm in no real hurry here. Making Kól wait shows him and his guards, who really holds the power here. "Your life is forfeit." The words are as cold as the smile I give him. Amused, as I watch the color drain from his face.

I've wasted enough time here. I signal for my men to follow me, and we head for the large, ornately carved doors leading into the great hall.

Chapter Two

ASHER

A servant approaches us in the courtyard. The worn fabric of his once deep burgundy uniform hangs from his gaunt frame, swallowing his slender figure. The man is obviously half-starved. As a matter of fact, outside of the guards...they all are.

He bows deeply at the waist, stumbling forward a bit, his feet unsteady with the motion. *"My Lord."*

"Go on then!" I huff, already pissed off from the earlier exchange.

He rises from his bow, steadier on his feet this time around. His full height rivaling that of my men. His ashen skin appears too tight over his prominent features. Crescent bruises mar the skin below his eyes, as if he wears a mask of death.

"This way, My Lord." With a slight tremor in his voice and his eyes on the ground he points us toward a towering wooden door inlaid with iron.

It takes two guards to open the massive doors. The carved panels depict a scene of what this kingdom had once been. They show the landscape abundant with lush trees and green valleys, a land teeming with life. It's nothing but a stark reminder of everything they lost once Kól became king.

We move no further than the atrium. The servant remains as a small eternity passes before he tentatively meets my gaze.

"Well?" A hard look from me has him moving swiftly to lead us on to the throne room.

We begin the journey through the dark halls. The lanterns barely give off enough light to chase away the shadows. They linger in the corners, their tentacles stretching out toward the dim light filtering in through the thin windows overhead.

The servant turns down corridor after corridor, and we stalk closely behind as we navigate through the labyrinth of hallways. The thick rugs lining the floors muffle our footfalls.

Where most rulers use gold and silver to adorn their palaces as a show of wealth, Kól has chosen iron. Every door is inlaid with it. Every fixture is made from it. Many believe that iron can kill us, though that isn't the truth of it. If we encounter large quantities, it can cause a type of blood sickness. It can even nullify a weaker Valore's power temporarily. But we wouldn't die from it unless it was used to remove our heads. But let's be honest, who wouldn't die from having their head removed? No one, so it's a moot point.

Wounds made with any other weapon will heal as if they had never happened, but injuries made with iron will scar. It is a disconcerting thought that she has been surrounded by it damn near her whole life.

The servant leads us to a set of large doors made of Rowan wood at the end of the hall. Two human guards of decent height stand to the side, opening it just as we come upon them, both sneering in our direction.

The throne room is poorly lit, just as I suspected it would be. Candles are lit around the edge of the room, creating little pools of light that don't quite reach the center of the hall. Sunlight trickles in from the thin windows that line the tops of the high walls. A long crimson rug leads us to a dais where their shitty king sits upon a throne of iron. His salt and pepper hair unkempt and desperately in need of cutting. The lines of his aging face are deeply carved into his skin, like a map of rivers. I haven't seen him up close since my father died nearly twenty-four years ago.

He stares at us with unadulterated disgust. My only response to all the hostility is a wide smile. After all, I'm winning.

"Kól, I hope I've found you well this afternoon." I couldn't care less about the old fuck. I just wanted to address him without his title. In response, his pale skin flushes with anger. It seems the offense didn't go unnoticed.

"Asher," he says in a raspy growl, trying his best to be intimidating. Though he still puts on a welcoming façade as servants enter with offerings of food and drink. I raise my hand stopping the servants where they are. I'd much rather get to business.

"We're not here to exchange niceties neither of us feels. So, let's get down to it, shall we?" That angry flush only deepens. But beneath it, I can see true fear. No doubt worried his reckoning has finally come—and it has. Just not in the form he expects.

His eyes narrow to slits as he regards me. "Out with it then! What will it take to get you and that demon-army away from my people?"

Like he cares for any of them. They wallow in filth, merely existing while ravaged by starvation and disease as they bury their loved ones. All the while he sits up here untouchable.

A serpent's smile plays on my lips. "Your daughter."

He practically sputters when the words leave my mouth. I'd bet in all his musings he never thought I'd ask for her. The one thing he can't afford to lose, and the one thing I won't leave without. If he knew how badly I needed her, he'd use it against me. Not even my men know why I want her, other than to deal a blow to our enemy. To possibly right a wrong done to our people when he stole her mother away.

Kól gives me three slow blinks before answering. "Why would you have want for my daughter? I have had her tested. She takes not after her mother."

I tense at the word 'tested.' My men all growl, no doubt

wondering what this old fuck did to a child in the name of *testing*. He either doesn't notice the tension that now fills the air, or he's disregarding the potential for violence that now ripples through the room. He just keeps right on talking. "In every way known to my scholars. She is—by all accounts—human."

Although I want nothing more than to remove his head from his skinny neck, I school my features into a mask of indifference. "I care not for your scholars' *findings*; I want her because it is my right to have her. It's the only true sign you will keep your end of the peace agreement. Besides, our children will be heirs to two kingdoms. They will hold power in two worlds," I reply, grinning at the bastard as if this were the whole reason I want her. His eyes light at the idea of having his tainted hands in two kingdoms. Sure, his daughter will give him a foothold in my lands.

"I think of this as more than just peace, but an opportunity for both of us to profit."

I can see the moment he decides this is worth the cost of selling his daughter in the name of so-called peace. I'm sure he's already thinking about how to kill me and whether he'll allow me to put my filthy hands on his precious daughter before I die.

"James," his beady eyes turn to the tall servant at his side, "collect Devany. Let her know her presence is required."

The servant pales slightly at the request, his shoulders creeping up toward his ears. He casts a quick look in both our directions before leaving the room.

There is no idle chit-chat to be had, nothing but tense silence. On their part, of course, not ours. The human guards stand at the ready along the perimeter of the throne room, waiting for an order that isn't going to come if Kól wishes to avoid war.

Everything is going as I had hoped. Though things could still go wrong, I don't see how it being anything we can't handle.

Kól stares daggers at me as the silence stretches on, but I pay him no attention as the delicate sound of heels clicking against the stone floor reaches my ears. It's time to take what I came for.

All that shit goes right out the window the moment she walks in. If her mother was considered beautiful, she could only be described as *devastating*.

I've never seen a lovelier creature. Her eyes shine silver, ringed in dark blue like the moon encased in midnight skies. A mass of curls that glimmer like spun strands of caramel and golden light frame a stunning face.

Her honeyed skin shimmers as if kissed by the sun, making her features even more striking. Delicately arched eyebrows lead down to the soft curve of her nose. My gaze falls upon full heart-shaped lips the pale color of crushed roses.

Greedily, I follow the graceful slope of her neck. My fangs aching to sink into the fluttering pulse of her vein and drink my fill of her. I imagine any man would gladly fall to his ruin to possess a creature as beautiful as the one approaching the dais.

"Ah, there's my beautiful daughter. Come here and sit with me, child. This is Asher of Draic, the king who has been marching across the human lands toward us and our people," he says it with more disgust than he did when we first arrived. His disdain is clear in the lines of his aging face. His murky blue eyes look upon me as if I am the very dirt under his shoes.

His tone is meant to taint her opinion of me. I could have told him he needn't bother. I shall make her detest me well enough on my own because I'm about to thrust her to the forefront of the war. Tearing her from her soft and sheltered life. I will show her the atrocities her father has and continues to commit against her own people, human and Valore alike.

"He has come with an offer of peace. An agreement that will bond our two kingdoms." A sick, greedy grin curls his lips, revealing yellowed teeth. His eyes alight in anticipation of her reaction.

"And what, pray tell, have you offered him for this peace?" she asks him, in a voice devoid of emotion, her tone suggesting she couldn't care less. But she doesn't remove her gaze from mine. That haughty air only adds to her appeal. I can see the cruel smile he gives her out of the corner of my eye as he turns to her. She knows the answer. She just wants to hear him say it.

"You." Her eyes close as the cold word falls from his lips with finality.

His smile grows with each second that passes without a reaction from her. She sits silently with her eyes closed, taking a deep breath. When she opens them, they burn like molten silver.

I had expected tears, not burning flames, but that's what I get. White hot fire scorching all those in its path. And I for one, can't wait to get burned.

Devany jumps from her seat so quickly that the heavy throne she sits on nearly topples over. The personal guard who accompanied her into the throne room catches it before it can fall. It all happens far too quickly for Kól or his guards to see, but I take notice. Whomever this man may be, he knows something of what she is.

This is the first sign that Valore blood runs through her veins.

"You gave me away... To him?" Devany swings her arm out, waving a hand in my general direction. Her tone is both enraged and resentful. But the truly sad thing is that she doesn't even sound surprised by this turn of events. Just furious. She'll need that fire for what's coming.

"You should've just offered him a cow and two fucking goats. Do I mean so little? You know what—" she says, shaking her head in clear disbelief. "Don't answer that." Fury comes off her in waves, filling the room with her displeasure. How the man believes her to be human is beyond me. The guards behind him shift nervously as she grows more agitated.

I swear, I have never had a woman act as if she would rather suck off a troll than marry me. Though I do like seeing that she has a bit of a backbone.

"You will watch how you speak to me. The child you will bear will rule two kingdoms, locking all those who would oppose us between two great armies." His greed is a physical presence: heavy, dark, and ugly. It tinges the air with its unctuous aura.

"Fuck. Your. Armies." Each word said with a slow measured step toward her father. The look that graces her magnificent face is full of ice and the smile she gives the man she calls father is cold and sharp, chilling the room.

The guard closest to Kól takes a hesitant step forward and moves as if to pull his weapon but gets no further than placing his hand on the hilt. The blade of Devany's young guard cuts through the air, the sound no more than an assassin's whisper. His sword comes to a stop against the unnamed guard's neck.

"Draw that weapon and I will gut you." The young guard's eyes darken with the anticipation of violence, the hint of a cruel smile curving his lips. He wants to hurt this man for thinking he had the right to harm her.

The older man releases his hold on the hilt of his weapon, raising his trembling hands slowly in surrender. He swallows audibly, hissing as the blade nicks his throat in the process. Glistening crimson droplets trickle from the superficial cut.

His reaction was so visceral I'm left wondering about the depth of the relationship between the two. Sharing has never been a strong skill of mine.

"Stand down, Kane." Devany's soft voice rings clear amongst the powerful voices growing louder around her.

Kane pulls his sword away from the man's thick neck without taking his eyes off him. Returning to her side, he angles himself into a defensive position, ready to intervene should anyone forget their place.

"I've already agreed to his terms. You will be wed in the morning and depart shortly thereafter. I will have your compliance!" Spittle flies from his mouth, his voice growing more agitated with each word.

Devany looks Kól in the eye as she replies. I'm not sure if he sees it, but I do—that glimmer of power.

"Yes, father." Her reply is full of steel and defiance.

With those two words she quits the room with Kane following silently in her wake. Now that the only significant person in this little meeting has left, I decide this was as good a time as any to take my leave and collect the life owed me.

When I put this plan into motion, possessing her was just my duty to my people. Now that I've seen her fire, felt it lick my skin. I can't wait for another taste. My lips curl in a sadistic grin. I think I'm going to greatly enjoy my new wife.

Chapter Three

DEVANY

Try as I might, I can't awake from this nightmare. With sleep abandoning me, I'm left to observe the night sky. I watched the light of dawn chase away the midnight sky—dissolving the shadows left behind—bathing the colorless stone of my room in warmth. To some I may be dramatic, I am marrying a king after all. But my place is here, with my people, protecting them from father's sadistic whims Not off gallivanting across the whole of Galandir.

I check myself in the full-length mirror and the eyes that gaze back at me are brimming with disbelief at my situation.

After my display of disobedience father had me sequestered off in this room with nothing more than my own thoughts to keep me company. Completely and utterly alone. I have no mother to help me into my wedding dress, to tell me what to expect of my wedding night, dispel my fears, or whisper how very much she loves me. What I do have is a father who cares very little for me, gleefully handing me away to a man I've hardly met.

The gossamer fabric of the wedding gown Asher supplied rustles as I step closer to the mirror. The sheer panels of lavender fabric are light on my skin and soft to the touch. The bodice cut so low that the valley of my breasts is on full display. The fabric clings to my body before the skirt flares out at the knee, brushing the floor with every step. We're it not for the thousands upon thousands of small amethysts and rose quartz crystals that cover it, it would be damn near indecent. Candlelight dances off each stone, twinkling in the mirror, chasing away the filmy shadows. A matching crown sits upon my head.

The only other jewelry adorning my body is a pendant of black obsidian inlaid with carvings of a language I cannot read. The onyx stone out of place against the soft muted colors.

Out of habit, my fingers lightly trace the edge of the pendant, feeling it warm beneath my touch. It's all I have left of the boy in the woods. It represents a promise ten years in the making from one broken soul to another. Proof that I'm not alone. That there's someone out there who cares whether I live or die.

I keep telling the girl in the mirror to smile, but I can't seem to muster one. There's truly nothing in this situation worth smiling about. The vast majority of my life has been devoid of any true joy since the death of my birth parents. I don't see why this should be any different.

By the Goddess, what am I going to do?

My breath stalls and my throat closes. Nausea rolls in my belly. A gasping half-sob leaves my throat and I push my hand hard against my mouth to keep the sound from escaping. *Fuck... I can't do this.* My eyes search the room as if I'll find a solution amongst the shadows that linger in the corners.

I'm a woman with too many secrets, too many people depending on me. I'm without a choice. I need to be within my father's territory in order to protect my people. Without me here, he will reign unchecked. On the other hand, there's no way my father would let me walk away from this marriage.

A fine tremor works its way through my hands as my helpless-ness and anger slip my tightly held control.

Surely Asher is no different from any other man I've encountered—egocentric and cruel. No doubt under the impression that he owns me. I'm sure to him I'm something to possess... to dominate and control. Well, I have news for him. It would take a very particular type of man to get me to bow before him and I'm afraid I just don't see that in his future. I'm sure he'll be greatly disappointed.

A loud knock startles me, pulling me from my rambling thoughts. The door opens almost immediately after, and a wave of nausea hits me, my limbs feeling as if thousands of small needles are stabbing me from the inside.

"Mistress, your father has sent me to inform you that it is time," says the maid as she nervously wrings her hands. Clearly, she expects me to kill her for being the bearer of bad news. I force a smile onto my face to put her at ease, though I'm sure it doesn't reach my eyes.

"Thank you, Tabitha." I keep my voice cold and disinterested, forever playing my part in my mother's plan, even if she has been dead a year now.

I take a deep breath and step out into the hall. My eyes take a moment to adjust to the darkness. The halls are dimly lit, small shafts of light penetrate the shadows from the windows high above.

Not a single soul is in the hallway outside my bedroom. Beneath my feet, a blood-red rug muffles my footsteps as I travel further down the corridors. At the end of the hall Asher's soldiers stand guard along the walls. Their eyes following me as I pass them before they fall in line behind me. I had asked Kane to wait for me in the courtyard, needing some time to myself. I regret that choice now. It's not that I can't take care of myself. Quite the opposite, really. But he creates a buffer between me and other people. If my father's court taught me anything, it's that people can't be trusted.

After the fifteenth soldier gets in line behind me, I lose control of my tightly held temper. Easily falling back into my royal cunt persona is like second nature.

"Don't you have anything better to do than follow me around? Or is your *king* so insecure in his position that he fears a slip of a girl will make him a fool?" My tone drips with annoyance and exhaustion, and perhaps a touch of misplaced anger.

The men don't look surprised or offended. The only look they give me is one you would give an errant child, which only pisses me off further. Taking a deep breath, poised to spew more venom at them when a feminine voice rings out with clear authority. She sounds none too pleased. I turn away from the guards to face her fully, primed to expel more of my poisonous words no matter how misplaced the action may be.

It takes everything I have not to gasp when I lay eyes on her. She is stunning. Exquisite, really. The sides of her hair are cut ruthlessly short, leaving longer chin-length strands on top. Her artfully disheveled tresses stick up in a way that gives it that unintentional *just fucked* look. The roots are dark purple and fade to silver white at the ends. Her porcelain skin glimmers in the early morning light coming in from one of the tall windows in the stone hall. But the true thing of beauty is her black eyes. I cannot discern where her pupil end and her iris begin. It's like falling into a beautiful abyss, uncaring of the dangers within.

"No, princess, they're not worried you'll run. They know you won't. You'll do what you're told like a good little girl." Clearly, she doesn't think too highly of me, not that I care.

I play the role my mother set for me well, but there is a new game afoot. One I don't know the rules to, and my people will pay the price if I lose. "What these fine soldiers were doing was a sign of respect and tradition. It's to show you they will be diligent and watch over you. That they will forever protect your back from those who would betray you."

Acting the spoiled princess might not be the best play. I may have a need for these people, but I don't know the best course of action. All I keep hearing is my mother's voice echoing in my mind. *"Every action has a reaction, every choice a consequence. Choose wisely because you have the lives of more than just your kingdom in your hands, nighean milis."* I turn to the soldiers once more.

"I apologize. I'm angry over how little choice I have over my own life currently and I lashed out at all of you. For that, I am truly sorry." From the looks on their faces, they did not expect that out of the spoiled princess the world thinks me to be. Their reaction would be comical if it weren't for the dire situation I find myself in.

The 'spoiled princess' is a disguise born out of necessity. It was all part of mother's plan and I use it to keep my spies safe from prying eyes with a well-placed barb or sultry smile to hold the attention on me where it belongs.

I'm good at what I do. One of the first lessons my adopted mother taught me when she brought me to these lands was how to hide in plain sight.

"Be the pretty spoiled doll they all expect you to be. Hide what you feel. Never allow them to see what you hide behind that lovely face. It's your biggest weapon because they will always underestimate you and it will be their downfall."

I just have to keep my head in the game, find out if my new husband is friend or foe. If it's the latter, then he dies. I turn back towards the woman whose name I do not know, not that I know anyone's name at this point.

Just as I walk past her, she reaches out and grabs my arm. I look from her hand to her face and back again. At this moment, I just don't have it in me to follow my mother's advice and I'm clean out of fucks to give.

It takes every ounce of willpower I have to keep up my mask of indifference. I'm leaving the palace. This not only puts me at a disadvantage but also in unknown territory. I continue to stare at her, meeting those black depths. Her gaze is filled with wicked amusement, while I know mine reflects on something a bit more dangerous. Her scrutinizing look says she's truly seeing me for the first time.

"There's more to you than just a pretty face, isn't there?" Her tone is quiet and assessing. I don't know these people; it would be bad to give them all my secrets, but it would be just as dangerous to be seen as prey.

"In nature, the most beautiful of creatures are often the deadliest." My reply is soft, but my message is clear.

Dropping my arm, her face breaks out in a smile so full of mischief that it lights up her eyes, making them sparkle like onyx jewels.

"Oh, I like you... Asher has got his hands full, and I can't wait to see it." With a graceful push bizarre, she falls into step behind me with the others, escorting me to the man whose ring I will bear by midday.

The wedding itself is a small and, at least for me, somber affair.

The large doors of the Temple are held wide open, giving me an unobstructed view of the aisle. A massive stained-glass window bathes the room in a complex pattern of color. The path is flanked by pews, leading to a heavy iron statue of the Goddess Livana at the end of the great hall. The Goddess of marriage and love... *What a joke.*

I step over the threshold and my eyes almost immediately find Asher, as if drawn to him. It was just the same yesterday afternoon. It had been difficult to pull my gaze from him, even as my father gleefully gave me away, the memory of father's eyes bright with greed reignites the flames of my anger. But it's the mocking smile Asher gives me that has me itching to draw the blade I have strapped to my thigh.

No good can come of this marriage. I know it, and he knows it.

With my head held high, I slowly make my way down the aisle toward a future I don't want. I hold Asher's gaze, showing I will not yield. His smile only doubles, displaying a hint of his fangs. A small shaky breath slips past my lips the closer I get to him.

Asher is an exquisite trap. All bronzed olive skin and captivating hazel eyes that hold you hostage with each glance he gifts you. His eyes are a kaleidoscope of browns, greens, and golds, changing with each emotion that crosses his handsome face. A closely trimmed beard surrounding his wonderfully full lips.

He stands tall on the dais. His mahogany waves pulled away from his beautiful face, revealing his finely pointed ears. Black studs wink in each lobe, sparkling in the colorful morning light. A reminder that he is far from human.

Tattoos and piercings are commonplace among the Valore, no matter their station. A far cry from humans, where you would only find them amidst commoners and soldiers.

As I get closer, his scent hits me. Campfires and winter nights. My steps falter, and the bastard's smirk only grows.

His tunic is made of rich vibrant silk, the color of midnight skies with gold embroidery that perfectly hugs what promises to be a strong, sculpted body. The cut of the jacket accentuates his broad shoulders and trim waist. In other words, my now husband has me wanting to make poor decisions.

And I just can't have that.

"Hello, *a stór*, don't you look ravishing?" His tone full of male satisfaction that comes with knowing everything I'm wearing he provided.

"Oh, stow it!" I hiss in reply, having reached my limit for the day.

He takes hold of my wrist for the handfasting, using it to pull me closer. I'm unprepared for the feel of his skin on mine. The slide of his hand leaves sparks of electricity in its wake, causing a delicate shiver to work its way up my spine.

I need to get out of here.

I turn to the priestess, a fake smile on my lips. "Please, carry on." I have no idea what to do.

Desperate plans swirl around the recesses of my mind as the need to run claws at my throat.

The moment the ceremony ends, I change out of that ridiculous wedding dress. There was no way I was riding back to his encampment dressed like some vapid little doll. My mother never prepared me for how to deal with a man like Asher of Draic. But if he's looking for a pawn as a wife, he won't be finding one here.

I send Kane to retrieve my horse while I change for the ride ahead. It's best to dress for the battle to come. I rip off the ridiculous wedding dress the moment I reach my rooms. My first real interaction with Asher of Draic won't be dressed as some insipid little girl. I may not have been adequately prepared for this life, but war is war. While some may wear suits of iron and steel, mine will be my delicately crafted courtly mask. The fine silk and meticulously laced corsets—my chain mail and plate armor. Unfortunately for me, our battles will be fought behind closed doors.

Because of this I'm well and truly fucked, this man is much too good looking for his own good, but mostly mine. He's type of man that can have any woman he wants and probably has.

While I'm well versed in the art of flirty distraction and sexual innuendo. Those things provided the cover I needed to hide my purpose within the palace walls. But when it comes to physical act itself, I'm more than a little lost... Sometimes in war, the best tactic is to retreat. That's why I'll be making a fast getaway later this evening.

Clearing the palace doors, I spot my stupidly handsome husband standing next to a majestic looking war horse of charcoal grey with a mane so black it appears to swallow light. What a beautifully behaved animal — the horse, not the man. The man I could take or leave... mostly leave. But the horse I would gladly take off his cold dead hands. Mostly likely wishful thinking, but a girl can dream.

"Well, hello there, wife. Are you ready to ride on to camp?" His tone glitters with a sensual promise I don't plan to answer. "You'll be riding with me. Come along, we're burning daylight."

I start to reply that under no uncertain terms will I be riding with him when I hear Kane leading my horse over. I release a deep breath and for the first time; I feel light. This animal has been my one and only joy living within these walls.

I place my hand on his head, slowly sliding it down his neck and through his beautiful mane. It's the color of the night sky, a lovely blue-black like the rest of his coat. He was the last gift my adopted mother gave me before she passed.

"You big, beautiful beast, you," I croon as I continue to pet him, reveling in the security and joy his presence brings me. He represents my mother's love and freedom from this dreadful place.

"Wife, do you plan to ride that beast side saddle all the way to camp? I can't see how that'll be more comfortable than riding with me." A smile colors his voice, even as Kane snorts a laugh at Asher's assumption I can't ride.

I turn to him, lifting one eyebrow, giving him an unimpressed look. "Bohan is the kind of beast best ridden astride." My voice is full of sexual swagger that I can in no way back up. But we're going with the *fake it until you make it* proverb.

Asher's eyes heat with my words, his mouth curving in a rakish grin as he closes the distance between us. He places one of us his large hands on my hip, walking me backward toward my horse. Out of nervous habit, I take a deep breath and lick my lips to suppress the quiver in my voice. His greedy eyes follow the movement.

"Is that something that interests you, husband?" I step away from him and move closer to Bohan to give myself some breathing room. It's hard to think when he's this close, which is something I can't afford. His heated eyes speak of the good times I'd find in his bed should I be so inclined. But that path most assuredly leads to ruin.

"If you're doing the riding... Absolutely." He moves in once again, invading my space.

His eyes glued to my lips like he's imaging what I taste like. I smile up at him sweetly, then place my foot in the stirrup, swing myself up into the saddle.

Once I'm firmly seated, I look down at him as if he matters little and in my best spoiled princess voice; I reply. "How unfortunate for you that the feeling is not mutual."

It doesn't elicit the reaction I was hoping for, given that the burning amusement in his gaze only seems to double. Not waiting to hear what may come out of his too sexy mouth next, I shift my weight forward and give Bohan three taps with my right boot and we take off at a quick clip, leaving Asher behind. An excited growl is the only sound I hear as he gives chase. Maybe this wasn't my best plan.

Chapter Four

ASHER

As it turns out, my little wife is quite the rider, outpacing us for most of the afternoon. It's as infuriating as it is arousing.

I spend the first leg of this journey monitoring every smile and laugh she shares with that guard of hers. It truly shouldn't be concerning to me what Devany may or may not feel for this human. She's a means to an end, nothing more. Her love would make the task ahead easier, but it is by no means required.

In an effort to distract myself from obsessing over their every interaction, I elect to observe the human.

What's his name again...? Ah, that's right—Kane.

It's always best to understand one's enemy and make no mistake, Kane is most definitely my enemy.

To the passive eye, he would appear distracted by her. But under observation, his ever-moving eyes take in the surrounding forest with a watchfulness that speaks to his training, consistently working to keep Devany within arm's reach in the event he may need to place himself between her and any perceived danger. I can't fault Kane for his protection of her.

His movements are designed to keep him ahead of Devany with her body unconsciously following. They move in sync with one another to a dance in which only they know the steps. The level at which they anticipate each other implies years of intimacy in some form or another. Though for his sake it had better be battle training, at the most friendship.

Trust me, I know I have no right to feel this way, and I refuse to look too closely at these emotions. But I'm liable to do any number of things to prove to whom she belongs. All of which I have a feeling would piss my little wife right the fuck off.

Ansel had our people move camp early this morning, bringing us closer to the neighboring kingdom of Naphal. I didn't want to stay too close to the Erabis' border once I had Devany in my possession. It's safest for all of us to put as much distance between us as possible.

I spent much of the journey in silence, allowing myself the opportunity to observe my new wife and her companion. It was almost as though the rest of the kingdom had chosen to do the same, there was not a peep from the creatures or birds of the forest. There was almost no sound at all save for the rustling of leaves and the quiet murmur of Devany's musical voice.

Every so often she'll look back at me and I'll be struck motionless by moonlit eyes—scarcely able to breathe—held captive until she turns away.

We make it to the new encampment by midafternoon. My people picked a beautiful spot, surrounded by lush, green woods. The soft hum of insects acts as background music to the hustle of building camp.

The outer ring of tents that house our unaccompanied soldiers has already been erected. These are our first lines of defense should we be attacked. Their tents are the least extravagant, opting for utility over comfort. The dwellings are made of canvas and wood. The next row in are the soldiers who travel with their families. These are larger affairs made with the help of our elemental magic users. Some made of trees woven together into huts of sorts, others with a mixture of stone and wood. The tents Devany and I will occupy are in the third row. The last is made up of four tents in the center of camp, housing the children and their matrons, as well as the sick or injured and our healers.

The buzz of voices becomes louder as we make our way to the common areas. The smell of campfire hangs in the air as our cooks prepare for the meat that the hunt will bring in.

We're only three days' ride from the border of Naphal and the sooner we get there, the sooner I'll have peace of mind. Kól isn't known for keeping his word, I sure as hell wouldn't put it past him to try and take her back by force, marriage vows or not. No doubt waiting for the moment we have our guard down, giving him the opportunity to kill me and get her back in one concise move. At least that's what I would do if I were in his shoes. Killing two birds with one stone.

I dismount my horse and hand my reins off to a stable boy before taking a final moment to watch Devany and her companion.

Ansel slaps my shoulder, his hand weighing heavily. "Well, brother, would you look at that?" The action startles me from my haze, and I can hear the smug bastard's amusement. This woman is a distraction, and she's gotten under my skin. At this rate, she's going to be the death of me.

As if she's heard my thoughts, the little minx looks directly at me, a smirk playing at her lips like she's winning this little game. She's so far out of her league that she can't even see the board.

Wishing I could choose to ignore him but knowing there's no way, I pivot only to see that his focus is also on Devany and Kane. Although his regard is filled with far more mirth than mine.

I fold my arms over my chest to keep from fisting my hands when Kane places his hands about Devany's waist to lift her out of her saddle, setting her softly on her feet. The smile she gives him is so sweet it has me fantasizing about ripping a hole in his chest and removing his heart with my claws. Would it be overkill? *Maybe*. Satisfying? *Fuck yes*.

"You might want to try seducing your wife instead of being your normal hard-to-like self, old friend, because it looks like the handsome young guard will be watering her garden soon enough... if you catch my meaning." His voice is so full of laughter that even his eyes twinkle.

Not that I'm paying him much attention because I'm solely focused on Devany as she walks through camp waiting for the soldiers to finish with the tent set up. She smiles and speaks with my people along the way, laughing kindly with them. Not a sign or whisper of the spoiled princess she has been rumored to be. She even stops to talk with the matrons as the children help with unloading the food stores. Anything that would give her an excuse to look down the aisles of tents.

With each soldier she passes, she makes a small mark on her hand with some sort of writing utensil. Each mark is made on a different portion of her palm.

I see her devious nature, but all my people see is a courteous, welcoming queen. It's all I would have seen as well; had I not been looking so closely. I'd have missed the calculated glimmer in her eyes as she counts the surrounding soldiers. Making mental notes of their locations. The way her eyes linger a moment longer than necessary, marking where each path leads.

My men are getting lost in her looks and innocent smile. They're underestimating her, as I'm sure many do, and not comprehending that my sweet, innocent wife is about to run— and I can't wait. The predator in me salivates at the notion of hunting our *a stór beag deas*. I'm also hard at the very thought of catching her.

This is going to be fun.

I'm willing to bet she gives as good as she gets. My eyes continue to follow Devany, and I decide to answer Ansel at last. My voice is absent as I report what I've seen, keeping my focus on the beautiful distraction currently weaving her way through my people as if she isn't plotting.

"My need for seduction or concerns of the guard's involvement are not of consequence because my sweet wife is about to run," I say much too casually for what it would mean for all of us were she lost. Not to mention what it would do to me.

"Well, brother, I think you underestimate her as much as everyone else does. She's clever. Hell, she'd have to survive a court like that. Even if you see what we don't, you miss what's right in front of you. She's a smart, beautiful woman and because of that reason and many more, she has the upper hand in this situation." That's all the advice he gives before he retreats, no doubt feeling as if he has endowed great wisdom upon me. It falls on deaf ears as the call of the hunt sings in my veins.

Maybe it's time to give my pretty prey a push, convince her to make her move sooner rather than later.

With a plan in place, I stalk Devany's every move throughout the day. I watch the way she moves, how her eyes track those around her. It's in the way she blends in that you see the beauty in her design. A predator among prey, moving with a grace bred of necessity. Hiding in plain sight, but I see her, and I have always preferred to hunt large game. Let's set the trap and flush out my target, shall we?

Chapter Five

DEVANY

The day was going so well until the moment Asher sought me out, wearing that serpent's smile that looks entirely too good on his handsome face. Mischief lightening his eyes, turning them the color of new moss, bright and free.

Nothing good can come from the look he's giving me. No doubt the same expression one might see on the visage of a demon right before he convinces you how wonderful it would be to fall. He only confirms my suspicions when he opens his mouth seconds later. Sounding entirely too pleased with himself.

"King Ivann of Naphal is expecting us in four days' time. You have until we reach the palace of Jamshid to prepare yourself for your role as my wife." " His tone reeks of expectation, like I am some pet that he could tell to sit and stay.

Every word out of his mouth only serves to reinforce my ever-increasing agitation. It grates on my already frazzled nerves and frankly I have better things to do than play these games.

Now that I'm no longer within the palace walls I'll have to find a way into the city proper without being seen. At some point

I'll need to establish a base of operations. But instead of working toward my new goals I'm dealing with his childish antics.

Take this conversation as an example; I know for a fact I'm giving him a look that speaks to all the ways I wish to harm him. Does he look worried that I'm fantasizing about killing him... No, he doesn't. He looks positively excited by the prospect of violence that he's damn near vibrating.

Probably thinking his pretty new pet has tiny claws. Well, he's in for a rude awakening because this pet's claws are far from small, and she knows how to use them.

He just keeps talking like I'm not trying to kill him with the power of my mind. "Until then, you will be afforded your own tent, which will be next to my own... But hear me now, you will entertain no men. Do not make me regret this luxury."

He is so proud of himself as he walks away, unknowingly giving me a means of escape. Tonight, when all is quiet, I'll be leaving this place. Kane will stay behind to give the appearance that I'm still nearby, allowing me enough time to put some distance between myself and my dear husband. Which should be easily done, given my speed and the help of a cloaking spell.

My tent is far more extravagant than I was expecting. Five trees stand along the perimeter, their spacing far too precise to be natural. The branches stretch overhead toward the center, interlacing to create a canopy that blocks out the evening sky. Heavy canvas is woven amongst the leaves and branches, giving some much-needed privacy. Obviously, the work of a Valore blessed in the earth element.

Lanterns illuminate the space, casting shadows along the fabric walls. The dirt floor beneath my feet is covered with faded rugs that muffle the sound of my agitated pacing. A large bed dominates the space, piled high with pillows and blankets made of scrumptious fabrics and pelts of fur, leaving just enough room for a small side table, and a changing screen.

Kane and I spend the next few hours quietly going over my escape plan. He's sure this is a trap, and in all honesty, it very well could be. But the possibility of escape is worth the risk. Most underestimate me, believing me to be wholly human. Asher, I'm sure is no different, so it's just a matter of timing and luck.

They announce supper shortly after the sun begins to set and I'm little more than a bundle of nervous energy from all this waiting. But as the night progresses, I'm pretty sure luck and the Gods are on my side. My dear husband and his horde of merry idiots began drinking well before the food was served, and everyone else soon followed, leaving only a few sober.

As a means to blend in, I nurse two glasses of elderberry wine, which has the added benefit of easing my anxiety. No one here truly expects me to socialize. So, with the darkening of the sky, I declared it time for me to retire.

A handful of hours have passed as I wait with bated breath for Asher to go to bed himself, hopefully alone... not that I care. I just don't want to be forced to listen.

Imagine my surprise when I hear him arguing with Kane at the entrance of my tent. Their voices are so loud I worry they may come to blows.

Kane is undeniably stronger than most humans. But there is no way to tell how he might fare against a Valore, much less one as powerful as Asher.

I quickly removed my shirt and shoes, roll up the legs of my pants, then cover up with one of my silk robes. Praying to the Gods that he's too drunk to notice. I take a fortifying breath before pulling back the flap to the entrance.

"What in the Gods' names is going on here?" I inject as much venom into each word as possible, making eye contact with each of them.

"This fool is trying to keep me from my bride. So, I'd say that the possibility of me killing him is what's going on here." Asher doesn't take his eyes off Kane, his voice frighteningly calm.

Kane being the ass he can be, smirks and winks at Asher, making like he's going to close the distance between us. Asher takes a threading step toward Kane and before I realize what I've done, I find myself acting as a barrier between the two men.

My hands rest gently against the fine material of Asher's jacket, and I silently curse myself for wanting to trace over the muscled form beneath it. My fingers trace over the golden embroidery of their own accord, the delicate touch bringing Asher's gaze to me. The awareness of his attention makes my heart skip a beat as I take in an anxious breath that I immediately regret as his addictive scent weaves around me, drowning me in midnight fires and winter air. My traitorous body fails me again as his strong hands rest against the curve of my waist before he walks me past Kane and back into my tent. A sensation overwhelms me, though I'm not quite sure if it's desire or fear.

This is bad, so very bad.

Being alone with a man like Asher is never a good thing when you're trying to leave said man. Asher has this way of surrounding you while drawing you in, and before you know it, he's got you.

"Why are you here, Asher?" I meant for the words to come out hard as steel and dripping with spite, only for them to sound feather soft.

Staring up at him, seeing the intense look in his eyes, is fucking with my head.

"Say it again." He goes preternaturally still. His hands tighten on my hips ever so slightly, giving me the impression of one of those great cats from the mountains of Naphal readying to pounce.

"Say what?" This time, my tone is decidedly more annoyed. Did he look as if he cared he was once again on my nerves? No... he didn't give two shits.

"My name—say my name again." Each word drips with

sloppy seduction. But his eyes practically glow at hearing his name on my lips.

Oh no, sir, we will do none of that.

I take a deep breath. Not that it does me any good, before I ask, "Why are you here, Asher?" Enunciating each word slowly, so his drink-addled mind can follow. The look I receive tells me he doesn't appreciate it.

"It's our wedding night, little wife. I can't very well be expected to sleep alone, can I?" The fuck he can't, but saying that will only make him dig his heels in. When I stay silent for too long, he opens his mouth.

I hold up my hand, cutting him off when he starts to speak. "I don't see how that's my problem." It's clear he's ready to argue his point before I've even made mine. Asher closes his mouth... but pushes out his lip in a pout. No grown man should be this attractive doing something so childish.

"You informed me just this afternoon that I would not be obligated to perform my duties as your wife until we made it to Naphal and would be afforded my own tent until then." A brief line appears between his eyebrows as his whiskey-soaked mind tries to make heads or tails of my answer.

I find myself staring at that small line, making a conscious effort not to reach out and rub my thumb over it.

Before I do something foolish like touching him—or worse, kiss him—I place my hand on his chest and step away. Asher opens and closes his mouth several times before finally settling on a reply.

"Yes, I said that, and I meant it. But my men expect me to spend the night with you to solidify our union. I had not taken that into account when I made my original offer." We'll be having none of that.

"Again, I'm not seeing this as any of my concern." Each word is said through gritted teeth, dripping with agitation, my eyes no doubt burning with it. "I will not be forced to share my bed tonight. Your men will just have to get over it." I should have known that my tone and statement would get me nowhere.

Instead of backing down, Asher advances on me, walking me back toward the bed. He's got a fixation with backing me into things. I hate it... ok I sort of love it, but mostly I hate it for how out of control it makes me feel. He continues to move until I collide with the bed, forcing me to sit in the process.

"Believe me, *a stór milis,* there will be nothing forced about it. You'll come all too willingly and enjoy every second, I can assure you."

Asher leans into me, placing both fists on either side of my hips, leaving me no choice but to angle myself back onto my elbows to keep the space between us.

His face is so close that his breath feathers across my lips just before he kisses me so thoroughly, I forget to breathe, and no longer care if I ever take a breath again. His tongue teases the seam of my lips and I open for him without thinking. He tastes faintly of whiskey and synder berries.

I've kissed very few in my life, but never a man like Asher. He owns every part of me in this moment, but the position of weakness it puts me in doesn't sit well with me.

He pulls away only a few inches, denying me the space I need to catch my breath. That infuriating smirk is back on his beautiful face, his eyes now the color of new leaves. I'm so busy staring into his lovely eyes it takes a moment for me to realize that he's still so close because my hands are now fisted in his shirt.

For fuck's sake, I need to get a grip on myself.

I drop his shirt with as much dignity as possible before asking, "Exactly what are you suggesting, then?" I keep my face neutral so as not to give voice to my inner thoughts.

I really need him to leave, but if I keep making a big fuss, he'll only stay to spite me or worse, get suspicious.

"I'm suggesting a compromise. Seems you're going to keep on lying to me and yourself about your attraction to me..." The arrogant bastard actually stops talking, like he's giving me a chance to speak up. A condescending grin dancing at the corn of his full lips, no doubt because of my reaction to his kiss. When he gets no response from me one way or the other, he continues, "And I'm not willing to cause unrest amongst my people by leaving. So, what I'm saying is that I'll sleep here tonight. If you don't give me any reason to believe you can't be trusted, your tent will once again be all yours until we reach Naphal. So, little wife, what say you?"

I'm trapped. If I don't agree, it's only going to make this worse. So, I do the only thing I can... negotiate.

"Fine, but you sleep on the floor." Crossing my arms, I give him my best *fuck you smile*, only to drop my arms the moment his eyes drop to my breast with a salacious grin crossing his face. He brings his gaze back to mine, a predatory glint shining brightly in their depths.

"No." What...? Did he just say *no*? My disbelief is written plainly on my face, only causing his smile to grow.

"You can't say no. That's not how this works, you barbarian!" The only reaction I receive is the lifting of one dark brow.

"I have agreed not to bed you this night, though it is my right as your husband. But I draw the line at sleeping on the floor." The cocky bastard rounds the bed and undresses since we've apparently reached the end of the conversation.

Unsure what else to do, I retreat behind the privacy screen to finish undressing, putting on my warmest bedclothes since it seems I'll be escaping in them.

"I'm going to see you in all your glory, eventually. No point in hiding, *a stór álainn*." The sound of his voice breaks through my careening thoughts.

I come out from behind the screen to find him already in my bed. The sight stops me in my tracks. In the dim light coming off the spent candles, I can just make out his tan bare chest and all that firm naked skin on full display and I'm momentarily struck dumb by the vision.

"Don't worry, I promise not to ravage you, *a stór milis*," he says, patting the bed beside him as if to show how safe it is to enter.

I stare into his eyes, trying to discern whether he'll stay true to his word tonight. While I know he's no gentleman, he does seem to have a code of honor. Which I find hard to trust having met many men of power without at one.

My curiosity gets the best of me, it seems, because I ask about something that's crossed my mind more than once. "You've called me different variations of that same phrase. What does it mean?"

I climb into bed beside the man I'm desperate to escape.

How did this become my life?

He reaches over, grabbing me by the waist and pulling me into the cradle of his powerful arms. I feel him smile against my neck as if the question humors him. The slight pressure of his lips lights a spark in my body. A reaction I won't be examining too closely.

"If you're a good girl, I'll tell you. Until then, you'll just have to wonder." For some reason beyond my understanding, I'm disappointed.

I close my eyes, pretending to sleep. I'm there for what seems like hours before his breathing evens out, letting me know he's finally fallen asleep.

His arm becomes a heavy weight around my waist, anchoring me to his body. Slowly, I roll onto my back, stopping every few seconds to give him time to settle. It takes a short eternity, but I manage it. I prepare to slip out from under him, only to be pulled more securely against his chest. His breath rustles my hair softly as he sinks back into sleep.

My heart beats heavily in my chest as panic sets in.

I must leave now!

The sun will rise soon and with it, the rest of the camp. If I don't go now, who knows when my next chance will be? At least with him in my bed, I know this is unlikely to be a trap.

It's now or never.

I take hold of his forearm, lifting it up just far enough to slip out and place it back down. For several seconds I kneel there, my eyes glued to his face, watching for any signs that he may be awake. Before I walk softly to the changing screen and grab my shoes, heading for the entrance.

Kane is waiting nearby when I exit, and with a quick nod, I head toward woods, sticking to the shadows, creeping past the last few tents.

Once I break the tree line, I stop to put on my shoes and get my bearings.

I need to head east to get back home to Erabis. Mum taught me how to use the stars and the heavens above us, leaving me with an understanding of which constellation of stars belonged to which God or Goddess and how to locate them. I make quick work of finding the grouping affiliated with the Goddess Ashlesha, knowing she can always be found in the east. With a smile and swift pace, I head back to my people.

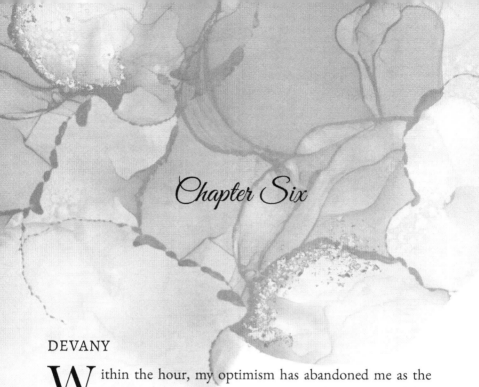

Chapter Six

DEVANY

Within the hour, my optimism has abandoned me as the sound of something or, more accurately, someone giving chase reaches my ears.

If I hadn't been paying such close attention, I would have dismissed the sounds as commonplace in the woods. The rustling of trees—the breaking of branches—animals taking cover.

But I know better. The bastard's caught up to me.

I had really been hoping for a larger head start, holding on to the belief that things went to plan on Kane's end, and he had gotten away before they were aware of my absence.

I increase my speed trying to stay out in front of my pursuer, yet he still gains on me. At this rate, he'll catch up to me.

My stomach sours, and anxiety weighs my limbs down. I hate to be chased. It reminds me too much of the day my birth parents died... of the day I met him, the boy in the woods.

A muffled growl to my left has me turning, only to catch glimpses of color before a body collides with mine, taking us both down.

After the hit, three things happen. First, my assailant twists us in the air as we fall, taking the full brunt of our landing. Next, he rolls us over, effectively pinning me to the ground beneath him with my hands pinned above my head. And finally, but certainly not the least significant, he pisses me the fuck off.

Not only did he catch me. He appears to be fully clothed right down to his boots. Like he had all the time in the world to catch me.

His handsome face is inches from my own and his closeness is doing all the wrong things to me. His pupils are fully dilated, giving his eyes a dangerous gilt. The outer ring is the color of autumn leaves. His beard is somewhat unkempt from sleep.

His body stretches over mine, and each point of contact sets my body aflame. And I hate it. It robs me of my self-control. I lick my lips and watch as his gaze drops to my mouth, following the movement.

"Let me up, you horse's ass." I buck my hips, trying to dislodge him. Anything to create some much-needed breathing room. Without lifting the full weight of his body, he restrains my legs between his.

"Woman, has anyone ever told you that you have a filthy mouth?" That playful smile of his is probably the thing I detest the most because of how much it entices me. The playfulness lightens up his face, softening the sharp edges of his cheekbones.

"I've scarcely said two words." I'm quick to point out, my voice dropping with irritation.

"Every dirty, unpleasant name you want to call me plays across your beautiful face." I don't doubt that to be the truth. He has this way of getting under my skin.

"Do I look like I give a damn what you think?" Giving him my best "you are beneath me" voice. His answering smile tells me he heard the change.

Transferring my wrists to one hand, he lightly grips my chin, forcing me to look him in the eye before he answers the question.

"No... not really, but you look damn good under me." His thumb brushes lightly across my bottom lip, drawing forth a shiver.

"Let me up, you pervert." Fear of the possibilities has my voice coming out harsh and cruel, though he doesn't seem fazed, only amused.

"Relax, let's get you back to camp and into bed, shall we?" He says the word *bed* with a wink before he stands up and grabs hold of my wrist, pulling me to my feet. The world moves around me and the next thing I know, I'm upside down with a close-up view of my husband's perfect ass.

"As it is, you won't be getting much sleep with this little excursion taking up most of the night. You're going to be dead on your feet." He continues to talk as if I'm not hanging over his shoulder thinking of all the ways I could kill him.

"I know that you've lived your life mostly behind the palace walls, but do you have any idea what types of beasts roam these woods?" His voice comes off more apathetic than laced with genuine concern. Even his steps are uncaring of the fact that I'm bouncing about on his shoulder. I grip his hips tightly to prevent my face from skipping off his ass with each step. The prick really is working my last nerve. "You're not even dressed for the cooler temperatures at night."

Oh, that's it. I lock both my fists together, pulling back and bringing them down as hard as I can from this position, aiming for his kidney.

"Put me down, you buffoon." His sharp intake of breath is music to my ears, but my reward is short-lived as he follows it up with a hard smack to my ass.

"Knock it off, brat, or I'll put you over my knee right here. Now, please tell me what the fuck you were thinking?" No, he did not just spank me. I pull back, fully intending to sink my teeth into his side, when his voice stops me dead.

"If you continue on with that thought, know that I will bite you back and it will end with me mounting you right here for anyone, man or animal, to see." Everything inside me goes quiet.

"Surely not, even you're not that much of a barbarian." He adjusts his hold on me, placing my stomach more solidly on his shoulder so my face is no longer up close and personal with his ass.

"Bite me, and let's find out, shall we?" Amusement rings clear in his voice.

The bastard.

Obviously feeling as if he's won, he continues to berate me for the stupidity of running into unknown territory. He carries me back through camp, much to my chagrin, seeing as most of the soldiers are now up to start their day. Many of them smile at us like we're some happy couple off playing games in the woods. My embarrassment knows no bounds.

The longer we walk, the more agitated he gets, as it sinks in that I truly tried to run. I'm not sure if it's the running or the potential for damage to myself that has him vibrating with anger. One thing I am sure about is this will not end well for either of us.

When I had pictured the possibility of entering Asher's personal space, it had been on my own two feet with my head held high. Being as we are about to enter his tent, I guess it'll be over his shoulder.

Asher walks calmly over to the bed in his tent and unceremoniously drops me on my ass. I quickly get to my feet, needing to be eye-to-eye for this conversation. There's no way I'll allow him a position of power for what's sure to come after my failed attempt at escape.

I keep expecting him to yell—he just continues, like he has all the time in the world, and I guess he does, but the waiting is killing me. Which is stupid considering the punishments I've received from my shit father. The years of berating. The pain... The fear. His continued silence has my anxiety mounting.

After removing his waistcoat and throwing it on the bed, where

I had been a moment ago, he unbuttons his shirt at the wrist and rolls each one up to his elbow, showing off corded muscle encased in coppery tan skin wrapped in whirling tattoos. I never considered the act of a male rolling up his sleeves to be sexy. I stand corrected. Apparently, when done by a man like my husband, it drips sex.

May the Gods help me... It should be illegal, or at the very least a sin to be that good-looking while also being an asshole.

"I have no intention of staying with you and your group of warmongers looking to further your own agendas." A humorless laugh leaves my mouth. "You can sure as fuck find someone else to be your pawn. I am Princess Devany of Erabis, heir to my father's throne, and I bow to no man." His eyes narrow as each word falls from my lips. For reasons I cannot comprehend, I can't seem to stop pushing him.

"No, dear little wife." Sarcasm colors the words as his smile mocks me. "You are now Queen Devany of Draic. You belong to me. You'd best make peace with that because I'll not give you up." Anger seethes from each word he utters.

"I am not yours in *any* way, dear *husband*." I place enough sarcasm on the word it's sure to piss him off.

I want him under no illusion regarding my feelings about the vows we took, because they mean nothing to me. I take great pleasure in rubbing in the fact that he's not yet had me. I'm sure that he assumes that Kane and I are sleeping together, which couldn't be further from the truth. Though the insinuation in my statement doesn't help to clear up the assumption.

The ire in his gaze turns to a black flame that leaves utter destruction in its path. It's proof enough that he understood my meaning, and now those flames lick my skin, but I'll not back down. He doesn't own me. I meant what I said, I bow to no man —certainly not him.

"You see, husband mine, you may have put a ring on my finger, but it'll end there. Nothing more, nothing less." My voice is full of cruelty, born of necessity.

I see the moment the switch between cruel king and savage beast occurs, his beautiful face becoming otherworldly.

The taste of magic, like wild herbs and lightning, saturates the air as his glamour slips. The space between us vibrates with power. Revealing yet another Valore trait; magnificent horns standing proudly from his head, curving slightly, and covered in the same golden tattoos as his body. It hammers home how truly inhuman he is.

Between one heartbeat and the next, he's suddenly before me —his speed uncanny— eliciting a shiver that runs down my spine. The heat of his body seeps into me, warming my skin. I have to physically fight the desire to close the distance between us.

"What do you think will happen, *wife*?" He gives my title the same treatment I gave his as he crowds me toward the only stone wall of the tent, likely raised by a Valore with earth magic to protect his vulnerable back. Violence, possession... and jealousy roll off him in waves. "Are you thinking of sharing this delectable body with that pretty human of yours... hmmm?"

Hearing him refer to Kane as *that human*, as if he matters little, just pisses me right the fuck off. He does not know what *that human* has done for me. Not just in his protection, but in his friendship. If it weren't for Kane, I would most assuredly be dead.

"He has a name, asshole! It's Kane. Show some respect and use it." Asher stares at me so intently that it almost feels like a physical touch.

I'm seething with righteous indignation, my eyes no doubt blazing with it as I stare back at him.

The hand that had been fisted at his side moves so swiftly it's impossible for me to gauge the action. His fist slowly closes around my throat, giving a quick squeeze. Not to cause pain. Only showing me... reminding me of how easy it would be to end my life. The feel of all that controlled strength beneath his skin only serves to spark my arousal.

"I don't give a fuck what his name is." Asher's voice is the soft whisper of an assassin as it feathers over my skin. "But if I find he's been buried between your pretty thighs, I'll kill him. So, know this, if you allow anyone in your bed that is not me, you have their blood on your hands, *a stór milis*." By the time he finishes his warning, my back hits the wall, expelling a hard breath from my lips. His body pins me there, all his hard lines pressed against my soft curves.

The scent of him envelops me, bergamot, fire, and a touch of oiled leather. My eyes flutter shut of their own accord. The closer he gets to me, the more my body surrenders, desiring nothing more than to give in to his mating call. With his free hand under my ass, he picks me up. Instinctively, my legs wrap around his waist. In an attempt to get as close as I can, I pull him in. I'm a mess of contradictions because with every breath I surrender, I push away twice as hard.

His hand slides from my throat to the nape of my neck, twisting in my hair. The sharp feel of his nails scraping my scalp has a gasp falling from my lips as he tilts my head back, exposing my throat.

He places soft, tantalizing kisses from the hollow of my throat to just behind my ear. But it's what he does on the way back down that's almost my undoing. His fangs scrape along the tendon of my neck, evoking a long, soft moan. The sound prompts him to smile against my skin. He holds my hair hostage as he pulls back, looking at my face. I can feel him hardening against me, stroking my arousal.

"You feel that, *a stór álainn,* because I can, the wet heat of you against me. Your arousal soaking through my pants to my hard cock. You may say you don't want me, but your body refuses to tell the lies that drip from your pretty lips." His tone is deeper and edged with violence. He pushes more firmly against me, and my thighs tighten around his hips.

I can feel the heated blush that colors my neck and face with each dirty word he utters in his dark, whiskey-soaked voice— caressing me—causing the continued betrayal of my body.

Desire drips down my thighs, further soaking his pants, and

I'm helpless to stop it. A predatory smile graces his perfect lips as each word that falls from them forces my body to prove what my mind refuses to accept.

He presses even further into me, the hard ridge of him putting pressure right against my core. I can feel the building of an orgasm as he rolls his hips. A feeling that until now, only I have given myself.

"Tell me, wife..." his voice is like velvet, "does this pretty blush speak to how innocent you truly are... hmmm?" he says against my throat, the sound vibrating along my neck with the ghosting of his lips. His fangs scrap across my collarbone, where he places a soft kiss in the hollow of my throat. "Does it run all the way down to the tight, hard nipples I feel against me?" Sliding his hand down to cup my breast, he runs his thumb back and forth across the hardened nub, causing such exquisite pain that quickly turns to pleasure.

"Open your eyes, *a stór*. I want you to see the face of the man who's making you come undone. To know who it is that brings you to ecstasy."

My eyes open slowly to bring my hooded gaze to his. I see the stark need written across his beautiful face. His eyes move between mine as if he's trying to memorize the moment. My legs shake as I fall over the edge, bright light and pleasure consuming me. My body is flush and trembling.

"That's it, *a stór,* give it to me." The rocking of his hips draws out the pleasure coursing through me.

The trembling of my limbs finally slows, and he gently lowers my feet to the floor. He takes hold of my face with both hands and what I see written in his stormy hazel gaze has my breath stalling in my chest.

How can one look convey so much? Lust and anger in equal parts.

Then his lips are on mine, seducing them to play with his, giving me a taste of what it could be like if I would just give in.

"You can fight this, *a stór milis*. In fact, I want you to. So that when you give your heart and soul to me—and believe me, you will…" He says it so softly, stroking his thumb over the apple of my cheek. "You will do so knowing that you fought the inevitable with everything you had. Because, My Queen, you were born to be mine. Of that, I'm sure."

With that, he quits the room, leaving me with my swirling thoughts about how the fuck things escalated so quickly.

Chapter Seven

ASHER

Last night keeps replaying in my mind. The way she felt in my arms—soft and pliant as her body curved against mine. The smell of her hair, the gentle sound of each breath she took.

Having her that way when she spends most of her time acting The Bitch is something that could quite easily become addictive for me. Don't get me wrong, I adore the challenge that side of her poses as well. Regrettably, these memories are now tainted with other emotions I prefer not to experience again.

Hunting Devany down when she inevitably ran was something I had looked forward to immensely. The two of us alone under the cover of night. Predator and prey. The hunter and the hunted. I skillfully placed my pieces on the board, giving her the incentive to run while also making her feel safe in the decision to do so.

Waiting on her to make the move felt like a small eternity. So, when she did, I dressed with care, being sure to give her a head start, not wanting the game to be over too soon. Once I hit the tree line of the forest, I immediately regretted having done so. The scents of the woods slammed into me and with it, the cold wash of fear. It's not an emotion I'm prone to feeling. Not since childhood, really. I've worked hard to prevent the need for such things. But this woman has a way of pulling emotion out of me far too easily.

A mix of scents had assaulted my senses. Her's soft and delicate, bringing to mind dreams of night blooming gardens along moonlit paths. Unfortunately, the strong smell of a full-grown hestra had also been present.

These cat-like creatures are native to the outlying woods of Erabis and Kannon. They don't pose much of a threat when they're young, but once they hit adulthood, they are prey too few. A female hestra can stand over a meter in height and has been known to snatch small children from the surrounding area much like a hadeon, which thankfully I didn't smell nearby. But their size isn't what makes them so hard to hunt. No, it's the fact that their skin changes to match their surroundings, making them damn near impossible to see, and one had been on Devany's trail.

I've never tracked anything as quickly as I did last night, nor have I ever been that furious. How could she run without being aware of her surroundings and devoid of a cloaking spell? It's like she has a death wish. I had to dispatch two smaller predators in my pursuit of her. I had expected their presence; these woods are teeming with them at night. The hestra had been an unwelcome surprise.

I caught the scent of the large cat before my eyes could focus on it, finding it several meters away from me. Not wanting it to see me too soon, I had taken to the trees, running along the branches so swiftly that they didn't even dip under my weight, easily keeping pace and then gaining on my prey. The woods blurred past me until I was less than a meter away from the creature, balancing on the lower limb of a nearby tree. It was a shame to destroy such a magnificent creature, but it hunted what was mine. With claws extended, I descended upon the creature, not allowing it time to make a sound, its fur exploding in a kaleidoscope of colors as I ended it.

Thankfully, Devany had not realized I was on her until it was too late. And now that I've had her under me, I can't wait to have her there again, spitting venom at me like the viper she is.

Traveling to the shores of Edling is going to take us the better part of a fortnight, with our civilian members and orphaned children that we picked up along the outer edge of the Barren Strait. Add the courtesy visits with each monarch, and it will be closer to a month before we're back on our own soil.

After Devany's attempted escape, I've decided it's best to leave a day early and put some much-needed distance between us and Erabis. I'm not entirely sure why she wishes to return so badly. Maybe she's been conditioned to react this way and that's why Kól was so willing to part with her. Whatever it is, it's very concerning.

I keep a close eye on my runaway throughout the day as everyone works to break down camp. Devany mostly walks around helping here and there; talking with my people, sharing that beautiful smile that I hope she will one day turn toward me. But at this rate, I won't be holding my breath.

The hairs on the back of my neck stand on end, and the beginning feelings of panic clog my throat. I turn searching for Devany, finding her no longer within my line of sight as something akin to fear crawls up my spine.

I seek Kane out, finding him exiting the stable. I'm closing the distance between us before I've the action true thought, doing my damnedest to rein in my emotions.

"Where the fuck is she?" I demand through clenched teeth, my eyesight wavering as my anger rises. I swear to the Gods of Old, if she's run again, I'm going to take her over my knee, and may the Gods help her because she will have a damn hard time riding that horse of hers when I'm done.

My stomach drops when Kane's head snaps up from the saddle he was checking, his eyes colliding with mine. The panic I see in their depths tells me what I need to know. Something is terribly wrong.

"What the ever-loving fuck do you mean, 'where is she?' You have an entire horde of men. How could you have lost her?" Kane's face flushes as his answering panic sets in, his eyes wild, and while I share his apprehension, I try to keep my voice relaxed.

"We'll find her," I say as if it's a foregone conclusion that we will, but if someone came into camp with none of us noticing... Fear is not something I'm used to dealing with, and as of late, it's becoming a growing problem. I weave my way through the packed-up carriages toward a group of six soldiers with Kane close behind. Keeping my step measured as I approach them, waving Bellicent and Ansel over.

"How is it possible you've lost your wife already?" Bellicent says. The woman has the demeanor of a pit viper with the training to make her just as lethal. I'm surprised by the affection in her tone. Her words are spoken lightly, but the undercurrent of worry only reinforces my concern.

"Did she run again? You might want to think about leashing your wife in the future," Ansel asks, a smirk playing at the corner of his mouth. Unfortunately, I don't share his mirth.

"I can assure you she didn't. Had she, I would know." With the stark look in his eyes, it's hard not to see the truth in Kane's words.

"I need a head count of all in our party to ensure no one else has gone missing." Two soldiers leave us promptly.

"You four, search camp. Look for anything out of the ordinary, no matter how small. But do it quietly, I don't want to cause a panic." I feel sick to my stomach when I realize something terrible must've happened. I almost wish she had run. At least then I'd know she was safe.

I feel my glamour try to slip as the need to find her becomes a physical pain. My frenetic instincts try to force my magic to react.

The four of us left split up, Bellicent and Ansel step aside to begin quietly questioning people. They speak in hushed tones to a few matrons who are packing the last few food goods into a carriage. Kane stalks to the southern tree line and I'll be taking the tree line to the north.

Movement out of the corner of my eye draws my attention to the children huddled in the middle of camp.

Toby paces in front of the small group, distraught. At thirteen years of age, it is easy to see he will grow to be a fine man, taking it upon himself to help care for the little ones. Currently, he has all of them sitting together, as he performs a headcount. With each pass, he becomes more agitated, starting over as if it will produce a different outcome.

"You alright, Toby?" He visibly tenses at the sound of my voice and brings his red-rimmed eyes up to meet mine as he tries to hide the tears.

"I don't know where Libby went. She is just a wee thing. It's my job to keep her safe, Your Majesty." He's shaking so much that words are hard to decipher through his anger and fear for the girl, but I get the gist of what he's saying.

"Toby, was the queen here when Libby was?" I work to keep my tone calm, not wanting to frighten the boy any more than he already is. If anything happens to Libby, Toby may not recover. He nods his head, confirming my suspicions.

The scents around me are muddled—far too diluted for me to get a clear direction on where they went.

Calming my mind, I feel the familiar itch that accompanies the call of my familiars. With a warning growl, twin wolves leap from my skin. One black as night, the other the color of starlight. Nox and Wren—they came to me on the eve of my sixteenth birthday, as is customary for familiars and Valore. They look at me as they await my command. Their massive bodies vibrate with unleashed violence.

"Find them!" The order is given life on a hard breath.

Nox and Wren sniff the ground around the young ones, casing the area in wider circles until they suddenly raise their heads to give the air a sniff and head straight into the forest east of camp toward the mountains with me following closely behind them.

We break past the tree line to find signs of a struggle. The overwhelming scent of Devany's blood and the growing sense of dread coursing through my veins has my instincts in a frenzy. I quickly out-pace my wolves, leaping over fallen trees, crossing running streams. Pushed on by the fact that the woman I've claimed as mine is wounded.

I round a large outcropping of rocks, skidding to a stop as my entire world tilts on its axis at the scene unfolding in front of me.

Devany stands guard in front of Libby. The girl's clothing is covered in rips and dirt. Her hair clings to her face, and blood stains her skin in so many places. Shit... in my panic, I must have missed the scent of her blood. Her arm is hanging at an awkward angle, a bone jutting out above the elbow, blood drips from her hand as she leans heavily on the rock behind her.

Armed with twin silver daggers, Devany stands before her. I didn't even know she had daggers, much less knew how to wield them. That's when I notice the deep claw marks across her stomach, but still, she stands in a fight stance, taking on a full-grown hadeon.

A beast of veritable nightmare that stands two-meters tall with the head of a large dog, two sets of eyes and ears, with six claws on each paw, and a large stinger at the tip of its tail. My reaction to the scene before me is rapid. A release of magic without conscious thought. The shredding of my glamour revealing claw-tipped hands and elongated fangs, all in preparation for defending my mate.

The growl that rips from my chest is the only warning the hadeon receives before one set of my claws embeds in his chest, the other slicing through that poison-tipped tail. It rears back on its hind legs, the claws of his front paw bearing down toward my exposed torso, forcing me to release it. The creature turns it's back to Devany and Libby now that a larger predator has challenged its right to the kill. Nox and Wren move in front of the girls, allowing me to focus on taking down the beast.

The animal sweeps his claw-tipped paw toward my neck, and I have to duck and roll to the side to dodge the blow. I drag my claw across his rear flank, leaving a deep, gaping wound. He turns, roaring into my face, spittle flying at me from its frothing mouth. He lashes out once more and I jump to evade the strike, the forward momentum taking the animal off balance. I don't allow him time to recover as I swipe my claws across his snout.

With each swing of its hooked nails, I land a strike of my own. Swing, swipe, miss, and repeat. With each rotation, the animal becomes more desperate to end this which gives me the opening I need to leap up onto the creature's back.

I slam my claws into its hide, anchoring myself to its neck while biting deeply into hadeon's throat. The need to feel his life bleed out between my fangs overwhelms my senses. Each frantic beat of the beast's heart forces more blood into my mouth, and I relish the taste of each mouthful, greedily drinking down my kill. A soft intake of breath breaks through the sound of blood rushing past my ears and has me turning my gaze toward the sound and Devany's wide eyes.

Once again, I expect fear. But as before, she proves me wrong because all I see is fire. These flames may very well consume us both. I drop the dead beast and head to her with a single-minded need to answer her mating call. I wrap her hair tightly around my fist and bare her throat to me. I lightly scrape my fangs along the tendon in her neck, eliciting a delicate shiver that works its way through her small frame. Just as my fangs are about to sink into her supple skin, she places a staying hand on my chest, stepping back from me though my hold on her is too tight to get much distance.

"Asher... she needs a healer." Devany's voice is cautious, like she's talking to an anxious animal, and I suppose in a way she is.

Shaking my head, I try to remember why I can't just have her... She's giving off all the right signals. But I can't think straight. Her scent is driving me crazy. Those beautiful eyes of hers are dilated and heated. Her nipples are tight and hard... but something's still amiss... *Is there another enemy?* I try to turn my head to find the new threat, only to have my female grab hold of my face with both her hands.

"No! Asher, I need you here! Libby's bleeding!" Her hand moves far faster than I would've expected and crashes into my face so fucking hard I taste blood.

The slap only serves to have me tightening my hold on her, a menacing growl from my chest. But it's the answering growl that comes from her that seems to break through the mindless brutality that clouds my mind. If only because of how unexpected it was. Though, it's by far one of the sexiest things I've ever heard. It gives me the break from my instincts that I need to better take in what's going on around me. When I do, I feel ill. I have Devany anchored to me by her hair. Her wounded body smashed against my blood-soaked chest. But it's the fact that I was so far gone I forgot about Libby. *Fuck!* I let go of Devany to kneel in front of the small girl.

"Hello, little one, let's get you to Marleen. She'll get you two all patched up, then you can tell me what happened, yeah?" I won't lie and say it didn't hurt to have her look at Devany before allowing me to pick her up, but... I understand. To see a full-grown Valore male functioning solely on instinct is frightening for adults, much less a child.

I carry Libby a few yards before I realize Devany is falling behind in her attempt to keep up. A sharp whistle has Nox emerging from the woods in front of us, having run ahead to scout out the path. With a nod from me, he heads in her direction.

"Climb on his back... He'll get you to camp in one piece and Wren will be our eyes." She looks at the two wolves and back at me several times before approaching him. Nox stands over a meter in height and must crouch down to allow her access.

"Your familiars, I take it?" Her eyes meet mine, glassy with pain. Valores heal quickly from most wounds, but hers are quite extensive and I have no way of knowing if growing up within those walls has hindered her abilities.

But the important part is she just admitted to the knowledge of familiars while she plays at being human. *I wonder how much more she knows of our kind.*

"I see you have knowledge of Valore maturity." Leaving the sentence open-ended, hoping she'll fill the silence in. And she doesn't disappoint. I just wish the answer would have been different.

"My father said that the best way to defeat one's enemy is to know them. Once you know them, you can systematically destroy them. He was trying to forcefully remove a Valore's familiar from their skin. I had the *pleasure* of being in the laboratorium for the months that he tried." Her voice hollows as she speaks until she gets to the word *pleasure*, which drips with so much disgust it speaks volumes about how she truly felt about her father's experiments.

"When did you receive your familiars?" I ask, wondering if it was different for her growing up behind the wards. She took so long that I wasn't sure the answer would ever come.

"On the eve of my fifteenth birthday, two ravens beat themselves against my window until the glass finally gave... They slammed into me so hard I was sure they had been sent to kill me. But as soon as they settled into my skin it was like... coming home." We stood face-to-face and it was only then that I realized we'd stopped walking. Ravens... the harbingers of death. I highly doubt that's a coincidence.

Chapter Eight

DEVANY

Asher is quiet the rest of the trek back and with that silence, I'm left with only my overpowering guilt. Like a crushing weight on my shoulders, it drags me into a dark void of shame. A fist forcibly closes my throat and squeezes my heart.

I almost got a child killed...

That thought plays on a loop in my head. I've spent so much time playing human, having it drilled into me. I've been so conditioned to blend in that when faced with a life-or-death situation, I forgot I had magic that could have saved this poor child from pain. That could have ended the threat before it escalated. Forever falling back on my mother's plan. A plan that, while good when I was a teenager, has no place in my life now. I'm not human, and it's time I acted like it, instead of denying that which the goddess has given me.

Thoughts of my failures drown out the sounds of Asher's steps. My vision is unfocused and hazy around the edges as the woods blur by in a mess of greens and browns as we make our way back to camp. The journey is slow going, thanks to mine and Libby's injuries, but Asher doesn't make one complaint.

Soon the soft melody of the woods is replaced by the sounds of people and horses milling about. Some stop what they're doing to stare—no doubt wondering if I managed to get this child hurt in an attempt to escape. Even if that's not true, I deserve their judgment. She was hurt because of my shortcomings.

"What the fuck happened?" Bellicent's voice rings out over the dull sounds around us. I lift my gaze in her direction and see that her face drawn tight. "And tell me you killed them." Her voice is more like a growl, suggesting more violence is on the way.

"Libby wandered off too close to the tree line and got snatched by a hadeon. Devany went after her." The words fall from his lips on a harsh breath. "And, yes, I killed it."

He doesn't elaborate further on the subject. Instead, he leads us to an ornately carved carriage with dried herbs hanging from the rafters. Nox follows obediently behind him. I'm in so much pain by this point I almost feel numb... almost. It's no less than I deserve for failing to properly protect yet another person. My blood soaks the velvety soft fur beneath me, lost within the pitch black that is Nox's coat.

Asher takes poor Libby straight to a woman with long ebony and silver hair, and bright golden eyes. Once we're all inside the cozy cottage-like carriage, I gingerly dismount Nox's back when he kneels for me. Marleen, the woman whose name I pick up through the conversation between she and Asher, begins working on Libby, using a spell to put the child to sleep before moving her hands over the wounds. She makes a series of complicated gestures as she collects and weaves the surrounding aether, pushing it into each injury and forcing them closed. The sound of bones snapping back into place is audible in the small space. Thank the Goddess the spellcaster could spare the child any added pain.

Pain is something I know all too well.

It's easy to tell the woman is a spellcaster. It's all in the eyes— the way they pulse and glow with power. One of the many things my sick excuse for a father taught me. His prejudice and greed colored my childhood. The pain and blood loss make it far too easy to slip into memories better left forgotten.

"Bring the child here, Tempest." I look up at Mother, but she's busy staring at father.

Her hair is pulled back tightly from her face, the skin along the hairline is white. Her features are more prominent than they were just a year ago. Her cheekbones and eyebrows are so sharp they look as if they could cut.

Her dark blue gown stands out in stark contrast against her almost-translucent skin, swallowing up her too-thin body. Anyone can see he's slowly killing her. From her hesitance, I can tell she doesn't want to do as he asks. Whatever is beyond that door must be truly awful for her to fight him like this. I don't want to go in there. From my growing sense of dread, I can tell that whatever is beyond those oak and iron doors will stay with me for the rest of my life.

"Come along, Devany. Do as I say. It's time you started learning something useful." As if this man has anything useful to teach me, but I look at him, nonetheless. I make sure to avoid eye contact as he speaks. He gets angry when I do; no doubt scared of what he may see looking back at him.

"She is only fourteen. These aren't things that should be told to a child. Especially one who carries Valore blo—"

"Enough." His voice is loud in the small stone corridor, even with the tapestries crowding the walls.

"She is my daughter, and she has shown no signs of your cursed blood. So, she will learn what's expected of her." Each sound out of his mouth drips with disgust, as he looks at mother like she is a disease that needs to be eradicated.

As if she had asked to be kidnapped and raped. Separated from the family she loved and forced into a loveless marriage. A trophy just to show the other kingdoms what he's capable of. But as bad as it sounds, these are also good things because it means he doesn't know what I am. At the very least, he's not sure, so in this we are safe.

"It's ok, Mother..." I'm not sure what else to say, so I turn to my

father and place my hand in his like the obedient daughter I need to be to keep my secret safe.

Triumph colors his eyes when I come willingly, giving him no cause to strike out at either of us. The smile that he gives me is no more than a slash of sharp, blunt teeth than something made to show approval. I have little time to think about how he looks when he smiles like that because his cold, callused hand wraps around mine. The other opens the heavy wood and metal door leading into a library type room. There are large tapestries lining the walls, with a monstrous fireplace dominating the far end of the room. Shelves and shelves of books and long tables in the center of the room that hold bottles, beakers, and burners. Oh, by the Gods, are those—? Jars containing horns, hooves, wings, and other things litter the far table. Why would he do this?

"Ah, darling daughter, I see you have noticed my pride and joy. Come, let's take a closer look, shall we?"

I look up at him, and for the first time, I see genuine joy in his gaze. This place of horrors puts that light in his eyes, that gleam of pride. He truly is a monster in the truest sense of the word.

I trail behind him to the table, being sure not to show him just how desperately I wish to run from this place. My body aches with the need to escape. But that would only result in me being punished again. So, I straighten the steel in my spine and harden my emotions like my mother taught me and follow him over the cold stone floors to the tables.

"You see all the jars here?" His pallid hand waves toward the table as if I could miss them.

He looks down at me with milky blue eyes to be sure I'm paying attention. Not waiting for an answer, not that he truly wanted one. That rounded face of his still sporting a sadistic smile and that terrible light still present in his gaze. With a nod of my head, he continues with his gruesome show and tell.

"Tell me, Devany, how can you tell a Valore from a human?" His look is expectant. There will be punishment for wrong answers.

I don't like when he plays these games, but I answer in a voice devoid of emotion. That speaks to how bored I am with being here. Just another way to keep my secret.

"A Valore has many traits, but all have long, pointed ears and fangs. Many also have animal features such as horns, hooves, claws, or wings. They are born with magic in their veins woven into the very fabric of their being. Their ability to control this magic varies depending on the strength and purity of their blood. The stronger ones being able to control the eight elements: Air, fire, water, earth, metal, electricity, ice, and weather. The Valore also have familiars that hide in plain sight, spelled to appear as tattoos or jewelry. They have the ability to glamour their identity, making it near impossible to detect them." He looks at me with so much pride it makes me sick to my stomach.

"And what are the traits of shifters and spellcasters?" His sick smile has grown as he gets excited about what comes next. But I answer in the same voice as before.

"Shifters carry their magic beneath their skin, allowing them to change from their human form to that of an animal. They can shift into a variety of creatures, from domestic to large predators. But they can't cast magic spells or control the elements, and they are also hard to detect. Spellcasters have an innate ability to see the aether around us. The very thing that makes up every living thing and with it comes the ability to mold it into spells. As well as healing others by manipulating the aether found within them. They draw people to them; they seem to glow from within, but it's the eyes that give them away—always more vivid than their human counterparts. They also have a darker side to them. If they allow a shade to live within them, sharing in their aether, their casting becomes something darker and far more dangerous. In doing this, they become Revenant." I hold his gaze as I recite everything.

"And what is a Shade?" The question throws me off. It's the first time he has ever asked what a Shade is. In fact, it wasn't even something covered in my lessons. I must take too long to answer because he's now giving me his full attention.

"Do you not know?" His tone speaks to his displeasure, but his eyes are bright at the idea of punishing me.

"No, father, I know the answer."

"Then why, pray tell, am I still waiting?" Damn.

"Yes... of course. Sorry, Father, a shade is a dark spirit that has passed into our realm from the veil."

"Very good, darling daughter, very good indeed." He pats me on the head like one would a pet, but at least he isn't hitting me.

"Everything you see around you is the future—a new way to win the war. Each of these jars contains a piece of a Valore, shifter, or spellcaster showing us how to better defeat them."

"Devany! Devany... are you alright?" Asher's face slowly comes into view.

"What happened?" My voice comes out hoarse, my mouth dry and my tongue thick.

"What's wrong with her?" Asher speaks softly while gently running fingers through my hair. The rhythmic tugging relaxes my sore, tired body.

"I'd say she lost quite a bit of blood. To be sure that's the only problem, I'm going to need to get her out of those clothes."

"I'm not taking my clothes off, absolutely not!" I push him away. The pain is all but forgotten in my panic. I'm too raw, my emotions running too high to let him see my body like this.

"A stór, you might as well get over that modesty of yours. One way or another, Marleen will look over your wounds." He stares down at me as he argues. "We have no idea what living behind those wards has done to you. And after that little fainting spell, I'm willing to bet you're in bad shape. So, sit down and let the woman do her job." His tone tells me he wholeheartedly expects me to do as I'm told.

"You know what you can do with those orders of yours? Shove them up your ass!" I am seething. Where does he get off? I'm facing off with him before I even realize that I moved. His eyes light up with sadistic excitement at the sight of my hostility.

"Don't worry, *a stór*, it's nothing sexual. I want you in top shape when I take you." His mouth curves at the corner, speaking to all the wicked delights he sees in our future.

"Pervert!" I cross my arms over my chest and turn my face away from him to hide the blush that always creeps up my cheeks when he mentions sex. Even in my current state, he still has this effect on me.

"Be that as it may..." The smile is evident in his words, "you're still going to al—" Whatever was going to come out of that too-sexy-for-his-own-good mouth of his is cut off by the sound of Marleen's voice.

"Your Majesties, may I make a suggestion?" She pauses to be sure that we're giving her our full attention, continuing once she's sure she has it. "Sir, I have been in your service for a great number of years and would never think to harm your bride. Why don't you take Libby to rest in one of the carriages, and I'll tend to the queen's wounds. Then, once she is dressed, you can appraise my work yourself." The witch's voice is tentative, but her back is straight, shoulders square, and eyes unflinching.

"Fine." The humor vanishes from Asher's eyes as he stares back at her before looking back at me. "We're not done here." With that said, he picks up Libby and quits the room.

"I don't know how much you know about Valore males, but it's extremely difficult for them to leave their mates, even more so when they're wounded."

"I'm not his mate. We barely know each other. I, for one, can't stand to be in the same room as him, and I'm sure the feeling is mutual."

"Nonetheless, you are who he has chosen." Apparently, we're done because she walks toward a chest at the end of the room and riffles through it. "Could you please remove your clothing, Your Majesty?" Her tone is soft with understanding, and those glowing eyes that see too much.

"Please, call me Devany." If she's going to see me naked, we might as well be on a first name basis.

"As you wish, Devany." A small smile graces her lips as she

replies. "But perhaps only when we're alone, one must uphold standards."

"I care little for standards; I've spent a lifetime living up to someone else's, and I refuse to carry on with the practice," I tell her in no uncertain terms. "If Asher doesn't like it, he can go fuck himself." I smile sweetly at her, and the small smile she gave me earlier returns, full and brilliant. Making her eyes flare brighter.

I take a deep breath and give myself a few moments to center my emotions. I haven't been naked in front of anyone other than Narcissa and Luna since I was thirteen. I start with my boots, then move to my pants with my shirt following shortly after. My movements are slow, though more from nerves than pain, each move meant to hold off the inevitable. I know the moment she finally sees my back by the quick intake of breath and the tentative finger that slowly traces the swirls of interlocking vines of night-blooming flora that cover the whole of my back. A tattoo embedded with magic so that it would cover the scars that cause me so much insecurity.

"I can feel the magic that pluses beneath the surface. A powerful spellcaster did this. How's that possible when your father has outlawed magic?" I smile at that. Luna would never let something like *laws* get in her way.

"There are ways to hide if you know how." My voice is a soft hush, as if I'm sharing a secret with her. But then her finger stops to retrace a piece of scarred tissue hidden beneath the tattoo.

"How?" The quiet horror in her voice shoots straight to the heart of me as she finally sees my shame laid bare before her. "It's difficult to scar a Valore, it would take—" The statement ends in a gasp when she finally understands, and it's that note of pity in her voice that has me stiffening my spine.

"Well, when that Valore is repeatedly tortured and too young to heal herself, while also living behind wards meant to hinder her kind... I suppose I should be grateful that he did it while I was too young to heal, because he would've killed me otherwise or had me collared like my mother." The indignant words tumble from my lips.

But Marleen doesn't call me on my ill temper or my rudeness. She simply hands me a warm washcloth and some sweet lavender soap to wash away the blood. Tears burn at the back of my eyes as I take these items from her.

Embarrassed by the emotion this small kindness has caused me, I merely put my head down and get to work cleaning my legs and arms, rinsing the washcloth out with each pass until the water is thoroughly stained with the sanguineous residue. Looking up from the bowl, I notice she has placed a new set of pants and chest binding on her cot for me to change into while she turns her back to give me the illusion of privacy. My voice is a choked sound in the back of my throat when I let her know I'm decent. She doesn't acknowledge what has just transpired between us—Doesn't give voice to the genuine fear I still carry within me. Fear of being judged as weak for not having the ability to protect myself. For being so unlovable that my father could do such things to me.

Once she is in front of me, I lower my arms from my torso to allow her a better look at my injuries which have healed to the point of being scabbed over. The only effects I'm still feeling are that of blood loss and pain. But I deserve those as a consequence for failing Libby. In truth, for failing so many before her. My mother's plan was faulty from the beginning. I did my best within the parameters of it, but so many suffered because of my lack of true action. I see that now. The strategy and machinations behind my father's great walls only did so much to protect my people. I should have done so much more. I deserve this pain. I relish the lesson it teaches me.

I meet Marleen's steady gaze head on, prepared to face many things, but it's the compassion and understanding that almost breaks my composure. With soft fingers and calloused palms, she takes hold of my face. Her luminous eyes, moving back and forth between mine.

"We each have our own monsters that haunt us. Whether they

be composed of emotion or flesh and bone, they have the power to wound or kill, but the only true power they possess is the power we give them. They're yours to slay. I can see it in your eyes. When the day comes that you decide to take back that power, you will leave nothing but destruction in your wake. You hold so much more than you realize." Her hand moves over my heart, and her eyes stare intently into mine. "You lack faith in yourself. But when you find it, may the Goddess help those who have harmed you and yours." The tears I had been holding back finally fall. With tender care, Marleen wipes them from my cheeks then pulls away to inspect my now healed wounds.

"You healed far faster than I expected, but you still seem to have some lingering pain. If you'll just sit back, I can—" I stop her with a staying hand, not wanting to see the look in her eyes when I answer. I turn away and put on the shirt that she had laid out for me.

"I deserve to feel this. There are lessons to be learned in pain." I give my response with my back to her, but she refuses to let me hide.

"And what lesson is there to learn here, Devany?" I meet her gaze and answer.

"That I'm stronger than my mother ever planned for me to be, and it's high time I act like it." With that, she gives me a sad smile and nods her head as if that makes all the sense in the world.

I think it's time for me to find Asher before he can corner me in this small carriage. So, I turn to leave, but the sound of Marleen's voice stops me. "Why cover it with a tattoo?" I consider her words carefully.

"I needed to turn something painful and ugly into something beautiful and free," I answer before walking out the door.

Chapter Nine

DEVANY

Upon exiting the carriage, I run face first into a wall of muscle belonging to none other than my husband. His spicy scent surrounds me and the heat from his body warms my skin. I have this overpowering need to bury my face in his chest to breathe in my fill and only just manage to stop myself from doing just that. What I don't manage to hide is the flinch that crosses my face or the arm that circles around my wounded abdomen on instinct. His eyes miss nothing, no matter how fleeting the expression may have been. His gaze locks on my arm for a few weighted seconds before returning to my face. He pulls me closer with his hands on my upper arms, being careful not to further exacerbate my wounds.

"Why?" That's all he asks. Not that I need more elaboration. He knows the only way I would still be in pain would be if I ordered it so, but this is not his choice.

"Because this pain is mine." My voice is quiet, the indignation and irritation ring clear with each word. "You don't get to decide what I do or do not feel. I assure you, I'll heal soon enough. Until then, I will carry the proof of my failure on my skin. It's the least that I can do to pay penance for the pain that I caused." I am once again drowning in guilt by the end of my impassioned speech. When I'm no longer able to hold his gaze, I look away to avoid seeing his reaction to my shame. With his fingers beneath my chin, he slowly lifts my face up to bring my eyes back to his.

"This was in no way your fault." His tone is firm with unwavering belief in what he says. His eyes flash with clear disbelief that I would think otherwise.

"Yes... it is. My shortcomings almost killed her—"

"Shortcomings? You can't be serious?" A humorless laugh falling from his lips. His voice is no longer soft, but now tight with disbelief. "What happened today had nothing to do with your *shortcomings* and everything to do with ours. Had you not been with her, she would be dead. There is no doubt about that. As it was, you took on a full-grown hadeon. Not only did you survive, but you held your own."

"This is my lesson to learn— my choice. I failed her, and whether you agree is neither here nor there. The pain will be fleeting. The least I can do is live with it, as a reminder."

His eyes move back and forth between mine as he tries to read my thoughts and get me to see reason. *Good luck with that, buddy.* These days, not even I know what's going on in my head.

"Fine..." The word is soft, almost like he's talking to himself. "If this is how you want to play, so be it. Until your wounds are completely healed, you will have guards with you to prevent any further injuries. You will spend the majority of your time resting in our tent. You will also ride with me until I deem you healthy enough to do so on your own."

"Who exactly do you think you are?"

"Your king."

Never in the history of language have two words been spoken with more arrogance. Again, the urge to hit him sparks within me, but is quickly smothered by his touch. "It's my job to command you." Those sinful lips of his curl up at the corner.

"Fuck. you." Each word is said through clenched teeth.

"That can be arranged, wife... Just say the words." I feel the soft glide of his hand as it moves to cup my jaw. His thumb stroking against my bottom lip. He leans his head in, lips brushing the corner of my mouth as he speaks. His breath warms my lips. Having him this close is intoxicating. Ruining my efforts at keeping him from being a distraction. His knowing smile only pisses me off further.

"No?" His smile only widens as I glare at him.

The ride to the next camp has been awkward and tense. Well... at least it was for me. Asher, on the other hand, doesn't appear to be having the same issue, if the heavy feel of him against my lower back is any indication.

All I can seem to concentrate on is the feel of him wrapped so tightly around me. The heat from his body warms my skin through my clothes and his large hand splays protectively across my injury. The whole thing is fucking with my head if I'm being honest.

Even that's not enough to keep my eyes from searching out Libby's carriage. The guilt over her injuries is crushing. Asher brings us up alongside it, having noticed me staring in that direction. It's a kindness I wasn't expecting but I'm grateful for it. I turn my head to thank him, which is when I catch sight of a young boy taking such attentive care of her. I've never experienced a love so purely innocent as the love he clearly has for her—not since my birth mother. Which is just plain sad now that I think about it. My second mother, while she cared for me, it was a subdued sort of love. Mostly, I represented the revenge she would one day take on the man who broke her. Her wolf in sheep's clothing. The nightmare he willingly allowed within the walls of his splendid castle... My father didn't believe in love or innocence of any kind.

Only pain and hate.

I watch enraptured as the boy runs his finger through her lovely copper hair, wiping her face down with a cool cloth. She's completely unaware of how tenderly he cares for her. Still blissfully asleep, thanks to the spellcaster. I continued to stare, drawn in by the way, he seems to see only her.

The sound of Asher's voice startles me out of the trance I had fallen into watching them.

"His name is Toby." His breath fans across the shell of my ear, causing an unbidden shiver to race down my spine. I turn my head so I can give him my full regard, bring our faces so very close that our lips almost touch.

"I didn't ask." Arching an eyebrow at him, sarcasm drips from each word. I've spent a small lifetime holding people at arm's length, not trusting one soul in my father's court. It's a habit that's hard to break, but it creates a wedge between Asher and me —and I need that space. It's the only way I know how to protect myself. Not that it bothers him, he seems to enjoy the verbal sparring.

"No..." his lips brush against mine, "but you wanted to." His answering smile only serves to piss me off because he's right. I did.

Movement out of the corner of my eye draws my attention back to the children, just in time to see Toby help Libby sit up, holding a waterskin to her lips since she doesn't have the strength to do so herself. With that image, I'm again drowning in guilt. *Not that I ever stopped. It seems to be my one constant as of late.*

The sound of Asher's voice brings my attention back to him. "It's not your fault. If anything, you're the reason she's alive." His voice is firm, leaving no room to argue. I decide the best course of action is deflection, not wanting to get into my decision to forgo healing yet again. The look he gives me tells me he knows what I'm doing. But he allows it, nonetheless.

"Are they siblings?" My eyes stray towards the children once more, watching them interact with each other. The beauty of it, a love so young, it's perfect.

"No, we came across Toby and Libby about two years ago

CROWN OF MY ENEMY · 83

along the outskirts of the Barren Straits, along the border of Naphal. Before that, they had spent three years with no one but each other. Toby provided for and protected Libby on his own. They're inseparable now. Wherever Libby goes, Toby follows, and vice versa." It was all said with a sad sort of resignation. But it's clear to see he holds affection for these two. Though my mind caught on to something else he'd said.

"The Barren Straits? My father touched briefly on the subject. I have always thought it odd that he never went into more detail. All he said was that Valore stripped it of all it had." My voice is quiet as my mind drifted back to my lessons and memories best forgotten. The phantom snap of my fingers being broken echoes in my mind, making my stomach revolt at the memory. It takes more than I'd like to admit to bring myself back under control.

"Well... he's partially right. The land represents the ruler, whether it be a Valore, human, shifter, or spellcaster. Our land is a reflection of ourselves. Minas, the false King of Froslien, found a way to strip the land at his borders of magic to strengthen his armies. We still don't know how he managed it. By the time their advancement was stopped, a quarter of Naphal had been stripped of all magic, causing their king to fall ill before passing. The Barren Straits are all that is left of the southern province of Naphal and the unclaimed forest between their border and Froslien." The information leaves me reeling. I didn't know the land reflected the monarch. The land was already bare when I came to live in Erabis. But it makes a sad sort of sense that land would be leached of all color and dead. Just like father's dead, shriveled heart.

I turn to Asher again and the movement brings our faces so close I'm momentarily distracted by the beauty in his captivating eyes. Flecks of spring and autumn flicker to life in his irises. They are so inviting I almost forget myself and kiss him. Realizing therein lies the path to ruin. It's no wonder I'm a little breathless when I bring myself back to the subject at hand.

"How were they stopped?" My eyes move back and forth

between his, gauging his reaction as he answers. I can tell that whatever he's going to say, I will not like it.

"Princess Lela of Aiteall," he says like it's the answer to all things.

I pull back slightly to have a better view of his face. "What does she have to do with this?" My brows furrowed in confusion. Asher raises his hand to my face, rubbing his thumb along the indentation between my brows, smoothing it out before dragging his fingertips back down along my jaw. His eyes are wholly focused on me.

"Princess Lela of Aiteall—younger sister to Queen Tempest of Erabis." He pauses as his eyes move over my face as he accesses my reaction to this news. My mind fills with white noise. The heavy beat of my heart is the only movement in my body. When I only stare back at him, he continues. "She beseeched the eight Elemental Druids, and they answered."

The breath I held shakes out of me in one word. "How?"

He closes his eyes briefly before continuing. "They blocked the path of whatever cursed magic Minas was draining the land with, creating a barrier along the new border of Naphal. But that only stopped Minas for so long. Our spies from within Froslien have informed us he began draining his weaker citizens of their magic—of their very lives—to continue strengthening his armies. In recent days, they have been able to breach the barrier. It weakens with each attempt. This is why we need to raise an army that can rival his because it's unnatural. The excess magic wears on the mind and body, turning them feral and damn near unstoppable."

I know what he was saying is important, but I don't care. There are questions that my soul demands answers to. "What happened to her? What was the price? What—What did she give them?" The questions are given life in one long breath. Wanting to know everything and nothing all at once. Asher's sharp intake of breath pulls me out of my spiraling thoughts. I mirror his actions. In. Out. In. Out. Until we were moving as one.

His eyes don't stray from mine even as his words break open my world and threaten to swallow me whole. "She died... ten years ago."

"My birth mother died ten years ago." A statement meant more for me than him. He answers it, nonetheless.

"I know." His reply is spoken so quietly that had it not been for the total silence within me, I never would have heard him.

My eyes bounce back to his at the quiet confession, with an equally quiet question. "How?" I ask, needing him to make sense of all of this.

If I hadn't been so lost in this moment, I would've resented him for it. As it was, my mind was still spiraling.

He looks back at me like he'd rather do anything other than answer me. "About ten years ago, a rumor came out of Hepha that Princess Lela lived and with her, the future of Aiteall."

"Future?" My voice sounded empty even to my own ears.

"Yes..." The word is a soft sound that ruffles my hair. "A daughter... the daughter of Princess Lela was promised..." He took a deep breath before proceeding. He seemed to be doing that a lot today. "She was meant to marry the youngest son of King Rainer and Queen Ophelia of Narci, cementing the treaty and reaffirming the friendship between the two kingdoms." His face draws tight as he waits for my response.

Well, he would just have to wait. My mother, or rather the woman who raised me after the death of my birth mother... She knew who I was... knew she was my aunt—my flesh and blood, and while she seemed to love me, she treated me as a pawn, a weapon to be wielded. Whether it be physically or politically. My father was much the same. A political weapon to reiterate his power in this war. And then there's Asher. How does he wish to wield me? If I had to guess, I'd say both. I can feel this blanket of sadness weighing me down.

My eyes snap back to him as a thought raced to the forefront of my mind. "You knew who I was when you came for me." Again, it's not a question, but a statement.

He answers it, nonetheless. "Yes, I did," he replies, with a hardness in his gaze.

"So, I belong to yet another man." The laughter that leaves me is hollow and sad. *Will I ever belong to myself?* Always meant to be something to someone else. I close my eyes against the onset of tears. Fight back the emotions that threaten to drown me. Even the feel of Asher's hand sliding along my neck to cup my jaw isn't enough to pull me from my sorrow. Not one to be denied, he tightens his grip slightly, not to hurt but to gain my attention. He leans his forehead against mine, waiting for me to open my eyes before speaking.

"You belong to me, and I'll not give you up." The words are as sharp and firm as foraged steel. His hand tightens further on my chin, eyes moving back and forth between mine to be sure that I hear him. "Know this, *a stór álainn*, you're mine."

Enough! I'm no one's pawn. No one's weapon. I know the moment he sees the change in me. That fire that flickers to life in my eyes answers the flames in his. If we're not careful, the two of us are liable to burn the world to ashes, leaving nothing but destruction in our wake. If his smirk is anything to go by, he'd let it burn for a chance to dance in the flames with me, and though I'll never admit it to him... so would I. "You know what? Fuck that. And fuck you. I meant what I said, I belong to no man, and I bow to no one." I try to pull back from his hold. To create some much-needed space between us. He only holds on that much harder.

He pulls my face closer, brushing his lip against mine. Just breathing me in for a moment. His eyes are solely on me. Those twin flames burning between us. His voice is so deceptively soft as he speaks. "Oh, *a stór milis*, one day you'll learn there's a difference between bowing and kneeling... and when you do, your king will be waiting."

I suck in a breath, ready to tell him what I think of him. Only to have his mouth crash into mine. Between one second and the next, we're devouring each other. Nothing but teeth and tongue as an unimaginable need to claw our way under the other's skin takes over. Always riding that fine line between lust and anger. By the time we rip our mouths apart, we're panting heavily. Those flames once again licking at our skin, only to look around and realize we're alone on the trail. The convoy had moved on without us.

"Well, shit," was all I could think to say. His husky laugh is the only reply I receive as he brings his hands around to take hold of the reins, stirring us toward camp, shaking his head in amusement.

"It's not that funny, asshole," I mumble as my face heats with embarrassment at what they must have seen as they moved on ahead of us.

His laughter only doubles. "Oh, but it is," he says, pressing a hard kiss to the side of my head. "It really is." I decided then and there that I really don't like my husband very much, and that we should most definitely not speak for the remainder of the ride. Just before leading the horse into a fast trot, he once again places a protective hand over my wounded stomach. How can he be such a horse's ass while also being so very considerate? He's a mess of contradictions.

Chapter Ten

ASHER

All I can think about for the rest of our journey is the way her lips felt on mine. How her nails dug into the skin along my neck. The woman hides so much passion behind those eyes of steel and midnight. It's a wonder it doesn't burn us both to cinders every time we collide.

What's truly frightening is I've come to crave it. The feel of it licking against my skin, dancing with my own.

I really should kill her for what she does to me. For becoming a weakness my enemies would surely exploit. It would be a kindness to do it myself—painless compared to what they undoubtedly are sure to do to her. I have a feeling it's too late for that now. So... we war against each other until we finally collide, leaving us bruised and battered with no choice but to succumb to our passions. And fuck me if I'm not looking forward to the next battle.

We make our way westward toward the Kingdom of Naphal, traveling through the Tanee woods. The tall, lush vining trees choke out the sun, leaving us encased in shadows. The spaces between them brimming with hostas, their large, waxy leaves in shades of yellow turned toward what little sunlight there is. Soft, dewy moss covers the ground. The smell of clear water and damp soil mixes with Devany's soft and delicate floral scent.

The rest of our trip is uneventful and silent. Though she's wound tight with tension. Whether it's from our fight or the kiss that followed, who's to say? But the further we journey from the western border of Erabis, the more agitated she seems to become, and the more convinced I am that they have conditioned her to run back to her bastard father. That in and of itself is disconcerting.

The sound of the Satran River greets us just before we break the tree line into the clearing where camp is being set. There's no fanfare upon entering, not a soul pays attention to us as we head for the stable.

People rush about erecting tents amidst the dwellings made of elemental magic. Those with the ability to manipulate the earth element create stacked stone from the soil beneath our feet or grow trees where there had been none, the branches weaving together, creating a canopy. Canvas is draped and interwoven throughout the area, creating a vision closer to that of a city rather than a traveling caravan. Others dig holes for fire-pits in perpetration for tonight's meal, while some head off to hunt. It's all a well-oiled machine from the days when we were only a nomadic army with no place to call our own. Lessons learned in the years before I conquered the beasts of Draic and became king.

We reach the center of camp, and a stable hand walks us to an available watering trough, where I swiftly dismount before helping Devany down. I take hold of her hips and lift her from the saddle, purposely sliding her body down the length of mine, staring into her beautiful eyes the entire time. Her hair tickles along my skin, bringing with it the scent of the forest mixed with her own. She shivers at the contact, and I watch her lovely eyes dilate with remembered passion. Blindly, I hand over Balius' reins, keeping my gaze trained on the dangerous beauty before me.

More than ready to burn for one more kiss, I brush my lips

against her tempting mouth. I'm met with a loud grunt as the impact of Libby's crying body knocks the breath from Devany's lungs.

The youngster wraps herself around Devany, burying her face at her hip. Giant sobs shake her slight frame, while she whispers, "I'm sorry," repeatedly. Tentatively, Devany wraps the child up in her arms. Her lovely eyes gazing at me with such a lost look that it makes my heart ache for her.

It's a look I haven't seen on her face often and it makes me wonder, not for the first time, what type of childhood she must have had. I bring myself to eye level with Libby, giving a lock of her hair a gentle tug to get her attention. She turns her tear-stained face toward me but doesn't release her hold on Devany's waist.

"Whatever do you have to be sorry for?" I ask, completely bewildered as to why these two females feel they're at fault for anything that's occurred. Her bright eyes are full of tears as she works through what she wants to say.

"It's my fault Queen Devany was injured." As I take a breath to respond, she continues. "I wandered off after Toby told me to stay put. He... always told... told me that... I had to do as he says... or someone could get hurt or... worse—die. And look what happened..." Great sobs break her statement up as she lets us know everything that has been weighing on her young mind.

"Sweet girl, you are not at fault for this. We are. It's our job to protect those in our charge. Toby told you that before because the two of you were on your own and you were his charge to protect... To keep safe. Now, you have us, and it is we who have failed you." I stop briefly to look up at Devany. "Both of you. We failed you, and for that I am sorry. I will be eternally grateful that you were better prepared to take care of each other than we were in taking care of you. We will not—" Stopping once more to look at Devany. "*I* will not," I stress the words, letting her hear the oath I'm making, "fail you again." I return my attention to young

Libby. "I beg your forgiveness?" She doesn't seem to know how to respond other than to nod, her lovely sunset curls bouncing around her slim shoulders.

"Now, with that out of the way. You've only just healed, and I don't want you running around. So, head over to your tent and rest up." Holding up one hand when she takes a breath. "And before you argue, your queen will be doing the same." I give said queen a pointed look to keep whatever argument she has poised on the tip of her tongue behind her sharp teeth.

Libby holds my eyes for a moment before heading in the direction of the children's tents. I stand and press my hand against Devany's lower back, leading her toward our own, where I'll be leaving her to rest while I help to finish preparing camp.

"Where the fuck are we going?" I just barely stop myself from smiling. She made it all of one minute before losing her shit. She turns around and shoves me in the chest, creating some space between us.

"Now now, wife. We had an agreement," I remark, unable to keep the amusement out of my voice.

Closing the distance between us, I lift my hand and trace her collarbone with my fingertips. Slowly I circle her, dragging my fingers along her shoulders with a serpent's smile on my lips. By the time I'm facing her again, her hands on her hips and she looks equal parts irritated and aroused.

"We had no such thing." Those quicksilver eyes of her burning bright. And like a fool who covets the sun, I can't help but move closer to her. Trailing the back of my fingers down her cheek to her jaw, it's as though I have no power to stop myself from running my thumb over her soft, pouty lips.

"Yes, we did." My voice is hushed, my lips drifting closer. "You decided to stay in pain. I decided that if you were going to insist on that decision, I would make sure you received no further injuries. So, you see, we both made our decrees and therefore we have an agreement, wouldn't you say? Unless you've changed your mind, in which case," I look her in the eyes to make sure she sees how very serious I am, "I'll call for Marleen, and you can be on your way to whatever mischief you have planned in that keen mind of yours." My eyes drop to her mouth while I give her a moment to answer before pulling my gaze from her lips back to her eyes. "No? Well, I guess we do in fact have an agreement, and that agreement states you will be spending your time in our tent. Now with that settled. Shall we?" I say, holding my hand out to her.

"I was to be given my own tent." the tight words are spoken between clenched teeth. Those eyes of hers say so much. So many things... Most are dirty words she wishes to call me, but there's a vulnerability most don't see. She's so good at hiding her emotions.

"No, sweet wife, you were going to have a tent of your own as long as you could be trusted..." My smile only grows the harder she stares at me. I do get a rush from these interactions. It's probably cause for concern, but that's a problem for another day. "Do I need to remind you of your transgression that has resulted in you losing your tent?" The more she looks like she wants to kill me, the harder I get.

"Please, *a stór álainn*, give in..." wrapping my arm around her waist, I pull her ever closer because it seems I just can't help myself.

"Give in to what exactly, husband?" The little minx leans into me, pressing her delicate breast against my chest. Allowing me to feel all her soft curves molding perfectly to me. "Cat got your tongue?" she says, her lips ghosting over my mouth while her eyes stay open, looking back and forth between mine. By the Gods, she's breathtaking.

I pull her tighter against my body and slide my hand into her hair, tilting her head back to give myself better access to her delicious mouth.

"To me, wife... Give in to *me*."

But before I can take advantage of that mouth, she places a

hand on my chest, pushing out of my embrace. A smile flirting with her lips.

"Where would the fun be in that?" Her reply said against my lips before leaving me to watch her enter our tent alone.

She thinks she's winning this game of wills. I'd tell her otherwise, but to quote my dear wife, where's the fun in that?

Chapter Eleven

ASHER

The day came and went, with me spending the majority of it in Ansel's tent going over where we're at on supplies and things of that nature. As well as which route will be best to take into Naphal. I was so occupied with making plans I hadn't noticed that night has fallen.

Neither she nor I have anywhere left to hide. So now is as good a time as any to enter our tent and see what the minx is going to throw at me next.

I stroll past Kane with a fuck you smile ready to once again verbally spar with my lovely wife only to be struck speechless by the alluring sight before me. Framed in firelight, dressed in a gown and robe of pale blue silk and campaign lace, stands my wife frozen as if caught committing a crime. The only thing she's guilty of is tempting me. Not that she is actually trying to. She was just born to stand out. The woman is perfection. Making me feel weak and that makes me want to tempt her as she does me. To put us once again on even ground.

"Well, hello, *a stór milis*, I see you've dressed for battle," I say to her, admittedly distracted. My eyes memorize every dip and curve.

I expect her to wrap her lace robe tighter around her. To hide that delectable body from me. But she rarely ever does what I expect her to do. With a defiant lift of her chin and a wicked glint in her eyes, she lets the lace slide down the length of her body to billow at her feet. And just like that. An invisible string is pulled tight, and I drift toward her without a conscious thought.

Devany's eyes track my steps with trepidation, and I get the satisfaction of watching the delicate movements of her throat as she swallows nervously. I raise my hand, trailing my fingers along her jaw, lifting her beautiful face. To bring her lips ever closer to mine. Those moonlight eyes say so much. I can't help the words that leave my mouth, knowing without a doubt she'll believe I'm feeding her lines.

"You are the most stunning creature I've ever laid my eyes upon." The whispered secret spoken across her lips moments before I bruise them with mine.

She's motionless for the space of a heartbeat, then she surges forward on the tips of her toes, tunneling her fingers in my hair to better anchor me to her. Devouring my kiss. Battling my passions with her own and we are once again burning.

I'm surrounded by everything her. The feel of velvety skin and smooth silk beneath my fingertips. Her scent, moon gardens and amber musk assaults me. It clings to my skin. The taste of wild synder berries and something purely Devany burst upon my tongue. Intoxicating. Utter perfection. Everything I never knew, I always wanted. The need to own this woman thumps a steady beat against my chest, making me deaf to everything except her quick gasps and soft moans. The subtle whisper of my name.

"The bath you requested is ready to be set up, your highness." A calm monotone voice tries to distract me from the wonders of my wife.

I pull away from her and she sways toward me like she just can't help it. Too helpless to stop it. She makes a disgruntled sound at being separated from my lips. Which just brings a smile to my face.

"Just a moment," I call out while placing my forehead against hers.

"Sorry to disappoint, *a stór álainn*. We'll have to pick this up later. I ordered this bath in the hopes that you may join me. What are the chances of me stripping you bare and getting you wetter than I already have? Hmmm?" I ask her quietly.

Her eyes open slowly, still swimming in seduction. But I can tell the moment my words register. She drops her hands from my neck, curling them into fists. Cheeks flushing further with embarrassment at having given in to me once again. She fights this so hard. Hell, at least one of us is.

Pleasure is something I can give her. But my heart... that's one thing I no longer have to offer. It's been blackened. Ravaged by all the things I've done to get us this far. Who knows what I may have to do yet? No, this is preferable. Her hate wrapped up in passion. Because the truth is she deserves better, she just doesn't know it.

"You pig!" I do enjoy her mouth. She'll need that strength for what's coming.

"Be that as it may, *a stór milis*." Toying with the thin strap of her nightdress. Threatening her with its descent.

"Sorry, husband, I've already bathed," she replies, lips tipped up at the corners.

I look her up and down, backlit by firelight. Skin flushed. Eyes bright. The mere sight of her is enough to damn well bring me to my knees. It almost has me saying fuck it to the bath and taking her to bed.

With a gallant effort, I take a step back from her, kneeling to retrieve her robe. I'm sure she would prefer to be covered before anyone enters. I walk around her, dragging the robe along the rug behind me before placing it around her shoulders. My fingers mapping the terrain of her neck, shoulders, and arms. My hands continue on their path until I can wrap my arms around her from behind. I pull her closer, placing my chin on her shoulder. Loving the little shiver, she gets anytime I'm this close.

"Bring it in," I call out to those awaiting entry.

I keep her close while we watch the copper tub being placed and filled. They bring in pails of hot water, one after the other, filling the space with steam. I watch them calmly while Devany is tight with tension. Trepidation seems to be her default emotion.

Which only makes me want to push her, to bring out the strong woman that lays beneath the surface. The one that will be queen... The queen I need by my side in this war. So, once they've finished, I nuzzle the side of her neck before taking a step back and walking over to the table near the tub. Keeping my back to her.

"Are you going to watch, little wife?" Throwing the taunting words over my shoulder.

I work on removing my weapons, placing them on the table. When no words come. I turn, giving her my full regard. But she just looks at me as if rooted in place. I remove my fighting leathers next. Unsnapping buttons and buckles maintaining eye contact with her through the entire process. Still, she stands, though her breathing has picked up once again. I would love to taunt her further with well-placed barbs. But I'm just as transfixed as she is. Reaching back, I grab my thin undershirt and pull it over my head, baring my chest to her. It's covered with an array of scars, both thin and thick, all from weapons made of iron.

When I open my eyes again, she's approaching me, and now I'm the one rooted in place. Afraid that any movement on my part and she'll stop. Her small hand lifts to trace the edge of a scar that runs along my rib with the tips of her fingers. I expected her hand to be warm like the rest of her, but they're deathly cold, quite the opposite of the fire she keeps just below the surface. Not once lifting her eyes to mine, tracing one scar after the other. I have to fight the urge to shudder at her touch.

"Iron." A statement, not a question. Her voice is painfully soft.

"Yes," I reply, placing my hand over hers, using my other hand to lift her face back up so I can see her eyes. Only to realize she's crying. Her eyes are glossy, eyelashes clustered in dewy spikes with drops of liquid clinging to them. I lean forward, placing light kisses, first to her lips, then to each eye. Tasting the salt of her pain and sadness.

"Why the tears, *a stór milis*?" My eyes move between hers, trying to discern the emotions I see swirling in their depths.

"I've seen scars like these before." Her hand falls listlessly to her side. Voice devoid of any emotion in complete opposition to her eyes. Those swirl with so many unsaid words. So much unknown pain. Pain she may never share with me.

If my suspicions are right, I'm going to kill her father slowly. And before I end it, I'm going to make him get on his knees and beg for her forgiveness.

The desolate look in her eyes is killing me. I prefer her fighting and spitting venom at me. Not broken and lost as she is now. With those thoughts in mind, I decide it's best to push her. Give her someone to fight. And when the time is right, I'm going to teach her to cut out the pain. To take the payment in the blood of her enemies. I'll line them up as an offering at her feet. Bare their throats for her blade.

"So, little wife, are you going to keep staring or do you plan on joining me?" I ask her, being sure that my voice drips condescension, arrogance firmly in place as I unbuckle my belt.

"Not that I mind you groping me, love." I grab her hand and place it on my cock. "But if you want my attention, best to place your dainty hand right here." Smirking at her as righteous indignation sets her eyes a flame.

Just as expected, she rips her hand from mine, bawling them into tight fists. Laughing, I turn toward the bath, giving her my back. This turns out to be a mistake because I end up face first in the water, having received a two-handed shove in the shoulder.

"You're such an asshole!"

I spin around in the tub so I'm sitting rather than drowning, still laughing under my breath.

She's once again across the room with her back to me, shoulders drawn tight, hands fisted. At some point, she must have removed her robe because I notice a tattoo that appears to start at the base of her neck traveling well below the back panel of the gown. The tattoo in and of itself isn't unusual, especially for a Valore. In fact, she should have ravens somewhere on her body.

The work is impeccable. Night-blooming flowers basking in moonlight. I stand up to step out of my now soggy pants and boots before returning to the tub, sinking beneath the warm water.

"Unusual for a human woman of your station to have tattoos, hmmm?" I ask as my eyes follow each dip and swirl of the artwork that climbs up her spine, fanning out over her shoulder blades to disappear around her ribs. The piece taking up the whole of her back.

"I think we've established that I'm very much *not* human." Her reply is quiet, as if she's worried someone may hear. So used to hiding what she really is.

"Have we? I've seen no proof either way. But back to the tattoo. It's truly exceptional work. Why did you get it?" The work is impeccable, the soft blues and purples playing beautifully against the glow of her skin.

"Thank you, I have several." The tone is so full of sarcasm that it brings a smile to my face. She really does snark well. "The artist is a young spellcaster by the name of Luna... She tattoos many of the townspeople, often weaving invisible protection spells beneath the art. Regarding your last question—none of your fucking business." She goes on giving far more information than I expected, but then she finishes up with a fuck-yourself-very-much at the end.

"Now now, wife, that's rude. How is a spellcaster hiding in your father's land?" This, I'm truly interested in. King Kól is known for hanging spellcasters from battlement walls or burning them along his borders. How did she come to know a spellcaster? I must ask out loud because she answers me.

"My mother knew her mother. I suppose I should say, my *aunt* knew her mother." Sadness once again creeps into her voice. It calls to something in me, that same loss of family. But in this world, we make our own and so can she. Something I'm sure Kól made difficult for her, and I'm sure it was done by design.

"Just because Tempest was your aunt by blood doesn't make her any less of a mother," I say hoping to ease her pain even just a little.

"No, Asher, I was her revenge. The wolf she could hide in plain sight. The danger he willingly let behind his high walls." She's only said my name a handful of times, but this is the first time I've heard her say it with so much resignation. As if that's all she will ever be. But she is so much more. More than even I gave her credit for.

"She was a sad, broken woman. That's no reflection on you." The words leave my throat on a growl. Pissed off that they made this woman feel less than. When she is everything... Everything they could never be and so much more. If I did nothing else, I'm going to teach her what she's truly capable of. Then sit back and watch them all burn.

"Isn't it though?" she replies, looking directly at me. Her strength clearly shining through. "That's all I've ever been, even to you." She is right in some ways and very wrong in others. For me, it's never that cut and dry where she's concerned.

"Tell me something else about you, Devany. I want to know something about you. Something more than what people have said you are." And I mean it. Gods, help me, but I want to know this woman. Heart, mind, and soul. I'm a selfish bastard. I want all of her, even if I can't return the sentiment.

She seems relieved by the change in subject and begins telling me a whole lot of things about herself without actually telling me anything. At some point, it must have dawned on her that I'm naked because her back is toward me once more. With each splash of water, her shoulders become more rigid, and I realize it's best to get out and dry off. I dress in a soft loose pair of charcoal gray sleeping pants that hang low, forgoing a shirt. After all, I do love her reactions to me.

"You can turn around now, little wife. I'm dressed." Her shoulders hitch up a little further. Obviously noticing the amusement in my voice and not liking it one bit.

She turns around and this time when her eyes land on my chest, there's a little more heat in them. I place my hand on her elbow, trailing it down to her hand, giving it a small tug and leading us to the bed.

"In you go, sweets." Pulling the soft furs back for her to get in. With a great deal of amusement, I watch her look back and forth between the bed and me. "It's not a snake, *a stór*, you can get in. I promise the bed and I won't bite. Well, the bed won't bite. But I promise when I sink my fangs into your soft flesh, you'll enjoy every minute."

She huffs while getting into bed, muttering under her breath. "I wouldn't count on it." Which only goes to further my amusement.

"What about you? I'm the only one to spill my secrets?" Not pointing out that she didn't really tell me very much.

"Fair is fair. What do you wish to know?" I say secretly hoping she asks nothing too probing.

"Where is your family? No one has mentioned anything about your parents." Of course, she asks that. I suppose it's only fair with everything she told me about Tempest.

With a deep breath, I reply, "My parents are on the other side of the Great Dome, within the Kingdom of Narci. When the wall went up, I was hunting in the Taritin Woods on that border between Narci and Hepha. I somehow ended up on Hepha's side of the woods, effectively shutting me out of my home." The word home said so quietly and full of longing. I know my family loves me. We lost so much during the war. Lives. Loved ones. Friends... Family.

"How old were you?" she asks, seeming like she genuinely wants to know. She lays her head in the space between my shoulder and chest, bringing her body close to my side. Not knowing what else to do, I wrap my arm around her waist.

"Eleven..." I trail off, distracted by having her this close while memories run freely through my mind, distant and vivid at the same time. "I was eleven when I was locked out," I repeat, to get us back on track, not that she notices my mind wandering in the past.

She looks up at me from her place on my chest, causing me to look down to see her eyes. "I was ten when my mother died. A boy in the woods saved me." Her voice is soft while her hand toys with a pendant hanging around her neck, drawing my eyes to it. Polished obsidian carved in the old language.

"What was his name...? The boy who saved you." My voice is as soft as hers.

She looks away from me before answering. "I don't know." A sadness full of longing creeps into her lyrical voice.

I place a finger under her chin to bring those eyes back to mine. Ready to ask more questions, but the hard look in her eyes tells me she'll answer none of them. I decide it's best to ask another day.

"Sleep."

Chapter Twelve

DEVANY

I wake up in a cocoon of warmth with an arm around my waist, molding me to the firm body beside me. The chest I'm currently using as a pillow rises and falls in tandem with the heart beating a steady rhythm beneath my ear. A deep breath surrounds me with a scent I'd know anywhere. *Asher...* He always smells like night air wrapped in winter fires. It's quickly becoming my favorite scent.

But that's not what has me distracted. It's not even all that tan, olive skin bare to my greedy eyes. No... it's the scars. There are so many. Some are thin, silvery, and white. While others are thick and raised. My fingers lightly tracing each one. The texture is so like the ones I also carry.

Asher takes a deep breath and releases it slowly, rustling the shorter layers of my hair — tickling my nose. I hold perfectly still, trying to breathe through the need to sneeze, so I don't wake him. A few silent moments pass before I continue on with my exploration.

I tilt my head back slightly to look up at him from my position on his chest, following the tendon of his exposed throat.

From this viewpoint, I can see all the sharp curves of his jaw, the steep slope of his ears and a halo of mahogany hair covering the pillow beneath him. With his head tipped back, it elongates the lines of his neck, making his Adam's apple more pronounced.

Intricate golden tattoos made up of shapes and vines intertwined with words written in the old language grace the sides of his throat, moving down his body, following the curves and dips of his muscles. The metallic ink shimmers in the lowlight of the almost spent candles.

Asher's beard is a little messy and unkempt from sleep. Unable to stop myself, I lift my hand, running it along his jaw. His beard is so much softer than I had expected, the thick hairs tickling my palm. I trail my fingers down the column of his neck, along the tendon and into the hollow of his throat. My touch is delicate and light. I shift my eyes back up every so often to be sure he's still sleeping soundly before I carry on.

I follow the curve of muscles around his chest to the metal bar in his left nipple, drawing my finger around it airily before carrying on. My fingertips trace the center path of his chest to his abs, snagging on a deep scar that starts below his rib cage and ends just beside his bellybutton. He's a warrior to his very core. All tight muscles and coiled strength. His scars are the only warning of how truly dangerous he is. Something menacing and lethal wrapped up in such a lovely exterior and like the ones I'm sure came before me, I'm falling into his trap.

I trace the scar to its end, only to have my attention drawn to a thin strip of hair leading beneath his gray sleeping pants, between the deep v of his hips. My eyes continue to track in the direction all signs point to, stopping at the large swell in the front of his pants. Taking in the full size of him has my breathing speeding up and every muscle in my lower belly clinching tight. Both in arousal and a little fear.

"Are you going to stare at my cock all morning, *a stór milis*?" A voice from above me asks in a sleepy rasp, my face flushing with heat. I'm sure even the tips of my ears are red.

"You barbaric bastard! It's not like I'm here by choice! Having been trapped by your arm all morning," I'm quick to point out. Anything to distract from being caught.

"Yes, such a hardship for you, my sweet little captive." His voice is a near purr, dripping with sensual sarcasm.

The arm he has wrapped around my waist lifts and his hand glides up my spine before tunneling into my hair. He gives it a sharp tug, pulling my head back so we're looking eye to eye. The quick act eliciting a startled breath from my lips. His golden green eyes track between mine as his head dips, moving slowly as if to give me time to say no. When no denial comes, his eyes light up with wicked delight. His mouth descending upon mine — devouring me in a way that only he can. He releases his hold on my hair to capture my thigh, hauling me over his waist to straddle him. Providing some much-needed glorious friction on my core.

So many sensations all at once. The heat from his body seeps into mine. Very much in opposition to the cold early morning air prickling against the exposed skin of my neck and back. The hard planes of his body press to mine. The feel of his hands on my bare thighs as he pushes the silk gown up around my hips, the sleek fabric caressing my skin. His fingers lightly flexing on my thighs.

A barrage of emotions swirl in my chest. Guilt and fear walking hand-in-hand. The anxiety of it all laying heavy in my stomach. And then there's the passion... By the Gods, so much passion. It's hard for me to reconcile the emotions he brings out in me. I never truly know what he's thinking or feeling, that alone puts us on uneven footing. But the passion within me works in tandem with his own, and I can't seem to ignore it. His fire calling to mine, singing to my very soul, caressing along the delicate edges.

I know this is a terrible decision, one I'll no doubt regret. But for the life of me, I can't find the will to care. So instead of denying my instincts... I follow them.

Shifting my weight on to my knees, I slip my hand between us and into his pants, where I wrap my hand around him, squeezing gently. My efforts are rewarded with a husky groan against my mouth. I open my eyes and withdraw imperceptibly, smiling against his lips. Squeezing once more before I slide my hand along the length of him, marveling at the feel. The contrast. Soft, silken skin over tempered steel. The weight of him in my palm. Another low, deep hum like moan leaves his throat. Needing to swallow that sound whole, I crush his lips with mine, slipping my tongue between his teeth and pouring all my emotions into it. Anger. Attraction. Disappointment. Hesitance. Insecurity. *Fear.*

I moan against his tongue as I give in to the passion. As I give in to *him.*

I pull him through my palm once more when Asher seizes my wrist. His other hand tangling in my messy hair, affectively holding me captive. He pulls my head back and studies my face with those ever-changing eyes of his, the color of bright moss with flexes of sunshine. What he's looking for, I don't know. Which makes me even more nervous and self-consciously shifting my weight. I have my hand on his cock... *And he's stopping me. What does that mean?*

He mutters under his breath. So low I almost miss it. "The gods themselves best bless me for my restraint."

I inhale to ask him what he meant by that. But I'm saved from asking any of the venerable questions I would probably regret later. "Wake up, asshole, we're burning daylight," A familiar voice says from the entrance to our tent.

"It sounds like someone likes you about as much as I do." I smile through the sting of rejection.

He huffs out a surprise laugh followed by a long shaky breath. Asher cups my face with both hands, leaning his forehead against mine. "Our first time will not be in a tent." He speaks these words softly just for me, pushing a lock of hair behind my ear and tracing the very human-looking curve. "I won't allow anyone to hear all the sweet noises you're going to make for me. Just for me, *a stór.* And certainly not when you're unsure." He places a light kiss on my lips. "When I have you, there will be no room for doubt. There will be only you and me."

"Time to go, you two," Ansel chimes in from just outside the tent, causing my face to flush with heat once again. Asher takes in the state of my face and gives me a rakish smile. All too pleased with himself.

"Up you go, He says, tapping my thigh lightly before lifting me off his lap and depositing me on the bed, leaving me to watch him get dressed.

My husband is very distracting to watch, corded muscles shifting beneath bronzed skin. A twist here, a turn there. I give my head a little shake as if to dislodge the sight. To bring my attention back to the subject at hand.

"Why are we burning daylight? Is there something we're supposed to be doing?" I turn my head to the side to get a better view of his ass as he bends over to pick up his pants. He straightens and turns around to give me his full regard, catching me staring at him yet again. An arched brow and flash of fangs are the only response I get. But I fully expect an answer to my question, and I say as much.

"I expect an answer, husband." Arching a brow of my own, smiling sweetly. But it vanishes with his answer.

"We're leaving today and pushing forward. With any luck, we'll reach the town of Lysia by nightfall. Which means you and I can stay in an inn tonight." I can barely hear him over the white noise in my ears. The next thing I see is Asher's face swimming in front of me. His hands hold my face. *When did he cross the room?*

"What the fuck? Devany? Talk to me, *a stór!*" So much concern in that voice. But I can't answer him.

The tension I've been feeling since yesterday has increased tenfold. My heart beats heavily within my chest, as if wishing to run back to Erabis all on its own. The scent of blood and death clings to my skin like I've walked upon a battlefield. With phantom screams echoing in my ears. Something is very wrong. *What's happened?*

"We can't leave," I whisper to him, holding on to his wrists. Feeling his pulse beat steadily under my fingers, grounding me to the here and now.

Until this point, the ominous feeling has just been lingering in the background of my mind. But faced with leaving, it returns with a vengeance. Almost like a warning bell has been rung, opening the floodgate of my power.

My head throbs, a pain behind my eyes so piercing that it feels like I may pass out. The mere thought of leaving, of moving further from the borders of Erabis has my stomach rolling and twisting. The room is spinning beyond Asher. *I think I'm going to be sick.* The misery behind my eyes steadily increases, and my skin feels too tight.

His eyes harden, losing all the softness they had held all morning. He straightens and his hands withdraw from my face, leaving my own to fall limply to my sides.

"No." That one word falls so hard from his lips that it feels like a physical blow.

"You don't understand. I can't leave." My voice is only shaking slightly now that the initial shock has passed.

"Yes, you can and will," he says with authority, as if he has any say in it.

"We will leave within the hour. The further we get from your father's borders, the better..." he pauses, and I think for a moment that he may see reason. But like an arrow to the heart that hope dies upon his lips. "You'll feel better once you're away from your father's influence." It's the pity I hear and see on his face that snaps me out of that vulnerable state. To light that fire within my soul and if he's not careful, I may burn him to ashes.

"My people need me here. How can you not understand this?" Incredulity rings true in my words. I search his face for some kind of understanding.

"I'm a king, of course I understand. The people in the tents outside. The people of Draic. Those are your people now. You are their Queen; they are who you need to worry about. Because we are hemmed in by two enemies and if your father gets a foothold here in Galandir we are well and truly fucked, Devany. And I can most surely guarantee that if he has you, he will. So, no... we're not staying. I don't know what kind of brainwashing your father's done to make you so loyal to him..." He stares at me with the most intense look. Agitation rolling off him in waves. I keep expecting him to treat me with the respect I deserve. To stop treating me like a spoiled child. What's sad is I don't even think he does it on purpose.

But I'm no child.

Turning my back on him, I grab a pair of riding pants and pull them on beneath my nightgown. Before I turn to face him once again. My nerves and anger lay heavy in my stomach. I rip my gown over my head and throw it at him. Though it loses some of the effect when his eyes are glued to my breasts, the Barbarian. I grab a corset from the nearby trunk, only just getting it tied before turning on him once again.

"Is that what you think? That I'm loyal to him? You do not know the things that I've been through. I won't leave my people to rot. I'm staying." Giving him a sardonic smile. Before turning my back on him and heading for the exit.

"The fuck you are." He reaches out, taking hold of my elbow.

"My gut is telling me not to leave. I won't abandon them, Asher." I twist around to face him more fully, though he doesn't release his hold on my elbow.

"It's the conditioning your father has put you through." His voice is coaxing and soft as he tries to get me to see it his way. His other hand reaching up, palming the side of my neck.

"I don't give two fucks about my father. The only way I'll be walking back to him is to take his head." True venom and hate drips from my lips, not the fake shit I throw at Asher. I don't actually hate him, not truly. But my father... that man does not deserve a peaceful death for the things he's guilty of.

"You think I'm weak..." Ripping my elbow from his grip, keeping my voice as soft as his. Patronizing him with the very tone he used on me. Admittedly, mine is dripping with sarcasm. "You don't even know me." With each word I take a step toward him, releasing the glamour that's protected me all these years. The magic slipping from my body like droplets of rain. Standing before him as I truly am. His eyes scour over my visage, taking in everything from the cutting curve of my ears adorned with silver and gold hoops to the sharp points of my fangs. He sucks in a sharp breath and lifts a hand as if he would touch me. But, with a hard look from me, he drops it to his side.

"I will not spend another life with a man telling me what I will and won't do. You had best reconcile yourself with that. Husband." I punctuate each word with a claw tipped finger to his chest. The scent of his blood fills the air. The last word said with a cold and bitter laugh.

"Don't follow me... If anyone does, you won't like what happens. I see you or any of your men. I will leave bodies in my wake." My voice is devoid of all the emotions it had once held.

"No... you won't." We were so much closer now, the warmth of his body chasing the chill from my skin. He takes hold of my arms — his hands curving around my biceps — holding me tight.

"Test me." The words are nothing more than a growl on my lips. Though not all my emotions are the anger I rightfully feel about leaving and having my voice all but ignored. Some of it, more than I would like to admit, is this hurt, hollow feeling in my chest. Which makes no sense at all. We're nothing to each other.

With both hands on his bare chest, I push out of his grasp. Walking backwards a meter toward the exit before turning my back on him.

"You know I can't let you walk away." The undercurrent to his tone sounds like resignation. Like he can no more control his need to keep me, anymore then he can control his need for breath.

"Can't or won't?" I turn to face him, needing to see the look in his eyes when he answers.

"Does it matter?" His face closes down, wiping clean of all

emotions. Eyes shuttering and with it all vulnerability they had no doubt once held, leaving me bereft with an odd sense of disappointment.

"More than you know." I hold his gaze, allowing him to see all the emotions he denied me. "More than you know," I repeat, the words only a whisper of breath. I give him a heartbeat to speak. To say anything that shows he hears me before turning my back on him and leaving. Bypassing several soldiers on my way out. My eyes connect with Kane's, staying him with a look.

"Don't worry, your king is fine. I was just leaving," I say, smirking at them as I walk by. Becoming the spoiled princess once more. I'll be damned if I let any of these people see my pain.

"What did you do now?" I hear Ansel ask, his tone suggesting that he's already exhausted and really doesn't want to hear the words about to come out of Asher's mouth. That makes two of us.

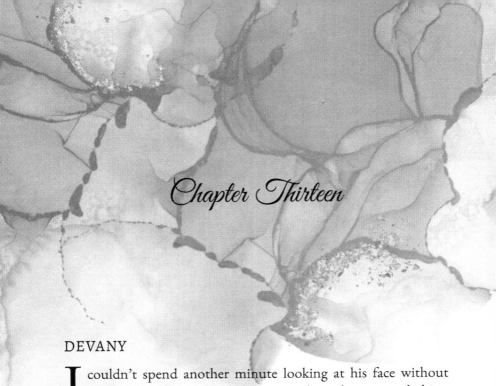

Chapter Thirteen

DEVANY

I couldn't spend another minute looking at his face without giving in to the overwhelming need to throat-punch him. That was over two hours ago, and I'm no closer to being calm than I was when I walked away.

That man gets under my skin in the worst way. For every step we take to move toward an amicable relationship that comprises respect and, at the very least, friendship. We take ten steps back, somehow unable to compromise. Sometimes I get glimpses of a man that's more than arrogance and brute force, only to have him open his mouth and prove I'm mistaken.

Add to that my undeniable attraction to him and I find myself just as likely to fantasize about punching him as I am to have him between my thighs. Either of these fantasies is a distraction I don't have time for.

But it's easy to see that with his help I can liberate my people. With only a small rebel army at my disposal I lack the manpower to free them myself. There are a few soldiers within my father's ranks that are loyal to me, and many others that would stand down if he were to go to battle against me. Unfortunately, there are far more that relish in the pain and destruction he allows them free rein to inflict on those outside the palace walls.

But if I had the backing of a legion the size of Asher's, we would have a chance. It's clear to see he needs something from me as well. I would gladly give him what he wants if it meant their freedom and happiness.

I'm jarred from my swirling thoughts by the sound of a small group moving toward camp from the east. The only thing it that direction is Erabis. *Has father sent men after us?*

I wouldn't put it past him. He gave me away far too readily for my peace of mind. I need to warn Asher... but first I must know what we're dealing with. I head for the group on quiet feet, being sure to stay hidden within the tree line when I hear a voice I know as well as my own. The fine hairs on my arms stand on end. Numbness filling my limbs as fear clogs my throat.

I break past the underbrush, bursting into the sun-drenched hillside, staring down at the small clearing in the valley below. My heart all but stops at the sight before me as I come to a halt just outside the woods. Ten of Asher's archers are positioned on the high ground within the trees opposite me. Their sights set on a large group of people in the field below us. *My people.* I take off toward the clearing, loose rocks shifting beneath my feet as I fight for purchase. I dig my boots in, trying to gain just a little more speed.

It won't be enough. I'm too far away to stop it.

I look back at the archers, trying to gauge how much time I have. Their arrows are notched, bow strings pulled tight, aiming for the caravan below.

I won't make it! The whoosh of the arrows as they slice through the sky is deafening. *No! No! No!*

"Narcissa!" That single word echoing through the earth beneath our feet.

My heart makes for my throat, strangling me. Flecks of light dancing before my eyes. Her head snaps in my direction, eyes wide, face leeching of color, paling her otherwise umber skin.

My hand lifts towards them, power painfully breaking free from its restraints, rocking me back on my heels. Rock and stone erupt from the earth, peppering my skin. The magic leaves a deeply dug channel in its wake as it heads straight for the heart of the two groups.

It's almost as if the world holds its breath for me. Pausing the universe, allowing me to see beyond the constructs of time. I watch the arrows take flight—displaying the air as they soar through the sky. When just as quickly my wall of stone and earth burst into being Creating a divide between the archers and my people.

Before the first arrow hits the ground, my legs are in motion, carrying me swiftly toward my best friend. A woman who as close to as a sibling.

Narcissa meets me at the edge of the field, the two of us falling into each other's arms with enough strength to force a breath from us. Not that we notice. This past week was the longest we had ever been apart.

I spent a few precious moments just drinking her in. From her almond and cinnamon hair fashioned in a plethora of thin braids that cascade down her back, to the beautiful glow of her umber skin and her eyes the color of honey with flecks of autumn leaves.

The only thing that mars the perfection of her face is a whitened scar that leads from her eye to mid cheek. A scar she received from father to punish me for showing her kindness. The bastard pushed her into a heated iron oven. I had snuck down through the servant's passage to her room every night for a week to check on her, then a week turned into months and then years. Now we're family and she's a sight for sore eyes.

"What happened?" I ask as she wipes tears from the apples of my cheeks. Forever playing the role of older sister. By the Goddess, I've missed her. But now's not the time for emotions.

"There's quite a lot to tell. Is there somewhere more secure we can talk?" Once again, all business. It's her ability to take control of most situations that's made her the only choice to lead my small army. I nod my head, pulling myself together. Showing those watching the united front, not the effort behind it.

"Of course. Let's get these people back to camp. Do we have any injuries?" My eyes drift toward Sam and a few rebel soldiers, standing between our people and Asher's men. Their stares unwavering.

"Unfortunately, yes," Sam answers in a strong voice, cutting through the growing noise as those around us talk over one another. All wanting to be heard. I'll need to speak with all of them in the coming days. Reassure them that they are safe.

"You there," looking toward the archers, picking one out at random. "Run ahead, prepare for our arrival. Get healers, food, and tents ready." Most of them weren't paying us any attention, standing in front of the wall with their heads tipped back toward the sky. Clearly shocked at the mere size of the stone wall I created. While the others look at each other, uncomfortable with the idea of leaving me.

"Your Majesty," looking toward the group that's now behind me. "We can't leave you behind," he murmurs, swallowing several times to clear his throat. Hands shaking slightly as he wipes them on the outer corner of his pants. The tone belaying just how much trouble they would be in if they returned without me in tow. It doesn't take me long to decide it wouldn't be a bad idea to have a few extra soldiers protecting my people from further damage.

The walk back is slow going with so many injured, and when we finally make it back, the encampment is a buzz of activity. I walk my people straight to the healers' tent in the center of camp. Where I spot Kane preparing sleeping arrangements, while Asher is standing outside the healer's tent directing people, having already called Marleen to oversee the injured.

I lock eyes with both of them, canting my head to the side,

heading toward my private tent with Sam and Narcissa on either side of me. Time to be the leader they need... To decide a course of action to deal with whatever horrors my father has committed now.

The scent of blood has only grown stronger, heavier, hanging in the air around us. One of them is injured, more specifically, Narcissa. I can see it in the way she keeps her arm close to her body. The rigid set of her shoulders. The tightness around her eyes and mouth.

Two guards pull back the tent flaps as I near and I walk in with Narcissa and Sam following me inside. The flaps haven't even finished falling closed before I'm turning on the two of them.

"What the fuck?" I say softly, grabbing Narcissa's arm and pulling it gently away to inspect her side. With her black clothing, it's hard to see the blood, but it shines in the low light of the lanterns.

"You're injured, and you said nothing?" I wait for an answer, but she isn't even looking at me. Her eyes are on the doorway and when I look over my shoulder, I see what snagged her attention. Asher and Kane are both standing just inside the tent.

"We're going to need a healer," I say as a way of greeting, holding eye contact with Asher as I walk her to the bed in hopes I can keep her there until a healer can get a look at her. It's silent for a beat while we have an unspoken conversation. His answer is a slight nod of his head before ordering one guard to fetch Marleen.

"Devany, do you want to tell me what the fuck is going on?" He says this as if I've somehow caused all this in the few hours I was gone. His shoulders set as if he's ready to battle with me once more. But it's not me that picks up the gauntlet he's thrown.

"You don't get to talk to her like that," Narcissa's strong voice rings clear. I watch her eyes flash and turn to steel. Those eyes can look so unyielding, but there is softness for those lucky few she loves, if you know where to look.

"She's my wife," he responds, staring her down with a look

I'm sure most men would run from. But this is Narcissa we're talking about. She backs down from no one, not even me.

"Doesn't give you free rein to be a complete and utter dick," she growls at him, jumping to her feet and crossing to the room.

"I don't know who the fuck you think you are, little girl. But, in this camp, among these people, I'm King. So, you had best check your attitude. Before I check it li-." He's all too happy to meet her halfway, growling right back at her.

"You'll do no such thing." The steel in my voice draws his attention back to me. I cross the room until I'm standing between the two of them, looking at Narcissa and pointing at the bed. "And you get your ass over there and sit down before you bleed out. I don't have time for temper tantrums from either of you," I state, looking back to Asher, who looks none too pleased. Well, fuck him, these are my people.

"You want to know who she is?" I ask, standing before him, fully prepared to take him on. *Why does he have to make this so hard?*

"Wouldn't have asked if I didn't, wife," he responds through clenched teeth, eyes as hard as stone, ready to continue our battle of wills once more. But at least his focus is once again centered on me where it belongs.

"She's my second in command of what little army I have. She and Sam also oversee the network of spies we have within my father's palace. So, if you could stop being an ass, I may be able to sort through this mess," I answer him, noticing that, at some point, Ansel and Bellicent had joined us.

"Careful *a stór álainn*, my patience is already wearing thin." His voice is the soft whisper of a lover, but his eyes tell a different story. Those are filled with anger as he turns to me more fully, placing his finger under my chin to bring my gaze back to his.

"And what, pray tell, are you going to do?" I ask, my voice taking on the same note, though there is steel in the undercurrent. I know he hears it because his eyes light up with devilish delight.

"Oh, sweet wife, there is so much I can do, and you'll love every minute, much to your chagrin."

Gently I withdraw my chin from Asher's grasp and take a step back to create some distance, before moving to the sitting area beside the bed. I take the chair opposite the one Bellicent commandeered for herself when she noticed all the tension. Never one to miss a good show.

"As Asher asked earlier, what's going on?" Ansel asks, bringing us all back to the subject at hand.

"Where do you want me to start?" I inquire, crossing my legs and leaning back in the chair as if I'm unbothered by all the heavy stares.

"How about the beginning?" Asher asks, his voice full of arrogance. But it's the intensity of his stare that has me working to suppress the shiver that wants to work its way down my spine. The fine hairs on my body standing up in response to the savagery in that one look.

I don't speak right away. The four of us all share a look. None of us are sure on just how much to share. But we've come too far to back up now.

"I'm the head of the rebel cause. As I said earlier, Narcissa is my second. She commands the infantry and our cachet of spies. Sam helps to coordinate the flow of information coming in and out of the palace and Kane watches my back for both the physical and proverbial knife." I tell them all this with the authority and regal air I was raised to wield. A queen, born to protect her people. A woman who will not be denied.

"And the spoiled brat routine?" Asher asks, as if he's truly seeing the full extent of the deception we've woven.

"A thing born of necessity. For many reasons, most of which I won't go into. But once I became old enough to draw attention, it became a way to keep all eyes on me. This allowed everyone else the freedom to move around when needed." The words are said practically, not betraying the things I truly endured. But from the look Asher is giving me, he knows something of what I lived through. Or at the very least, suspects.

"You have the world fooled with that act... Well done. When did you start building an army?" Bellicent's voice draws my attention to her. The only one in the room who's not livid. At least outwardly.

"That was our parents' doing. Father began enlisting willing fighters to train in the Taritin woods. A few older retired soldiers from various armies around the continent helped lead it," Kane answers Bellicent's question. He does so, looking Asher right in the eye. As a show of solidarity, I'm sure. Asher just flicks his gaze away from him to focus on me.

"I take it this was all done under the nose of Hepha's Monarchs?" Asher asks me directly, sounding none too pleased with this new information.

"And the spies?" Ansel cuts in, trying once again to bring us back on track.

"That ball was put into play early on. The five of us noticed how many shifters and Valore were hiding in plain sight among the staff of the palace," Narcissa states plainly.

"It didn't take long to have a large backing within the staff. When they knew father was having some nobles over to bitch about something or another, we would manipulate who was on service that night. Those fucks never paid attention to the ones who served them," I state, unable to hide the disgust I hold for most of my father's courtiers. While he had a few who did not share in his cruelty, most did.

"Something we kept from her mother. That woman always had her own agenda. Even at the expense of Devany." Narcissa never cared for my mother. There's no missing the disdain that drips from each word.

"Our spies brought in information that went beyond petty quarrels. We had in our possession information of tax drops, slave convoys, and so much more," I state as a way of moving the subject on from my mother. In no mood to look too closely at her motives after everything I've learned recently.

"I began overseeing the infantry. Once I took complete control from dad, we sent that information out to them, and they began hitting the carriages. The money funded our efforts, and we had the added bonus of retrieving the slaves," Kane states, his voice strong and devoid of emotion.

"Out of curiosity, what did you do with the slaves?" Bellicent once again got in on the conversation. Though her voice is deceptively calm. As if she's hanging on every word while also keeping her emotions in check.

"Those that wanted to fight were trained to do just that." Sam's smile was a cruel, twisted thing. The type of pride that comes from having trained those men and women to be more than those bastards told them they would or could ever be.

"And those that didn't?" Her lethal tone enough to scare any sane man, but apparently we're short on sanity here. Because Sam looks like he wants to toss her over his shoulder for some sexy time. It seems Narcissa is inclined to agree with him.

"The ones that wanted to move on were given money and escorted to Hepha," I reply, wanting to be sure they knew we took care of these people. Got them to safety.

"Back to the situation at hand, *a stór*," Asher says crossing his arms, his body practically vibrating. He's the picture of impatience.

"I guess that's a question for them to answer." Looking toward Narcissa and Sam, hoping they can tell me this isn't the shitstorm it appears to be. While knowing in my very bones this is just the beginning of the bad news.

"Your father brought in a revenant named Astra. She cast a widespread spell and for some thirty seconds, we all lost control of our powers. It was the most terrifying thing I've ever experienced." Narcissa's voice shakes slightly, a reaction that speaks volumes coming from her.

She's no stranger to fear having lived on her own since her

mother's death when she was only seven. We're all just a bag of parental issues. It's one of the many reasons we're so close. Our soul's pain recognizes itself in another.

"We couldn't hold our glamour, Devany," Her gaze snapping to mine, letting me see the genuine fear still behind her eyes. "The shifters were forced to change. If we hadn't had soldiers nearby, it would've been a bloodbath."

"How many dead?" I ask softly, the tone decidedly un-queen like. When neither of them answered. I repeat the question, looking directly at Narcissa.

"Ten... We lost ten souls." Unable to hold my gaze, her eyes dropped to her bloodied hands. Sam, while looking at the both of us, carries on with the report.

"Our human spies are still in place and with them, the flow of information. We're in good shape, considering everything." His tone is quiet, but strong.

"You've got to be fucking kidding me? Good shape, my ass!" Unable to hide the self-loathing. I really should have been there. My hands ball tightly into fists at my sides, the tips of my nails bringing blood to the surface. The bite of pain is no more than I deserve.

I rise from my seat and begin pacing as I try to think of any plan that may aid me in getting the rest of my network out of the palace.

"My queen." When I don't answer or even acknowledge him, Sam tries again. "Devany." It's the soft steel in his voice that catches my ear, causing me to stop and listen. "They're there because they wish to be, because they believe in you." I'm sure they believe in me. But I don't deserve their faith. I've proven that time and again. I can't keep them safe.

"They don't get to make those decisions," I growl, looking back and forth between Narcissa and Sam, needing an outlet for this fear and anger.

"You want us to follow you... to trust, believe in you and what you stand for. To follow you into battle. Then you need to do the same. You need to trust in us. To trust that we will be where we must. To trust that we can handle ourselves and what's coming." Narcissa holds my gaze. While her words are whispered, they are no less powerful.

"Luna?" I don't bother elaborating and by the way they look at each other I'm not going to like what they have to say.

"She stayed behind." Narcissa's eyes show me she's as devastated by this turn of events as I am. After all, it's been us against the world for as long as I remember.

"We need to get them out," I reply softly, desperately rearranging plans in my head.

"No." It's silent for a beat, the word stopping me in my tracks as I turn sharply to face her more fully.

"What?" Is all I can ask. Staring at her as my brain tries to make sense of what she just said.

"She wouldn't come. You know it and I know it. Get that thought out of your head. It's too dangerous for you to step foot in that kingdom without a larger army at your back." She's right. I know she's right, but I can't leave them.

"They're not safe we nee—" I try again, desperate to find a different outcome. She cuts me off, stopping the desperate words.

"To let them do their jobs. Luna is hidden away, monitoring everyone left behind. She has a direct line to the infantry and the spy network. If something further happens, we'll know." As her voice rings with strength, I realize I'm not talking to Narcissa, the person I've chosen as family, but the woman who leads my Army.

I'm not even sure why I'm pushing for answers when she's clearly hurting. I can see it in the set of her shoulders. Her skin paling from blood loss.

"Let's get you to Marleen. It's unlike her to not come when summoned. She must still have her hands full with everyone else." Making my way toward her. When she feels better, we'll talk more. As it is, she's going to be pissed if anyone sees her like this.

"I haven't received my answers yet, wife." Damn that man for always making things too difficult.

"I don't give a flying fuck about your answers. You were already privy to things I wouldn't, under normal circumstances, have told you. So why don't you piss off somewhere? Because my sister is in pain and has been so during this entire conversation and I won't be allowing it to carry on any longer." I hear her sharp intake of breath at the word sister. Being alone has left scars on her soul.

I help her to her feet, only to have her legs buckle. I look at Sam and he quickly picks her up. "Take her back to the Infirmary and ask for Marleen. I'll be following shortly." With a small nod, he leaves the tent.

"How did they find you? We've been traveling for days. Not taking a single known road. But they found you. How?" Asher's tone is firm, but not unkind. It doesn't take a genius to hear that his patience has reached its end. He's not going to like my answer, however.

I dart a quick look at Kane.

"He didn't ask the question," Asher says, moving into my line of sight. Effectively blocking my view of anything but him. "How did they find you?" He repeats. The question is little more than a growl at this point.

"Blood oath. They're all bound to me by blood. They'll be able to find me anywhere and I them." I stare at him with steel in my spine and icy flames in my eyes. Even my skin feels colder as we face off. If he thinks for one moment, I'm leaving these people behind. He's out of his ever-loving mind. Whether or not I need him, they will always come first.

"Someone could use them to track you." Agitation is shown in his tone and movements. The way he prowls in front of me, his hands behind his back.

"My people wouldn't do that." Now it's my turn to growl at him. I mean, where the hell does he get off?

"They probably won't be given much of a choice," he states quietly, almost devoid of emotion. Then turns to address Ansel, as if I'm no longer part of this conversation.

"We're leaving at first light and traveling straight through to the capital of Naphal. We'll have to take some drastic measures to make sure our people are safe." He doesn't elaborate on what he means by drastic measures. His eyes leave Ansel's and zeroing in on me.

"You should've told me." There's a quiet reprimand in that sentence that I don't like.

Maybe I should have, but I wasn't willing to have my people trade one monster for another.

"You know, contrary to popular belief, I don't owe you a damn thing and I don't need your permission. The sooner you realize that the better off you and I will be. Because these are my people. They have lived with things that would cause most to curl up in a corner, begging for the end. You can take yourself in hand and get fucked. If you think I'll be leaving them behind. If they leave..." Once again advancing on him until I'm all he can see for a change. Making sure he sees the truth in my words. "I leave." With that, I quit the room. In desperate need of fresh air.

I'm halfway to Marleen's tent when I feel a vibration under my feet. As if the ground itself is trying to warn me. The wind picks up, carrying with it the scent of iron. The more I use my powers, the more things I notice. Something's heading this way. I pick up my pace, running toward a group of soldiers.

"We're under attack." Those are the only words to pass my lips when the screams come from the outer row of camp.

"Move!" I yell, directing women, children, and the wounded into the healer's tent. It'll be easier to protect them if they're all in one place.

"Everyone to the back of the tent. Sam, you get in front of them. If this doesn't work, you're the last line of defense." He answers with a nod of his head, and pulls out twin axes, standing in front of those who cannot stand for themselves.

I let the glamour slip from my body. Releasing the tight hold I have on my power. I feel the earth, wind, and water rushing up to answer my call. The ground moving beneath our feet, trees growing where none had been. The magic takes hold, building a barrier between us and the advancing soldiers.

I register the heavy clank of steel-on-steel moments before the magic snaps into place, effectively closing us off from the outside. The lack of sound was so intense that if not for the overwhelming sound of my heartbeat in my ears, I would've thought I'd gone deaf.

From behind me comes the hushed voices of scared children, whispering, afraid that death has come for us. Their fearful voices tugging so heavily on my heart. I turn away from the entrance and kneel before them, taking in their frightened faces. They're all so young, too young to live through all they have. And now they fear for their lives. Because those fucks outside think it's their right to kill as they wish.

"None of you are going to die," I quietly promise.

"How can you be so sure?" One of the older children asks, not disrespectfully but fearful curiosity.

"I know because I won't allow them," I reply, leaving no room for arguments.

With a flick of my wrist, two bushes with lovely azure leaves and white blooms sprout next to the children. The little ones whispering about the pretty leaves, distracting them from the chaos going on outside the barricade. They smell the blossoms and touch the leaves with awe.

I return to the barrier and with a snap of my hand and the elements part for me, closing behind me just as quickly.

The soldiers, both the invading troops and Asher's men, take an enormous step away from me. That little display of fear brings a smile to my face. Though it must not be too welcoming if the look on their faces is anything to go by.

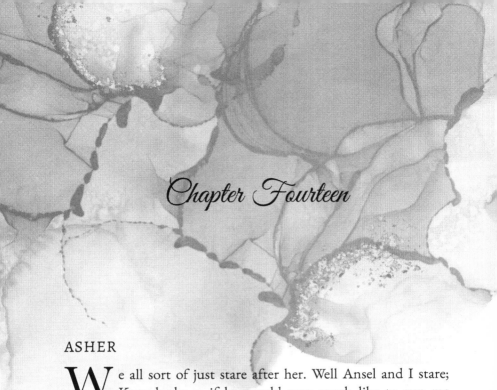

Chapter Fourteen

ASHER

We all sort of just stare after her. Well Ansel and I stare; Kane looks as if he would very much like to run me through with his sword and Bellicent looks inclined to let him. Also, I'm pretty sure she just told me to go fuck myself. The woman has a mouth filthier than most men. It certainly makes for interesting exchanges.

When she's using that filthy mouth, all I think about is how much I want to occupy it.

The cold steel in Kane's voice has me blinking out of my stunned stupor to find his gaze fixed on me. His eyes no longer hold any amusement, all there is to see is the cold malice he hides so well behind his pretty face. In this moment, he is the man that has no doubt killed countless people to protect her and will potentially kill countless more.

"You have no idea what she lived through in that place..." his voice was so cold you would think that it had never known warmth. "Sure, she seems spoiled to you, and maybe she is in some ways. But as a child, were you ever tied to a whipping post in the courtyard of your home... for all to see? Then beaten because you were kind to a servant or showed any other undesirable emotions, like generosity or compassion?"

His glare holds nothing but contempt as he stares me down. "No... Well, she was! She was whipped so often that she bears scars. It should be impossible with the Valore blood that runs through her veins, but as it turns out, recurring trauma doesn't heal. It was just one of the many ways Kól proved to himself that she was more human than Valore. The sick old fuck!" He slowly prowls toward me as he speaks until he's within arm's reach.

"Keep pushing her asshole and you'll lose her before you've ever had her." Turning his back on me, he heads for the exit, no doubt to go hunt her down. But I can't let him leave just yet because I must know.

"Are you speaking from experience...? Hmmm, tell me Kane, has she ever looked at you as anything other than a brother and a protector?" The disdain I feel for this man is clear as crystal with each chipped word.

Jealous... I've never once been jealous in my life, but I am of this man. I feel it in my stomach every time she smiles at him. He has her in a way I don't, and it pisses me off. She's mine and he's going to be a problem. He needs to take a step back before I fuck up his pretty face.

Kane doesn't turn from the entrance, his eyes still staring in the direction I'm sure she took. "Her mother used to tell her that her heart wasn't hers to give away..." Where his words had once been tempered steel, they were now as lifeless as the plains that surround Erabis. "I had once thought that she meant Devany's heart belonged to her people, to remind her she serves them, not the other way around." His head tips back on his shoulders as a laugh leaves his throat, the sound of it dull and hollow.

"When Devany was fifteen, she found me in the stable one afternoon... her looks were teasing, her smile enticing." Shifting back around to face me, he continues with a self-deprecating smile. "She was the most alluring creature I had ever seen in all my seventeen years. When she pulled me toward her, I went all too willingly. The Queen's voice had interrupted us just as our lips touched." His jaw ticks and hands fist in retroactive anger at his lost moment. Looking away from me, he carries on. "She looked from me to Devany and said, *'your heart is not yours to give away.'* Her voice was soft, as if it pained her to say it. Devany left the stable with her eyes on the floor, refusing to look at me while walking out without so much as a goodbye, leaving me with her mother. Storming passed the Queen, I asked why her heart wasn't hers. To which she replied, *'she gave it away to the boy in the woods."*

Walking away from me, he throws one last remark over his shoulder. "I guess we're both shit out of luck." But the remark was lost to the roar of my heartbeat running rampant in my ears.

Screams ring out before Kane passes the tent flaps. The four of us run toward the shrieks of pain and the sound of steel. My heart is in my throat as I desperately search for Devany. Five men head toward us, swords drawn... *Iron.*

The bastards brought iron.

Kane engages first, blocking the guard's strike with the cross-guard of his dagger, pushing the blade of his sword forward through the man's chest. He's barely pulling the blade free when a second man comes at him from the side, forcing him to jump back, narrowly missing the strike. Using the man's momentum, he takes hold of his wrist, pulling him forward, impaling him on his dagger. Before stepping over his body.

A guard comes at us with his sword above his head and a scream on his lips. His eyes are wild with hatred and fear. Wielding dual short swords, Ansel closes the distance between them. His attacker comes at him with a wide arching strike. Ansel crosses the blades and blocks the overhead blow before landing a hard kick to his opponent's knee with an audible crunch. His hand moves in a blur of motion, leaving behind a gaping wound in the guard's neck. His body dropping lifeless to the ground.

Ansel's head snaps in Kane's direction, his eye narrowing. He tosses his sword in the air, catches it by the blade, and throws it. I watch as it spins blade over hilt, landing in the chest of the guard attacking Kane's unprotected back. The two dispatch the last man in quick, efficient moves.

Our attackers have already made it past the outer row of our tents.

"We need to get to the middle of camp. To the children's tents and the infirmary. They're unprotected if they're already passing the outer tents," I yell over the noise surrounding us. The tang of blood is already saturating the air.

My men are holding their own, but we're outnumbered five to one if my counts are right. I sent a large number of soldiers off to hunt and scout our next campsite. They'll never make it back in time. As we pass yet another row of tents, we stumble upon anarchy. My soldiers are standing between a small army and those who are too weak to fight. The sound of metal on metal is deafening.

Several men notice us, breaking out of formation—swords drawn. It's a mistake that costs them their lives. In three moves, I've killed two men, the blood sliding from the tip of the blade on the downward strike, painting the dirt beneath my feet. When I look up, I find that Bellicent has finished the other two.

I catch Devany's scent, but I don't see her. *Where the fuck is she?*

I only make it a few meters when four more men attack, once again impeding my progress. If the sounds coming from behind me are anything to go by, the other three have their hands full as well. But I must trust in their abilities to hold their own.

I block the first blow, and sparks fly from the blades as they shift against each other. The guard grunts, spit flying from his mouth as he pushes forward, trying to get me to give an inch. I look down at him, the corner of my lips tips up and I twist my wrist, locking our swords together, pressing my weight into his body. My clawed tipped hand rips into his lower abdomen and his life's blood coats my fingers. Bloodlust sings in my veins. The next two men are sloppy, and I decapitate them with ease. The last, however, puts up a bit of a fight, until he too lies lifeless. Though he manages to inflict minor wounds to my face and hand. As well as a glancing injury to my side with his blade.

My eyes keep sweeping the fallen, expecting to see Devany's body on the ground. *Where is she? What if she's dead?* That fear has me fighting with my heart in my throat.

Most think we rely heavily on our magic, and some do. But the men and women in my army are proficient in both. So, it's only a minor hindrance when these humans appear to deflect the magic being thrown at them.

So much magic hangs heavy in the air. It crackles around me —dancing along my skin—coating my tongue with the taste of it. But somehow, it's not affecting these very human soldiers. Despite this unforeseen obstacle, we're holding our own.

They caught us unprepared because I didn't think he'd come at us like this. I overestimate Kól's care for her safety. The ground beneath my feet rumbles. The sound growing louder until suddenly the earth around the center tent cracks open. Trees sprout and mature before our very eyes. The water from the river behind the tent joins it, building a dome of earth and water.

"What the fuck is that?" Ansel asks in a hushed voice. I'm inclined to ask the same question. But I didn't expect an answer.

"That's Devany's power off its leash. They've really pissed her off now." The sound of Kane's voice draws my attention to him. But his eyes are on the dome.

Both armies, his and mine alike, take a healthy step away from the living dome made of earth and water. The elemental wall parts and out walks my wife, hair flowing in an unnatural breeze. The elements ready to answer her call. As soon as her feet touch down outside the dome, the magic snaps back into place. Effectively blocking anyone from the entrance.

More men rush us, though I have a feeling they won't get very far. With a snap of her fingers, black and gray flames erupt, circling most of the attacking army. We fight our way to the ring of fire, hoping to find a means to get in so we can finish this. I watch in fear as men draw their bows tight, arrows aiming for her chest. My people continue to fight around us, but all my focus is on her.

"How are we going to get in?" Bellicent's yells over the screams coming from the other side of the flames. They're testing the boundaries, trying to see if they can get through.

As if in answer to her question, the flames drop before us, allowing passage. We enter behind what's left of the mercenaries sent to slaughter us. My eyes locked on the far end of the battlefield. We watch shocked as Devany walks through the flames completely unharmed. *How the fuck that's even possible? I don't know.* It's a worry for another day. But the sight causes total chaos to break out. Some would rather take their chances with the flames, then the vicious beauty that controls them.

I would like to say that it burnt them painfully, but quickly. That is not the case. It's as if she can control the very rate at which the flames burn them, and she makes it last. She makes it hurt.

Making my way toward the center of the small battlefield, I fight with a single-minded focus. Get to Devany. My attention is divided between her and the battle. I kill one after the other, leaving nothing but death in my wake. My blade is thirsty for the blood of my enemies. But she hasn't engaged in hand-to-hand combat. In fact, she hasn't really moved from her spot just inside the flames.

Three more men block my view of her. The one to the right engages first, but he's cut off by an attack as the man in the center tries to strike at the same time. These men are not used to fighting in open battle, much less with each other. They're only used to using their weapons on the defenseless. This wouldn't have been much of a fight if they didn't have the numbers and a way of deflecting magic.

The blade of the center man's sword bears down on me from overhead, forcing me to use my wrist guard to deflect the blow. The strength of the impact pushes me back a step. Hoping to take advantage of my distraction, the guard to my right decides now is the perfect time to strike. He pays for that decision with his life as I run my sword through his chest. I take a step back, pulling my sword free from his body. In a wide arch, I slice my blade through the air in front of me, the other two jumping back to avoid the strike. With nothing more than a thought, flames engulf their swords, the blade turning bright red then white. The metal melting into skin and bone within seconds, dropping both men to their knees. I look down at them as they cradle their ruined hands and feel nothing but contempt. Following the downward strike of my sword, their headless bodies slump to the blood-soaked earth.

"Asher!" Her panicked voice carries across the battlefield.

I whipped my head around in time to see a soldier raising his sword behind me, mirrored in the blood upon my weapon. There's no time to stop the blow. I have no time to do anything but look at her beautiful face, wanting her to be the last vision I see. Only for her to turn into shadows and smoke before my eyes.

The sound of a grunt and a soft intake of breath has me turning around in time to see the guard pulling the sword meant for me from Devany's chest. I catch her as she collapses, keeping her body upright.

My arm swings out while I hold her close, my lips pressed to her sweaty head. The nameless soldier's head tumbles to the ground, followed by the thump of his body. But I pay it no mind. The beautiful creature in my arms holds all my attention. I gently lower my lovely Queen to the ground and stand, releasing the glamour that holds my power at bay. My sword becomes a living flame and the very air around us answers my call. Sucking breath from lungs, burning flesh. But just like before, they're only slightly affected. Denying me my vengeance.

The softest touch to my ankle brings my attention back to Devany.

"They wear talismans that protect them from the bulk of our magic. You'll have to fight them hand to hand. There's no other way. I'll try to burn the charms from their bodies." Raising her hand to do just that.

"No, *a stór*. If you use any more magic, you'll die before I can get you to a healer," I tell her with a staying hand. The scent of her blood is clouding my good sense, because right now, what I truly want is to burn her father's tainted kingdom to the ground. Then drag him out by his neck to that barren land that surrounds his palace and slit his throat, feeding the land that he's bled dry.

She doesn't have much strength to argue as I lean down, brushing sweaty hair from her exquisite face. Her eyes flutter shut and with it the flames that had encompassed us. What's left of the army is handled quickly. Their screams follow me as I pick up Devany, heading toward that living dome as the water recedes back to the river it came from and the trees part to let us pass.

Chapter Fifteen

DEVANY

"She lost too much blood. Her body's using energy it doesn't have to heal. Basically, Your Highness... her body is eating itself," Marleen says in her soft, lyrical voice. The words seal my fate because I think I'm dying.

The scent of winter fires and midnight air surrounds me, and I know instantly I'm in Asher's arms. The heat from his body chasing the chill from mine. The shivers racking my spine intensify as the two temperatures war with each other. His fingers brushing my no doubt blood caked hair from my face.

"She needs blood, my king, or you will lose her," she says, drawing Asher's attention. The statement is so quiet that I almost miss it over the roar of rushing blood in my ears, warping all the sounds around me. Even my vision is blurring. Shadows creep in from the outer edges and bright white light dances in front of my eyes. I feel hot and cold at once. My skin is coated in a thin mist of sweat. The worst of it is the numbness of my limbs.

"She's fed from me before." Kane's strong voice breaks through the tangent of my thoughts. His large form takes shape to my left. His hands loosening the buttons of his tunic to expose his thick neck, my mouth waters at the mere thought of his tangy blood on my tongue, moistening my dry mouth, quenching my thirst.

I must make some sort of desperate noise because Asher's gaze comes back to mine, his beautiful face drawn in a deep frown. That powerful jaw of his clinches and the tendon along his neck stretches tight, drawing my attention. My hand moves as if of its own accord. Reaching out, I run my fingers along his jaw, through the soft hairs of his beard, watching his throat work as he swallows.

"So beautiful." The whispered statement said with reverence. Those lovely lips break out in a smile that could light the sky, even if it's strained.

"You're not too bad yourself, but you're going to need blood, *a stór milis*," he responds, concern clear in his tone. His ever-changing eyes dance with so much emotion. More than he's ever shown before. *I must really be dying.*

My fingers feather along the tendon in his neck, following it to the large vein that rests where the shoulder and neck meet. It pulses beneath my fingertips, strong and steady. My instincts scream at me to take what I need. The throb in my fangs keeps time with my heartbeat—hard and demanding—my body insisting that I feed. Overwhelming me with each minute that ticks by as my life's blood seeping from me slowly.

My glamour wears thin as exhaustion sets in. My body diverting magic from it to more important endeavors, such as keeping me alive. Until finally my glamour slips away. Asher brings my weak body more securely into his lap to give me better access to what I need.

"She's fed from me multiple times; I can handle this." Kane's aggravated tone distracts me slightly. He knows how I feel about feeding. It's an intimate thing not to be taken lightly and can often lead to sex for most, the two going hand in hand for Valore. Though Kane and I have never crossed that line.

"She won't be in the future. I can guarantee that. If you knew anything about Valores, males and females alike, you would know better than to suggest feeding from another's partner. I would kill you before I allowed you anywhere near her in that capacity. I have a feeling that Devany may try to kill me if that happens," he says this with a disgruntled smirk. Almost like he wouldn't mind trying to kill Kane if he thought he could get away with it. "With that said, she fed from you out of necessity. Valore blood contains magic. She'll heal quicker with my blood in her system."

"Now isn't the time for your ego. Besides, she's hardly yours." I can almost *hear* the look he's no doubt giving Asher. If he doesn't knock it off, Asher may very well try to kill him. Obviously, he doesn't care about the barely leashed violence vibrating just beneath my husband's skin because he just carries on talking. "Taking someone from their ho—" I've had enough talk... My fingers thread through Asher's silky hair, pulling tight as my fangs sink into smooth, unmarred skin. The taste of sweet, savory blood laced with power floods my mouth and overwhelms my senses. His deep groan vibrates my fangs, tickling my lips and he pulls me tight against his body.

All that controlled strength, yet he holds me as if I am something precious.

Out of the corner of my eye, I see a female step toward us and the growl that rips from my chest surprises me enough that I momentarily stop drinking. Though Asher's having none of it. He places his fingers in my hair and once again runs them through it, causing me to relax into him once more.

"Everyone out, there's too many people around. It's causing her some distress," he whispers softly against my temple as he continues to stroke me like a house pet. Which would normally piss me right the fuck off, but since it feels so nice, I'll be angry later.

Right now, I just want to get my hands on him.

Diligently I work to get my hands between our bodies. Just as my fingers graze to the laces of his pants, he grabs my wrists, pulling them behind me, holding them to the small of my back. I growl in the back of my throat. Only to have him tighten his hand in my hair, keeping me in place.

"There'll be none of that, *a stór álainn*. The first time I have you under me, I want you in complete control of your senses. Knowing it was your own choice to be there. Not an act of pure instinct. Though I'm sure we'll have some of those moments too. But not the first time, no matter how badly I crave you." His voice sounds both pleased and aggravated.

I'm unsure how long I feed for, overwhelmed and lost to sensation. The only thing I remember is being lifted in powerful arms and carried to a soft pallet of furs, encompassed by a scent I've come to crave.

There's this sense of timelessness as I drift in and out of consciousness. The soft sound of voices wakes me, distracting me from sleep's sweet embrace. I'm unclear how much time has passed, but I'm so tired.

"I've never seen flames the color of night... the color of death... You know more than you're letting on, Asher. Who's her father? Because I can guarantee he's not human. There's nothing human about that girl." Ansel's voice was quiet with concern and a healthy dose of curiosity. Well, he could get in line because I'd also love to know. It was the one thing my birth mother would never tell me. I knew the man I called dad wasn't the one that sired me, but little else.

"I do know more and there's much I won't tell you. But I don't know who her father is," Asher replies.

"What are you planning to do when the wall comes down and the man she was promised to wants her back?" Ansel asks softly, that stoic concern of his ever present.

"I'll not give her up." His answer is a heated whisper before I once again fall into a dreamless sleep. Wrapped in this new sense of protection, I find myself in.

I'm roused from sleep once more by a gentle rocking motion and the sound of Asher's soft, smoky voice.

"Devany, love, you need to wake up and eat something," he states in a tone both coaxing and firm. This man is always a mess of contradictions. The very epitome of hot and cold. Not that I'm much better, but I'm a woman... It's my prerogative. At least that's what I tell myself.

"Go away before I stab you." It's the only response I have for him as I pull the blanket over my head. I'm beyond tired, and it feels like I've been dragged behind a pair of runaway horses. As if I caught fire and burned from the inside out.

"I'm sure you'd love to try. But unless you eat, it's unlikely you'll have the energy to carry through with my demise." I can practically hear his smile, *the prick.*

"Why does it feel like I have been burnt from the inside out?" I decide to ask because I've never felt this way before. Everything is so sensitive, that even the slide of the sheets hurt. This is the most pain I've felt in quite some time.

"Magic burnout... It's what happens when we burn through magic quicker than we can replace it." The words were matter of fact, but I can hear how upset he is.

I pull the blanket away so I can glare at him better. But as soon as the blanket is no longer covering my head, my senses are assaulted with the most mouthwatering scent I've ever come across. My body decides at that moment to make its need for food known with the loudest sound I think I've ever heard it make. My cheeks heat as I push myself into a seated position. His soft chuckle has my ears heating too, no doubt pink from embarrassment.

Asher collects a bowl of broth from a tray laden with food beside him. Bringing the spoon to his lips before blowing on it, once it's cool enough, he feeds it to me. Before repeating the process with the next spoon full.

My eyes glued to the motion, tears stinging the back of my

eyes at the gesture. I have had very few take care of me since the death of my birth mom. My mother... I mean Tempest. I'm not sure how to refer to her now that I can see things as they were. I guess it doesn't matter. Nothing to be done about it now. She was never much of a nurturer. Though I'm sure father beat that softness out of her years ago. I'm broken from my morbid thoughts by the sound of Asher's voice.

"Sometimes I feel you fight me, just for the sake of fighting with me," he says, giving me a pointed look while continuing to feed me one spoonful at a time.

"I could say the same of you," I'm quick to point out. I mean, if I'm guilty, so is he. Plus... the snark distracts me, because as much as these tender actions speak to the neglected parts of my soul. It's also equally unnerving. We sit in silence while he feeds me. Broth, roasted meats, and bread.

"Aren't you going to eat?" I finally ask, unable to eat another bite. But he doesn't answer, merely hands me a glass of water. Which I happily take.

As I wash my meal down, I study his face. There's tension around his eyes and mouth. His hair sticking up haphazardly, as if he's been pulling at it. He's foregone his glamour, standing before me as the Gods had meant him to. Horns tall and curved, poking through his mahogany waves. Golden tattoos lace around them. The sharp points of his ears stand strong and sharp. He's the picture of everything that makes Valores different.

He takes the water from my hand and returns it to the tray. After which he rises from his seat and heads to the entrance. These things are all done in silence. I notice the ridged set of his back and shoulders. That barely leashed agitation that he seems to carry with him always.

Pulling back the heavy flaps to our tent back, he allows them to bring in the tub. The small space fills with steam and the smell of scented oils. I give it a valiant effort to get out of bed. But I lack the energy to complete the task. I guess almost dying really takes it out of a girl.

Before I can give it another go, Asher picks me up and carries me to the tub. He places me gently on my feet, turning me around to face away from him. His long capable fingers move my blood caked hair over my shoulder, and he begins to unlace my corset. The action itself surprises me, and I attempt to turn around to stop him. But he only grabs me by the shoulders, gently faces me forward once more.

"Let me take care of you." His hushed plea is the only sound in the small space outside of my heartbeat.

My corset falls loose from my body, and it promptly gets thrown to the side. Next, he takes hold of my once white silk blouse, pulling it over my head and it to joins my corset. His fingertips skate across my skin, along the lines and swirls of my tattoo. His hands slow as they read my pain and abuse with every scar. He doesn't say a word. Merely spins me around to face him. He kneels down before me, unlacing my breeches and sliding them down my legs. His fingertips trailing down the back of my thighs, removing one leg at a time. I watch him during the entire process. Swallowing thickly at the unnamed emotion clogging my throat. Just when I'm ready to take a step back, he looks up at me, gliding his hand up my calves.

"I'm going to kill him." No need to elaborate. I know exactly who he's speaking of.

"Not if I beat you to it." The sadistic grin he gives me lets me know how much he approves of my answer.

I try once more to step away from him, but he's having none of it. He continues to glide his hands up my body until he's standing before me. He picks me up and places me in the tub.

"Your clothes are going to need to be burned," he says, picking up the offending items. Presumably to have someone burn them. I don't care much, they're beyond repair.

Asher returns, sitting just out of sight—quiet. But I can feel his eyes on me. The physical touch of all that attention. It's enough to damn near make me breathless as I go through the motions of cleaning my skin of all the dirt and blood coating it.

The aches and pains in my muscle unwind in the hot water, a byproduct of whatever oils and herbs that were added.

I brace my hands on the side of the tub, attempting to stand as my legs give out beneath me. Before I'm able to cause myself any other damage, I'm swept up into the safety of his arms. His strides are tense as he brings us back to the bed, taking a moment to dry me off before placing me underneath the furs, foregoing any clothes. Under normal circumstances I would've complained, but as it is, I have no energy. The bath zapped what little I had. Asher circles the pallet, removing his clothes along the way, and slides in beside me. He reaches for me and gently pulls me into the cradle of his arms. With my head on his chest, I listen to the steady beat of his heart.

"You could have died." The whispered words bring me back to alertness. With a finger under my chin, he tips my face toward him, so we're eye to eye.

"Never do that again." There's a lethal note to that statement, a feeling that I pushed him much further than he was emotionally prepared to go. But I reply honestly, nonetheless.

"I can't and won't make that promise to you." His eyes move back and forth between mine as he gauges how serious I am about that statement. More than he'll ever know, because something in me rejects the very idea of him coming to harm. There's no telling what I'm liable to do. I'm not sure how we got here, but here we stand.

Chapter Sixteen

ASHER

"Y ou may very well be the death of me." I say it lightly, but I mean every word.

Staring down at the woman who took a sword for me. I can still hear the sound of her breath as it left her body, the scent of her blood, the feel of it slipping through my fingers. My stomach threatens to revolt at the thought. It's no wonder that I have no appetite. I don't see that'll be changing anytime soon. Despite her concern.

"Right back at you." She fires back without missing a beat, a little smirk playing across her tempting lips.

Unable to stop myself, I move forward, overcome with the need to taste her. Just to remind myself that she is alive and safe in my arms. Just a soft brushing of my lips against hers, simply breathing her in.

She lays her head back on my chest, the fragrant scent of something solely her surrounds me. With each breath, her body slides against my own. It's all too distracting. My mind drifts to things I have no business thinking about. Now would not be the time to give in to my base instincts when she's in no state to reciprocate. Though my blood healed her chest wound, she's still favoring her right arm.

Needing a distraction from imagining all the ways I could dirty up my wife, I decide to share a little about myself. Maybe give her a brief insight into what makes me... me. Staring toward the ceiling of the tent, my eyes follow the folds of fabric.

"I spent nine nights and ten days wandering the woods after the wall effectively locked me out of my home." I'm not sure why I chose this particular experience to share with her. It just seemed like the right start. She interrupts with a question.

"Why were you alone in the woods?" It's a quiet question, one she seems unsure of asking. I look down to meet her gaze when I feel her look up at me.

"I wasn't... I was on a hunting trip with my brother. He was teaching me how to track large game. But I had traveled too far south in the Taritin woods and somehow ended up in Hepha. So, when the wall went up, it separated us," I say, my voice devoid of emotion. It still hurts to think of them. The family I may never see again. Deciding it would be safer to carry on with my story, I continue. The last thing I need is to fall down the rabbit hole of longing for things I cannot change.

"I was luckier than most. I had a stocked pack. We had already decided to stay in the woods for the week. Although, by day five, I had run out of water and was painfully low on food. Two days later, I had officially run out with no plan on how I was going to survive. On day ten, I stumbled across a caravan. They were making camp. But what drew my eyes was the fire-pit. The smell of roasting meat was wafting to me." I can still feel the phantom twists and pains of starvation. The dryness of my mouth. How thick my tongue had felt. The pain that came every time I swallowed. If it weren't for the Sadeen River flowing from the Neven Mountains of Narci I would have died. It's for this reason I will never allow my people to go hungry. I know what that feels like and wish it on no one.

"The next day I decided I was going into that camp after dark and stealing some food. It was the first time I'd ever tried something like that, but it was also the first time I had ever gone hungry." She's staring at the side of the tent. Her breath is even and slow, but I know I have her undivided attention by how stiffly she holds herself.

"Sneaking in was far easier than I had expected. But there was a reason for that." I feel a smile come over my face. I had never been more frightened than I was that night. "Their scouts had spotted me the day before." A huff of laughter slips past my lips. "I only made it seven meters into their camp... Only made it that far because they let me." I shake my head. It's funny how eleven-year-old me was so sure I could steal from a group of warriors. The motion draws her eyes up to me. A little indention appears between her finely arch brows. I reach forward, rubbing my thumb over the small indent, smiling at her.

"They took me before their council, which comprised three men. Not even given a chance to plead my case. They simply pushed me to my knees, placing my hand on a stump. They were some of the most imposing men I had ever seen. One asked in a voice so deep it scared the shit out of me, *'Do you know the punishment for stealing, boy?'* A laugh traveled around the group. Which pissed me off. If they were going to kill me, they needed to get on with it and I said as much. My reaction only made them laugh harder. With a twinkle in his eyes, he brought the sword down toward my wrist. Stopping just shy of breaking skin. I looked up at him when I realized I still had a hand. Moving down so we were eye to eye, he said, *"Best to not get caught, boy."* The group around us cheers and stomps their feet. When I made no attempt to move, he nodded to the men holding me. *"Go on then, make yourself a plate."* That was all he said before turning his back to go on about his business. That... was the day I found my new family."

Placing her dainty hand on my chest, she pushes herself up so she could look at me more fully. Instead of looking confused as she had earlier, she was now looking at me as if I were an idiot. Which only made me smile at her more. When I make no move to elaborate further, she huffs out a breath, muttering something about me *"being too stupid to live"* as she retakes her place beside me. I do love that mouth of hers.

The two of us lay there quietly for some time. Watching the flickering light of the candles as they burn down. Just soaking in each other's company. Happy to share space. I thought she was asleep when my own eyes started to droop. Her soft voice breaking the silence.

"Why did the dome go up in the first place?" She was hushed, as if speaking too loudly could break the quiet spell that had fallen on the room.

"Because two kingdoms' hearts had bled from their losses and decided to let the rest of the world burn." Unable to hide my sadness for those losses. I want her to understand how their actions affect her, both of us, really. "For the kingdom of Aiteall, it was the loss of their princesses... Your mothers," I elaborated so she would understand the significance of that loss. "And for the kingdom of Narci... they lost their king. He had died trying to protect those very princesses From King Kól... So, you see, the heart can do very selfish things when it's hurting." I never really understood how they could've done what they did. Not really... that was until I saw her bleeding out in the dirt. In that moment, I realized I would have done far worse.

"Asher..." Her sweet voice cuts through the thoughts in my head. It hits me in the gut anytime she says my name. Unable to speak through the unnamed emotion. I hum my response, letting her know I'm listening.

"I don't want to be like those two kingdoms. Forsaking all others in the name of my own pain. Help me save my people... Back me against my father. Help me. And I will back you in any way I can." It was a quiet request; one I would have granted whether she had asked for it or not.

"You need only ask, *a stór milis*. If it is in my power to give. It's yours." With a tender brushing of my lips to hers, I repeat myself softly. "You need only ask."

She surges forward, bringing my mouth back to hers when I pull away. Her fingers twisted in my hair, pulling me closer. Practically crawling into my lap, she winces slightly, even though she tries her best to hide it.

I groan into her mouth and try to pull away once more. So, I can see her eyes. She doesn't let me go far. Throwing a leg over my hip, seating herself more fully on my lap.

"You're in no shape to be doing this." I try to get her to see reason. Not wishing to cause her further injury.

"I think I can decide for myself what shape I'm in." The damned woman purrs against my neck. Her lips feather across my skin, trailing kisses down my neck before scraping her fangs along my collarbone. If I hadn't been hard before, I was now.

"Please, Asher. I just want to feel alive... Please." Sensing my hesitation, she sits up.

A look of defeat crosses her face before she looks away. But it's the desperate note in her voice that has me grabbing her chin hard to bring her face back to mine. In her gaze, I see that fire I've begun to crave so much ignite within her moonlit gaze.

"*A stór álainn,* you beg for nothing." I growl the words at her with a hard look in my eyes.

I lift her from my lap moving much too fast for her to react; her back hitting the bed softly with me landing between her thighs.

"Is that what you want, Devany? Hmm, to know you're alive?" I ask, closing a fist around her throat, tipping her head back.

I make my way down her neck much as she had done to me. Sucking the delicate skin over her pulse into my mouth, teasing the skin with my teeth. Her legs tighten around my hips. Grinding her sweet little clit into me and driving me out of my mother-fucking-mind.

"Answer me or I'm going to stop." I tsk in her ear, tightening my grip on her throat.

"Don't stop."

"Then tell me what you want." My hips rocking and grinding into her, heightening both of our arousal. The scent of her driving me crazy.

Unsure. She looks up at me, biting her lip. A pretty blush blooms across her cheeks, making the light dusting of freckles on her nose stand out. Embarrassed to tell me what she wants.

"What do you need, wife?" The question a whisper upon her lips, tempting her to play with me. To take what she wants like the queen she is.

"Asher..." Breathing life into my name. Halting for only a moment before setting my world on fire. "Make me come."

As soon as the whispered command slips past those soft lips. I angled her head, exposing her throat to my greedy mouth and kiss my way down the column of her neck, my tongue traveling the length of her collarbone. I lay soft kisses down along her sternum. My hands caressing her skin, blazing a path down her body.

I nip and kiss her sweet skin, scraping it with my fangs. Not drawing blood, just threatening her with the possibility. Paying homage to each breast, my lips drift over her skin from the valley of her breasts to her nipple, circling it with my tongue. I suck the harden tip into my mouth. Her back bows off the bed—fingers tighten in my hair, holding me to her. I flick the pebbled nub with my tongue, listening to her fevered moans as they get louder. No doubt drawing the attention of anyone nearby. My tongue glides along her skin to give the other the same treatment. Tasting her skin upon my tongue before moving down her body.

My fingertips ghost over her tattoo of two ravens in flight along her ribs. Their wings shining in a kaleidoscope of color against her shimmering bronze skin in the low light of the candles.

By the Gods, she's a distracting woman, an otherworldly beauty. From the sharp slope of her ears peeking out of a mass of curls. To the delicate fangs barely visible over her lower lip. And because I can't help myself, I press my lips to hers and she opens for me immediately, her tongue playing with mine. Soft gasps and little moans, music to my ears.

Her sides quiver gently as my claws lightly graze the side of her torso, leaving goosebumps in their wake. I drag them along the outside curve of her hip. My mouth once again making its way down her body. Kissing a path from the hollow of her throat to the swell of her breasts. My hand continues along its path, gliding along the underside of her thigh, hiking her leg higher up on my hip. My claws leave faint marks behind from hip to knee.

I kiss her just below her ribs, my tongue trailing down the valley of her breast—kissing a path toward my quarry, I nip and suck her sweet skin, making my way to the soft swell of her hips.

I curl my hand beneath her thigh, pulling it over my shoulder, doing the same to the other, settling myself between them. I cup the inside of her thighs, spreading them further apart to give myself better access. I turn my head to the side and lay a kiss to the inside of her knee. Slowly moving up, nipping the tender flesh of her inner thigh. My tongue trailing the soft vein, humming with power. Until I reach the delicate folds of her sex.

"Asher!" Her voice slightly panicked, as her legs tighten hard on my shoulders.

I pull my eyes from my new home for the evening to meet her gaze. She appears almost scared, and that gives me pause. *No. It can't be.*

"Devany, are you... have you been with a man?" Complete and utter disbelief is what I feel right now.

Her head turns to the side, looking away. Cheeks coloring further and I know I'm right. Her body flexes as if she's going to pull away. But I tighten my hold on her thighs. I had been possessive before, but now knowing I'll be the only man to touch her... Has me wanting to roar at the sky. To mark her so deeply that my name is burned into her very soul.

"Look at me Devany." I'll not have her hide from me. Not in this. She takes her time, but eventually gives me her gaze once more. Sweet relief is what I feel when I see that defiant fire in her eyes. *Ever the queen.*

"Let me give you pleasure," I demand of her, but it is more of a plea than I care to admit to myself.

She doesn't speak. Just merely loosens her legs, allowing her knees to fall open. I keep my gaze on hers as I once again place soft nips and kisses along her sweet inner thighs. Lightly blowing on her soft wet sex, watching her eyes flutter close.

My tongue runs between her folds. My first true taste of her bursts to life on my tongue. But it's the shocked gasp that has me smirking before I take her clit into my mouth and suck softly. That gasp turns into the sweetest moan I've ever heard. This woman will wreck me if I let her.

She grabs hold of my horns, pulling my face closer. The gods be damned if I don't love every minute. I slide a single finger inside her and feel her muscles resist the intrusion. I flick my tongue against her clit, my finger moving shallowly until I feel her body relax, pushing a little deeper each time. When her muscles begin to tremble around me, I add a second finger, increasing the suction on her clit. Her breathy moans play in tandem with my heartbeat as it runs wild within my chest.

My fingers curl inside of her, caressing the front wall along the sensitive nerves and as she tightens around me, I nip gently on her clit, and she cries out so sweetly as I push her over the edge into orgasm. That sound alone has me painfully hard as I continue sliding my fingers in and out of her slowly. Her clit throbbing against my tongue as I alternate between licks and kisses, bring her down.

I remove each of her hands from my hair, now a tangled mess from her questing fingers, and place them at her sides. Working my way up her body, I leave kisses against her fevered skin. My lips once again connect with hers, allowing her to taste herself on my tongue. Devouring her moans one at a time.

When she once again buries her hands in my hair, I gently remove myself from her embrace. Rolling to the side and taking her with me. But apparently, she's having none of it because her hand begins to slide down my chest toward my very erect cock. I grab her roaming hand and bring it to my mouth to place a gentle kiss on the inside of her wrist. I bury my other in her hair, pulling her head back, giving myself better access to her mouth. I place a not so gentle kiss on her sweet lips. When I'm finished, I look into her liquid silver eyes and find that she's pouting. But beyond that, I see trepidation and nervousness.

"But... you... ah didn't." Her cheeks flame so red I can practically feel the heat coming off of them.

In everything she has confidence for days, but not in this... I'm going to enjoy teaching her. Using the hand in her hair, I push her head back to my chest, patting her other hand.

"Shhh, this wasn't about me. Now go to sleep. We have a long day's ride ahead of us."

Chapter Seventeen

DEVANY

I wake to the sounds of camp being broken down around me. It seems in light of my father's attack; Asher has decided we're moving on to the kingdom of Naphal first thing this morning.

It's a move that has me leaving behind many of my human allies within my father's palace, as well as the magic users choosing to stay behind in the outer villages. Even though I'm unhappy about this turn of events, I understand the reasoning behind it. I need them to be my eyes and ears, and I'm trusting Luna to keep them safe.

Word has undoubtedly spread to my father by now of my little display yesterday, and he will be none too pleased. I don't doubt for a moment that he didn't have a scout watching the entire battle unfold. So sure he would win, even knowing what Asher was capable of.

Though I have to admit the amulets worked far better than I thought they would when father had first spoken of them. The revenant working with him must be incredibly skilled. He always was a hypocrite, using magic when it suited him.

The sooner we get our civilians into Naphal, the better.

I head to the large healer's tent to check on the injured. The smell of blood hits me before I even make it past the last ring of tents circling the center of camp. But the biggest shock is the sheer number of people wounded. A few of them no more than teenagers.

My father did this...

I've failed... yet again, managing to only protect the children and the sick. I had been expecting something underhanded and cruel. But the aggressiveness with which he attacked us was unexpected. It is a mistake I won't make again.

We'll need to find a workaround for the amulets, or this war could end before it has even begun. He's obviously no longer afraid of the threat Asher poses. Especially not with the revenant by his side. In truth, why would he be? Until yesterday, he had never lost.

I mean, frankly speaking, he was able to sneak into Aiteall, kill a king and steal not one, but two princesses. What he cannot see is the threat I pose to him and his rule. Not only am I a magic user like those he persecutes. But he's shared his entire plan for the war he's waging against those born with magic in their veins, all in the name of humanity. Though let's be honest, he cares little for them. I'm a wealth of information in his enemy's hands. And I'll be exploiting everything I know.

When did I start thinking of this conflict with my father as a war? *I'm not sure... But war it is.*

If Asher is correct, more death is on the way from Froslien. It's hard for me to admit my ignorance, but I know very little about Froslien and its false king, or its inhabitants. I'm sure their lives are filled with pain and cruelty at the hands of a tyrant king, just like those who live behind my father's walls. Something will need to be done on their behalf. But before I can turn my attention to those foreign walls, I must first look toward my home.

I will need a plan. *Correction... We* will need a plan. Now that Asher and I have finally come to an agreement. His help in freeing my people in exchange for whatever it is he needs from me. Even with the unknown cost, it's a fair trade, because I would've given him much, much more.

I come across the healer's tent to find Bellicent outside, directing the spellcasters to those who still need their attention. Injured men and women surround the tent, sitting wherever there's space for them. Some are sprawled out on the ground, others curled up on benches. Many of them hold bandages to bleeding wounds, but at least they're all alive. Those who are unharmed tend to the others, cleaning their injuries, bowls of water murky with blood litter the ground.

My mother used to say I had a knack for healing. It's something Valores aren't known for. Is that a clue as to who my father is? Who's to say? But it is a skill that will help to ease the suffering of these warriors who have fought tooth and nail. In some cases, quite literally. To protect those who could not protect themselves.

I walk into the tent with my head held high, only to come to an abrupt halt. Toby, the young man who tended to Libby's injuries so sweetly a few days ago, lies on a wooden table. Asher and Kane hold him down while Ansel presses an already bloodsoaked rag to a gaping hole in the young man's abdomen. They ran him through with a large weapon, most likely made of an iron-silver alloy. My father's pride and joy, designed to kill two birds with one stone, or in this case, shifters and Valore alike. The wound is much too large for his natural healing ability to kick in. We're going to lose him if Marleen cannot manipulate enough aether to repair the damage.

Sweat coats her brow and her hands move in a blur of motion as she takes in far more aether than a spellcaster should be capable of. If she keeps this up, we'll lose her as well. Her lips take on a bluish color, which is concerning.

"Enough, Marleen. We'll end up losing you both if you keep this up." Asher's powerful voice pulls me from my scrutiny of the woman's appearance. Repeating my concerns out loud.

"Almost there... Just a bit more." Her voice, breathy and thin as she throws more of her own aether into the spell.

"Enough!" He shouts at her, but it's too late. She crumples to the ground in a heap.

Without her controlling Toby's pain, he jack-knifes off the table, his screams filling the space.

Asher immediately goes to Marleen's side, checking to see if she is still among the living. But I can tell from here that her heart is still beating. Just barely, but beating, nonetheless.

I head to the table and look down at Toby, taking hold of his hand. I wipe sweat soaked hair from his face and he looks at me with glassy eyes that beg me to make it stop.

"We'll make it better," I whisper to him, before glancing at Kane, giving him a subtle nod, and he takes hold of Toby's legs.

"Hold him down, this is going to hurt," I say to Ansel, not taking my eyes from Toby.

"What the fuck do you mean this is going to hurt?" Ansel asks incredulously, though there is some underlying fear as well. I guess my little display yesterday left an impression. Well, that feeling is about to increase.

"For fuck's sake, just hold him down," I respond, not having enough energy to explain. I'm still tired from yesterday, and this will not help. But leaving this boy to die isn't an option.

"Do as she says!" Asher barks, obviously frustrated with the situation. As he sits on the floor, cradling Marleen's head in his lap.

I close my eyes, working to bring that dark, cold thing that lives in the depths of my soul to the surface. The shadows unfold —sealing every crack and smothering the light within me. Bringing attention to all the dark things I hide from. I sense the shadows flowing from my body and coating the floor at my feet. It is both terrifying and liberating. Like embracing an old friend, whispering songs long since dead to me. Completely attuned to those around me. The feel of every soul nearby, the beat of life as it flows through their veins. I can feel what souls are still tethered to this realm and those whose ties have thinned. Picking through them all, searching for the ones still holding on as life slips away.

I find their threads and pull them to me. My eyes open as my shadows enter their chests, filling up every corner. Toby's screams increase. The pain of having his injuries healed all at once; tendons and muscle stitched, bones mended. The agony so over-whelming his body goes limp, his mind sparing him the anguish.

But it's incomparable to what the healer must go through. In her attempt to pull the boy from death's embrace, she infused the spell with her life's essence. There are prices to pay when you do such a thing. She was prepared to pay the price. Her life for his. She just didn't have enough. So now her price is pain. A smile dances across my lips as the screams begin, the cold thing within me relishing the pain.

The shadows have completely consumed me now, I willingly to give into them if it means bringing others back from the brink.

"Enough, come back to me, *a stór milis*." A whiskey-soaked voice pulls at my mind.

"A price must be paid."

"The price has been paid," that voice growls, once again tugging at my mind.

"No." My voice rings out with finality.

"Give Devany back," he growls as if he has any say, the silly man. We may keep him.

"Foolish man. We are Devany... Devany is us." A hint of laughter in the response.

"Damn it, Devany. Pull back." That soulful voice says before his lips are on mine. Sucking the shadows into himself and breathing fire into me. Relieving some of the pressure in my mind. Warming my soul, giving me what I need to tighten my reins and pull the shadows back. To push them back down into the box, I keep them in.

The adrenaline leaves my body abruptly, and with it, my ability to stand. I sag against Asher's chest, his arms the only thing holding me up. Each breath I take feels like I'm inhaling sand. The noise of the tent muffled by ringing in my ears.

"Fucking hell," are the only words spoken, Ansel's tone breathless.

I'm inclined to agree with him. It's getting harder to deny that there's something very wrong with me.

"We're leaving immediately..." Asher states quietly. I feel his head lift to look at someone over my shoulder. "Ansel, tell the soldiers to be on alert. There's no telling what kind of creatures felt that." His arms tighten around me just enough for me to feel it, even in my numb state. As if he's preparing to carry me off before something comes to take me away. Ansel whispers yes almost too quietly for me to hear over the rush of blood in my ears. I feel Asher look back at me before looking over his shoulder.

"Bellicent, how are the injured?" I didn't even realize she had come into the tent.

"They're well enough to travel. Whatever she did healed them all. Shadows encompassed the entire camp, Asher. What the fuck's going on?" She sounds genuinely perplexed. Not afraid, just confused about the circumstances we find ourselves in, because I'm a freak of nature. Her awe is misplaced. I'll only end up getting them killed.

"You should leave me behind. Keep yourselves safe." My voice is stronger than I feel. This is the best choice for everyone, the only choice really. I'll protect my people from afar, and Asher will be their king. "It's for the best."

"Stop speaking nonsense, woman. You're going to stay right beside me where you belong." His statement brokers no argument. In one swift move, Asher sweeps me up in his arms and carries me over to a cot.

"I want to be on our way within the hour," he states softly to those in the tent.

I hear a shuffling of feet, then all is quiet except for Toby's deep breathing. He blessedly passed out from the overload of pain. I don't blame him. I feel the need to pass out myself. Asher smooths my hair away from my face, but I can't muster the strength to open my eyes.

"Wake me when it's time to leave," I mumble just before sleep pulls me under.

"As you wish, My Queen," are the words that chase me into the void.

Chapter Eighteen

DEVANY

The rhythmic trot of the horse wakes me. Encompassed in what I assume are Asher's arms. His warmth seeps into me, chasing away the chill that has permeated my very being.

"I thought I said to wake me up." Decidedly more irritated than I have any right to be.

"I tried. You were sleeping like the dead. So here you sit. You're stuck with me for the duration, I'm afraid." He huffs laughter under his breath. *The bastard.*

"You sound entirely too happy about it." I turn my head to get a better look at him. But only get far enough to see his chin. He smiles and only gives me a quick look before facing forward once more.

"And why shouldn't I? I've got you right where I want you." A shiver works its way up my spine as he runs his teeth along my neck from shoulder to just behind my ear.

"Pervert," I respond, panting just a little, unable to hide the effect he has on me.

"I don't see how that has any bearing on the situation." He

whispers the words close to my ear, his voice dropping an octave as it slides across my skin like a caress.

"My head hurts," I say, deciding this was the perfect moment to bring this up, needing a distraction from the things my husband makes me feel.

"Speaking of which, what happened back there? You shouldn't have been able to do something like that." Since I really don't know how I can do half the things I can, I decide deflection is the best course of action.

"I don't think Ansel likes me."

"So you're just not going to answer the question?" He doesn't sound mad, just curious. Well, get in line, buddy. I would love to know too.

"If I had answers... Who am I kidding? I probably still wouldn't tell you." This time, I feel his laughter against my back, and for some inexplicable reason, I find myself smiling. Which is a completely inappropriate response. When I don't speak anymore on the matter. He responds to my previous statement.

"Ansel was the first to be taken in by the caravan. Bellicent and I came along about a year later. He's always taken on the big brother role with us... He's convinced you'll be the death of me." It's all said with little to no emotion. As if he couldn't care less one way or the other.

"And that doesn't bother you?" I ask, wanting to understand how his mind works.

"No, why should it?" I tilt my head in his direction once more, trying to unravel the puzzle that is my husband.

"You should, because he could very well be right." Frustrated with him for a completely different set of reasons now. I mean, really, who acts so nonchalant about the possibility of dying?

"It doesn't matter one way or the other. This is the path I've chosen..." He looks down at me as if to make sure I'm listening. "You. are. mine." He whispers each word slowly while tilting my face up to meet his lips, just a soft brushing along my own, ghosting over my jaw before ending at my ear. "And I'll not give you up." A confession that brings with it another shiver. He pulls back from me as if nothing at all has transpired.

"Now, back to what I was saying. Ansel has always played the big brother role. It's very hard for him to be without some measure of control. He probably hasn't been without it in some form or another since we were kids..." He trails off, lost to memories that span the small lifetime they've all been together.

Family... Something I've had in short supply in my years within the palace. Even though I have Narcissa, Kane, and even Luna, we could never openly be around one another. To do so would have been to turn my father's eye toward them, and that was something I was never willing to do.

I covet their freedom to care for each other openly. I lived in fear my father would harm them as a new way to cause me pain. We all understood why I had to stay away, but the absence was felt. Asher voice pulls me from my swirling thoughts of family and envy. But it's a word that catches my attention or, more accurately, two words.

"Wait, did you just say portal magic?" I had to have heard him wrong. "But that's an exceedingly rare gift, is it not?" I realize after everything I have done in the last couple of days, being awestruck seems silly. But that is exactly what I am. There are kingdoms that would put him in a collar for that gift.

"That's not a safe gift to have, Asher. Believe me, I know. There are slavers within my father's borders that would gladly chain him." Nauseous at the thought of what they would do to him. My eyes strayed in his direction as he rides out on our right. His eyes coming up to meet mine head on as if he feels my stare. Asher turns his head toward Ansel as well.

"They could try." The quiet steel of those words, leaving no doubt as to what he would do if they ever did.

"Tell me about the shadows, Devany" A soft demand, but a demand, nonetheless. It seems he only uses my name for serious matters.

"There's not much to tell," I say as I look around for Narcissa, finding her behind me with Kane out in front. Anything to distract from the conversation I know is coming.

"Devany, I need to understand what it is we're dealing with." He reaches around to tilt my face toward him, running his thumb along my chin. "Help me protect you... to understand." There was a softness to his demand that makes it feel so much more like a plea. That I answer him.

"There's always a ripple of darkness beneath my skin. A... Shadow... The constant companion to my soul." I take a deep breath. I've never told another living soul about this. Kane and Narcissa know. But have never asked me to explain. Most likely because they know I don't truly understand it myself.

"What is it?" he asks, his lips close to my ear, placing a soft kiss on my shoulder. The feel of his warm breath brushing along my neck, a small distraction.

Not wanting to be sucked in by the intimate moment. I look around to watch the trees move by. Listening to the sounds of a nearby stream. The feel of a soft breeze skating across my skin.

"It feels as if two types of magic are battling for dominance within the very fabric of my soul. I lived in fear of what my father would do had he ever found out. The things he did to magic users." A quiet confession. Tempest tried to keep the horrors from me in the beginning. But it's hard to hide those atrocities even from a child when they're everywhere. I have no doubt had father known, he would have done far worse to me. Child or not.

My throat closes and I can see the charred remains of magic users hanging from battlements. The scent of burning flesh carried on the wind. My spine locks tight with each memory that enters my mind. Asher tightens his arm around my waist, pulling me more firmly into his body. Most likely scenting the fear I work so hard to hide.

I have known since a young age that the man my birth mother raised me with was not my true father. Because, as Ansel had pointed out, there is nothing human about me. No matter how much I wish I could be. To be anything other than this. I look toward the stream, blinking the moisture from my eyes, and swallowing past the lump in my throat. Asher waits quietly while I pull myself together, running his thumb over the exposed skin above my riding pants.

"From the moment my magic made its presence known, I have worked tirelessly, striving for stability. Learning to control whatever this is... Without knowing where it comes from." The words whisper softly, as if someone may overhear and tell my father. "As I'm sure you figured out by now, control was something I could never quite achieve." I shake my head, laughing under my breath, though it sounds hollow. He doesn't speak. I'm not even sure he's breathing at this point. The only movement I feel is his thumb as it continues its path along my skin.

I look down at my hands as if I can see the magic dancing across my fingertips. Disgusted by what's locked below the surface.

"I was only ever able to lock it up and shove it down." I spit each word out as if I can taste the foul magic on my tongue. "But the true problem, Asher... is that every time I give in to the shadows, I can feel them consuming me a little more." A fine mist of sweat breaks out along my skin, quickly cooled by the breeze, leaving goosebumps in its wake. I fear the day I lose the battle. Finally, losing the fight against my emotions, the tears spill over my eyelashes.

"Shh, you're so much stronger than you give yourself credit for, *a stór milis*," he murmurs so no one else can hear. Tucking my head under his chin, wrapping both arms around me.

"You don't understand... Every day it pulls at me, bringing me one step closer to the fall, and I have no idea what's on the other side." I softly give a voice to my genuine fear. What happens when I lose the battle against the shadows that weave in and out of my soul?

I reach up to wipe the tears from my face, only to have Asher stay my hand to do it himself. Embarrassed, I attempt to hide, but he grabs my chin, his grip unyielding. Painfully, I pull my face around to meet his. Pissed off, I yank my face from his grasp. His smile grows when faced with my displeasure.

"There she is." That seductive voice of his curls around me. Though the angle is still painful, he takes hold of my face once more. With gentle hands this time, brushing my lips with his. "There is nothing weak about you, wife. I'll not have you thinking otherwise," he purrs against my mouth and heat pools low in my stomach, causing my cheeks to heat.

I pull away once again. Only this time for a completely different reason. The need to hide the effect he has on me. I turn away and scan the surrounding area. But if the light dancing in his eyes is any indication, he wasn't fooled. But says nothing, allowing me my dignity. It's the first time I notice we're completely alone. It seems he allowed me to maintain more of my dignity than I had previously thought, keeping my meltdown between us.

The horse takes off at a quick gallop, easily closing the ten meters between us and the convoy. But almost as soon as we are upon them, I feel it. Something whispering in the wind, sliding over my senses. I raise my hand, stopping the group with the motion.

Apparently, after the battle with my father's men, my magic is quick to react to perceived threats. It wasn't even a conscious thought to release my glamour. My magic causing the ground beneath us to rumble.

"Careful my warrior queen, these men are friends, not foe," he whisperers in my ear. Before calling out to the trees in front of us. "You should show yourselves before Devany decides she's willing to chance another battle."

"Yes, we heard about that." There's laughter in that voice, but Asher goes rigid behind me. The arm around my waist tightens slightly.

"And how, pray tell, did you hear of that?" It's said lightly, but there's an undercurrent of violence. He's prepared to fight with this person. Friend or not.

"Relax old friend." The humor in his voice seems to only increase at the threat of violence now lacing the air. "We mean your mate no harm." Asher takes in a breath to respond, but I beat him to it.

"We're not mates, and I'm the one you should be concerned with." I say every word with authority. My head held high. Back straight.

"You heard my queen. It's best you show yourself, Ivann." If I had thought Asher would treat me as a child throwing a tantrum, I was wrong. He treated me as his equal, even if I was threatening one of the rulers of the sixteen kingdoms. "She doesn't suffer fools lightly."

"Trust me, he speaks from experience," Ansel cuts in, breaking the tension. I have to say it's the first time I've heard humor in his voice when referring to me.

"Indeed," the man responds, coming into view for the first time.

He is quite handsome, to say the least. His gaze dances with so much laughter, I could practically feel the warmth coming off his brown eyes. His smooth ochre complexion offset by his hair—so black it appeared blue in the late afternoon sunlight. The only hair on his face was a mustache that curls dramatically at the ends. But all this is eclipsed by the rakish smile he was currently pointing in my direction. Those warm eyes of his dragging down my body so thoroughly it was damn near scandalous.

"Rumors of your beauty have been heard across all sixteen kingdoms, but none have done you justice." I can hear just the hint of an accent in his husky voice. If I were any other woman, I would most likely find it terribly attractive. But I merely arch a single eyebrow at the obvious enticement in his voice. Since I already have my hands full with the asshole behind me.

"That'll be enough of that," is Asher's disgruntled response. It takes a great deal of effort to keep from smiling as he motions the horse forward through the grouping of soldiers, bringing us alongside King Ivann. But his only reaction to my husband's irk is a wink in my direction before turning his horse around, keeping pace with our fast trot.

By the time we enter the woods, our men have closed rank. Kane staying out in front, Ansel moving to our back with Narcissa taking his spot to our left, Bellicent to the right. It's all done so seamlessly that one would think they had done it a hundred times before. We might be on allied soil, but we're taking no chances. My father has already shown he's not afraid to start a war.

Neither Narcissa nor I have ever been outside of Erabis. It is quite literally a whole new world. Beautiful and strange all the same. We've never seen such beauty, from the villages dotted throughout the woods to the Covenia river that divides the surrounding terrain. Places I've only seen on maps. But none of it compares to the sight of the mountain pass opening before us. Revealing a vast desert surrounding an oasis. A beautiful city standing tall amongst lofty trees, leaden with fruit. Walls made of sandstone stretching toward the sky. Foliage of purple, pink, and white spilling over the tops, softening the hard edges. Lovely round top buildings that shine in a kaleidoscope of color in the light of the setting sun.

I can't help but gasp at the magnificence of it all. It's simply breathtaking.

"If you find this worth gasping over, just wait until you have me between your thighs, wife." The bastard says it loud enough for everyone around us to hear. The men all chuckle about it. I've decided at this moment all men are bastards. The tips of my ears are no doubt as red as my cheeks.

"Pervert," I respond with a harsh breath. He really is a bastard sometimes.

"Yes, so you've said before," he whispers in my ear, dragging his nose along my neck placing a soft kiss behind my ear.

"Keep it up, husband, and you'll never find out," I say it just as loud, causing the group to laugh even harder.

"It seems you've met your match, Asher," King Ivann points

out while still laughing under his breath. But if he thought to get under Asher's skin, he was mistaken.

"I know. Imagine how spectacular it will be when we collide," he murmurs his answer against my skin. That arm of his pulling me firmly into him to feel him hardening against my backside.

Chapter Nineteen

ASHER

The sun has nearly set by the time we make it to the city proper. The soft pinks and purples of dusk paint the sky in a bright wash of color. It reflects off the metal dome roofs of the buildings and shimmers off the water in the beautiful stone canals that bring in freshwater from the mountain pass. The aqueducts weave along the city streets to fountains and wells, bringing in much needed water to this desert kingdom. Vegetation covers the walls and spills from pottery, softening the sharp edges of the carved stone walls. Devany's not wrong, it really is a breathtaking sight.

Just walking through the streets, you see the prosperity of the kingdom and the warmth of its people. Ivann is beloved and his people are happy.

The streets are full, and even with night fast approaching, the bazaar is still humming with activity. The scent of fresh bread and spices assaults the senses. Children's laughter echoes in the streets melding with steady buzz of sound from the marketplace. This is what Erabis, and Kannon were once like, twin kingdoms with a friendship that went back a millennium. All destroyed by the greed of one man. Now both lay in ruin. Devany will never know what they were like before Kól betrayed Kannon's young king. Slaughtering him and his only heir, a sister.

She and Narcissa haven't stopped admiring the many sights laid before them. Awe plainly written along their features. It's then that it occurs to me that neither has ever been outside of Erabis. That's just disheartening to have that broken place be all you've ever known. The sound of Ivann's voice draws me from my thoughts.

"So how long are you in need of board, old friend?" he asks, serene and unhurried. As if he doesn't feel the breath of war breathing down his neck the same as I do.

"Just until we rest up. We don't wish to impose. It's been a busy few days. My queen needs rest." She's been through quite a bit in a short period of time.

I'm not sure she's fully grasped what she may, in fact, need to do. It's one thing to say you'll kill your father. It's an entirely different situation when it comes time to follow through, no matter how deserving he may be.

"That's not a problem. Let's get you all settled. We will serve dinner soon. Nyra is excited to see all of you. She won't shut up about it." It's said with exasperation, as if he doesn't love her more than life itself. He spoils the woman. I pity the man who must live up to all he's provided.

"Nyra?" Devany asks, pulling her eyes from the many stalls that line the street, her lovely voice skating over my skin, sinking into my bones.

Though I'm not surprised she doesn't know of her, Ivann has done well to keep knowledge of her to a minimum.

"Yes, my dearest little sister. It's been sometime since we've all been together." He's right, it's been almost a year since last we were all together. Only last time it was on Draic soil.

Once inside the city walls, the ride to the palace is short and sweet. Members of the staff meet us within the inner courtyard. My infantry knows their way around. So, with weary bodies, they drop their horses off and head toward barracks for a hot shower, a meal, and some much-needed rest.

I look up to see several handmaids heading our way; the pack led by none other than Nyra. Her blue-black hair is tied back in a long braid that hangs over one shoulder with delicate wisps of hair framing her face, softening her cheekbones. She and Ivann share their father's coloring. But she gets her bright green eyes from her mother.

I jump down from my horse and turn to Devany, helping her down. Being sure to drag her body along my own. Once she is on her feet, I take hold of her hand, leading her toward the palace doors. The two of us stop to observe Kane and Ansel approaching Narcissa to help her dismount from her horse. Only for her to swing her leg over the saddle and jump, landing on sure feet. She gives neither man acknowledgment, walking with purpose into the palace. Devany gives an unladylike snort, shaking her head before she too is heading toward the palace. Leaving me standing there. I'm not sure where Bellicent is, but I'm sure she finds all this highly amusing.

With nothing else to do, I follow in my wife's tantalizing wake, stopping just inside the grand foyer. The space is dominated by a staircase carved from a single piece of sandstone that leads to the overlook. Throughout the room, every door, banister, and window ledge is made of rosewood native to this region. Its vibrant red undertone contrasts beautifully with the warm natural sandstone. Giving the space a pleasant welcoming feel. Large hand-painted tiles cover the floors in every direction.

"Since your group is much larger than in times past, you'll be taking up the eastern wing," Emma states as she greets us, smiling warmly.

She's been running Ivann's household for as long as I can remember. Before that, she was their nursemaid, the closest thing either of them have to a mother. And if you don't watch your manners, she'll box your ears no matter how old or big you think you are. We all absolutely adore her.

"Ladies, you will be to the left. You two gentlemen to the right." She directs Bellicent and Narcissa to one side, gesturing with her hand to the right for Kane and Ansel, knowing that they would all prefer to have people pass by them before getting to us.

Emma turns back to Devany and I, her eyes bright with unshed tears. Taking hold of our hands, she smiles at us both with so much pride that I find myself swallowing thickly. If she knew that I practically stole Devany from her home, she would be highly disappointed with me.

"You and your lovely bride will take the Center rooms which overlook the west gardens. They're beautiful this time of day." She leans forward, kissing Devany on her cheek, startling her slightly, still unused to friendly contact. To keep Emma from looking too closely at her reaction, I draw her attention back to me.

"Hey, and where is my kiss?" Emma turns to look at me, her cheek pinking a little. But before she can do anything, I pick her up and spin her about the floor. Before placing her on feet, she smiles wide enough to show her straight white teeth, giving my arm a swift smack.

"You great big flirt," she says it admonishingly, though there's still a smile on her face and she's a bit breathless from laughing at my antics. She gives my arm one more smack before gesturing to the stairs once more.

"Go on now, get cleaned up. Supper waits for no one," she says to all of us before quitting the room and heading toward the kitchen.

"Thank you," Devany whispers, without looking directly at me. I can tell the whole interaction has left her out of sorts.

"There's nothing to thank," I whisper back, keeping my eyes forward as she had. She does glance at me before looking forward, and we continue our trek to our rooms in silence.

Not wanting to give her time to think about the room arrangements too much. I cut straight to the point.

"Clean up quickly. I'd rather not be late. Emma will box my ears. She finds it highly rude." To this, she smiles.

"I have half a mind to be late just so I see this with my own eyes," she replies, smirking at me.

"Oh, *a stór*, everything she does to me." For dramatic effect, I pause, giving her a slow perusal. Remembering exactly what she looks like without her riding leathers on. "I'm going to take it out on that lovely backside of yours." I'm satisfied when I see that lovely blush blossom on the apple of her cheeks.

"Tonight, will be informal. Tomorrow night will be the official banquet, the fanfare of one king welcoming another. A show of respect, if you will," I state dismissively, with my hands in my pockets, I turn to face her.

"What should I wear?" Seeming unsure. The small indention between her brows deepening. It never ceases to surprise me how she can fret over such small things. While also showing so much confidence in others.

"Devany, wear whatever you choose. No one within my court will ever push their expectation on you." She wasn't born to take orders; she was born to give them. She says nothing about this, just stares at me.

"I'm going to check on Ansel and Kane. Make sure they haven't killed each other," I state deciding that it was best to give her space. She acknowledges me by nodding.

Our night starts out with introductions. Nyra formally introduces herself, along with Ivann's four wives. First, there's Eva, a rare beauty, and the daughter of one of the largest merchants in Galandir. She's also his oldest and dearest friend, having been betrothed since childhood, her dark hair and dark eyes are reminiscent of those from Naphal. She's a delicate creature in comparison to his second wife.

Which brings us to Chloe. She comes from a warrior tribe located near the Southern border of Naphal, near the barrier along the border it shares with Froslien. Her father comes from a long line of large cat shifters. He had taken a human for a mate and until Chloe, all their children, were born with the ability to shift. Knowing how hard things would be for his youngest daughter, he trained her to become a lethal weapon to be wielded. Ivann was out investigating a border breach when he came across her and that was it. They began courting.

Regrettably, I know little about the other two. Outside of the fact that they're twins, Sibil and Tasha, the youngest of the four, with a quiet beauty about them.

Last, Ivann introduces Jasper, his second. The broody bastard gives us a stiff formal hello. Never giving much away.

We spend much of the night in a haze of camaraderie. Each of us shares loud stories of our misspent youth. Free flowing drinks and sweet-smelling tobacco for those of us who indulge. Devany watches all of this quietly. The occasional smile gracing her lips. It's late when we finally make it to our rooms.

I remove my clothing with little to no fanfare. While listening to the rustle of cloth coming from behind the changing screen. Devany emerges in a pale pink nightgown, the silk hugging every alluring inch. There's no seduction in her hurried steps, diving quickly beneath the sheets.

Instead of getting under the covers, I crawl up the bed and hover over her body, trapping her not only by the sheets, but by the weight of my body.

I rest my forehead on hers. Just breathing her in and allowing her scent to surround me. My lips brush hers, grazing the corners of her mouth with light teasing kisses that leave her breathless and chasing my lips when I pull away. Her lovely eyes glassy with lust.

"Asher," she whines, wiggling beneath me, attempting to get her hands out from under the sheets.

"No touching *a stór*, you need your rest." It seems she doesn't like that answer because she's once again wiggling beneath me. Which causes me to harden against her and by the look of triumph on her face, she got the result she was looking for.

"Let me put my hands on you." Her face colors the same shade as her gown. Unable to even look me in the eye as she makes her request. Rolling off of her, I lay down beside her.

"Alright love, you can put hands on me, but turnaround is fair play." Her eyes widened slightly. If she thought to control this interaction, she was very wrong.

Chapter Twenty

DEVANY

My heart beats frantically in my chest like a bird against a pane of glass. I'm about to have my way with Asher of Draic. Nervous energy courses through my body, my stomach takes flight, and my hands begin to tremble. I inhale a deep calming breath, filling my lungs with Asher's intoxicating scent, winter fires surrounded by sweet night air.

I throw my leg over his hip, covering his body with my own, much like he had. I sit up in his lap and look down at his handsome face. He's all sharp angles and rakish looks. A light beard covers his powerful jawline, and his hair hangs unbounded to his shoulders in a mass of mahogany waves. The tips of his ears visible amongst the velvety, thick locks. His olive skin shimmering in the moonlight from the window.

Lightly, I glide my hands up his chest, the heat of his skin brands me and without thought I drift closer. The bastard smiles widely, putting his hands behind his head and gets comfortable, watching me with hooded eyes.

He's right about turnabout being fair play and I intend to

have quite a bit of fun. With a daring smile, I take hold of my dressing gown and pull the silky fabric over my head slowly. I'm rewarded by the sharp sudden intake of breath and the tightening of his hands on my thighs—I hadn't even felt him move. I take my time opening my eyes to meet his gaze.

"You are the most beautiful creature I've ever laid eyes on." The words are spoken with reverence, his eyes glued to my face.

There's an intensity in his gaze I can't put into words, an unnamed emotion I lack the experience to place. No one has ever looked at me as Asher does. Like I'm all he sees.

He raises his hand and tucks a lock of hair behind my ear, the tips of his fingers trailing down the outer edge. He cups the side of my face, and I can't help but lean into the touch, closing my eyes briefly. Just soaking in the warmth of his skin. His fingers glide slowly down the soft slope of my neck, his hand closing around my throat, squeezing gently.

My pulse jumps wildly beneath his fingertips as he holds me still. His dark fathomless eyes hold me motionless. His pupils are blown wide, the irises only a thin green-gold ring. My reflection stares back at me from their depths. My lips are slightly parted, my eyes hooded with lust. He releases my throat, drawing a slow line down my chest, his fingertips tracing the swell of my breast. He brushes my nipple lightly with the backs of his fingers before running his nail across the peek. My breath catches somewhere between my heart and my throat. Cool night air brushes over my skin, cooling the heated flesh leaving behind goosebumps.

It's equal parts overwhelming and empowering to have all his attention solely focused on me. He makes me feel like this beautiful, confident, powerful thing he claims me to be. It gives me the courage to do and take what I want.

With my eyes open, I lean forward, placing a soft kiss on his mouth. His hands automatically tangle in my hair as he tries to deepen the kiss. But I pull back, stopping him with a look when he tries to pull me back.

"Tread lightly with your power, *a stór*," he growls at me, eyes burning bright like an autumn fire.

With our gazes locked, I lean forward once more to place a kiss just to the side of his nipple before tracing the bar with my tongue. He shudders beneath me, his grip on my thighs tightens almost painfully. I wiggle against him, unable to stop myself, needed friction of some kind. A deep groan leaves his throat, his chest vibrates with the sound.

This is a reaction I like very much. I kiss my way down his chest, paying homage to his piercings. Listening to every tortured sound he makes. Each breath is taken through clenched teeth. I worship every scar, tracing each crease and divot with my lips. Once I reach the blanket around his waist, I stop—unsure. What do I do next? My heart is once again that frantic bird beating on glass. It's the sound of his voice that drowns out the noise.

"You don't have to do anything you don't want to, Devany." His fingers skate along my jaw, tilting my chin to bring my eyes to his. They hold so much warmth and understanding that it makes my heart pick up an extra beat, fucking with my head in a way only Asher can.

I turn my head to place a tender kiss on the palm of his hand before I turn back to his waist. My tongue maps the expanse of skin between his hips. Which earns me another deep groan. Like I'm killing and pleasing him all at once. I quite like the sounds he makes. With sure hands, I sit back and drag the satin sheets down from his hips, uncovering his thighs. My eyes were on his for a moment before lowering them.

There he is in all his glory. Very hard and very erect. And not for the first time, I wonder how that's going to fit.

He takes my quiet perusal of him for something it's not and repeats himself.

"You don't have to do this," he says softly as his hands grip my waist to move me. I shake my head, and he stops and lightens his grip.

I reach between us and take hold of him, lightly gliding my

hand from base to tip. Taking in the contrast of textures, soft silky skin wrapped around hard unyielding muscle.

He sucks in a deep breath through his nose. His eyes fluttering shut. His grip on my hips tightens, and I'll no doubt have fingertip bruises by morning. But I can't find it in me to care one bit.

I think back to what he had done to me with his mouth and lean down, licking him from root to tip in one long stroke. His hands tighten almost painfully as he whispers my name. I do this again and again, my hand following behind my tongue. With each pass, my hands become surer as I learn him. On the next upward pass, I decide to take him into my mouth, sucking gently. He fills my mouth over and over again; my name becomes a chant and a prayer. His hands tangle in my hair, using it as leverage to glide himself in and out of my mouth. Each thrust a little faster than the last as he chases his own release. When suddenly he tries to pull me off.

"Devany, stop, *a stór*." To this I suck harder, bringing him further into my mouth, holding his hips down with both hands.

"Shit... love, I'm sorry." My brows furrow, trying to figure out what he could be sorry for.

Then it happens. He moans low and long. His release fills my mouth. I work hard to swallow it all. But having never done this before, it's less than graceful.

I sit back, feeling oddly satisfied. But the next thing I know the room is spinning and my back hits the mattress, his mouth on mine as he swallows my next breath. His tongue sweeps in deeply and I wrap my legs around his waist, pulling him deeper into my embrace. He breaks the kiss, lowering his forehead to mine.

"Woman, you're going to be the death of me." His panting breath ghosts over my lips. He closes eyes and slides his nose a long mine, his face is soft with pleasure.

"I think it's time for fair play, don't you, *a stór*?" he says with a wicked grin.

The look he gives me steals the breath from my lungs because nothing good can come of it. He looks more like a demon of temptation getting ready to sweet talk a mortal out of their soul.

We spend the rest of the night with his head buried between my legs as he does his due diligence to make sure I scream his name loud enough for the world to hear. Not that I'm complaining by the time I fall into a dreamless sleep.

Chapter Twenty-One

DEVANY

Bright early morning light filters behind my closed eyes. The warmth of it dancing along my skin, melting away the last remnants of sleep. My mind floats somewhere between rest and wakefulness.

The moment passes in the still and quiet of the room as I wipe the slumber from my eyes. My mind comes to wakefulness gradually. I lengthen my body—arching my spine—stretching my neck and back to relieve the sleep induced tension weighing them down. Asher's faint scent hangs in the air, tempting my mind as well as my body as memories of last night play freely in my mind. I reach back for him, finding only the soft glide of cool sheets. Clutching the linens to my chest, I sit up quickly, my eyes snap open. I find the space empty and there better be a damn good reason for why I'm waking up alone.

I glance around the room, hoping for some kind of clue as to where he may have gone off to this morning, *without saying goodbye I might add*. But the only thing I find is a tray filled with what must be my breakfast resting on a small table in the sitting room.

It had been too late for me to get a good look at the bedroom last night, but to see it in the light of day takes my breath away. Sheer lightweight drapes sway in a soft breeze blowing in from the balcony. Dawning light filters in the through the open French doors, illuminating the room, giving it an airy glow. Beautifully dyed pillows in vivid hues decorate the space, from the tiled floor to the intricately carved furniture in all shapes and sizes. Hand-woven rugs in the same colors as the sunset reflecting off the domed roofs of the city soften the painted tile floors. The room is intimate and cozy with a lived-in feel.

It's best to get my day started because I know full well Narcissa plans to put me through my paces. One can never be too prepared. I love the woman half to death, but she can be terrifying when she wants to be.

It takes no time at all to get to the cliff's edge above the training grounds. Thanks to the heat, I'm already regretting my life choices. Naphal is known for its warmer climate and dry air, which translates to... you guessed it, boob sweat. *Yay me.* My only reprieve is a faint icy breeze blowing in from the south. The air carrying with it the scent of snow, salt water and a hint of decay. The wind most likely blowing in from the tainted shores of Froslien.

Movement catches my attention, drawing my eyes to the training grounds below. Men of all shapes and sizes occupy the sparring rings, both kingdoms competing in different sports and exercises. Voices and laughter mix with the sounds of steel-on-steel echoing off the rock-face.

It appears this is where Asher went this morning. *Did I mention he didn't say goodbye?*

He and Ivann occupy one of the sparring rings on the outer edge. They're both standing beneath a bar that's roughly a half meter above their heads. A large group of yelling soldiers surround them, calling out numbers. It takes me a moment to realize they're all placing bets.

Ansel and Jasper approach them, secure one of their arms

behind their backs. Effectively hindering each of them. Asher and Ivann bend at the knees before jumping as one, grabbing hold of the bar with their free hand. They hang there for a moment before pulling themselves up, bringing their heads above the bar.

"Are you planning on staring all day?" I was so engrossed in the games below that I hadn't noticed Bellicent until she placed her hand on my shoulder, startling the shit out of me and forcing an ungodly squeak from my throat.

"What the fuck are you doing? Sneaking up on me like that!" I snap at her because she fucking scared me and that just pisses me off.

"It wasn't like I was trying to sneak up on you. Maybe you should pay more attention to your surroundings instead of drooling over your husband." The laughter in her voice only furthered my irritation. The glare I throw in her direction would cause most to turn tail and run. But all I get is a very unimpressed look. The men below roar and cheer, snapping me out of my staring contest with Bellicent, drawing my attention back to them. Asher and Ivann are once again back on two feet. Breathing heavily.

"What are they doing down there?" I wave my hand in the general direction of the rings below as my curiosity gets the best of me. Father's training grounds never looked like this. Even Kane seems to enjoy it. Taking part in the games. Completely in his element.

"Surely, you've seen training grounds before. Sparring rings? Grappling pits?" Her eyes moved back and forth between mine. The look she's giving me is a strange mix of puzzlement and concern.

Rolling my eyes, I answer her. "Yes, father had... *has* all those things. But there is no enjoyment to be had. You fight or you die. There was a time when my father would go down to the villages and have all the boys between the ages of twelve and twenty line up in the square." My stomach turning sour at the memory of those who were torn from their homes, beaten for resisting. "He would pace up and down in front of the young men, dragging out the process. He enjoyed the fear he induced in both the families and the boys. He'd take all of those with the right body type or potential and rip them from their families. Only one of the many fucked up things he did."

"Sweet Goddess, every time you open your mouth about that place, it's a dark tale." Her voice hushed, as if she's sad for me. But she can keep it. I don't need her pity.

My eyes drift back to the rings below us. Where men have just finished jumping from post to post, all of which are raised at varying heights off the ground. As soon as the two men step out, Ansel and Jasper move on to the next ring and obstacle. For this one, each of them has ten javelins. They must throw them through five ring targets several meters away at different elevations. The group once again places their bets. Asher holds up five fingers, placing a wager of his own.

I stare at him as he stands there with sunlight glistening off his olive skin, his mahogany hair escaping its leather wrap, sticking to the sides of his neck. He throws his back and laughs so freely that I can almost imagine that I can hear it.

When Bellicent doesn't say anything, I repeat my earlier question because I just can't deal with the weighty silence.

"It's the Relay Games. Draic and Naphal have done them for the last couple of years. As a way to be on good terms with allies." Now that grabs my attention.

"Let me get this right." Turning my body to give her my full focus. "We fight our allies, causing injuries of varying degrees in order to keep them as allies. That may be the most feeble-minded thing I've heard." Truly baffled, I mean, I don't know a lot about the working relationships between allied kingdoms. But it stands to reason that bloodying them up is the opposite of what we want.

"They're men," she says this like that's an answer in of itself. Thankfully, she doesn't leave it at that because I don't get it. "Sometimes they just make little sense. But in this case, there's a little more to it. We train with them a few times a year as an act of good faith. Giving away our fighting styles thus putting each at a disadvantage should we ever face each other in battle. The tournament though, has only been going on for the last couple of years."

Her eyes light up as memories seemed to play behind them.

"A few years ago, the four of them were in their cups and started arguing over who was better at what. So naturally that turns into those four jackasses going outside in the dead of winter, challenging each other to various physical feats. None of which they had the center of gravity to complete. But they made so much noise that they woke up the entire barracks. Once they realized that there was no threat, the soldiers promptly began placing bets and, with that, the tournament was born." I couldn't contain the unexpected smile that took over my face.

I could almost see the entire scene play out in my head. The overwhelming urge to laugh bubbling up inside of me. Such a light feeling. One I haven't felt often. I return my gaze back to the training grounds to hide from Bellicent's probing looks, feeling embarrassed for so many reasons. But primarily because I'm unused to exposing my feelings, good, bad, or indifferent. I stare out at the grounds, not really seeing anything. When Bellicent once again places her hand on my shoulder, her voice breaks through my thoughts.

"Few people know this, but Ansel and Jasper are distantly related on Ansel's father's side. At the end of the Great War, Ivann's father sent him to Jasper's family for safekeeping. At this point, The Elemental Druids had placed the barrier, stopping the drain of magic. But it was too late for Naphal. The kingdom had already lost a third of its land. With each monarch being tied to the land, the loss of magic took its toll on Ivann's father. He was too far gone to save... And it was a slow death. He wanted to err on the side of caution, sending Ivann away for safekeeping. The land's transition from ruler to ruler can be dangerous. Everything has a cost and to bind yourself to the land, you must make a sacrifice. This leaves the new ruler weakened. Ivann's father was unaware that Jasper's parents had passed in the last siege. By this point, Jasper has been living with us for a few months. The caravan had a habit of taking us strays in. Because of this Ivann was with us for a few years. All four of those men are closer than brothers, with bonds born in fear and bound by blood. Which is one of the many reasons Draic and Naphal are such close allies."

I let all that information sink in, knowing she is trying to help me find my footing without feeling like she's crossing a line or betraying Asher. I decided to focus on the games while my mind makes heads or tails of everything I've learned.

The soldiers are once again surrounding a ring, this one occupied by Asher, Ivann, Ansel, and Jasper. The four of them suspended from a set of rings. They begin to move, pulling their bodies up and spinning in a smooth, slow circle. Before coming back to the beginning point, only to start again. Their arms push out parallel with the ground as they pull themselves up once again, their legs lifting out in front of them. A series of gravity defying movements ensue.

Every move is disciplined and flawless in execution. The four of them are a sight to behold. But my eyes are drawn to Asher, which shouldn't be all that surprising as they always are. They each hold in a different position before dismounting, flipping in the air, landing on the balls of their feet. I feel rather than see Bellicent walk away, leaving me to scrutinize my husband as I contemplate my next move.

With their dismount, the games below come to an end. Which is good timing, being as I see Narcissa looking for me down in the sparring pit. She's all healed up and ready to train. So am I, for that matter. It's the whole reason I'm out here to begin with, dressed in fighting leather in this ungodly heat.

The walk down to the training grounds takes no time at all.

I scan my surroundings, my eyes sweeping across the training grounds, looking for a particular person. It doesn't take long to find Narcissa running practice circuits, having already appropriated one of the far rings for us. Her beautiful chestnut braids are piled high on her head. Close fitted leathers, very similar to mine, hug her curves. Each strike against her imaginary foe is smooth and true, like watching art in motion.

They all watch her as she flows smoothly from one move to the next. Some stare, seeing her for the threat she is. Believe me, I understand. She's an imposing sight. Others stare on with blatant lust. A few are even brave enough to approach her. I search Kane out, watching for his reaction to the scene playing out before us. And when I find him, I can tell by his ticking jaw and hard eyes that he's taken notice. But instead of doing anything about it, he simply turns his back and continues with his match.

She plants her sword into the sand, meeting the men head on with a sultry smirk. An ease to her sexuality that I've always been jealous of. I'm the married one and yet I'm no more comfortable with sex than I was before my vows. She nods her head; no doubt having secured a rendezvous. She pulls her sword from the sand and resumes her training exercises. But not before shooting a quick look in Kane's direction as a look of disappointment covers her lovely face. With one last look, she turns her back on him, picking up where she left off once more.

Her eyes collide with mine as I approach. Soldiers watching every step we take as we close the distance between us. Most know me by reputation, thinking of me as the soft and spoiled princess. Asher's soldiers eye me with apprehension because they've seen what I can bring about when pushed. Ivann's men think I'm incapable of causing any serious damage. Little do they know.

"Where've you been?" she says by way of greeting. Being hostile for no good reason. So, I guess it's going to be one of those days.

"Lovely to see you, too," I reply, deciding to push her right back. "You need to get laid," I state with a *fuck-you* smile I've perfected over the years.

"Not that it's any of your business, but I've already set that up." Returning my *fuck-you* smile with one of her own. She turns, giving me her back, grabbing a nearby water skin.

"Then what's your problem?" I'm exasperated by how hard-headed she can be sometimes. As comfortable as she is in her sexuality, I don't think she'll ever admit to the feeling she has for him.

"Nothing, just go arm up." Her voice goes from irritated to somber. With my hands on my hips, I continue to stare at her back for several seconds before heading for the weapons table and doing as I'm told.

The flat surface is covered in a small arsenal of forged steel. My fingers dance along the hilt of each weapon, taking in the craftsmanship and beauty. There's all manner of weaponry here, from spears to daggers and everything in between. After testing the weight of several blades, I settle on a lightweight short sword made of Alanus—a black and gold alloy only found within the Brynhild kingdom. It's rare to find items made from this metal outside of Brynhild. The sword is magnificent, the black and gold weaving and bending with each other, creating this beautiful wave pattern.

"Ok, let's run through a few basic refreshers before moving on, shall we?" she says calmly, once again centered and in her element.

My mind clears with the repetition of motion. My body reacts without thought to the rhythmic beating of my heart and breath. Each of my movements is slow and precise. Once I'm in my zone, Narcissa advances, the clink of steel ringing out with each strike. We move to a song she and I have danced to dozens of times. But the blank headspace I've achieved is interrupted by Asher.

"Getting a workout in, are we, *a stór*?" He's such a horse's ass sometimes. Though he's lucky, I can see the teasing humor in his evergreen eyes.

"Remember, husband, while I may not have used magic to fight before a few days ago. I've been fighting with iron and steel for most of my life," I point out. It really pisses me off when people underestimate me. Though it does work to my advantage.

"Would you like to put your money where your mouth is,

wife?" Head held high, he does his best to appear haughty, but struggles to keep his mouth in a straight, respectable line.

He just stands there waiting me out, crossing his arms over his large chest, showing off the masculine curve of his forearm encased in tan skin, veins standing out along the muscles. His smirk finally wins out when I don't immediately reply.

I turn back when I hear Narcissa. "Oh, this is going to be fun," she says, barely able to keep herself from laughing. Asher no doubt thinks I'm in over my head, always underestimating me. He really should know better. By now, Kane and Ansel have joined us.

"That it is," Asher says, prowling into the ring as Narcissa steps out.

We pace the outermost edge of the sparring ring, sizing each other up. Well, I'm sizing him up, he's drinking me in, in a slow appraisal. His eyes start at my thick, tightly-laced knee-high boots, following up the closely fitted fighting leathers, stopping at my face. That look alone has left me feeling stripped down and bare. His tongue sweeps along his full lower lip as if he's imagining what I taste like.

"Are you sure you wish to do this, *a stór álainn*?" His smile tells me he finds it cute that I think can take him on in a sword fight.

If he only knew. Well, I guess he's about to find out. I look him in the eye and watch him twirl the hilt of the sword within his grasp. It's then I notice we've drawn a crowd.

"Oh, but the question you should ask is, are *you* sure, husband mine?" I reply with the sweetest voice I can muster.

The glint of predatory excitement in his eyes is the only answer I receive before he's on the move. His sword swings in from the side, only to be met with mine in a mighty clang of steel on steel, sparks flying in all directions. He applies pressure, forcing the blades further into my space. His eyes dance, and that infuriating smirk of his plays across his lips. But I answer it with one of my own. I raise my foot, landing a solid kick to his stomach, sending him flying backwards to land on his back several meters away. Unfortunately, he gets to his feet quicker than I would have liked. Instead of being met with anger and a hardened gaze, I'm met with heat and hunger.

"Well. Well. Well. My sweet, it seems we have quite the game afoot here." His voice now laced with sensual amusement.

Asher captures so much of my attention that it takes a moment for me to recognize the rising buzz of sound around us as soldiers call out bets on our duel. I can't hold back the satisfied smirk that forms with the knowledge that these men have no idea what I'm capable of.

My movements are fluid as I advance on him, the sword nothing but an extension of my arm. I'm met with his blade on my downward strike. His parry has more strength behind it than the first, as if his opening attack had been merely to gauge my strength.

Now that he knows I'm not a novice, he's moving quicker, each blow working to throw me off balance. But I won't be going down that easily. If he wants to beat me, he's going to have to work harder for it.

We use more strength with every strike we land. Each counter-move quicker and harder than the one before. A thin layer of sweat coats our skin as we move faster and faster, surrounding us in a tempest of dust. We break apart, retreating to the outer edge of the ring, pacing back and forth, neither one willing to look away. His hand continues to flex on the hilt of his weapon. I twirl my sword out to my side in a wide arc, watching him, waiting for his next move.

Absently, I notice that the crowd around the ring has quieted as they take in just how evenly matched we truly are, though I must acknowledge that he's still holding back. At long last, he makes his move, lunging forward. His sword heading straight for my chest far quicker than I had anticipated. I lift my weapon to counter his move, only to have him beat left, finally taking me off balance. His arm twists in such a way that he sends my sword flying across the ring. Seconds later, he somehow locks my arm under his own. A smile on his face as he clearly thinks he's won this bout.

Well, if he's expecting me to admit defeat, he's sorely mistaken. I pull my head back, slamming it forward sharply, resulting in a satisfying crunch. His grip on me loosens and I land a knee to his inner thigh, hard. Asher staggers back, dropping his weapon, and I use his distraction to put some much-needed space between us.

He stares at me from a few meters away, having already retrieved his blade. With his left hand, he wipes blood from his upper lip as the other twists the hilt of his sword. He circles the sparring the ring, keeping his eyes on me, tracking my every movement, as if being disarmed suddenly makes me his prey. His first mistake was challenging me. His second is not realizing that I've been holding back as well.

Using the speed I had yet to display. I move forward, dodging his weapon, placing a foot on his leg, and using it to climb up his body. I swing my leg around his neck, using my momentum to flip him to the ground, dislodging his sword in the process. I land on top of him, pinning his shoulders to the ground with my knees. Which has the unfortunate result of bringing his face up close and personal with my core.

My face flushes further when his eyes drop from my face to my spread legs. The breath in my lungs catches when his gaze finally returns to mine. The heated look is filled with wicked delight that has every one of my lower muscles clenching. But it's the following smirk that pisses me off.

"I can't say I'm opposed to this position, *a stór*." I'm so riled up by the laughter I hear in his voice that I don't react to his powerful hands on my waist until it's too late. Suddenly, the world is moving as he switches our positions, effectively pinning me to the ground with his legs on either side of my hips.

"It seems I win this round, wife." His breath ghosting over my lips as he moves in to kiss me. With his lips seconds from touching mine, I reply, my lips brushing his with each word.

"Are you sure about that, husband?" My eyes dropping between us to the blade I hold inches from his cock. His eyes drop to follow mine, his stare leaving a trail of heat in its wake. When his gaze once again meets mine, his lips curl into a full smile.

"It appears I was mistaken," he concedes, his tone still filled with mirth.

"Never drop your guard, husband. You never know when your opponent has something up their sleeve." I smile sweetly up at him. Though my body is primed to answer the seductive look in his eyes.

"I'll bear that in mind in the future, *a stór álainn.*"

Chapter Twenty-Two

ASHER

I get to my feet and offer her my hand, which she takes without pause, gripping it firmly as I help her to her feet. With a sharp tug, I pull her lithe body into my arms. My hand wrapping around her body, fitting against the small of her back — holding to me. Each deep breath I take fills my lungs with the scent of night-blooming flowers and something that's wholly Devany.

It always hits me in the gut anytime I have her in my arms like this, feeling too damn good for my peace of mind.

My fingertips dance over the arch of her hip, gliding up along the curve of her waist, my thumb tracing the outer edge of her ribs just below her breast. Devany shudders in my arms and pushes closer to me.

Gently I tip her chin up, bringing her gaze to mine, trying to read what's going on in her head. But the moment I look into her eyes, it knocks the breath from my lungs, leaving me momentarily dizzy.

I've never held a more enchanting creature in my arms.

I slide my hand around the nape of her neck, tunneling into her messy curls, the slightly damp strands slipping through my fingers. A soft sigh passes her lips when my nails scrape lightly along her scalp before I wrap her hair tightly around my fist, using it to tilt her head back further.

We stand there, our chests brushing faintly with each breath we take to calm our racing hearts. Her pulse fluttering against my wrist, her pupils blown wide. Like the sun who covets the moon, I lean in to take her mouth, unable to help myself.

I've been imagining the feel of her lips since she stepped into the sparring ring with me.

She doesn't close her eyes, holding my gaze unwavering. A challenge in their depths. Our lips a hair's breadth away when she puts her hand to my chest and gently steps out of my embrace.

I have to lock my limbs down to keep from grabbing her. The woman intrigues me more with each passing day. All that fire living beneath that chilly exterior, she shows the world.

Devany's eyes linger on mine before she turns on heel and leaves me in the ring, not even bothering to look back. Narcissa easily falling into step beside her as they leave the training grounds with most of the men and quite a few women staring after them with a mix of awe, fear, and hunger. *It's the latter I have a problem with.* Though I note with some satisfaction that most are quick to look away when they notice that they've drawn my attention. Many of them opting to leave all together.

I nod to Ansel and leave the training grounds as well. A world of things that must be done, but my thoughts circle around Devany. How beautiful she'll look when she comes on my tongue and cock.

With much disappointment, I bring my errant thoughts of seduction to heel. Because tonight's banquet is more than just one king hosting another. It's a show of power. A statement.

Erabis and Froslien aren't the only kingdoms with a lack of regard for life. We need to keep those on Galandir that would take advantage, afraid. Or we could end up losing more than any of us are willing to part with. The weak paying the price.

That's why tonight's banquet is so important. Many of

Ivann's high-ranking courtiers shall be in attendance, several of which are his most conniving. And this is by design. Their fearful whispers will get the word out of the stronghold we're becoming.

I round the corner and draw to a halt, coming upon Devany and Narcissa talking in hushed, hurried tones. They stand surrounded by the lush manicure garden, hidden within the shadow of the palace wall. Their stances are rigid as they face off with one another. My lovely wife is talking wildly with her hands. *Whatever are these two up to now?*

I clear my throat as I close in on them. Not wanting Devany to think I was spying or sneaking up on her. She can be very touchy about some things. Both their heads snap in my direction, eyes narrowed. Their reactions eerily similar to each other.

"We all have a formal dinner to prepare for ladies. So, you'll have to plan world domination some other time." The words are chipper and sarcastic. A bright smile on my face. Irritation sparks to life in Devany's eyes, which only makes my smile grow.

She looks magnificent. Her liquid metal eyes burning a path between us. Hair slightly mussed, with errant strands sticking to her face. Her skin misted with a light sheen of sweat. That body of hers is a work of art.

"Mind your business, Asher." Her tone suggests that I'm on her nerves. Too bad for her, I get off on being there.

"Oh, but wife, you are my business." But before I can say more and aggravate her further, Narcissa steps in with a disapproving look in my direction.

"He's right, this is your first official appearance as queen. Best that it's on friendly soil where making a mistake won't be so much of a faux pa. We can discuss this further at a later date." Already walking in the other direction before my wife has a chance to respond. Not that it stops her in the least.

"This isn't over," Devany calls loudly to her back. To which Narcissa's only response is to raise her hand with two fingers up. Never once turning around.

Calmly, I walk up to my pissed off wife and offer her my arm.

She looks between it and my eyes a few times before cursing under her breath and taking it.

The walk back is silent and uneventful. But even in the calm, the tension builds between us. We gravitate toward each other, closing the distance until our bodies brush with each step. The heat of her body seeping into mine and pooling low in my belly. I can't even look at her for fear of taking her right here against the wall for all to see.

I fill my lungs—breathing deep—feeling drunk off her scent.

It takes every ounce of self-control I have to get back to our rooms without giving into the temptation that is Devany.

Her fingers tremble against my arm and I'm left to wonder if she fears following through with the seduction she's helped weave. If she regretted what was to come, it would kill me. It's best to take it slow, even if it pains me.

We step over the threshold, and I head straight for the bed, throwing myself on to it, crossing my legs at the ankle with my hands behind my head. I watch her carefully, looking for any sign of the vixen from the training grounds.

She stands in the foyer by the closed door, looking everywhere but at me. What I wouldn't give to march over there, strip her bare and fall to my knees, worshiping her with my mouth like the Goddess she is.

When her eyes finally meet mine, she's fidgeting nervously, looking very un-Devany-like. It's that soft, unsure look that has me taking pity on her and breaking the silence.

"These rooms have their own bathhouse just through there." I direct her to the right with a nod of my head.

Goddess knows I would like nothing more than to join her.

"You can go in first." Unable to stop myself from pushing her just a little. "Or I can go first." Stopping to look her up and down, licking my lower lip. "And you can watch." My smile flashing her just a hint of fang. She swallows nervously before her eyes sparkle with that fire I love so much.

"Pervert." There's little heat behind it. The word's become more of a pet name at this point.

"No...?" I stop, pretending to give her time to think about it. "Well, off you go then." With one last look at me, she slips from the room, closing the door behind her. It takes a great deal of willpower not to follow her through those doors.

I close my eyes and listen to the sound of the water lapping lightly against her skin — the soft sighs that pass her pretty lips — I can almost imagine her beckoning me into the water like the siren she is.

"Asher." A feathery voice drags me from the fantasy my mind had crafted.

When I open my eyes, I find her standing before me, covered in only a towel, dripping water on the rugs beneath her feet.

For a long moment, I just simply take her in. From the burnished, metallic strands of her hair to her moonlit eyes and shimmering skin. Every piece of her is exquisite.

Getting to my feet, I take a step toward her and that beautiful blush of hers makes its presence known. As I'm struck silent by the sight before me.

"Asher," she says my name softly once again, with just a hint of embarrassment. It's that note in her voice that has me dragging my gaze back up to hers. Though I do it slowly. Taking my time to memorize every exquisite inch. Only after I've taken my fill do I look her in the eyes.

"Yes, love?" Her blush deepens at the sound of my voice.

Her fingers playing with the end of the towel that barely covers the things she wishes to hide. Fuck, I'm going to have to thank Ivann for this. Her legs look amazing, painted in droplets of water.

"I have nothing to wear for a formal dinner." My eyes stay glued to her legs when I hmmm my agreement. "Will you please look at me? What am I going to wear?" Her tone is stronger thanks to the irritation sparked by my lack of an answer.

"I am looking at you." In fact, I've been painfully hard since I opened my eyes, needing to be inside her more than I need my next breath.

I close the distance between us in four wide steps, towering over her petite frame. Sometimes I forget how much smaller she is compared to me. All that attitude and fight, she's larger than life.

The tips of my fingers glide up her biceps, painting a path through the droplets of water coating her skin. *And by the Gods, what I wouldn't give to lick each drop from her body.* Her breath hitches as my fingers trace along her collarbone, my nails scraping lightly.

I circle her throat with my hand, and she shivers in my hold as my grip tightens ever so slightly. Her breath coming out in soft, choppy pants. The scent of her sweet arousal teases my senses and has me fantasizing about ripping that towel from her delectable body.

Tenderly, I caress the side of her neck before I tilt her head back with my thumb, giving me a better view of her beautiful eyes. Twin moons shining brightly in blackened skies. Her irises were nothing more than a thin ring of silver.

I take one step forward, then another, walking her backwards. A delicate gasp falls from her lips when her back makes contact with the wall.

Music to my ears.

"You could wear just this, *a stór álainn,* and I would be a happy male." Tipping her head to the side, I expose the long line of her neck.

I place a soft kiss in the hollow of her throat before scraping my fangs up along the tendon to whisper in her ear. Her panting breath my reward.

"But if you do not wish to wear a towel, there are many outfits in the armoire." Her eyes briefly touch the wardrobe before she meets my gaze once again, staring back at me with bright, heated eyes. Daring me to make the next move.

She's so beautiful.

I brush my nose along hers, and her eyes drift close, denying me their beauty. For a quiet moment, I admire the soft curves of her face. The rise and fall of her chest and the warmth of her skin. I give her neck a light squeeze and she opens her eyes, sucking in a silent breath.

My gaze falls to her mouth, her lips just begging to be kissed. I'd like to say I made the first move. But where I hesitated, she did not. Taking hold of my shirt, she surges forward, pulling me closer despite my hand around her throat. And the moment her honeyed lips touch mine, I'm lost.

Gods, the things she does to me.

With my other hand, I scoop her up, her legs instinctively twisting about my waist. I press her more firmly into the wall, taking a moment to admire just how good she looks wrapped around me. The pretty blush staining her neck and chest, her damp hair clinging to her shoulders.

She is breathtaking.

My eyes touch every exposed piece of skin until I reach where her towel has split open, revealing the perfect view of her sweet core. I feel like a fiend for all the dirty things I want to do to her. All the places I want to put my mouth. To taste her. To feel her supple skin break beneath my teeth. My fangs embedded in her flesh.

It's my turn to suck in a shuddering breath when her velvety lips taste my skin, her fangs scraping roughly across my collarbone, leaving goosebumps in their wake. She winds her arms around my neck, pulling me closer, forcing me to remove my hand from her throat. With nothing in her way, she deepens the kiss. Her thighs tighten around my hips as she grinds into me, trying to find some much-needed friction. Her hands fumble as she works the laces of my pants—her intention clear.

I take hold of those busy hands, hoping to gain some control, quieting their movements. I cup the nape of her neck, my finger shifting through the damp strands, and I rest my forehead on hers.

"Are you sure?" I ask her, admittedly a little breathless myself.

"Yes, I'm fucking sure," is her disgruntled response, and I can't help but huff out a short laugh.

She tightens her arms and legs around me as I pull away from the wall, holding tight while I walk to the bed. I sit on the edge with her in my lap, keeping my movements slow as I loosen the knot holding her towel up, giving her ample time to protest. When she makes no move, I let the fabric fall to the floor and my breath is painfully knocked from my lungs as I take in every glorious inch.

Devany stares down at me with a soft smile playing at her lips. Her hair hangs over her shoulder like a thick curtain hiding us from the world. She leans forward, her mouth brushing mine in a kiss so soft my chest aches. But it's not enough. It'll never be enough.

I wrap my hands around her waist, dragging her forward against my body. Encouraging her to move on my lap, her sweet body grinding against mine. Even through the thin layer of my pants, I can feel her damp heat seeping into my skin with each glide of her body, the sensation drawing a ragged breath from my lungs.

She arches her back, and I take full advantage, tasting her sweet skin. My lips ghosting over her tight nipples. Whispered moans tumble from her lips each time her core connects with my aching cock. She closes her eyes and goes fluid in my arms, her head falling back on her shoulders. I've never seen anything more beautiful or felt anything more tempting.

"*A stór*," I whisper against her fevered skin, waiting for her to look at me before sucking her nipple into my mouth gently. My hands working her hips as she gets lost in the feel of us moving together. She buries her face against my neck as her body flushes with pleasure.

I'm painfully hard, and this is the most exquisite torture.

I reach up, gliding my hands along her spine, gathering the heavy mass of hair in my fist so I can get a better look at her face. Her eyes are hooded, and her lips are slightly part. She's ravishing, like looking upon the sun in all its splendor. I bring her mouth to mine. Devouring her. Stealing the very air from her lips.

By the Gods, this woman does things to me.

She continues to grind against me. Driving me out of my mind. The scent of her, the feel, her heat... all of it. She makes this small, disgruntled sound in the back of her throat.

"Do you need something, *a stór*?" I ask against her lips. With bright, timid eyes, she gives me only a slight nod.

I grab hold of her chin with my other hand, placing a light kiss to her lips before asking, "What do you need, Devany?"

"Touch me, husband..." she quietly demands.

"Gladly."

I reach between us to find her clit. The bundle of nerves, hard and throbbing beneath my thumb. With short, firm circles, I work her higher as she rides my hand, my fingers gliding along her slick folds as tiny moans leaving her mouth.

Using my grip on her hair, I yank her head to the side, exposing the long line of her throat. The sharpness of the action drawing a gasp from her beautiful lips. Her breathy moans music to my ears. I've wanted nothing as much as I want her to come undone on my lap with my fingers between her pretty thighs.

Her grip on my arms tightens, breaking the skin, when I drag my fangs along the curve of her neck. She shivers in my embrace, her head falling back on her shoulders. Her pulse fluttering against my tongue as I suck the skin into my mouth. My fangs aching to sink into her petal soft skin. I feel her get wetter, drenching my hand as my fingers tease her entrance.

There's not much I can do to prevent the pain from coming, but I can sure as hell help her enjoy it.

She tenses slightly when the tip of my finger enters her; I take my time working it in and out slowly. Kissing her mouth until she softens and then adding another. The palm of my hand rubbing along her clit with each small rock of her hips. My fingers stretching her—teasing her sensitive front wall—preparing her for me.

Knowing I'll be the last male to touch her—The *only* male—nearly unmans me.

I grab her by the back of the neck, forcing her to look at me.

"Open your fucking eyes," I growl at her.

I have this compulsive need to see her eyes swim with need, then crash into pleasure as she comes undone in my hand. The first of many I plan to ring from her body.

She blinks, glassy eyes filled with lust and hunger. Humming in the back of her throat when my fingers graze a particularly sensitive spot deep inside her. Her muscles tighten around my fingers in response and more of her sweet arousal coats my palm as she rocks against my hand, fucking herself. I ache to be inside her.

I realize in this moment that this woman means something to me. That there isn't a thing I wouldn't do in her name. I would gladly scorch the world.

"Don't you dare close your eyes. Do you understand me?" She doesn't answer, just nods jerkily, riding my hand faster. Her inner walls tightening at the command.

Her eyes are bright and fathomless, like the night sky and brimming with need. It won't take much to throw her over the edge. I need her pleasure like I need my next breath.

Holding her gaze, I lower my head to take her nipple into my mouth. I keep my motions slow, watching her as she tracks my movements. Her chest rises and falls with each shuddering breath she takes. My mouth brushing over her supple skin before capturing her nipple between my lips.

She continues to ride my hand, my fingers moving in long strokes as I tease her. I suck her nipple into my mouth, running the flat of my tongue over the firm nub, feeling it pebble further, her skin breaking out in goosebumps.

Her walls tighten around my fingers, and I bite down. To give her a flash of pain to heighten her pleasure. Her claws tear into my skin as her glamour falls away, leaving her ethereal beauty on display. Sharply pointed ears, shimmering skin, and eyes that glow with power.

The need to have her... To claim what's mine overwhelms my good senses.

I stand and lower her to the bed, desperate to get my clothes off. She watches me closely as I undress. Her teeth sinking into her full lower lip. I groan at the sight and the little minx smiles because she knows exactly what she's doing. Reaching back, I pull my shirt over my head. Uncaring of the blood on my arms. Her eyes take me in, tracing the lines of my chest down to my hips. Where my pants lay undone from her busy hands.

I can't help but smirk as her eyes widen on my heavy cock. Though, it's the look she gives me when she meets my gaze that has need singing in my veins.

Even as I know, I can't rush. It's almost painful to hold back, when all I want to do is rip my pants off and bury myself so deep inside her she feels me for days.

I stand at the foot of the bed and rip what's left of my laces, removing my pants quickly. Her gaze never strays, her attention feeling like a physical caress. I give her a moment to look before I grab hold of her ankle and give it a sharp tug, dragging her to the middle of the bed. I can't help but smile at the startled breath that leaves her lips at the sudden moment.

Slowly, I crawl up her body, settling between her legs, my nose grazing her inner thigh. The scent of her fills my lungs, driving me crazy. It seems unnatural to want her the way I do. To be consumed with thoughts of her day and night. It's something I don't wish to look too closely at.

I trace her skin with my tongue, trailing up to the apex of her thighs. Devany moans unrestrained when I push my tongue between her folds. Humming against her clit in appreciation as her flavor rolls on my tongue. Like sunshine and summer festivals.

She covers her mouth to muffle the sound. While her other hand tangles roughly in my hair, pulling me closer, demanding I give her more. But I want every sweet sound she makes. I want it all and I won't be denied. I grab her hand, lacing out fingers together, concentrating my efforts on her clit, working my fingers if my other hand into her once more. I wind her tighter with each flick of my tongue. Her hips tilt up, chasing my mouth, silently asking for relief.

"Asher, please," she pants, begging me to give her what she needs. And Gods, if I don't love every minute.

"Not yet, *a stór*, the next time you climax, it's going to be with my cock buried deep inside you." My voice is husky and harsh, foreign to even my ears. She's the only woman to have this effect on me.

I make my way up her body, laying feather light kisses as I go, first to her hip and another just below her breast. Getting lost in the scent of her skin. The taste of her. I hook my hands under her thighs and pull them roughly apart, settling myself between them once again.

I line up with her entrance, my need hitting a steady beat inside my chest. But her eyes show a hint of fear, and that I cannot have. I lean forward, placing a soft kiss at the corner of her mouth, only a brushing of lips before I take her mouth more fully, kissing her so completely that there's no room for fear, only desire.

I press forward—entering her slightly, but it's enough that her eyes fly open. My arms shake with the effort to hold back while my body begs for me to take her in hard, deep strokes. My heart pounds against my rib cage like it's trying to get to her. Just this little taste of her makes me dizzy with pleasure.

"Take a deep breath, *a stór álainn*," I tell her before thrusting forward, taking her completely. We each suck in a harsh breath. My sight whiting out, all my nerve endings firing off at once. Her eyes squeezed shut tight as her skin pales slightly from the pain.

"I'm sorry, *a stór*, it can't be helped." My stomach knots as I hold still, waiting as she adjusts to the feel of me.

While she lets loose a slow, shaky breath, I kiss each of her tightly closed eyes, followed by the tip of her nose, moving down to her lips, kissing them thoroughly, as I steadily building her desire again. When she tightens her legs around my hips, I pull back slightly before thrusting forward and it's my turn to take a shaky breath as I slowly build speed. Her body is so tight I have to fight her grip on me to get in a full stroke as I'm completely lost to sensation and drowning in pleasure.

I wrap her hair in my fist, pulling her head back to get a better angle on her delicious mouth. Nicking her lip with my fangs. She presses her chest further into my own, moaning with her eyes closed. Shamelessly, I swallow each sound she makes. Greedy for more. We move together, sweat coating our skin, pushing us higher and higher.

The scent. The feel. The taste of her makes me lightheaded.

My hand glides along her side down to her hip, dragging my claws lightly over her thigh, pulling it higher on my hip. I feel her fluttering around me but not falling over.

"Give it to me, Devany," I growl at her, needing to feel her again before allowing myself to follow.

I slide my hand between us, using firm circles on her clit. My mouth ghosting over her neck. As I thrust harder and faster, her claws raked down my back, no doubt drawing blood. But when she bares her throat to me in silent invitation, it's almost my undoing. I strike hard and fast—bury my fangs deep—drinking my fill. Her taste dances on my tongue like the sweetest synder berries. She screams out her release, tightening down around me, pulling out my climax.

I lower my forehead to hers while I catch my breath, running my fingers through her thick strands. I open my eyes and lean back, taking in the beautiful sight beneath me. Her face is flush, and a light sheen of sweat coats our bodies. Her body wrapped around mine as if she wishes to hold me nearly as much as I do her. Her eyes are closed, but when she opens them, I'm struck speechless. They shine with some unnamed emotion that I want to bask in.

Kissing her alluring lips, I roll off her, bring her body with me, nesting her under my arm. She hides her face in my chest as if embarrassed. Terrified she'll second guess herself, I reach down, placing my fingers lightly under her chin, tipping her head back so I can see her beautiful eyes, still bright with passion.

"Are you ok?" My voice is hoarse, feeling oddly unsure. I could never forgive myself if I hurt her.

"Yes, I think so," she answers softly, but she doesn't hide from my gaze, which I take as a good sign.

"I do believe we're going to be late, husband," she states, laughing under her breath.

"Let them wait."

I lean down, taking her mouth in a deep kiss. She throws her leg over my hip, bringing her core up against my rapidly hardening cock. At this rate, we really will be late. Not that I can find it in me to care. Because to have her in my arms like this feels far better than it should.

Chapter Twenty-Three

ASHER

As it turns out, my wife rushes for no one, not even a king. But as she steps out of the dressing room, I realize it was worth every fucking minute. Her lightweight skirt just kisses the floor, with a band that sits high on the waist. The asymmetrical top ending where the skirt begins, giving the smallest peak of skin. With each step, the iridescent fabric shifts color from purple to teal and back again. It's quite sexy in its modesty. Her hair braided back from her face, embellished with chains that crisscross over the thick plait. Skin shimmering in the fading sunlight of the setting sun, with her finely pointed ears standing proud, adorn with long earrings that barely brush her collarbone.

No glamour tonight. Friend or not, we'll be walking in with our power on full display.

"Asher, it's beautiful," she says with a hint of wonderment as she fingers the spider silk. But I couldn't give two shits about the dress outside of how she looks in it.

"Yes, it is," I reply, my attention solely focused on her. She looks up at me, most likely having heard the huskiness of my voice. A pretty blush colors her cheeks once she realizes my focus is on her, not the dress.

That unnamed emotion is once again clogging up my throat. I offer her my arm. Which she takes without hesitation.

"Off to meet the lions, *a stór*. Are you ready?" I ask with a wink, but when I look at her, her expression was quite serious.

"I've dealt with vindictive courtiers my whole life. This won't be anything I haven't handled before," she states, and of that I have no doubt. With a small nod of my head, I hold my hand out in front of me toward the door, following her over the threshold, heading toward tonight's debacle.

The sandstone halls are free of guests as the staff runs from here to there, their steps echoing off the tiled floors as they prepare to fulfill the court's every wish completely unseen.

At the end of the hall stands the entrance to the ballroom inset into the smooth stone wall. The doors carved out of a single piece of rosewood. Etched into the wood is a dream oasis. Palm trees heavy with fruit sway in the wind surrounding a city built of stone. From high on the city walls, flowers spill over, softening the harsh lines of the battlement. As the sun bathes the land in its blessed light.

Two valets stand on either side of the entrance, waiting quietly for my signal that they may open the doors.

I turn to Devany, stopping us a few meters away, so our conversation will remain private. "Are you ready?"

"Yes," she replies calmly, leaving no room for any doubt.

She pulls her shoulders back, straightening her spine and lifting her gaze to meet mine. Her face holds no emotion, but the haunting air she wears so well. She exudes control.

I take hold of her chin, lifting her face a little higher. Her eyes flare and pulse with power as I tighten my grip, drawing her to me. With my eyes open, I lean in, brushing my lips faintly against hers. A delicate shiver skates through her body and I deepen the kiss. A barely-there moan slipping from her lips. My mouth swallowing the sound before it could be heard. When we break apart, we're both panting.

Staring into her bright eyes, I nod imperceptibly, signaling the valet to open the doors.

The music hits us the moment the doors are cracked open, spilling into the space, drowning out the sound of our heart's beats. She curls her hand around my arm, giving it a nervous squeeze. Though, outwardly, she's a picture of confidence. I caress the back of her hand with my thumb, leading her over the threshold and into the ballroom.

The night moves along relatively quickly, filled with thinly veiled insults wrapped up in compliments like pretty gifts.

Though Devany handles it all beautifully, working the room and smiling sweetly as she navigates the backhand compliments with ease. Playing the game so well.

I'm standing beside her quietly while she speaks to a rather loud couple, when a man announces that dinner is to be served and two large doors at the end of the ballroom swing open. Leading to a spectacular site indeed. They've set the banquet hall with two long tables taking up the center of the room. Several chandeliers made of lightning glass hang from the cathedral ceilings. All this leads to a table sitting upon a dais looking down on the room.

I lead her down the center aisle to the dais where Ivann awaits to formally greet us. His face holds a bright, welcoming smile. To anyone looking, they wouldn't see it for the illusion it is. However, I can tell from the ticking of his jaw to the seriousness of his eyes. There's something weighing heavily on his mind. But ever the gracious host, he leads us to our places at the table.

As soon as we sit, our plates are presented and placed in front of us. The dish is so laden with food it is a wonder it didn't break under the weight.

Ivann makes a show of sniffing his elderberry wine before taking the first bite of his food, humming in approval as is custom in formal events.

The dull din of quiet conversation and cutlery tapping against porcelain quickly replaces the quiet. Most of the courtiers keep quiet, content to listen to us in hopes of hearing information that may benefit them later. Not that will discuss anything of importance in earshot of others.

Nyra's curious voice breaks the silence at our table. "Is it true what they say about Erabis? That King Kól has gone mad? That the streets run with the blood of magic users?" I feel Devany go rigid beside me with each question she asks. Every pair of eyes from the surrounding tables swing in her direction.

"Nyra!" Ivann's wife Eva gasps, her dark eyes rounding in shock, saving Devany from having to answer. Exasperation clear in her tone, having tried for years to train curiosity out of Nyra. Convinced a good princess is quiet and goes where she is led. But I'm afraid that ship has sailed. And I think she's better for it.

"Leave her be, Eva. It's good to question things. Who needs a princess that questions nothing?" Chloe cuts in before Eva can go on some tirade about how a princess should act. They're always quick to fight. Sharing Ivann's bed can't be easy for them, sharing his love even harder.

"Too right, my sweets," Ivann replies, raising Chloe's hand to his mouth kissing her fingertips. A delicate blush colors her cheeks, which seems almost out of place on her harder features.

She was born and bred a warrior. Her crimson hair shaved on either side of her head; the rest braided down her back as is custom for her people. Keen eyes the color of steel. Her arms are muscular and well formed, with an accumulation of scars from years of swordplay. She's a beautiful woman. The picture of a warrior's perfection and every bit her father's daughter. I wonder if Ivann will still feel that way when he finds out she's teaching his sister to fight and has been for quite some time.

Devany's cuts up her food in small pieces, eating one morsel at a time, repetition seeming to calm her nerves. It would seem as if this were the part of the night she dreaded most.

"What she needs to do is concentrate on her studies and stay where she'll be safe. She has no business on the battlefield," Jasper states like he has a say in the matter, finally joining the conversation. Nyra looks at him and I see the hurt that flashes in her eyes before she closes it down. But as usual, he doesn't see it. Nor how she looks at him.

"And why is that?" Devany asks, her words sharp and authoritative, dropping her cutlery with a clink against the porcelain.

I can't help the smile that takes up residence on my face because he now has four very lethal women staring at him. Not a smart move to tell Nyra her place isn't on a battlefield in front of four women who are formidable in their own right and will likely play a large role in the coming war.

It's the first time he's looked up from his plate since we sat down. To his credit, he doesn't balk at the heavy stares pointed his way.

"With all due respect, Your Majesty, but her place is here within the palace walls, learning her role within them. I'm sure you of all people understands where her place is, as well as your own." Now he's gone too far.

I notice Bellicent and Narcissa smirking at the fool, because if he thinks he's getting away with talking to her like that, he's out of his ever-loving fucking mind. If he wishes to disrespect Nyra, there's not much I can do if Ivann's going to allow it. No matter how I disagree. But he will not speak to my wife like that. In the peripheral of my vision, I see Kane take a step toward him. Even Ansel looks ready for a fight. Devany merely lifts her hand, stopping us all.

"Yes, I do understand. Far better than you. I spent a lifetime living up to a man's expectations." The quiet words were easily heard over the dull noise of the room.

But it's the fierce look in her eyes that finally has him realizing how disrespectful he's been. Opening his mouth to most likely to apologize. She once again lifts her hand, stopping him. I've never met a woman who can control an entire room with a mere hand like my wife, and it's got me painfully hard.

"Do you have any idea what I plan on doing to him... my father? Hmmm No... Would you like to suffer the same?" Lifting one delicate brow, every bit the queen she is. The words said so casually that it takes a moment for the threat to register, his face paling slightly.

"My apologies, Your Majesty." I don't think I've ever heard him contrite before.

"It's not I you owe an apology to. No, it's the women around this table because they could very well save your life one day." She holds his gaze until looking down like he no longer matters.

Her leg shakes slightly under the table. But other than that, she shows no outward signs of how upset she is by the confrontation. My hand lands lightly on her thigh, causing her to startle faintly. Again, not enough for anyone to notice outside of those who know her well. Rather than removing my hand, I stroke her thigh softly until she relaxes into the touch. What I'm not expecting is for her to take hold of my hand interlacing our fingers.

Ivann claps his hands loudly. Bringing our attention to him, though, Devany doesn't look up. Still working to get her emotions under control.

"Shall we retire to the lounge for tonight's entertainment?" he announces loudly, more than happy to move to a more intimate environment. Best to prevent our conversation from being overheard.

Devany turns her head in my direction, lifting her face slightly to speak into my ear. Her breath feathering over the outer shell, causing me to swallow a groan.

"Entertainment?" she asks quietly, her lips brushing my cheek.

"Naphal has some of the best dancers in Galandir." I tilt my head towards her, bringing our mouths ever closer. My eyes on hers as I answer, just staring into her moonlit eyes. The moment broken by Ivann's loud voice.

"Galandir, my ass, the world is more like it," Ivann is quick to point out. Laughing as he leads us through an ornately carved archway.

The lounge is a large round room with walls and floor covered in rich mosaic tiles that reflect the low light coming off the hanging lanterns. Seating arrangements with curved sofas and floor pillows are scattered throughout the room. All pointing towards a beautiful four tier fountain that provides a magnificent focal point.

Everyone scatters around the room, taking up different vignettes. The energy thick with excitement, the dancers are quite a treat. There's nothing like it, as Ivann so humbly pointed out in the world. I'm eager to see Devany's reaction, knowing that she wouldn't have seen anything like it before.

The music starts almost immediately, drowning out the dull sound of conversation and leaving us open to discuss more sensitive matters. I look at Ivann, ready to move on to more important things.

"What's going on?" I ask directly, not in the mood to dance around the issues. Before he even speaks, I can tell he plans to deflect. I know he wouldn't outright lie to me. But he would talk round the question. So, I'm going to nip that in the bud.

"Cut the shit, Ivann. What's going on?" My voice was just loud enough to be heard over the music in the booth.

I lean back on the small sofa, sliding my arm along the back behind Devany. My leg brushing against hers. The innocent touch makes me hyper aware of her presence. It takes so much effort to keep from pulling her into my lap, knowing full well that were I to act on that desire, it would piss her off.

I simply stare at Ivann, waiting him out.

"I'm having border issues," he states, grimacing slightly. Knowing what he's asking of me before he does so.

"I thought the borders were protected by elemental magic?" Devany questions, most likely thinking about the fact that her mother paid the price for that barrier.

"It is, but the magic has begun to fail." I can see all the questions forming in that keen mind of hers.

"Unlike with the northern wall, which has magic fed into it daily. The magic preventing Froslien from draining the surrounding land was part of the bargain made between princess Lela and the Druids. It was only ever meant to be a temporary patch. If it's failing, it means whatever the deal was must be coming to a close." Sorrow fills her eyes at the mention of her mother.

She looks down, hiding her watery eyes. I reach over, intertwining our fingers, lending her my strength. I rub light circles into her palm. Offering comfort.

"I've lost men trying to investigate. Is there a way to patch up the weak spots in the barrier?" Bellicent and I share a look before I answer. One that Devany doesn't miss if the narrowed eyed look is anything to go by.

"We can help you," I assure him easily. Even though Devany looks like she wishes to argue but thankfully she holds her tongue. Though I know I'll hear it the moment we're alone. Not that she doesn't wish to help. She's just scared, even if she hides it well.

"I'll ride out with you to the border, where we'll meet with Chloe's father. He'll have a better understanding of the situation," he replies with a firm nod of his head.

Chapter Twenty-Four

DEVANY

I've never been to the border, nor do I like the idea of Asher going there. There's no way of knowing what may happen. But one thing I can guarantee is it's not safe.

They don't even seem worried about what's to come, while I sit here silent, like a fool.

Having spent so much of my life secluded, I still don't know how to interact in these types of situations now that I no longer have to hide. Luckily, I don't have to decide one way or another when the volume of the music increases, drawing our eyes to the center of the room.

Five beautiful women file out of the doorway, black swirling tattoos cover a good amount of their skin. The inked scenes come to life with each movement of their bodies. Their skirts are made up of a single panel of fabric draping between their full thighs, matching bands wrapped around their chests. Each graceful motion brings a light ringing from the plethora of bracelets on their wrists and ankles.

The women all produce a stick out of thin air and dip it into the fountain. With the flick of their wrist, it bursts into flames and the dancers twirl and spin. As the batons spin faster and faster, a scene cast entirely from flame takes shape. I've seen nothing like it before.

My eyes stay riveted to the performance as the picture moves, showing a maiden dancing, calling on The Elemental Druids. That's when I realized this is the scene of my mother calling on The Druids to save their lands from Froslien.

It's then that the tears swimming in my eyes finally fall.

These people don't know who my actual mother was, so they couldn't have known what this would do to me. But as I watch the scene of my mother as she dances around the ceremonial flames calling on the eight elements, my heart breaks open.

I hadn't noticed the conversation around me had ceased until Asher places his fingers under my chin, tilting my face toward him. His gaze holds so much compassion that I swallow thickly for an entirely new reason. No one has ever looked at me the way he does with those ever-changing eyes.

I break eye contact and pull away gently to look around. I have the attention of everyone in our booth, but thankfully we're in a private vignette, surrounded by thick velvet drapery. Quickly, I wipe the tears from my face, smiling weakly at everyone.

"It's exquisite," is all I say as I dodge Narcissa's probing looks.

My mind continues to close in on itself with memories of my mum playing on repeat as I watch the dancers move from sequence to sequence. Memories of how she taught me that very dance when I was just able to walk.

"What do you plan to do with Kannon and Erabis?" Jasper asks, bringing my jaunt through memory lane to a halt. We all stop and look at him.

"I assume you plan to kill her father, so what do you plan to do with the kingdom?" he elaborates. His tone is firm as he holds our gaze, obviously having some opinions on the matter.

"Yes, we plan to kill him." Asher's words are practically made of steel. He wanted to kill my father on principle—but now the reason is so much more personal for him.

For me... it's always been personal.

"I only bring it up because the human monarchs may have a problem with the two of you collecting kingdoms," he says it with a forced lightness, but there is a peculiar undertone to the statement that borders on fear.

"Well, we won't have much of a choice. We can't very well leave them unprotected. You must not understand how twisted my father's court is. Of course, there are some who don't agree with him and treat their people well. But they are far and few in between. Most revel in the pain they freely inflict. It will take us time to weed them out and replace them. Then decide on a new leader." Goddess, I'm exhausted just thinking about all the things that have to happen.

"You may have another option, at least where Kannon is concerned," Ivann replies. Now *that* has my interest.

"How do you mean?" I ask, giving him my full attention. Well... most of my attention. I'm slightly distracted by Asher's fingers playing with the hair at the nape of my neck.

"Easy, my dear. Place Kannon's heir back on its throne," Ivann replies, his warm brown eyes sparkling in their intensity.

"Impossible. My father was thorough in his destruction of their home and bloodline," I state evenly as my heart breaks for yet another family he's destroyed for his greed.

"Supposedly, her personal bodyguard—an alpha shifter—was able to smuggle her out before the fire consumed the palace. If this is to be believed, the last heir to the Kannon throne lives," Ivann says as I stare at him, trying to gauge how much he believes this rumor, because it changes things.

"Where are they now?" I ask, as if everything hinges on it.

Putting her back on her throne leaves me open to deal with the corruption within my father's land.

Much of Kannon's great army scattered to the four winds after the assassination of their king. But I bet if she came back, so would they. And if she did in fact live, I can't believe she hasn't spent this time building a new army. It's what I would do.

"My sources say you can find them in Serpent's Cove in the service of Queen Nalin," Ivann responds, leaning back in his chair, crossing his ankle over his knee and smiling brightly.

"Your sources? What makes you think that they're right?" Asher snorts while he continues playing lazily with my hair.

"They're the same sources that told me about your brief battle against King Kól's men. I'd say they're quite good at what they do." Asher stiffens slightly beside me, but I don't have time for their male horseshit.

"Can we get back on point? The Pirate Queen? Why would he take her there?" I need to understand everything if this is going to be a viable option for us.

"Because it's the furthest he could get her from your father. Until such time she is ready to kill him, that is. At least that's what I assume, mostly because that's what I would've done," Ivann answers with a very matter-of-fact tone, having a similar thought process to mine. It's probably very similar to the plan he has in place for his very own sister.

"She's going to have to get in line," I respond in much the same manner. If anyone's going to kill my father, it's going to be me.

"Be that as it may, you're going to have a hard time convincing her not to kill you," he says critically.

Though I think he's more concerned with what Asher would do should someone try to kill me.

"I'm not so easy to kill," I'm quick to remind them both.

Suddenly, there's a glass in my face. My gaze rises from it to Bellicent, who merely grins.

"You looked like you could use a drink." I snort at the understatement, which brings a genuine smile to her face.

Asher and his men left for Naphal's southern border before sunrise, accompanied by Ivann and a few of his guards. The group heads to strengthen the wards along the barrier holding Froslien's army back. With each passing day, the barrier weakens. Soon there will be no way to patch it and when that happens—may the Gods help us.

Thank the Goddess my husband let me sleep, after spending most of last night in a blur of alcohol. My brain and body still aren't happy to be here. I feel like shit as Chloe, Narcissa, Bellicent, and I stand around the table in Ivann's war room staring at a map of Galandir, trying to iron out the logistics of combat.

I hate to say it, but Naphal is going to be ground zero in this war, sharing borders with both Froslien and Erabis. Though if we kill my father and put Kannon's heir back on the throne, we may be able to bring two more kingdoms into the fold.

Chloe leans over the map, one hand on the table with the other pointing out our enemies from within Galandir itself—which is more significant than I had thought.

Besides my father, there's the kingdom of Sólális as well as several influential families scattered throughout the other kingdoms. All of which deal with the slave trade.

If you add that to what Aiteall and Narci did by erecting that dome and cutting themselves off from the rest of us while we were left to fight and lick our wounds alone... Well, the other nine kingdoms—not to mention the shifter clans—may not feel so inclined to align themselves with us. All of which leaves us with a short supply of allies.

"We need to find a workaround for Kól's amulets," Bellicent states, looking at me. She's not wrong, but most of our allies—if we can find any—will be human. So, it's a moot point.

"We'll get a message to Luna," Narcissa replies before I can. I hate that Luna stayed behind. Not having her here with me is like having a piece of my soul cut off. I have to keep reminding myself that she's a strong spellcaster, she can take care of herself. I just wish someone would explain it to my heart.

"Though we may have to rely on more conventional means. We held our own. If it weren't for being surprised, it would have been over much quicker. We just keep it in mind moving forward," I add, deciding to put in my two cents on the matter.

"What you should do is speak to this caster friend of yours about duplicating the amulets. Think of the protection it would give our human counterparts," Bellicent points out.

We continue to discuss where soldiers will need to be deployed, who we think will stand with us, and what they bring to the table. We argue for hours about how best to convince the Kingdom of Hepha to ally with us. It'll be a battle in and of itself, with them being neutral territory. If we can convince them, it will be the first time they've taken an active role in a conflict.

But the room goes silent when Ansel and Kane enter the room, followed by several soldiers. You can practically feel the unleashed violence in every step they take.

"What's wrong?" Two simple words leave my lips on a demanding breath. The two men exchanged a look before addressing me.

"We were ambushed, Devany," Ansel replies, speaking in soothing tones as if he's talking me off a ledge. Never before have four little words had the ability to bring my entire world to a standstill.

"Shit," is the only response in the quiet room. I have no idea who says it, though in all reality, it doesn't really matter.

All I can do is shake my head at him as emotions clog my throat. I need to lock them down and pull them together because it's time to be the queen I am.

"How many can you portal with?" I ask Ansel with a tone that rings far stronger than I feel.

There's a spark of irritation in his amber-colored eyes. Mostly born out of that fact, Asher shared his gift with me, but he keeps that to himself, for now.

"Ten, maybe twelve," he says in a flat tone. I point to the man behind him.

"You gather as many men as he can safely carry, preferably shifters or Valore. These men are from Froslien, we'll need to fight magic with magic. I won't risk human life and it's pointless to risk it in a battle they can't win." This situation hammers home the need to replicate those amulets.

My nerves fray at the edges and my patience is all but gone. My husband could be dying as we speak, and we're doing nothing. We need a plan. But when he doesn't move fast enough, my control slips and I snap.

"For fuck's sake, move!" The words are so loud, pushed on by my magic. They echo around the room, the very building shaking in response to my anger. That seems to shake him out of his trance.

"Where's Ivann?" Chloe's question is quiet and wrecked with fear, and it's then that I realized mine isn't the only husband missing.

Before Ansel can answer, I speak. "No matter what, we'll get them back." I focus on her, so she knows she's not alone in this. She gives me a single nod and begins arming up, as does Bellicent.

"There's no need. Ivann is with the other men trying to get to Asher." His voice is riddled with irritation.

"Explain." A one-word order, and for once he doesn't look pissed to follow.

"When we realized we were being overrun, he caused an avalanche of rock to cut the majority of us off, trying to save as many as he could. Right now, there are about thirty Froslien soldiers hopped up on magic against him and a hand full of ours." He was rightly pissed. And as soon as I save my husband's ass, he and I are going to go around about this.

"Can you take the men directly to Asher?" He shakes his head before I even finish the sentence.

"The barrier displaces magic. It's part of what keeps the false king from being able to drain the magic of the surrounding land."

It's the first time that I've been able to hear the underlying worry in his voice.

"Okay, here's what we're going to do. You're going to get the soldiers as close as you can. You'll help Ivann's men dig out the pass. Kane, go with them." Both men give me a quick nod before turning on their heels, leaving me with the other women.

"You three should head out with them," I state as I turn to leave the war room.

"What will you do?" Narcissa finally asks.

"Go get my husband, of course." I give her a little cocky wink before leaving the room.

I step outside to a bustle of activity, soldiers moving into position around the palace, the others heading out into the city proper on the off chance that Froslien has men on their way here. I watch as Ansel organizes the group he's taking with when he notices me. His steps are chipped as he makes his way toward me like I'm some errant child and not the woman who burnt an entire army.

"Where the fuck do you think you're going?" All I do is lift an eyebrow and cross my arms beneath my breasts, cocking my hip for good measure.

"Come again?" He deflates slightly.

"Please, Devany, Asher will kill me if anything happens to you," he pleads. I know he's right, but there is no way I'm staying back. I give a nod of my head and watch as his shoulders sag in relief, thinking that he's talked me out of it—silly man.

I walk over to a clearing in the courtyard, letting that final glamour fall away from my visage. Wings of black, iridescent feathers burst from my back. With one hard beat, my feet lift from the ground. Two beats. Three beats. Four beats, and I'm in the air, headed for the open expanse of the sky. The fading sound of shouting follows me as I head toward the pain in my ass... It's sad to say that even in my mind, I use sarcasm to hide from how much this man has gotten under my skin.

Chapter Twenty-Five

ASHER

We're going to die here.

Fighting this close to the barrier is a double-edged weapon. One that works more in our favor than theirs at the moment. They're cut off from their magic reserves the same as us. But where we are level-headed, they are crazed by an excess of magic. It makes them incredibly strong and unpredictable. But that same unpredictability also makes them sloppy, and irrational, putting us on more even terms.

I'm not sure how so many of them could slip through the barrier, and at this point, it doesn't really matter because I don't see a way out. There are just too many. I count at least thirty, maybe more.

The magic crazed soldier swings his weapon wildly. Spit flies from his mouth as he screams with exertion, the sharp metal coming at me far quicker than I was expecting. The tip of a blade nicks my chin as a sword slices toward my neck, forcing me to bend back. Our swords contact on his next strike, pushing me back a step. My rear leg sliding in the dirt and gravel before I'm able to dig my heels in, stopping my backward momentum.

They've nearly pushed us to the pass, not that it'll do them any good. I brought the walls around it down over an hour ago, blocking us all in.

I hear the soft whisper of a bow being drawn seconds before four arrows fly by my head and the bodies of four enemy soldiers fall before me. Arrows protruding from various places. Eyes. Neck. Chest. A sense of indifference sliding through my chest. The horde merely steps over their fallen comrades, as their death is of little consequence.

Jameson staggers back and falls to his knees. A dagger sticking out of his shoulder. His assailant follows him to the ground, pulling his sword back, preparing to inflict the killing blow. My short sword leaves my hand and in a moment that is both fast and slow, I watch my sword twist in the air, blade over hilt, before slicing through his assailant's neck.

I pull my longsword over my shoulder, turning around to step back into the fray when two more arrows sail by. My eyes land on a Froslien soldier on his knees before me, two arrows protruding from his neck. That was far closer than I care for.

Out of the corner of my eye, I see two of my men drag our wounded back toward the rock wall behind the line of our archers, giving them cover. A new wave of Froslien soldiers push forward and we lose another meter. We're bruised and bleeding.

Another soldier comes at me. I block his first strike and counter, my blade's edge slicing deeply through his bicep. Blood saturates the hilt of his sword, the weapon slipping through his fingers. I act quickly, slashing my blade forward, gutting him and moving on to the next.

"I'm out of arrows!" Toven yells from somewhere behind me.

"I'm down to two!" Gunter calls.

"Here, make 'em count!" Samuel response, presumably tossing them more arrows.

Tristan steps forward, pulling out his longsword. "This day is as good as any to die. Might as well take as many of these fucks with us as we can."

They'll soon over run us. Then they'll use our dead bodies to climb into Naphal. The further inland they go, the more magic they'll have at their disposal. We need to thin the herd, make it more manageable for Devany and my soldiers.

Fuck... the thought of her beautiful face, those midnight eyes flashing with defiance, comes to the forefront of my mind and I ruthlessly squash it down. It's a distraction I can't afford. Not if I want to keep her safe.

We step forward as one, but I have my sights set on this real nasty bastard. He stands about a half a head taller than me. His skin is a sickly color, bled free of life. With thick purple veins that pulse with tainted magic, standing out in stark contrast to his paled skin. All of them have a similar coloring and build.

I barely step forward when the world around us darkens as if something has blotted out the sun. I keep my eyes on the devils before me, bracing for whatever ambush this may be. But they back up, huddling together in the defensive pose.

A rhythmic beat fills the air, bouncing off the jagged rock face, echoing back tenfold and the scent of midnight gardens drifts in on the breeze. I take my eyes off our adversaries and look up to find a creature above us. I hear the intake of a collective breath as I lean back to get a better look. But all I can make out is a large silhouette with the halo of sunlight encompassing it.

The silhouette dives toward us, the rate of speed increasing as they close the gap, wings tucked in tight. A steady hum soon replacing the rhythmic beat.

Meters from the ground, their wings snap out, catching the updraft in the valley and slowing its sudden rapid descent. A few more flaps of those powerful wings, and an impossible body slams into the ground, landing in a crouch before me. And by impossible, I mean my wife.

She straightens to her full height, her shoulders back and head held high, every inch the queen she was born to be. Glorious heavy wings hang from her back, the black feathers coming to life in the late afternoon light. Highlighting the shift in color from blue to purple, pinks, and reds and every color in between.

Her wings flex and her feathers ruffle before tucking tightly against her body and vanishing. She looks back at me and winks like now is the perfect moment to flirt. This woman is going to be the death of me. I know I've said this before. But I'm really starting to believe it.

"How many more times will I need to save your ass, husband?" Her delicate brow arched, a smirk playing with the corner of her full lips. She walks forward, ready to engage with the enemy soldiers that have now recovered from their initial shock.

I guess if we're going to do this, we're going to do it together. Six soldiers step up, spreading out beside us. Toven, Gunter, and Samuel notch the last of their arrows, slicing their thumbs along the arrowheads. There's power in blood, after all.

Devany reaches for her belt, and I watch in fascination as it unfurls in her grasp. Each link elongates, extending out from the segment before it, until it reaches the ground. Sharp spikes protruding from each joint, ending in a honed obsidian pendulum. An enchanted weapon, no doubt a gift from her spellcaster friend.

When she flicks her wrist, the moment is like a whisper in the wind. The chain whip lashes out, going through the throat of the nearest enemy soldier and as if it's an unspoken signal, pandemonium breaks out around us before his body even hits the ground.

I've seen Devany fight before, of course I have. But this was poetry in motion. With every flick of her wrist and turn of her body. Another corpse falls.

"Look alive gentlemen, watch each other's backs." That's all I say to our remaining soldiers as I move into the fray, making my way to Devany.

She flings her arm out in a wide arch; the whip wrapping around the neck of her opponent, and she pulls tight, nearly decapitating him. Sprays of blood paint the floor at her feet.

I make my way through two more combatants, receiving a

minor wound on my forearm. But nothing that would stop my forward momentum.

I make it to her in time to block the strike of Froslien soldier coming up on her from behind and remove his head. Promptly, I take my place protecting her vulnerable back. We don't acknowledge each other. We don't have to. I can feel her energy flowing in and around me. So, I trust my instincts. Listening to the silent push and pull of her body.

Soon we're moving to a rhythm all our own. She twirls her body, moving fluidly, whirling the whip above her head. With every flick of her wrist, I strike with my sword. She spins and I pivot. With each rotation of her hand, the whip twirls around us, slicing through muscle, tendon, and bone.

We're quickly swallowed up by both sides. Lost to the melee. Devany and I fighting back-to-back amongst the warring factions. The sound of rubble reaches my ears. Shouts and grunts echoing off the walls of the valley. They must have cleared the gorge.

Several combatant soldiers shift toward the pass, making the herd of soldiers more manageable. I hear rather than see a spear coming toward us. The high pitch whistle races through the air. Grabbing Devany, I twist us, protecting her body with my own. The spear connects with my thigh. The impact drawing a grunt from my chest. The pain doesn't even register.

"Asher!" Devany voice rises above the battle.

"I'm fine. Stay the course."

The wide arch of a blade comes for our necks. Reaching out, I grab the shape edge with my bare hand. My palm slices on the blade as I use my strength to keep him from pushing forward. Devany turns around slamming her claw tipped hand into his chest.

The heavy clang of steel-on-steel rings out around us. The steep walls amplify the harsh sounds so much it becomes all I can hear. Through all this, we continue to move, a flick of a whip, a strike of a sword. We move within this beat for what feels like minutes, or it could be hours, until we look up through the haze of blood to see none of our enemies still standing.

The thick stench of blood hangs in the air, and our surviving soldiers have the gruesome task of making sure our enemy is dead. Others remove our wounded and our lost. This is but a small sample of how ugly war can be.

When the dust has finally settled, I look her over, checking for injuries. Her skin and clothing are painted in blood and her eyes are bright with adrenaline. Her face is flush, her cheeks pink. A fine mist of sweat coats her skin, leaving strands of hair and dirt sticking to her face.

She has the beginnings of a bruise on her cheekbone and blood dripping from a cut above her eyebrow. Gently, I trail my fingers from her temple just below the gash to her jaw, slipping damp hair behind her ear. My fingertips sliding along the sharp point of her ear, eliciting a shiver from her.

Without warning, she launches herself at me. I just barely have enough time to catch her. Those lovely long legs wrap about my hips, and she twists her fingers in my hair, devouring my mouth. Her tongue dancing with mine.

I adjust my hold on her, bringing her body closer to my own. My hand slips up her spine, tangling in the hair at the nape of her neck, wrapping it around my fist. A sharp tug exposes the long lines of her throat, allowing me to place soft kisses below her jaw before scraping my fangs along the tendon. A throaty moan is my reward.

My racing heart is trying to claw its way out of my chest and into hers. The only thing I can hear is our ragged breathing and her soft moans. Everything else is background noise, like a conversation muffled by water. I take a deep breath, trying to reel in my instincts. Before I end up fucking her right here on the rough ground for all to see. I rest my forehead on hers, my panting breath rustling her hair. Those beautiful liquid silver eyes staring back at me.

I'm prepared to see a range of emotions. What I don't expect to see is her lovely face wiped clean of any actual feeling—that impenetrable mask she shows the world in place.

"Don't hide from me Devany." My voice is so low it's barely above a whisper, my throat closing with emotion. I try to swallow the sensation. It feels something close to what I imagine swallowing rocks would feel like.

I hold Devany's gaze while I give orders to the surrounding soldiers, picking five men at will to help close the gap in the barrier. The wards need to be stronger and there's no telling what sacrifice the druids may require.

"Asher, what now? How do we restore the barrier?" she asks breathlessly. I can feel her words skate across my lips with every exhale.

"We fix the wards," I reply quietly, knowing she will not like what comes next.

"I thought there was no magic this close to the barrier. How do you set wards without access to magic?" she asks, looking slightly confused. Those tiny lines appearing between her brows as she looks around trying to figure out how we'll be accomplishing this. I take a slow breath before responding.

"A sacrifice. Something to appease The Elemental Druids." I feel her body tense so tightly she practically vibrates.

Her fingers dig into my biceps, her claws drawing blood. She stares through me, scarcely breathing and lost in thought.

"What type of sacrifice?" she asks so softly I can barely hear her over the heavy wind rushing through the valley.

"Blood... Even this close to the barrier, there's always magic in blood," I answer thoughtfully, running my thumb along her bottom lip, releasing it from her teeth. Smoothing over the indentions her bite left behind.

She still feels wound tight beneath my hands. "Several of us bleed, painting the words in blood asking for The Druids' blessing." Her wide eyes connect with mine and it nearly brings me to my knees. It's rare I see fear in this woman's gaze.

"What if blood isn't enough?" Her voice is stronger, but still has a shaky note to it.

I want to ease her fears, knowing this will bring her mother's sacrifice to The Elemental Druids to the forefront of her mind. It's actually the one reason I hadn't brought her along this morning.

"Blood will be enough, *a stór milis*. Do you feel the energy flowing beneath our feet?" She gives me a small nod. Staring into my eyes.

I raise my hand to tuck another piece of hair behind her ear, allowing my hand to trail down and grip the back of her neck. "The vibrations will give off a sort of humming noise when those chosen have gotten close to the barrier. The tone increasing the closer they get. The chosen will then get on their knees, cut their palms and bleed on the earth. Asking for the gift of protection while writing the runes into the wet soil beneath them."

The dull drum of noise around us quiets, and I see we have everyone's undivided attention. Uncomfortable with them, witnessing what feels like a very intimate moment. I deflect by sending the soldiers up one at a time.

Each one walks up to the barrier, and they all wait to feel the energy flow change. So far, it hasn't. I try to release her hand so I could step forward and take my turn. But she tightens her hold on my fingers, drawing my attention to her.

Devany meets my gaze, and I see the determination in her eyes. She must've decided she was going with me no matter the outcome, and I respect her more for it. Knowing it must be terrifying for her. Her mother's unnamed sacrifice hanging between us.

She squares her shoulders, and I witness that defiant lift of her chin. I love it so much. There's still fear in her eyes, but there's strength, too. I give her hand a gentle tug and we walk toward the barrier together.

The vibration of energy increases and with it comes the humming noise. It gets louder with each step we take toward it.

Gods. I really hope it's me that The Druids want a sacrifice from. She's bled enough in this life, and she's frightened of The Druids. With her mother's unknown bargain hanging over her head, I don't blame her.

"Step back, *a stór*." She releases my hand and steps away.

I go to my knees before the barrier, placing a hand on the invisible wall. You can feel the static, like tiny pinpricks of electricity against your palm. So much magic flowing through it. But the humming is getting softer the further away she gets.

My stomach drops and a sinking feeling twists my insides when I realize they do in fact want her... just as I know she'll do what must be done, if only to protect our people. I turn toward her, looking up at her beautiful face, trying to find the words to tell her what is required. But she is already walking toward me with a blade in hand.

Devany gracefully kneels beside me with an elegance born of her station, a slight tremor working its way through her body. She holds her hands out stiffly to mask the shaking. The need to hold her is so overwhelming that I snake an arm around her waist, pulling her into my lap. We sit quietly, the wet earth beneath us. Her back to my chest, facing this together. Something about it just feels right.

With my arm wound tightly around her waist, I hold my other hand out in front of her and she places the dagger in my hand. A shiver works its way up her spine and her teeth start to chatter. Her breathing becomes shallow and increases significantly.

"Shh... I've got you," I whisper, pulling her closer, holding her in the cradle of arms.

We sit in silence as the seconds tick by. Just breathing each other in. Once the worst of her shaking subsides, I take her hand in my palm, placing the blade against her soft skin. "*A stór?*" As soon as she looks at me, I capture her lips with mine, first cutting her palm and then my own.

I hold our combined hands above the earth beneath the

barrier. Not only do we hear the energy, but we feel it leap for our blood as it drips to the earth.

I pull my lips from hers; the energy demanding we finish the ritual. With her eyes on mine we reach down as one and I draw the runes into the blood-soaked earth, one stroke at a time.

The drain is immediate and painful. The Druids take their price in magic, extracting it from our veins. Devany sucks in a sharp breath and sags in my arms, her body succumbing to the drain. I tighten my hold on her, pulling her more firmly in my lap.

She becomes heavy when sleep takes its hold. Her head lists to the side, exposing her throat. She looks so young. So fragile. With bloodied hands, I smooth the hair from her face, settling her head on my shoulder.

I feel the all too familiar drag of fatigue as I draw the last line of the rune and the magic snaps into place, knocking us all back. I land in the mud with her safely in my arms. Unharmed but out cold.

The only reason I'm even conscious is an act of sheer stubbornness. Motivated by a singular understanding that she's not safe here.

For a moment, all I see is open sky when a hand appears before me. I drag my tired eyes from the beauty of the heavens to see Ansel standing over us. "Do you want me to take her?"

"No," I grumble, slapping my hand into his. He pulls us up, holding onto me as I reorient myself.

He reaches forward once again as if to take Devany from my arms. A hard look and he backs away, hands up. Though he doesn't wipe the smirk from his face.

"You're an asshole," I state, which only makes him smile wider at me.

"Be that as it may, we need to get the two of you out of here. This place is much too open for my peace of mind," he says, looking around as if to make his point.

I lumber up to the newly cleared pass, feeling exhausted down to my very bones. The walk to my horse is slow and painful. My insides feel as if they've been scorched, I can only equate it to magic burnout. Even with my slow pace, Ansel stays nearby, knowing I'll need him to help me mount my horse.

It somehow feels lighter on this side of the pass. The sun is warmer. Brighter. The sounds of nature ever present. But on the other side, there is no noise. If not for the battle, it would've been as still as death. And just as cold.

We reach my horse, and I reluctantly pass Devany to Ansel. It physically hurts to be separated from her since performing the ritual, but I grin and bear it. I get my foot in the stirrup, but it takes several tries to swing myself up into the saddle. Enervation weighing down my limbs. Immediately. I reach for Devany.

"Everyone, rest when we get back to the palace. We're taking our leave in the morning," is all I say as I take off in that direction, toward safety and some much-needed sleep.

Chapter Twenty-Six

DEVANY

It's early morning when I wake up in Asher's arms. My body aches all over and exhaustion leaches the strength from my limbs, making my head too heavy to lift. Every time I tap into my magic, it wipes me out. Which is a problem I can't afford to have.

I lay with my head on Asher's chest, listening to the steady beat of his heart. His arm is a heavy weight around my waist—holding my bare body against his. The soft rise and fall of his chest the only movement.

The room is as quiescent as the grave. The quiet is so comforting that I lie motionless so as to not break the silence.

I watch specks of dust float within the sunlight that bleeds into the room around the curtains, the diffused light chasing away the midnight shadows.

My mind drifts to thoughts of yesterday.

I hadn't been afraid of facing down that tainted army, even with the numbers stacked against us. Fear had not crossed my mind. I knew he would not let me fall. We may only be friendly enemies on most days. But one thing is clear, we're in this together.

Though that fearless strength soon faded when faced with the bloodletting.

I was fully prepared to stay by Asher's side should the task fall to him. But I hadn't prepared myself to take part.

All-consuming fear threatened to lock up my muscles, it had taken a great deal of energy to force my body to move. First, to remove the ornate silver dagger from my ankle holster. Second, to walk toward him, one step at a time. The dirt beneath my feet gave way to mud the closer I got to the barrier.

The pulse of energy that radiated around us seemed to leap toward me. The hum became so intense that it felt like it not only came from all around me but also from within.

Asher dropped to his knees and placed a reverent hand on the barrier. Even though I couldn't see it, I could feel it. Like standing too close when lightning strikes.

I was so scared of what they would ask for. That perhaps blood wouldn't be enough. All I could think about was the deal my mum made. Not knowing what she actually gave up. Sensing my fear, Asher took matters into his own hands, protecting me when I couldn't protect myself. I remember little beyond that.

I allow the steady beat of his heart beneath my palm, and the rhythmic sound of every breath he takes to relax me. I draw idle circles lightly on his chest, feeling the difference between the unmarred skin and the scars.

Thinking over everything that has happened until his hand covers mine, halting my nervous movements.

"Good morning, wife," he says with a raspy quality to his voice from sleep. I mumble my morning platitude in response.

"How are you feeling?" The question is hesitant and laced with concern. Still treating me as if I'm made of glass. But I don't break so easily. If my father hadn't been able to do it, then nothing will.

Though I'm not ready to discuss my mother or my reaction to the bloodletting. I'm used to sacrificing blood for my people in one way or another. But The Elemental Druids cause me bone-deep terror.

It's not knowing what my mother's deal was. Did she pay the price, or will I? It's the unknown that I find terrifying.

I shrug my shoulders in response, like that's all that needs to be said, as I avoid all eye contact. Just because I don't break, doesn't mean I'm not a coward in some respects, and talking about this is one of those things. I've spent my whole life keeping myself separate to protect those I care about. So much so that now I find it damn near impossible to express how I feel. So, giving voice to these things, breathing life into the genuine fear that I will pay the price for my mother's bargain is beyond my capabilities.

The hand currently resting on my ass slides up my spine to tangle in my hair. He uses it to tip my head back, so I have no choice but to meet his gaze. The other traces along the length of my neck. His eyes become impossibly dark as he stares at my lips. Even as his brows furrow and the corners of his mouth turn down imperceptibly. He doesn't repeat his question, just simply waits for me to speak.

"I don't want to think or talk about it just yet." The response is so quiet, it's almost as if there is someone here to judge my feelings.

"Then what do you want to do, Devany?" he replies on a hard breath, not angry but just not understanding.

He leans forward, placing a soft kiss on my forehead, his breath rustling my hair as he just holds me. The moment feels beyond intimate. I slide my arm across his chest, holding on tightly. As if this will end all too soon.

But this fear is my problem to deal with, only I can ease it. I need a distraction from all the things running wild in my head.

"How were you able to cause an avalanche so close to the barrier?" I ask, canting my head as I look at him. Once again, he takes a deep breath, releasing it in a rough exhale. His eyes rolling up to mine and that one look tells me he knows exactly what I'm up to but doesn't call me on it.

"The pass was a way from the barrier, and I like I told you, there's magic in blood. I bled and asked the earth druid for a blessing. If Froslien's army wasn't so insane with excess magic, they would've been able to do the same thing." He speaks calmly but pulls me close, his arms tightening around me ever so slightly.

He tucks my head beneath his chin while he continues. The skin along my neck and back tingles as his fingers slide through my hair in gently caresses.

"How do you feel about joining me in the bathhouse, *a stór*? We'll get nice and clean before discussing our trip to Serpent's Cove to meet with Nalin. See what she knows of Seiko and where we can find her." I place a hand on his chest, pushing myself up so I can look at him. My hair cascades over my shoulder, forming a curtain blocking out the light from the window. He takes the heavy mass in his hands, pulling it away from my face, and holds it at the base of my neck.

He's so beautiful, it almost hurts to look at him. I stare into his lovely ever-changing eyes, that today are the color of autumn leaves just as they begin to turn.

"I think I'll take you up on that, husband." I smile sweetly at him, my thumb dragging back and forth along the bar in his nipple. His pupils dilate, swallowing the iris, wiping them of all color. I can feel my body mirror his, and the smile I receive is so bright it makes my heart race.

Asher releases my hair, allowing the strands to cascade over my shoulder once more. He slides out from under me and walks around the bed to carry me into the private bathhouse connected to our room.

It's absolutely stunning. The entirety room is covered in pearlescent tiles that reflect shimmery rainbows in the early morning light. Three large windows take up the whole of the wall to our left. They run from the floor to the ceiling, ending in pointed arches. The ceiling is a beautiful work in shapes and angles, covered in the same delicate tiles.

Three chandeliers made of lightning glass hang parallel to the windows over a deep pool of water, so warm you can see the steam rising from the surface. The room smells of lavender and rosemary, most likely coming from oils added to the pool. The tub is sunken into the floor, running the length of the room. Crystal-clear water glitters like jewels as the light bounces off its surface.

He doesn't break stride, walking straight to the tub, taking the steps, and wading into the water. I switch position to wrap my legs around his waist. With one hand, he maneuvers us to the middle of the pool. He easily keeps me afloat with a hand under my ass while treading water.

I look up to meet his gaze as his free hand grips the back of my neck and his mouth collides with mine. His tongue pushes past my lips in a soul-stealing kiss. I push up in his arms, my fingers tangling in his hair, pulling his head back to get a better angle on his mouth. Asher feels my response and pulls me closer. He holds me hostage, though in this moment, not that I'm trying to get away.

"Stop distracting me, wife," he says, panting heavily, eyes dancing with amusement as he presses his forehead against mine.

"Sorry, husband, but that was all you," I am quick to point out, even as I laugh quietly under my breath, smiling at him brightly.

He lifts a hand to my face, cupping my cheek, his thumb tracing lightly along the underside of my bottom lip.

"This is the first time you've smiled at me like this. It makes your eyes sparkle like moonlight off still water." His voice is quiet, eyes scouring over my face like he's trying to memorize every nuance.

Uncomfortable with the observation, I try to look away. But Asher refuses to let me hide. He kisses me softly before using one hand to once again wade us through the water before stopping to place me on the bench built into the side of the pool.

He's so gentle in his care of me, picking out a bar of lavender soap and a cloth from the basket on the tiled floor behind us. Working the soap into a lather, he gently wipes it along my neck and across my shoulders. He gives each arm the same treatment. Next, he takes my hands in his, pushing his thumbs into my palm, working out tension I didn't even know I had.

He moves on to my breast, skimming the soft, soapy cloth over my nipple, causing goosebumps to form in his wake. When he does it again to the other side, I suck in a sharp breath. His eyes slowly lift to mine, darkening into a deep green. His fingertips trail between my breast and down over my stomach to dip beneath the surface of water. His touch is both light and intense as his hands run from my hips to my thighs, spreading them wider so he can press closer. His nails scrape lightly along my skin as he moves a hand to the center of my thighs, slipping between my folds to find me slick from both the water and the intimacy of the moment.

Asher rubs my clit in small, slow circles, making my stomach clench and other parts of me throb. He doesn't take his eyes off of me as I squirm, needing more—which he's more than happy to provide. Sinking one finger into me, he moves it slowly until I relax into the pressure. Then he adds another, keeping the movements unhurried until my hips move in time with his hand. Steadily increasing the speed on my own, but when I'm unable to push myself over the edge, I give him a pleading look. He finally gives in, adding another finger and increasing the speed, building the pressure as my lower muscles wind tighter and tighter, and then suddenly—I'm soaring, lightheaded and panting while light dances before my eyes. He lightens his touch, bringing me back down slowly before he resumes bathing me. The soft cloth skates over my sensitive flesh to clean away my release.

Asher places the washcloth on the edge of the pool, removing a bowl containing a soft, whipped soap from the basket. He scoops out a generous amount, taking his time working it into my hair before rinsing it. Once done, I watch as he repeats the process for himself.

Though I've already climaxed, I find myself squirming as I watch his hands glide over his beautiful body, tracking the rivets of soap and water as it slides down the divots and curves of his muscles. The suds slip from the contours of his chest and into the strong creases of his abdomen, then drift away on the surface of the water.

My eyes move back up his body to land on his face, where I find the asshole smirking at me with one of his brows arched in amusement. I open my mouth to give him a piece of my mind, but he dips under the water to wash the soap away. He comes back up and pulls me into his arms, having apparently deemed us clean enough to get dressed and meet the others. I guess there's no time like the present.

It's time to set the board and watch our enemies fall.

When we arrive in the war room, everyone is already discussing strategy. Or should I say *arguing* strategy? But all discussion ceases when we walk in. Narcissa and Kane each give me a quick once over before turning back to the map.

The room is all dark wood with recessed panels covered in bold green wallpaper. They've positioned tan leather chairs around the perimeter of the room. The map itself is a large hand-painted table measuring one meter by two meters. It contains all the sixteen kingdoms and the shifter clans. The wood is inlaid with copper and its carved legs depict large fig trees and desert cityscapes. In short, it's beautiful. There are curved wood pieces representing each kingdom's infantry positioned around the map.

They dismiss us quickly, turning back to the map and resume their arguing.

"Stop." It's all I say, but everyone quiets down again. Once I have their attention, I turn to Ivann, smiling sweetly.

"Your Grace, please brief us on where we're at as a whole," I request, deferring to him. We are in his kingdom, after all.

"There's no way to truly tell which kingdoms will support us in the upcoming days. Especially with your father still committing mass genocide. Add that to the wall, and the monarchs are going to be less than hospitable." Ivann's response is straightforward, but his mouth is turned down and there's a tightness around his eyes.

"We can call for a meeting, invite all sixteen kingdoms and the numerous shifter clans, hold it in the Kingdom of Hepha—neutral territory for all those involved," Bellicent suggests. It's a smart play, allowing us to get a feel for the other monarchs.

"But first, we'll have to deal with my father." As I say the words, I feel my stomach turn sour. I hate the man with everything I am, but I also fear him. To this day, I still carry around the invisible wounds and the physical scars.

"To take on your father, we're going to need more able bodies than what Asher has with him. Let us keep an eye on him," Narcissa interjects, stopping briefly to meet my eyes before she carries on. "We still have spies behind the palace walls and with it the flow of information is open. Sam and I will stay here and notify you should anything happen." Her shoulders back and head held high, every inch the commander she is, and her tone leaves no room for argument.

I look at her for a few long moments, my emotions warring within me. On the one hand, keeping them here gives me someone to monitor the situation. On the other hand, I'm putting the woman I consider family in danger should anything go wrong. But I guess we all have our parts to play. Besides, the look in her eyes tells me she won't be deterred.

"Fine. You will have several men with you, including Kane. You make no move without my expressed consent." I ignore everyone else in the room, keeping my eyes solely on hers. "Do you understand?" Her reply comes as a sharp nod of her head. "Good, shall we move on?" I ask, casting my eyes across the room. Kane looks as if he would argue, but with a look from me, he wisely keeps his mouth shut.

"Well, with Narcissa and Kane staying here to monitor the

situation. You, me, and the others will head towards the coast of Edling. If we ride hard, we can be to the boats in two days' time. Ansel and the rest of our people will head to Draic. I've been gone for some time, it's best that someone make contact. Ansel will find homes and jobs for those of your people who wish to travel on with us. You, Bellicent, and I, along with the rest of the soldiers, will take the second boat and head for Serpent's Cove to see what Nalin may know." His eyes move from mine to look at Ivann. "The wards have been reinforced. They should hold them back for a while, at least. If there's anything else I can help with, let me know." Asher dips his head to his old friend in respect, and Ivann returns the gesture.

We go over several plausible scenarios. But without a true number of allies, it's hard to plan beyond the battle with my father.

Chapter Twenty-Seven

DEVANY

It took two and a half days to ride to the port in Edling, where our ships were being safely docked. Another three weeks to sail to Serpent's Cove.

It's late afternoon on our final day of travel, and the sun is relentless in its pursuit to make this day unbearable. So, when the floating kingdom comes into view, I almost weep. The crew begins to run about, preparing the ship to dock. Four men lower the sails and tie them off while several others pull the rigging, securing the boom. Once we're within range, they drop the anchor and throw the spring lines.

The moment we're safely in port, Asher leaves to secure our rooms at the inn. Which I'm most grateful for, because apparently the open sea and I don't agree with each other. I'm already loathing the return ride to Draic as I wait on the deck of our ship, looking at the wonderland before me.

The barge floats in the ocean off the shores of Aiteall. Not that you can see it with the living elemental dome encompassing it. Their shoreline is craggy and littered with driftwood, boats, and ships that lay abandoned in derelict piers. The waters are rough, beating upon the shore. In some areas all the way to the cliffs. As if the ocean itself is angry with them.

The pirate kingdom, on the other hand, is a vision to behold. The barges connect to each other in a crescent shape. It has tall buildings that house their citizens on either side of the entrance point. Just beyond that are six more buildings that stand slightly taller, each painted a different color to represent the vice they cater to. In the center, there's a gilded building that towers over the rest, which I assume is Nalin's home. Vegetation cascades down along the tops of every building. I can see trees heavy with fruit and wells full of rainwater. The scent of salt surrounds me, stinging my eyes and coating my tongue.

Movement draws my eye to the pier where Asher comes aboard. He walks toward me with that effortless swagger that I love as much as I hate. I admire the fine cut of his tunic and the way his trousers mold to his thighs. I can't seem to drag my eyes away from the way his trim waist and broad, muscular shoulders flex beneath the fine fabric. My eyes move up to his body to land on his face. Those ever-changing eyes are the color of moss today. Beautiful, curved horns that stand tall and proud and all I can think about is what they look like when his head is buried between my thighs and my hands are wrapped around those horns. My mouth goes dry and my blood heats in my veins. The bastard smirks at me like he knows exactly what I'm thinking about.

"We're checked in, wife. The crew will bring in our belongings. You, Bellicent, and I will head for the pleasure barge to request an audience with Nalin."

Bellicent slides up next to me. Smiling much too brightly. "This is going to be fun," she says excitedly, her bright eyes bouncing to me.

"I'm not sure I agree," I mumble even as I accept Asher's hand and allow him to lead me away.

As soon as we cross the threshold, Asher leaves Bellicent and I to our devices while he tries to procure an audience with Nalin. I wander the pleasure barge with her as my ever-present shadow until I finally stop in front of a wall with... by the gods, is that? I look back at her because surely, I'm mistaken.

"Are those... paddles?" I can feel my cheeks heat as I whisper the words. She apparently finds my discomfort hilarious as she stifles a laugh.

"Why yes, they are," she replies, nodding while I'm simultaneously shaking my head at her.

"Why in the Goddess's name would anyone want to be... to use..." I'm at a loss for words and now she's outright laughing at me.

"You'd be surprised," is all she says as she leads me away from the wall and toward the bar. I'm thankful—because I could use a drink.

The bar area is full of dark wood and rich reds. High top tables fill the room, each with a scantily clad man or woman dancing on them. The patrons surrounding the tables lay down gold and silver pieces while servers weave through the tables, dropping off drinks and taking orders. The room smells heavily of incense and tobacco.

"Hey, beautiful, what can I get you?" I startle slightly, having been so distracted by everything going on, I hadn't realized the bartender was waiting for me.

"Oh, sorry... elderberry wine, please." Feeling slightly embarrassed by the wide-eyed look I must have as I take in everything.

"No need to apologize, love." His eyes heat as he licks his lower lip, giving me a once over before finally landing on my face. He begins to speak, only to be cut off by another man.

"I haven't seen you in here before, sweets." He stresses the word 'seen,' suggesting he would very much like to see more of me. "Tell me, sweets, are you here with someone?" This is the pickup line he's going with? I know little about these kinds of things, but these seem kind of generic. Surely, he can do better than this. He looks at me as if he expects me to fall at his feet or something. I mean, he's pretty, but *not* that pretty.

"Yes, I'm here with someone," I state flatly as I look around, trying to locate Bellicent. Where the hell did she go? I jolt when I feel his fingers glide along my cheek to tuck a lock of my hair behind my ear.

"What can I call you, my sweet?" he asks, slinking into my personal space. Not wanting to be boxed in, I knock his hand away standing up from my chair.

"You can call me Queen if you must know." The horse's ass actually laughs.

"Queen of what?" His tone suggests he thinks I'm flirting.

"Of Draic," Asher's voice cuts in, causing both of us to look in his direction. I expect to see him staring a hole through this fool, but he has eyes only for me. "*Wife.*" That one word holds so much authority and sounds less than pleased.

"Husband." The word slips off my lips, full of seduction and promise. While his eyes do heat at what I'm offering, he still looks terribly angry.

"Wife?" The pretty fool decides to bring our attention back to him.

If the violent look Asher gives him is anything to go by, it was the wrong thing to do. He takes a threatening step toward the pretty fool and draws the attention of the surrounding patrons. The hushed voices around the bar are steadily rising. The best course of action to keep him from killing someone and getting us kicked out is to intercept and distract. Pushing off the bar, I close the distance between us. The tips of my fingers trailing up the inner line of his tunic, sliding up his chest as his arm takes hold of my waist, pulling me to him.

"Yes, I'm Queen Devany of Draic, formerly Princess of Erabis," I say in my best, you-are-so-not-worthy voice, with a side of you're-so-fucked. His skin pales dramatically as my weight of titles registers in his mind. I smile brightly at him. *Yes, pretty fool, I'm that bitch.*

"Ethan, get out of here before they kill you," says a man as he approaches us, sounding all too bored.

Ethan apparently doesn't need to be told twice as he turns on heel and walks away as quickly as he can, though none of us acknowledge his quick exit. My attention is focused solely on the man in front of me... Just who is he? Even though I can feel Asher's heavy stare like a physical touch on the back of my neck, I continue to stare at the newcomer. Asher's attention stays fixed on me and if it weren't for the pounding of his heart beneath my palm, I would believe him unbothered by the interaction. His hand closes around my throat, tilting my head back to look into my eyes. He says nothing, just simply looks at me. A strange question in his eyes just before they soften somewhat.

"She'll see you now," The newcomer cuts in once again, drawing my attention. His voice is cultured and refined.

His chestnut complexion was rich in a way that only a Valore's could be. Dark and vibrant, offset by his light hair that seemed to be spun of pure gold and eyes the color of sunshine. The sharp slope of his pointed ears confirms my suspicions of his heritage. He wears practical clothes, made from fine fabrics. And while he carries a few weapons plain to see, only the goddess knows how many others there may be. Not that he needed any. It's obvious he's lethal.

A tattoo of a viper twists up his arm, the head peeking out above his collar, and I could've sworn the scales shifted in the light, most likely his familiar. Snakebite piercings adorn his lower lip with another at his eyebrow. There was an undeniable and deadly grace about him.

"Lead the way, Cyrus," Asher replies, though he continues to look at me for a moment longer before placing his hand on my lower back while he holds the other out in a silent command to follow.

"Who is he?" I whisper to Asher, keeping my voice just quiet enough not to be overheard.

"Cyrus of Nysar—consort to Queen Nalin."

"Nysar? That's an island kingdom, yes?" My father was more concerned with the kingdoms within Galandir than those beyond, so my knowledge is limited.

"Yes, though it's actually two kingdoms, Nysar is ruled by Queen Cora and her wife, Queen Finley. Then there's the under-water kingdom of Gali, home of the sea-folk, ruled by Ryuu." I have so many questions, but now isn't the time to ask.

We weave our way through the tables to a doorway at the far end. Which opens into what appears to be a gambling hall. We continue through several rooms, each decorated uniquely to itself, catering to another vice. You can feel the slight rocking motion of the ocean surrounding us.

From what I gather, what started out as a few barges roped together has become a kingdom unto itself. Completely self-contained. It is now a beautiful cityscape, a floating wonderland of debauchery.

One story that I had heard was of Queen Nalin, herself. It was said that she had once been a slave, chained and collared for her ability as a siren. To add insult to injury, her owner lost her in a bet to a pirate. I know little of how she went from slave to queen. But I feel it stands to reason that she must be quite strong in character.

We finally come upon large oak doors, guarded by two female sentries. They open that door as we approach, allowing us to enter without breaking stride. A small gasp leaves my lips as we enter. They've covered the room in dark wood, much like the bar with gold gilded accents throughout. A beautiful chandelier made entirely of sea-glass hangs from the vaulted ceilings with a rich purple carpet leading from the doorway to the dais.

There, a beautiful woman sits upon a massive, gilded throne. Her hair is long and thick, hanging well past her hips, in a red so vibrant it reminds me of living flames. She's wearing tight leather pants with a matching corset over an untied silk blouse. The ensemble is finished off with a pair of low-cut heeled boots. The queen herself sits lazily on her throne with one leg thrown over the arm while she picks her nails with a dagger.

Cyrus walks straight to the dais, standing beside her and placing his hand on the back of the throne. He wears a careful mask of boredom. But it's a mask I know well, as I've worn it many times myself. Her eyes finally drift up to meet ours and she raises a delicate brow as if to say, *why aren't you bowing?* I hate to be the one to tell her this, but I bow to no one. So, I raise a single brow of my own and we stand locked in a battle of wills, waiting to see who will come out on top. After several intense minutes, she gives me a bright smile and sits back.

"Nice to see the rumors are true," she says, but I can't tell whether it's a good or a bad thing.

"It's been a while since you last visited us. I'm sure it will disappoint the girls to hear you brought your wife," she says all this very critically.

I try hard not to react. I really do. But I can't stop myself from looking at him. And from the look of triumph in her eyes, I played right into whatever game we're playing here. So, I react the only way I can think.

"I'm sure they'll live another day, otherwise they can take it up with me. Though I don't think it's in their best interest." My tone is cold enough to freeze water, and the threat is plain to hear. I may not have wanted a husband, but he's mine, nonetheless.

She smiles benignly at me, pulling out a cigarette and placing it in her mouth. As she reaches for a silver matchbox, Cyrus takes hold of her chin roughly, turning her face toward him. He leans forward so they're eye to eye before he blows lightly on the tip of her cigarette, lighting it. The room fills with the sweet scent of tobacco. The act itself is so blatantly sexual that I feel like a voyeur. They continue to stare at one another, and you can tell from the looks on their faces that the room has faded away.

"What brings you here, Asher?" she says, not taking her eyes off Cyrus and sounding like she really couldn't care less.

"I'm looking for the heir to the Kannon throne. We were told we could find her here," he says, sounding entirely too high handed.

"Why are you looking for her?" It's asked casually, but there's still a sense of violence in the air. I cut in before Asher can speak.

"We wish to place her back where she belongs." She stares into my eyes, and I allow her to see my truth.

"And your father?" she asks with more curiosity than hostility.

"He's a dead man walking. At this point, it's whoever gets to him first," is my monotone reply.

Her eyes light up at the causal mention of my father's death. I see he's made no friends here. *That's good to know.* She stares at me for a long moment, willing me to show my hand. But she'll get no more from me. She seems to realize this when I simply just stare back. She turns to address Asher once more.

"She and Alaric are currently re-homing resources," she tells us as she sits back, crossing her legs.

By re-homing I'm sure she means stealing, not that I give a shit. She looks at me as if she's waiting for me to object. So, I answer the question in her eyes just so we can move things along.

"As long as you stay away from Draic ships and those of our allies, I couldn't care less what you do," I say in a way that ensures she and I completely understand one another. Nalin nods her head as if this is acceptable before turning to speak to my husband who has been unusually quiet during this entire interaction.

"They should be back in the morning. I'm assuming you wish to stay in the city?" she asks, sounding bored once again.

He doesn't answer, just simply nods his head. Two men step forward, bowing deeply at the waist, holding out a hand, indicating we have effectively been dismissed. I wait for the doors to close behind us before addressing Asher quietly.

"Are we safe here?" I whisper.

"Yes, but it's still best to keep your wits about you," he replies.

"Then where the fuck did Bellicent go earlier?" That gets his attention, and he finally turns his head to look down at me.

"She came to find me when she saw you being approached by Ethan. Not wanting to make you look weak by stepping in," he says, sounding like he's still pissed about the whole thing.

"I can take care of my-damn-self," I mumble under my breath, decidedly put out by the assumption that I could not.

"Of this I have no doubt, My Queen," he tells me softly, just as I feel the heavy weight and heat of his hand on my lower back urging me forward.

Chapter Twenty-Eight

ASHER

Devany is uncharacteristically quiet as we follow the attendant. We trail behind him through the impressive floating palace, passing room after room of dark fantasies come to life. Whatever your vice may be—they have it here.

She holds herself as regal as ever and to the untrained eye she looks completely at ease. But I've spent a great deal of time studying my wife and I can tell from the heavy set of her shoulders and sharp line of her back that she can feel all their eyes on her.

They're practically foaming at the mouth, looking for any weakness they can exploit.

Very few of Nalin's people were born within the kingdom, most have relocated from other territories. It's probably safe to assume that many of these people came here because it was the furthest they could get from Erabis, fleeing from her father's greed and lust for bloodshed.

Many of them would love to take a shot at her, to use her to punish Kól by proxy. Though they must know what would befall them, should they act on that desire?

We pass scantily dressed men and women milling about the

halls and rooms. Each gives us a practiced smile made of smoke and mirrors.

The attendant leads us to a grand hallway and bends at the waist, holding his hand in the direction he wishes us to go. Making no move to go down the hall, we simply wait him out, and I swear it's like he can sense my irritation because he takes his time standing back up.

I turn to him in time to see his lips twitch at the corner like he's fighting the urge to smile, once again pointing toward the hall.

"This is your concierge for the duration of your stay with us." My eyes are on his as I contemplate whether killing him is worth the trouble.

I step into the fool's space and wrap my hand around his throat far too quickly for his human reflexes to gage the movement. I tighten my grip, lifting him from the ground, the toes of his boots scraping along the hardwood floors. When his eyes begin to water, I lower him to his feet and close the space between us, pinning him with my stare. Though he visibly shutters, I get no other reaction from him. That in and of itself pisses me off for reasons beyond my comprehension. The man really hasn't done anything to earn the level of hostility I feel toward him. *But it's like I'm being compelled.*

I hear a very subtle intake of breath, so low I doubt any of the surrounding humans heard it. It's a sound that would've drawn my attention one way or another, but when it's accompanied by a series of sharp tugs on my hand, it grabs my complete attention. I bump into his shoulder as I turn slightly to see what's caught Devany's attention.

The hardwood floors beneath our feet transform into a plush burgundy rug. The shade enhances the rich, dark juniper-colored walls. The painted surface somehow swallows and reflects the candlelight from the lanterns hanging low from the ceiling. The bottom half of the wide hallway is covered in opulent wood panels.

But none of those things are what have caught Devany's attention. No, that honor goes to the pretty human sitting on a velvet chaise lounge the same shade as the rugs.

She looks up at us with cosmic-blue eyes that glow with power... a spellcaster. Now the aggression makes more sense. The little bitch is casting. This is poor form. Nalin and I will be having words on this—alliance or not.

"You may leave us, Jeffery," she states to the attendant at our side.

But her eyes never leave ours—or should I say they never leave Devany's. I look over at him to see the crooked grin he's been fighting finally win out as he turns and leaves us.

I turn my attention back to the unknown woman. She has thick, black, bluntly-cut hair that hands to her shoulders. Her skin is so pale that it stands out in contrast to the brightness of her blue eyes.

A light blush of color stains her high cheekbones.

She stands gracefully and walks toward us dressed in a black front-laced corset with ties loose at the top, baring her breasts. Her shoulders are covered by a high-collar lace cape fastened at the throat with a cameo brooch carved of jade that hangs in the hollow of her throat. A matching lace skirt sways around her mid-thigh.

Our guards tense as she closes the distance between us. But she pays them no mind, stopping less than two steps away—very much within striking distance. When she raises her hand toward Devany, I grab her by the wrist before she can touch her. The woman's eyes roll up to meet mine and she looks at me from beneath her lashes, an easy smile on her lips. However, it's the calculated look in her eyes that gives me pause.

"I mean no harm, Your Majesty," the woman states with a liar's smile upon her red painted lips.

Devany places a hand upon my shoulder to bring my attention to her. "It's alright." Just two words, that's all she says.

It is, however, enough to remind me we have an audience

looking for a weakness in any form. I tug the woman to me by the wrist I hold hostage, so we're almost nose to nose.

"You try anything. I'll kill you," I tell her, my tone low and quiet, but the malice and violence are plain to hear.

Wryly she smiles up at me, all emotion absent from her gaze. I shove her away and the little vixen turns toward Devany, reaching to take a lock of her hair, twirling it around her finger before she looks up shyly. A look that has undoubtedly worked for her in the past.

"Your Highness, may I join you this evening?" Suddenly sounding timid, her voice even quivers slightly.

She's an excellent actress.

A pretty blush rises to Devany's cheeks as she takes this woman in. Her lips part slightly, and my attention is immediately drawn to her mouth.

"Your name?" Devany asks, giving the woman a pointed look.

"Rayne, my name's Rayne." She shifts her weight from side to side and Devany takes an audible breath before her eyes harden.

The spellcaster senses the change, the shift in the energy around us.

"Did you just ask to join me in my bed? The one I share with my husband?" Her voice takes on that quiet quality that conveys a great deal, despite its volume, as the temperature in the room drops several degrees.

"I'm sorry, I didn't mean—" The spellcaster trails off as she seems to look for the right words.

Her eyes frantically look for someone to help her. But those same people who moments ago were looking for a weakness to exploit are now backing away from us as Devany's power fills the many corridors. The corner of my mouth twitches as I fight a grin of my own because it seems they've pissed off my sweet wife.

"Make any offer like that to either one of us again and it will not end so well a second time." Devany's voice echoes through the hallway as she stares at Rayne.

I don't have to turn and look at those around us to know many are nodding their heads and backing away.

"We won't be needing your assistance. *For anything.* I hope we've made ourselves clear?" I query, bringing her attention back to me. Whatever she sees in my eyes has her taking a step away from us. The scent of her fear fills the wide space and I cant my head, giving her a predatory smile that displays my fangs. Our little concierge continues to retreat, nodding sharply before bowing low.

"Of course, Your Majesties. I apologize for my misstep," she replies in a small voice, backing up further before slipping through one of the many hidden doorways.

I worry that Nalin may be playing head games with Devany. Most likely trying to see if we're worth backing in the war against Froslien. And if I'm being honest, we need her.

Froslien has a formidable armada to contend with. We'll need Nalin's warships. If we can add Edling and Sólális, each with a small naval reserve, as well as Gali and Draic' size-able forces... Perhaps it's wishful thinking to have all these things fall into place, but if we can do even half that, we may have a fighting chance.

We continue down the hall, stopping at a heavy wood door with ocean waves carved deeply into it. The detail is so lifelike, I can almost hear the ocean breaking on the shore. I reach forward and turn the knob with a flourish, winking at Devany as I throw the door open.

The room is a masterpiece. Ornate dark wood panels cover the walls from floor to ceiling. Large tiles span the room covered by blue rugs with white details. Opposite the door stands a four-poster bed with two windows on either side.

Through the window, I can see Aiteall's abandoned shores and a sense of sadness washes over my heart, weighing my shoulders down. Our homes lay just beyond that cursed dome of magic.

Bellicent checked our room out while we were talking with Nalin for anything dangerous or out of place. She gave us the all-clear once we arrived but left us alone shortly after. No doubt in search of more pleasant pursuits. Which is alright by me. Devany has reached her fill and if she were to have a breakdown, I would prefer it to remain between us.

I settle into one of the two brocade chairs in the seating area, watching Devany pace from one end of the room to the other. With each of her hurried steps, I think back on the earlier meeting that went far better than I had expected. But then again, Seiko wasn't present. Only the Goddess knows how she'll react tomorrow. Not that I blame her, but if she tries to kill my wife, I won't hesitate to snap her neck. And let's be honest, that's no way to start an alliance.

Devany nervous pacing practically wears a hole in the carpet beneath her feet. Not to mention she's bitten her nails down to the quick, it's a wonder they're not bleeding.

Her beautiful face is scrunched up, creating creases along her forehead and in between her delicate brows. Worriedly she chews on her lip, wringing her hands nervously. I'm not sure what got her so railed up, she handled Nalin and the spellcaster beautifully. If Seiko can't be persuaded, then we'll figure something out.

It's obvious she needs something to do with all that excess energy. Something to take her mind off things.

Devany's so engrossed in whatever is occupying her mind that she doesn't notice I've moved until she runs into me. She attempts to take a step back, but I don't allow her to get far. I pull her to me, wrapping my arm around her waist and taking hold of her hand. Her free hand automatically goes to my shoulder, and I sway us to the music that plays through the walls from one of the nearby pubs.

Devany doesn't look at me as we move around the space. Her eyes drift to the side, denying me the intimacy of looking into her eyes. Our movements are slow and sensual as we spin around the room. Her beautiful body moving in rhythm with mine. My breath stirs her hair with every exhale and her long, caramel curls brush my fingertips with each sway of her hips, surrounding me with her lovely soft floral scent.

She slowly relaxes, as several songs pass while we're twirling around the stately room. No words are spoken, we simply just dance. I make it a point not to look at her, staring at the wall above her head. When I feel her eyes on me, I look down at her. Wordlessly, I stare into her eyes, waiting for her to speak.

"What if Seiko refuses our offer?" Her voice is small, breaking at the end. The indentation between her brows deepens.

"Then we find someone else to sit upon her throne and back them with the full might of our armies. See if she's able to get it back then." My reply is cold, the words hard.

Leaning over, I cup her face in the palm of my hands to soften my words. My thumb tracing the apple of her delicate cheek.

"Let's get you to bed. There are some things I'd like to show you." Leering at her playfully, which brings a smile to her face as I had intended. "Before our meeting with Nalin and Seiko tomorrow evening," I state tenderly, my voice softening toward the end. Realizing all that's come to pass must be overwhelming for her and we're only just getting started.

I take a step back, turning her in my arms. My fingers deftly work the laces of her corset loose, watching the fabric slacken before sliding down Devany's delectable body to pool at her feet. Next comes the silk blouse that I promptly pull over her head, revealing that beautiful tattoo.

It covers the whole of her back. So many types of flowers, all in colors of purples, blues, and mints. My fingers slide along her spine, vertebrae by vertebrae, eliciting a bone deep shiver. I love the way her body reacts to me.

She's silent while I undress her. The only sound she makes is the panting breaths that leave her lips. I turn her around once more, and kneel before her, making quick work of untying the laces of her leather pants, then gliding the supple fabric down her firm legs. She steps out of them and attempts to move away. Not that I let her go anywhere. I wrap my hands around her thighs and pull her back. My lips glide over her skin from one hip to the other. I tilt her hips forward slightly, my tongue sliding between her folds to taste her on my tongue.

Her fingers dive into my hair, holding me right where she wants me. Her nails scrape my scalp, but I'm already standing up, sweeping her into my arms and carrying her to the bed. I place her on the cool satin sheets, her beauty literally takes my breath away. Her eyes are soft and hooded. Lips slightly parted with a pretty blush on her cheeks. My eyes devour every inch of her as I remove my clothes before climbing into bed beside her. I spend the rest of the night taking her nice and slow, showing her what she does to me without words.

Chapter Twenty-Nine

ASHER

Devany fell asleep some time ago, wrapping her slight frame around my own. Her leg thrown over my waist and her head resting upon my chest, over my heart. Something I've noticed she does often. Lush caramel curls drape over her slender shoulder, fanning out across the pillow. The fresh floral scent of her hair surrounds me, seeping into my very soul.

The sun has barely filtered in through the window, casting shadows along the wall when a knock sounds through the door accompanied by a formal voice.

"Your Majesties, your presence has been requested for breakfast," a muffled voice states before I hear its owner stepping back from the door, giving us privacy.

The slight commotion rouses Devany from her sleep, and she burrows closer into my side. Tucking her hands between us as if cold. As tempting as it is to stay in bed all day with her, our presence is required.

"Time to get up," I tell her softly, placing a kiss on top of her head. Lightly brushing her hair off her shoulder.

"What time is it?" Devany asks around a yawn, her voice raspy with sleep, snuggling deeper into my side.

"Nalin has requested our presence. She wishes us to join them for breakfast." I do my best to sound formal and courtly while I look down at her laying on my chest, her head moving with each breath I take.

Reluctantly, I loosen my hold on her body, allowing her to sit up, watching as she stretches her hands to the sky. Completely at ease with her nudity, I lean forward to brush her nipple with the back of my fingers, watching as the silken skin puckers and hardens with my touch. She gasps faintly as I trail my fingertips along the curve of her breast, sliding them across her rib cage to trace the outline of her raven tattoos.

"Is Seiko here already?" she asks around a loud, lengthy breath, stretching further. Her eyes suddenly widened. "Oh, shit, is Seiko here? I thought that would be later today. I'm not mentally ready for this... to see her." Her voice gets quieter as she stares at her hands as if they're stained with all the blood her father's spilt in the name of greed.

I reach over, tipping her face up so I can see her beautiful eyes brimming with tears as she works so hard to hide them from me. Tiny droplets cling to her lashes, brightening her eyes and enhancing the color. Her teeth sink into her lip to hold back a fragile whimper.

She doesn't meet my eyes, her gaze drifting to the wall away from me, and I've had enough. No one has the right to make her feel less then. I grip her chin roughly and scowl at her.

"His sins are not your sins. Do you hear me?" She nods faintly, almost pulling her chin free from my grasp.

Her eyes are subdued and somber with misplaced guilt. I cup her face with both hands, letting her sleep-warmed skin press against mine while my eyes move back and forth between hers.

"You are not at fault for any of the things he did to them..." I rest my forehead on hers before I continue. "...For what he did to you." I enunciate each word, watching as she absorbs them.

Devany makes a hiccupping-sob and she bits her lip once more, trying to keep the sound from escaping. I kiss her gently, tasting her tears and sweet blood from where her teeth have cut into the soft tissue of her lip.

"Remember, we bow to no one. Not even the monsters that haunt our past," I whisper against her lips.

We walk into the dining hall as if we're prepared for battle and that's not far from the truth if last night's events are anything to go by. Devany opted for a combination of warrior and queen. A sheer silk high-low dress encased in a leather corset with a matching pair of tightly-fitted leather pants and knee-high boots. The short train of light fabric flows behind her as she walks with purpose into the room.

I went for a much simpler look. Buckskin pants with a black tunic to hide the array of weapons I brought with me this morning, choosing function over fashion.

Devany keeps her glamour firmly in place, having not yet become fully comfortable with her true form after having spent years hiding it. I choose the opposite route, foregoing my glamour all together to remind them what and who sits among them.

We walk to the wide planked table, set for seven. Two seats notably are empty. It doesn't take a scholar to surmise who is missing.

Nalin sits at the head of the table, her bored persona on full display. She wears a crisp white shirt with a high collar bound in a wide leather belt with her thick crimson hair braided over her shoulder. Cyrus sits to her right, his body relaxed, but his hand hovers over his hip, where I'm willing to bet he carries a weapon of some sort. To her left is one of the empty chairs and to the left of it is the other. Last, Rayne sits at the end of the table. Her hands in her lap, eyes on the table. The line between us couldn't be clearer.

A young server ogling my wife rushes over to pull out her chair. I growl at the boy before he can, doing it myself. I don't trust these people.

"Is growling at my people really necessary?" Nalin asks while lightly swirling the wine in her glass, sounding all too bored. She has some fucking audacity after what she pulled last night.

"After you sicced your little caster on us... I feel that growling and is more than required," I reply, slamming my hand on the table. Devany is quick to cover it with her own, giving me a subtle squeeze.

Nalin's reaction is almost immediate. Her glass slamming on the table, cracking from the stem to the rim, wine sloshing over the edge. She stands slowly, swinging her lethal gaze at me.

"That's quite the statement. What exactly are you accusing me of?" Her shoulders heave as the tips of her fingers pale against the table.

I look at her, trying to discern whether she's lying. But before I can come to a conclusion, Devany speaks up. Not even bothering to rise from her seat. This slight deviation from etiquette does not go unnoticed. Especially since Cyrus is looking at her with a raised brow.

"That is a question for Rayne, is it not?" Devany responds, eyes on Nalin, before cutting her gaze towards Rayne. The spellcaster can't contain the shiver of fear that skates down her spine.

"What have you done?" Nalin asks, her eyes now on the spellcaster as she rounds the table, walking toward her.

"Why do you believe them over me? After everything we've been through." Rayne tries to deflect, her eyes narrowing as she glares up at Nalin, her anger surfacing now that the initial fear has worn off.

"Simple, there would be no point in lying when I can pry the truth from your lips. As you well know," Nalin states as Rayne now openly cries, shaking her head profusely.

"Now, are you going to speak your truth? Or are you going to force the issue?" Nalin asks calmly, but Rayne stubbornly turns her head, wiping the tears from her eyes and when she turns back around, her eyes have hardened.

"Do what you must, My Queen," she whispers. The words quiver with anger and fear. Her eyes cut to Devany and I.

"What did you do?" The words seem to chime from Nalin's lips, and I find myself fighting to resist answering her question. Even though I have done nothing wrong... lately.

"I did it because I love you. We have no business involving ourselves in a war on Galandir soil. King Minas will slaughter us all and more than likely enslave you." Rayne's eyes are glassy with more unshed tears as she looks up at Nalin, trying to implore her to see it from her point of view. "He promised if I eliminated them, he'd leave you and our people untouched," she states the last part quietly, staring at her hands.

"Who told you that?" I ask her, standing from my seat, stocking toward her.

"You're not my king," Rayne responds, her defiant eyes attempting to intimidate me.

"Answer the fucking question. You're a disgrace and have tainted our honor with your actions! What do you have to say for yourself?" Nalin once again slams her hand on the table, leaning forward so she's eye level with Rayne.

She stares at her, waiting. And when no answer is forthcoming; she stands shaking her head, turning her back on Rayne. "Get her out of my sight."

"What will you do with her?" Devany inquires, being no stranger to violence.

"She'll be put to death. Hung over the side of the battlement and left for the sea dragons to feast upon. We are a hard people, betrayal is unforgivable and punished harshly," she states matter-of-factly, once again at ease.

Two more people join us as Rayne is dragged away. They must be none other than Seiko and Alaric. Devany tenses slightly beside me.

The woman couldn't be older than her late twenties. Her

smooth black hair is cut short, shaved on one side and chin length on the other. Seiko's golden skin seems kissed by the sun. Delicately upturned copper eyes sit within a slightly rounded face. She's dressed similarly to Nalin, only her blouse is blue. The man, whom I assume is Alaric, is easily over two meters in height. Dark brown hair is plaited close to his head, both sides shaved close to his scalp. His piercing blue eyes seem to take in every detail of the room. A beard the same color as his hair hangs long past his chin.

Seiko smiles at us as she takes her seat, Alaric following suit. Nalin clears her throat, suddenly uncomfortable with the situation at hand. She looks back and forth between Devany and Seiko before huffing out of breath and resigning herself to the fact that this is happening one way or another.

"Allow me to introduce you to Queen Devany and King Asher of Draic." I watch the realization dawn on her face moments before she draws her sword and swings it out toward Devany's exposed chest. Without thinking, I reach my hand out, catching the blade with my bare hand. My blood stains the white tablecloth. I don't even feel the pain as the blade cuts deeper into my palm as she tries to push the sword past my hand into Devany.

"Enough. What have I told you about weapons at the table?" Nalin speaks out as if she's addressing two children. Seiko drags the blade back, allowing it to cut deeper into the palm of my hand. With a simple thought, the sword heats, causing her to drop it, blisters already forming on her palm.

"The next time you strike out at either my wife or myself, the consequence will be more than a burnt hand. My wife is not responsible for the sins of her father, and I will not allow others to punish her in his stead." Holding my hand up to show the deep gash in my palm. "And that," I gesture to her hand with my chin, "is for this."

When I once again take my seat, everyone else follows suit.

"They're here to offer you your throne back. To back you in your bid to recover your kingdom." Nalin is the first to speak, causing us to break eye contact to look at her.

"Give me back my throne? Something that already belongs to me?" A humorous laugh falls from her lips while her eyes harden.

"They're looking for allies in the upcoming war," Nalin informs Seiko with a hand under her jaw, thumb resting on her chin.

"No." Just one word. No negotiation. No explanation.

She can't possibly think she'll get her throne back without an ally.

Rising from my seat, I incline my head to first Nalin then Seiko, giving them the respect as due their station.

"Then we're done here." I turn toward Devany, holding out my hand. A silent command. "Devany?" When she places her hand in mine without the normal arguments, a slightly relieved breath leaves my lips. I never know if this is one of those times she decides to push back.

Once I've secured her hand, I help her rise from her seat. But before we can exit, she turns to Nalin.

"Thank you for your hospitality. I hope you'll consider our proposal."

She looks at Seiko. "I would say I'm sorry for your loss, but it will appear contrite and disingenuous. But what I can tell you is that I know my father's cruelty firsthand. Only time will tell if I'm anything like him. But you should at least choose for yourself. Get to know me, then make your choice." The quiet power in her voice resonates throughout the entire room.

"We'll take our leave shortly."

We walk quietly through several halls before we make it to the outlining piers where our ship is ready to set sail. Our items were already being brought aboard, courtesy of Bellicent. I hold my hand out to assist Devany as she steps onto the gangway. But before she can take a step on it, we hear our names being called. Cyrus closes the distance between us only to be stopped by three of our soldiers. He doesn't address them, merely looks at me as if he thinks I'll just let him pass. *Not likely.* I simply stare back at him with an arrogant smile on my face. I can practically feel the irritation rolling off him.

"May I speak with you?" He stares me down as he huffs out the question. I just look at him and when he says nothing else, I turn Devany back toward the gangway. Then I hear his voice once again.

"May I garner an audience with you, Your Majesty?" he asks, his voice sounding as if he's swallowed rocks. His hands twisted at his sides as he stands rigid before me. I'm fully prepared to make him wait it out when I hear Devany's voice.

"Forgive my husband, you may speak, consort," she says in that quiet way of hers that has all those around her stop and listen. While she gave him the right to speak, she also put him in his place by reminding him we are not equals. He's a better man than most, taking the reprimand with respect and bowing at the waist.

"My queen wishes for me to tell you that no matter how Seiko may feel, she is still open to an alliance and looks forward to meeting with you in the future," he says with far more respect than he's ever shown me.

"Please tell your queen we look forward to it as well." She looks at him with a soft smile as she waits for him to look at her. When he does, she dips her head courteously. The grin he gives her almost pisses me off, being that I've never seen him smile at anyone outside of Nalin.

"I will, Your Majesty." His voice was a surprised whisper. She gives him a slight nod of her head before turning around and boarding the ship. I'd say something to the bastard, but he's already turned away. So, I do the only thing I can and follow Devany aboard.

Chapter Thirty

DEVANY

We sail into a fog so thick I can practically feel it slide along my skin, chilling me to the bone. The dense haze blinds me, amplifying the sounds of the water lapping against the sides of the ship and with it the briny scent of the ocean.

The sounds of creatures breaking the water's surface—birds calling to one another—the creak of the wood deck below my feet. The sounds so crisp without my sight.

The serenity of the moment pulls at my soul, lulling me into a sense of peace.

A pair of arms circle my waist, dragging me back against a hard chest. "Careful, *a stór*. You're safe," Asher says to me, a hint of humor lacing his words.

If only that statement were true. But it can't be when everywhere I look, I see a war we'll need to fight.

I shift my weight, leaning back into him, soaking in his heat, and allowing it to warm me. With a wave of my hand, I gesture toward the scene in front of us, then realizing he couldn't see the motion through the haze.

"What is this?" I whisper, though the words echo around us as if bouncing off hollow walls.

"This is the spell that protects the rest of the world from Draic," he tells me gravely.

I turn my head to look up at him, even though I'm unable to see through the fog.

"Shouldn't that be the other way around?" I ask him, frustrated that I can't see his face to gauge his answer.

I hear him take a breath as if to answer when the fog breaks and I gasp at my first glimpse of Draic.

Before me stands a mountain so tall it disappears into the clouds. A waterfall descends from the summit, cascading this way and that way until it reaches the ocean below. The water seems to glow a beautiful turquoise blue, vivid like a jewel reflecting the sunlight.

At the base are twin cities on either side of the water flowing back into the ocean. Buildings made up of gray stone are carved from the massive outcroppings before the mountain with flat slate tile roofs of varying sizes are spread across the landscape. The windows are bright with warm light, some with smoke billowing from their chimneys to ward off the chill coming in off the ocean. A large stone bridge connects them. Ships and boats line the large ports, but it's the palace carved into the mountainside itself that takes my breath away.

Magnificent balconies of all shapes and sizes are scattered along its sharp surface. Some with small waterfalls spilling over the edges, others with stairs and walkways connecting them. The ornately carved windows and archways cover the mountainside.

Separating the twin cities and the mountain palace is a high wall that is almost impossible to see beyond. Within the enclosure is a grand stone gateway that leads to a massive door so tall that even from here I can make out the decorative silver panels and hinges. It's framed by two mighty columns that hold up a massive stone header.

I can hear the dull murmur of conversation and the laughter

of children playing—even the rich smell of food assaults my senses.

If a kingdom represents a ruler, what does this land say about my husband? Because while it's beautiful... breathtaking, really, it's also sharp and looming, one wrong step and you would fall to your death. *Well, now that I think about it... It's exactly like my husband.*

"Welcome home, *a stór álainn,*" Asher whispers, kissing me gently below my ear, eliciting a shiver from me.

I'm so engrossed in the view that it takes me a moment to realize that it's no longer daylight.

"Where is the sun?" I ask, not that the sun was missing per se... But it was definitely darker than it had been.

"There is only twilight and night here," Asher says with a heavy sigh.

"How's that possible? It's not like we're on a different plane of existence..." I say, laughing nervously. "Are we?" Admittedly, I'm a little anxious now that I asked the question. But Asher's laughter sets me at ease, even if it was at my expense. *The bastard.*

"Always so thirsty for knowledge, *a stór.* No, we're still on the same plane. But it exists by its own rules because the creatures that once roamed this land, well in all truth, still roam this land, didn't care for the light, so they willed it away. It's called Draic for a reason. Winged demons walk these lands and guard the skies," he tells me quietly, pointing above us. My head automatically follows, and what I see once again draws a gasp from my lips.

"Dragons," I whisper as if they'll hear my voice and come eat me. Because let's be honest... They could.

I watch large, winged shadows fly above the cloud cover. Long tails dance behind them as they dip and dive within the clouds.

"Shifters would be more accurate," he responds sadly. It's that note in his voice that has me pulling my eyes from the sky to look at him again.

"Shifters?" I ask quietly, but he's already nodding in answer to my question.

"Cursed to stay in their shifted form. Until they became more animal than person." He stops talking, eyes drifting back to the sky. "My father had once told me the story of this island. Of how its strong people were betrayed by a friend they considered family. Trapping them on this island so they couldn't prevent him from doing horrible things." His eyes come back to mine, and they burn with vengeance, but not for himself, for these people. His people.

"Who did this to them?" This time I'm the one to look up. Feeling a deep sadness for these people.

"Minas, the False King of Froslien." The muscle along his jaw jumps with each word.

This false king is much like my father. He has hurt far too many. Regrettably, I know little about him. That's something I'm going to have to remedy in the near future. In order to beat one's enemy—you must first know them. It's the one and only lesson my father has taught me that was worth a damn.

"How are you king here, if beasts rule this place?" I'm not sure why he smiles at me. But it makes my stomach dip despite the subject at hand.

"I asked." I pull back to get a better look at him.

"You asked?"

"Yes. I climbed that mountain and sat before them, asking them to follow me, promising to find a way to cure them and their children. To return them to their families." He waves a hand to the people milling about, the children in the streets, and that's when I realized all these people lost their loved ones to something much worse than death. They're here, but not. This is so much crueler than death.

"These are their mates and children that weren't affected by the curse. Human, Valore, spellcaster, they've all been looking for a way to bring their loved ones home, to no avail." The magic around us stirs and something in my soul responds. In this moment I know without a doubt I could break their curse, at the very least, ease it some. I would just have to give myself over to the very thing that scares me.

"When do I have to...?" I look down at my hands, my words tapering off as I remember the bloodletting and that all-encompassing fear that came with it. Asher takes hold of my chin, bringing my eyes back to his.

"It won't be the same, I promise." His voice is so soft with understanding. But I feel the humming beneath my feet, the call of the ocean and the land begging me to bleed for them.

Asher takes hold of my hand, leading me off the boat past the men and women hustling about, working to get the sails down and stowed.

We exit the ship, following the pier to the cobblestone streets leading into the cities. Up close, they're even more spectacular than I had first thought. The buildings are carved from the very landscape. Quite literally, one with its environment. Upon closer inspection, the slate roofs are indeed flat, but they appear to be some sort of landing for the dragons. The taller structures seem to have open balconies spanning their length.

Asher and I follow the bright blue river that flows toward the sandy shore and into the ocean. We pass men and women, children, and families. All of them, despite their hardships, seem so very happy. They wave and smile at Asher, even approach him, expressing how thankful they are for his safe return. He takes the time to introduce me to each one, and while they respond kindly to me, they are much more subdued.

A small family is making their way toward us. The mother is distraught, her eyes rimmed in red and her hair a mess.

"Your Majesty, is Marleen available?" the woman asks, swallowing several times past the emotions clogging her throat.

"No, she stayed behind to help with Ivann's wounded," Asher responds, taking in her disheveled appearance—the way her husband holds her close to his side.

Her hand covers her mouth as a choked sob breaks free, as if to smother the sound. She holds the babe in her arms tightly to her bosom, her arm slightly shaking. Her husband closes his arms around her, and she buries her face in his chest with the babe safe between them. When Asher looks upon them, it's with a more critical eye.

"Marcus... Jess, what's happened?" His voice was coaxing, the type of tone that inspires a belief that everything will be alright.

"It's our Marbel. She's not doing so well, sir." It's not Jess who answers but Marcus, he holds her as she cries softly against his chest.

Before Asher can speak, I step in. I want to help in any way I can. "May I see the child?" I asked them softly, feeling like an intruder in this moment.

"Who are you?" Marcus's tone is steeped in suspicion as his eyes swing in my direction.

"Marcus, allow me to introduce you to my wife, Queen Devany." The man's eyes widen marginally as he takes me in. His wife is too lost in her grief to notice.

Marcus mutely nods his head before turning and leading his small family silently toward the lower houses. The matching stone dwellings are only distinguishable by the brilliantly painted doors. Each home displays large planter-beds and potted gardens teeming with a variety of fruit trees and vegetables, herbs, and flowers. The vibrant colors give the subdued stone a warmth it lacks.

We stop in front of a lovely stone cottage marked by a brightly colored purple door. Four wide windows with ornamental boxes overflowing with flowers flank the door. Three large planter beds sit on either side of the walkway and the porch is crowded with potted trees and berry bushes.

I halt at the gate just looking up at the beautiful home before me. I can't help but think about the last proper home I had. The one I shared with my birth mother and the man who raised me as his own. I don't realize I'm crying until Asher is in front of me, cupping my face with both hands, wiping the tears from my cheeks with his thumbs.

"Are you alright?" he asks me quietly enough that the conversation is kept private. His eyes move between mine, gauging my reaction.

I take a deep breath before replying, "Yes, I'm fine. This isn't about me." Looking away, I try to escape the intensity in his gaze.

He tightens his hold on my jaw, causing my eyes to jump back to his. He leans forward, merely brushing his lips against my own. His hands fall away moments later before he turns and enters the home.

I cross the threshold and I'm hit with the overwhelming humidity that smothers the home. The soft whimpering sounds of a small child hangs heavy in the air.

"Where is she?" I ask the room in quiet demand. When no one answers, my gaze swings to the parents. Marcus and Jess seem so small curled around each other. The woman's sobs calm enough for her to respond. Her hands shake slightly as she points to a door on the far side of the room.

"What will you do?" Her voice sounds small, but there is steel in her eyes. The innate instinct to protect her children.

"Heal her, of course." I smile at her softly, even though she hiccups on yet another sob. I wish I could make this easier for them. But I can't.

"Don't make promises you can't keep. Even here we know your father and by proxy—you," her husband states from behind her, each word dripping with misplaced anger and hopelessness.

I look over her head, my gaze colliding with his. "I'm not my father, you'll realize that in time... Now I'll be needing a moment alone with her," I respond firmly, holding his eyes, waiting to see what he will say.

Marcus has no response, obviously stuck in his indecision. When he says nothing, I cross the space and enter the child's room, shutting the door behind me. I use a small blast of air to keep the door shut while I work on the poor girl.

The room is simple but decidedly girly. An ornate vanity with a near perfect mirror sits in the room's corner. Two large windows take up the far wall overlooking the garden of planters. Each one opened slightly, the scent of flowers drifting in on the chilled breeze. A beautiful silver chandelier hangs over a carved bed frame. The bedding is made up of white cotton and violet lace.

But it's the small girl that couldn't be more than ten that draws my attention. Thick flaxen waves blanket her pillow, and her tan skin is pale from whatever illness runs rampant in her veins. Marbel doesn't move and makes no sign that she's aware of my presence. Her pain-filled whimpers permeate the otherwise silent space.

My glamour slips away. The energy releasing into the world around us. My shoulder muscles stretch as they take on the heavy weight of my wings. I adjust my stance—rolling my shoulders back, rotating my neck from side to side to ease the tension. Next, I block out the world. Deep breath in. Deep breath out. When everything fades away, I loosen my hold on my shadows and pray to the Goddess for some semblance of control.

The shadows rush forward, blasting through the small crack I made for them, filling the room and choking out what light there is. The door vibrates against someone's repeated assault. I can barely hear Asher giving the order to back away before all is silent. To err on the side of caution, I push more air against the door, reinforcing it.

My shadows quickly overtake the home. The air becomes thick, and I open my eyes to find the world in shades of gray, the only colors are the glowing threads of life. Marbel's glows a brilliant sapphire, blinding in this in between place. Once I hold the child's strand within my shadowy grasp, I repair the harm caused by the illness. First the damage to her lungs—then the lining of her stomach—followed by the bruising of her kidneys. Each pained sound she makes breaks my heart, but I'm unable to make it easier for her.

Marbel doesn't wake right away, but her thread is well anchored in this world, the steady beat of it is like music in the shadowy silence of this place.

I take stock of my body, feeling the power writhing within my grasp—so wild and foreign.

The more I actively tap into this power, the harder it is to control. I feel like a conduit for a power my body was never meant to contain.

The shadows pull away, thinning out, stretching my senses and making my hold feel flimsy. The harder I try to draw them back to me, the leaner they seem to become.

Breathing deeply, I focus on the pulse of energy beneath my feet. The pull of the Elemental Druids. *Please, give me the strength to draw the shadows back to me.* I wrap my senses around them and pull. At first, they resist as if caught on something before rushing back. The impact pushes me back a step across the black stone floor. My body feels as if it could burst under the pressure. I grit my teeth, holding in the pained sound that wants to fight its way out. A light sheen of sweat coats my body. *Just a bit more. Almost done.*

"Hello," a small voice interrupts my mental tangent. Her voice rough from non-use. "Who are you?" It's a simple enough question. But for some reason, I find it hard to answer.

She tries to sit up, and I rush over, placing pillows behind her back. Her wavy flaxen hair hangs slightly tangled around her shoulders. Her large brown eyes blink up at me as she waits patiently for an answer to the question.

"I guess the simplest answer is that my name is Devany. I'm Asher's wife."

"Silly, doesn't that make you Queen Devany?" A smile brightens up her cherub-like face.

"I suppose you're right," I respond, replacing my glamour and releasing my hold on the door.

"Where'd your lovely wings go?" Marbel cants her head, sounding genuinely sad to see them go. By the rounded shell of her ears, I would say she's human. But that means nothing here. From what I've seen of Asher's kingdom, the populace is greatly diverse.

A wave of dizziness crashes over me so swiftly I have to grab the footboard of the bed to steady myself. Before I can call out, Marbel parents burst through the door. Marcus's angry eyes swing toward me, taking several threatening steps in my direction. He doesn't make it far before Asher's on him.

He slams Marcus into the wall. An elbow across his throat, cutting off his ability to breathe. Marcus's face turns bright red even as he struggles to get to me. Vaguely, I recognize the sound of Jess openly crying and laughing as she presumably holds the young girl in her arms.

"You dare to threaten my wife?" Asher growls at him.

But the arguing ends there as Marbel calls out for her father. "Papa?" she cries, her voice quivering with fear. No doubt scared of the struggle between her father and Asher. At the sound of her voice, Marcus's eyes shift to her, and a tear rolls down his red cheek.

"Asher," I softly call out to him, bringing his attention to me. He drops Marcus abruptly. Between one heartbeat and the next, I'm in his arms, heading for the door. Each step is heavy and angry. He holds me tightly to his body, fingertips digging into my skin.

"Thank you, My Queen," Marcus says as we're leaving the room, kneeling before his daughter. Her hands clasped tightly in his as he kisses them. I can't hear what he's saying, but it brings a smile to her face.

The room feels lighter now that the undercurrent of pain has lifted from the atmosphere.

"You're Welcome," I reply quietly as we walk out the door.

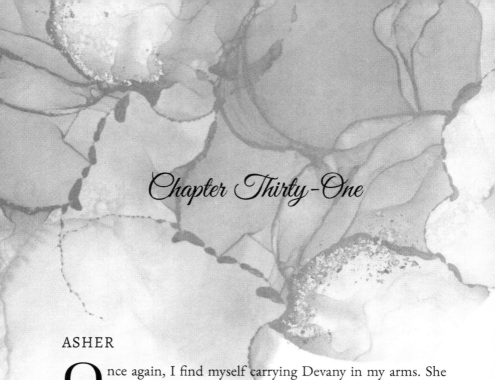

Chapter Thirty-One

ASHER

Once again, I find myself carrying Devany in my arms. She keeps pushing herself, and there's nothing I can do about it. I have no knowledge of what these shadows are, and therefore have no way of helping her.

I sigh heavily; I pull her closer, fearful of what tomorrow may bring. She tightens her arms around my neck, taking on some of her slight weight. Her closeness eases some of the tightness in my chest.

"Why does this keep happening?" she asks, leaning back to get a better look at me, her eyes bright with power, those delicate fingers of hers playing with the hair at the nape of my neck.

There's still a slight tremor in her limbs, though she's recovering quickly enough. Her features are pinched from the lingering pain and the parlor of her skin is pale and misted with a light sheen of sweat. Her skin cools quickly in the icy breeze, causing her to shiver in my arms. But other than that, she seems unharmed.

I still don't like this... Not that I have much of a say.

On the upside, I've noticed that her recovery time is greatly improving. Maybe this weakness is just her body adjusting to using magic after years of going without. At least that's what I'm hoping the cause is.

We reach the end of the lower row houses just before hitting the main road that leads to the courtyard. I know Devany would much rather enter our palace of her own accord, so I stop and lower her to her feet, holding on a moment longer to be sure she's steady before letting go completely.

The wind whistles by us, bringing with it the sound of the water crashing against the white sand beach, almost drowning out the distinct murmur of voices coming from the main road. The light has dimmed considerably since our arrival. Soon enough, nightfall will be upon us.

Devany looks up at me from beneath her lashes. Her beautiful moon lit eyes holding me captive while her hand slowly rises to brush a lock of hair from my forehead. Her cool fingers trail from my temple to my jaw before she lets her hand drop. I catch her wrist, bringing it to my mouth and with my eyes on hers, I place a kiss on her palm.

Her breath catches when my lips touch her skin, and I can't help but smirk against her hand. I do love the way she responds to me. Devany yanks her arm from my grasp with a narrow-eyed glare. Promptly turning on heel and leaving me behind, she heads for the main road. Her reaction only makes my smile double.

More than amused by her antics, I follow in her tantalizing wake. The temperature drops as the wind coming off the ocean water increases. The streets darken as we move from twilight to nightfall. Devany stops several meters from the main road. Her hands flex at her sides, tightening and loosening as she seems to hesitate.

A gust of wind howls through the mostly empty street, picking up her hair and allowing her caramel locks to float on the breeze. The wind rustles her thin silk blouse, causing her to visibly shiver.

I jog up to her, easily closing the distance between us. She doesn't turn to look, nor does she acknowledge me. A breeze once again blowing by, eliciting another shiver. I grab her by the elbow, turning her in my direction, noticing her lips have taken on a bluish tint.

Removing my tunic, I hold it out in front of her and when all she seems to do is stare at me; I give it an impatient shake. Several moments pass by while she contemplates her next move. Until she finally rolls her eyes and shakes her head in disbelief, mumbling beneath her breath. Wordlessly, she shoves her arms into the garment with rough, jerky movements. I drag the coat up her arms and shoulders, trapping her hair beneath the collar. Gathering the heavy mass of curls in my hands, I move it out from underneath the fabric, and drape it over her shoulder.

Devany eyes me for a moment before she drops her head, resting her forehead against my chest, her body riddled with tension. Not knowing what else to do, I wrap her up in my arms, pulling her closer. I rest my chin on top of her head and sigh heavily against her hair, disturbing the strands.

"I'm no one's queen, Asher," she confesses to me, stepping out of my embrace, her eyes fixed on my chest.

As the seconds tick by, Devany stares at my chest after she gives me that shit response. Her voice barely registers over the breeze.

I take hold of her face, leaning down so we're eye to eye. Her breath is shallow and jagged, and each cool exhale brushes along my lips. She grabs hold of both my wrists. Her grasp strong—fingers digging in—nails leaving crescent moon indentions. Much like she had in Naphal.

Her tongue swipes along her lower lip, reminding me how much I love the way she tastes and because I just can't help myself. I gently brush her soft lips with mine, allowing myself that small taste.

"Yes, you are! You're my queen!" I tell her firmly with my eyes on hers.

"But... I..." she stutters, clearly frustrated, having been through so much in such a short time.

"Talk to me, Devany," I whisper across her lips. The words said so low that it feels like it could drift away on the breeze. My thumb trails along her lower lip, my eyes trained intently on hers.

I slide one of my hands into her hair, tilting her head back as I pull her closer. With each breath she takes, her delicate breasts brush my chest, making me acutely aware of the way she feels in my arms. Her soft curves pressed against me. That floral scent of hers surrounds me, teasing my senses. I don't repeat myself, just simply wait as she puts her thoughts in order.

"Your people aren't safe if I'm here. No one is. My father will come for me, especially now with the rumors of what I've done." Her response is practical... matter-a-fact even. But it's the quiver in her voice that gives her away.

"He doesn't matter... You are no man's secret. Least of all his. Let him see the wolf he allowed behind his walls. See the woman who shall end his life..." I trail off, looking back and forth between her eyes. "One day very soon. Let them all see, *a stór milis.*" Devany sways towards me, erasing any space there was between us.

She lifts on the tips of her toes, curling her hands around the back of my neck and I watch spellbound as she draws me into a kiss. Her lips sweep over mine so faintly that had I not been standing so perfectly still I would've missed it. When Devany's eyes open, the silver has almost been swallowed whole by her pupils.

It has to be unnatural to want her the way I do. My body's reaction to her always feels... inevitable. Her lips connect with mine once more, licking at the seam, and I open for her, more than happy to give in. When the kiss breaks, it leaves both of us panting. She kisses the corner of my mouth before gliding across my cheek to my ear. Her sweet breath skates along the shell, eliciting a groan that rattles in my chest. My grip tightens around her waist even as she pulls away to look at me.

"I'm so tired, Asher... I'm so very tired," she confesses softly. Tears pooling in her eyes, making them glitter.

I lean forward, brushing my lips over each eye, tasting the salty liquid on my lips. With both hands in her hair, I pull her forward, and she opens for me without hesitation.

Devany's addictive taste bursts on my tongue. Just that small sample has me groaning into her mouth. Clearly enjoying my reaction to her, she wraps her arms around my neck, clawing at my shoulders in an attempt to get closer.

We break apart breathlessly and Devany's eyes timidly meet mine. Her tears finally win the battle and spill over onto her cheeks. Gently, I wipe them away with my thumbs, placing a soft kiss on the top of her head.

"We're going to meet quickly with Ansel, then head to bed." She nods in response.

I can only imagine what this must be like for her. She seems to get herself under control as she gives me one more small nod, but I can still see the tension around her eyes and the rigid set of her shoulders.

I raise my arm, holding it parallel to the floor. Without hesitation, she places her hand and arm over mine. While this position is overtly formal, it has the added benefit of giving her something to lean on.

We make our way to the main road. Walking swiftly, following the water canal to the town center. The lanterns along the street lighting the way. We pass homes and stores before coming to a stop at the city center. At the far end stands the Great Wall, built of stone mined from this very mountain, a scene of dragons in flight carved into the rock face. Beyond that wall are moon gardens made up of flowers that only bloom in moonlight.

The center of the town square is punctuated by a large fountain standing three meters in height. Dedicated to paying homage to the four corners. Each corner is represented by a stone dragon with metal wings in a kaleidoscope of color. Their claws hold the embodiment of the eight Druids: water and summer, fire and autumn, air and winter, earth and spring. The glowing blue water flows through it, cascading over the five shelves, each larger than the last, before pooling in the large stone basin.

Ansel meets us at the large gate, breaking up the stone wall that surrounds the palace. He moves forward, grabbing my forearm just below the elbow, pulling me into a hug. When we pull back, I scrutinize my friend. His beard is a little unkempt and his hair longer than it has been in quite some time. But looks no worse for the wear.

"You look like shit," I say, grinning widely at him.

"You don't look much better," he volleys back, like the smartass he is.

I take a breath in preparation to verbally spar with my second in command. Which is sure to devolve quickly into half-hearted insults... But let's be honest, that's half the fun. Devany cuts us off and she couldn't care less how we feel about it.

"Did you run into any trouble while we were away?" Short and quick, my wife never one to fuck around. Her eyes locked on his, categorizing every movement.

Ansel's eyes narrow in her direction. His lips press into a thin line clearly holding back all the things he'd like to say. But I know he respects me too much to act on it. He turns his full attention to Devany bowing at the waist, showing her the respect of her station. Even if it's a bit stiff.

"We ran into no problems, Your Highness." The reply is very matter-a-fact, and his voice lacks warmth as he remains bent at the waist eyes cast down as he replies.

He rises from his bow, looking Devany over. His keen eyes take in everything, paying close attention to the tightness around her eyes and shoulders and the almost translucent parlor of her skin as fatigue sets in.

He looks straight at me before he looks at Devany once more. "Perhaps calling it a night is in order," Ansel says this more to himself than to us before turning and walking toward the grand palace doors, certain that we will follow.

I look more closely at Devany and realize that she's dead on her feet. *I wonder how she would react if I picked her up?*

Ansel waits for us just inside the foyer as I keep my steps slow and measured for Devany's sake. Once we step over the threshold, he turns away once more, leading us toward the grand staircase carved out of the mountain wall. The wall across from the stairs has a small waterfall that cascades down the roughly honed stone, flowing steadily into a spring embedded within the floor running the length of the spacious room then disappearing beneath large slate slabs, creating pathways.

Devany follows Ansel up the slate staircase, and I'm not far behind. We bypass the second floor, heading straight for the third, where my private rooms are. The pops of blue in the furniture contrast with the dark gray stone and give the space a relaxing feel.

Once we reach the third floor, I nod at Ansel and lead Devany to the rooms on the right. We cross over the threshold, and I head for the large sea glass doors leading to the balcony, I open them letting fresh air into the room. On this side of the palace, we have a clear view of the ocean and the thick mist that hides us away.

I can hear Devany shuffling her feet nervously behind me.

"Through those doors there," I point with my head as I fiddle with the locking mechanism, "you have a private bathtub connected to your rooms. You'll find fresh clothes in the next room." She doesn't acknowledge me, at least not verbally. I can feel her heavy stare on my back before she relents and heads for the bathtub. We're finally home.

Chapter Thirty-Two

DEVANY

My bathhouse, though small, rivals Naphal's in opulence. The honed walls glitter in the candlelight. The iridescent veins breaking up the black stone, looking like the night sky with stars lighting the way. There's an ornately carved bath basin that stands in the middle of the room, constantly being filled with water flowing in from the ceiling above. The excess water flows back into the stone below.

It feels good to finally wash away the ocean's grime. I close my eyes and let my mind drift. How my life has changed so much in so little time is beyond me. But here we are.

With great effort, I pull myself from the bliss of the hot water and make my way to the bedroom where I find a nightgown laid over the bedding.

The sheer silk panels drape over my body in a rich dark blue that stands out against my skin. I stare at myself in a large full-length mirror that leans against the stone wall with the night sky glittering behind me, my hair hanging in loose curls down my back.

It feels both frightening and exhilarating to look at my reflection without my glamour. The two competing emotions war within me.

The curve of my wings sits just above my shoulders, their iridescent feathers shine in an array of colors under the low light of the lanterns. The sharply pointed ears adorned with a series of hoops in mixed metals peeking out of my caramel curls while the shimmer of my eyes and skin gleam richly with power.

I barely recognize the otherworldly creature staring back at me from the mirror's glass.

I watch as she lifts her hand and traces the outer shell of her ear, following the sharp line of her throat. Her fingers graze the obsidian pendant that lays warm against her skin. I close my eyes to block out the vision before me, if only for a moment, to calm my emotions.

"You're beautiful, you know?" His whiskey-soaked voice breaks through my thoughts, my eyes jumping to his in the mirror's reflection.

I watch the play of his muscles as he prepares for bed. The way his charcoal gray sleeping pants hang low on his hips. The expanse of bronze skin encased in intricate golden tattoos, interlocking vines that spiral and twirl. His curved horns stand tall and graceful, covered in the same golden tattoos.

Turning away from the mirror, I watch him wring the water out of his hair with a towel—his shoulders and arms flex with each movement. Droplets of water slide between his shoulder blades, following the line of his spine. The sight makes my mouth go dry. May the Goddess help me, but I'm hapless to stop my attraction to him.

I no longer have a heart to give this man. Not that he's asked for it.

He notices he has my attention and throws the wet towel on a nearby chair, walking over to me. I tilt my head back, as I maintain eye contact. I refuse to back down from the intensity I see in his hooded eyes, even if being the center of his focus is always overwhelming.

Slowly reaching out, Asher rubs his thumb along my lower lip. A shiver I can't control works its way down my spine and he smirks down at me, loving the way I react to his touch. *The bastard.*

His fingers continue on their path, trailing along my jaw, down my throat to skate across my collarbone. His touch is light and seductive. When his fingertips meet the edge of my pendant, he strokes it casually. His eyes ask a silent question begging to be answered. His focus is so intense that I find it hard to keep from squirming under the weight of it.

"You never take this off." Not a question, but a statement.

"I can't. I've tried. Luna said it was spelled and bound by blood. It can only be removed by the one who put it there," I answer, feeling a little breathless from his touch. But then again, I always do when he's this close.

"And who, dear wife, placed this around your pretty neck?" His tone is deceptively soft while those beautiful long fingers trail across my collarbone, his calluses scraping the delicate skin.

"Once upon a time, a young knight saved a girl in the woods. To let her know that she wasn't alone, he placed a pendant of stone about her neck." I keep it a vague and whimsical story, pretending that my heart doesn't hurt when I think about it. I loved him as a child. When I was lost and broken... May the Goddess help me, but the man in front of me... His broken pieces call to mine. We fit together like a puzzle box. But I still can't keep from pushing him.

"Does that make you jealous?" I taunt him, though the words lose some of their effect with how breathless I am from his touch.

His darkening eyes are on mine as he answers. "Why should it? You're mine." He heads for the large balcony at the far end of our bedroom. His shoulders are tense and there's a rigidity to his steps as he walks away.

"A ring does not denote ownership." I'm more than a little pissed off when he dismisses something that helped me survive all the beatings. It represented another living soul who cared whether I lived or died. And he has the balls to act as if he owns me.

He turns to look at me, eyes on the pendant. "No piece of jewelry does." He prowls back as barely-leashed violence vibrates beneath his skin. Each step is measured as if he's working to keep himself from lashing out at me.

"I'm jealous of a man who doesn't exist," he says with a shallow laugh. His words are angry, but there was an undercurrent of hurt I can't quite place.

"Just what the fuck does that mean?" My anger rises to the surface. But he keeps talking as if I hadn't spoken at all.

"How about I tell you a story, wife?" his words drip with sarcasm. I open my mouth to respond to his question, but the look he gives me has me closing my mouth painfully with an audible click.

"Once upon a time, a boy found a lost princess in the woods. She was running from dragons," he said the words so quietly, but his eyes were hard—almost cruel. Tears sting the back of my eyes while my mind tries to reconcile what he is actually saying.

"And for the first time in a long time, he wanted to be the hero. *I wanted* to be her hero. So, he slayed her dragons. One. At. A. Time." Each word is punctuated with a step. He cants his head as he watches me struggle for breath.

"Imagine the pain I felt when I stood in front of that princess after spending ten long years fighting my way back to her. Ten years trying to become worthy of her, only to have her look at me without an ounce of recognition in her beautiful eyes. To have her look at me as if I were unworthy." The words were still barely more than a whisper on an angry breath.

"Asher." That one word is ripped from my throat as I finally lose the battle with my tears.

Each one leaves a salty trail along my skin, and he leans forward, licking up one and then another. Before taking my mouth in a kiss so achingly soft that it feels like my heart is breaking. His hands reach behind my neck and release the clasp on my necklace. For the first time in ten years, I feel the weight of it slide down my neck and into his waiting hand. Asher turns his back on me before heading for the door.

"Where are you going?" There is so much noise in my head that I wasn't sure I had asked the question aloud until he answered.

"Out... I can't be here with you right now." It felt cruel to have him leave me here like this. But it's probably for the best. Who knows what the two of us may say to each other right now? But I just need to know one thing before he goes.

"What happened...?" I suck in a shuttering breath when his sad eyes turn to me. "What happened that night? ... please."

My eyes move to my necklace in his fist. Watching his knuckles whiten as he squeezes that much harder.

"I followed your scent back to your cottage. Your father was already dead, but I heard voices and laughter coming from the back of the house..." he trails off while his eyes stray to the floor. His tone is so devoid of warmth that you would wonder if it had ever known joy. "I'm sorry, they damaged your mother beyond repair. Her attackers died painful, but the one that had your scent on him." His eyes snap back to mine, now burning with hate. "I took my time with him. He died slowly, one piece at a time." His eyes soften slightly as he looks at me.

"I knew who you were the moment I saw your mother. We were traveling back to my family when your aunt came upon us. I have no idea how she was on that road at that time. It seemed serendipitous. She took you and told me to come back when I was worthy. I placed this on your neck so you would know I was out there—that you weren't alone. So, you would have something to remember me by." His voice was once again soft, his eyes no longer brimming with hate. He looks down at the necklace in his hand. "A lot of good that did me."

He turns, giving me his back once more and leaving me alone

in the empty room staring after him with tears freely falling from my eyes. The pain coming from inside of me is so intense that I curl in on myself, wrapping my arms around my stomach, hoping to hold it all in. I crawl into bed, allowing oblivion to take me.

Chapter Thirty-Three

DEVANY

I've been laying in this bed feeling sorry for myself far longer than I care to admit. My eyes stray to the door for the hundredth time, begging the Gods to make him walk through it. When he again fails to do so, I get up and start pacing the room. Do I stay here? Or do I hunt him down?

I stop abruptly, my eyes wandering to the open balcony door. The sheer curtains bellowing in on the salty ocean breeze. *Fuck this.* I will not wait around for him to grace me with his presence. *Absolutely not.* I'm going to climb to the top of the mountain and cement my connection with the land. The mountain begins to hum as if it heard my thoughts and wholeheartedly approves.

It's probably best to start my climb from here, because if anyone were to see me leaving, they'd run and tell Asher. So, I dress with care, pulling on warm clothes for my icy climb up the mountain.

I walk out onto the balcony, tilting my head back to get a better look at the rock face. The mountainside is jagged enough to give me plenty of places to grip. I'm thankful for it since I'm not secure enough in my wing strength to fly to that dizzying height. I make my way to the edge and step up onto the rail, bringing myself closer to the rock wall. Reaching up, I get a good grip before leaning out to get a foothold and step off the rail completely.

It takes several hours of pulling myself up one rock at a time, stopping whenever I come to a ledge large enough for me to stand on. If I were human, there's no way I could have done this. As it is, my arms and legs burn from holding up my weight. Sweat slicks my skin and pastes my hair to my face. My eyes feel gritty from the wind blowing dirt into them and even though the temperature has dropped, my skin is flush.

After a small eternity, I reach a substantial plateau. The problem is that it's currently occupied by dragons. Three adults and two children. They're as magnificent as they are frightening. The young ones are slightly taller than Asher, and he has at least a quarter of a meter on me. The other three are the size of small buildings, though one is just a hair smaller than the other two. All of them vary in color. The younger two are playing in what must be a hot spring because I can smell the sulfur in the air from here. The other three are watching on, though the larger ones are paying more attention to their surroundings.

A few pebbles cascade over the side as I adjust my hands. The rocks barely make a sound, but they hear it just the same. All three of their heads snap in my direction, baring their teeth at me. The one I assume to be a male approaches as another stands in front of the two younglings and what appears to be the mother.

If I'm going to plead my case, it's now or never. "Please, I mean you no harm. My name is Devany... I'm Asher's wife. I only mean to bleed for the land and possibly help with this curse business. I don't want to get anyone's hopes up, I may not be able to do anything. But I would like to try, nonetheless," I hurry to say, not wanting them to eat me. *Please, Goddess, let them understand what I'm saying to them.*

The dragon in front makes a series of growl-like noises as he communicates with the others. When he finally turns back to me, his eyes hold a dangerous glint. Just before he runs at me in a full sprint. On instinct, I raise my hands to protect my face. The sudden movement knocked me off the small ledge. In my panic, I forget I have wings of my own. The scream ripped from my lungs is immediately swallowed by the wind, and I come to an abrupt, painful halt as a rough talon circles my body, plucking me out of my free fall and slicing shallowly through my fighting leathers, drawing blood. It scares the shit out of me.

"Calm yourself, little Valore, I mean you no harm... Yet." His rich, dark laughter fills my mind.

I try to stave off my rising panic. I really do. But I make the mistake of looking over my shoulder to see the ground so far away. If my heart pounds any harder, it's going burst from my chest. My stomach bottoms out when he banks left and spirals higher. Then we crest one of the many peaks before diving into a break in the mountain. We come to a stop, and he hovers before he sets me down with great care.

I look up to find myself surrounded by dragons, their tails shifting back and forth violently. Malevolence bleeds into the atmosphere as the shifters shuffle from foot to foot, agitated with the intrusion on their territory. Many of them growl and bare their teeth. The others closing rank around the entrance of a cave where they cut off my view of their young.

A growl deeper and darker than the rest rings out around us, echoing off the steep walls. It sounds like it's coming from everywhere and nowhere. Several shifters step back to reveal a dragon substantially larger than the rest. This must be the alpha. His coloring is a rich royal purple that iridescently shifts with each step he takes toward me. I don't bow, but I incline my head in respect.

"I hear you are the new queen of this land and have made promises you have no way of keeping." I bristle at the assumption and the sarcasm. I realize these people have been through a lot, which is the only reason I let the slight slide.

"Firstly, I made no such promise, only that I wish to try.

Second, out of respect, I came here to introduce myself. Whether you like it or not, I am queen," I reply evenly. After all, if you must yell to get your point across, you don't deserve to lead. If a dragon could look surprised and amused, I'd say that was the look crossing his regal face. You can almost see the man beyond the dragon.

"So, the question is, are you going to allow me to try, Alpha?" I ask him sincerely. These are his people—that makes this decision his.

"You may." His tone is somber, as if he's already disappointed.

I place my hand against the ground, reaching for the energy bond to this kingdom and release a trickle of magic, waiting for the answering pull. I sift through the magic tied to this land, looking for the spell binding them to their shifted forms. I stand with my shoulders slumped. How do you tell a group of people who have suffered so much that there's only so much you can do? *My heart breaks for them.*

"Go on, tell me how there's nothing you can do. How you tried, but you've raised my pack's hope only to disappoint," he growls, baring his teeth. Even the voice inside my head has a slight growl to it. I don't fault his agitation. He's had no way to help his people as he watches them suffer year after year with no end in sight.

"I'll say nothing of the sort." Surprise once again crosses his remarkably animated face.

"What then?"

"The curse can't be broken," he growls at me again, cutting me off, but I hold up my hand to stop him. "Let me finish. Quite a few of your pack mates are too far gone to pull back. I'm sorry." I stop to allow that to sink in and carry on when he nods his head. "Now there is a workaround. I'll be able to give you back the ability to shift, but only while you're within the mist. In order to leave, you'll have to be in human form. You'll be unable to shift outside these borders." I lay out the parameters of what I'm offering while keeping my eyes on his.

He nods his head, and I give him one final warning. "You may want your people to land. This could be disorienting for them." He lets out the loudest roar I've ever heard, wreaking havoc on my sensitive hearing. I cover my ears, falling to my knees as pain pierces through my head. Dragons drop from the sky, presumably to land wherever they find a place.

Not bothering to get up from my knees, I pull a sliver dagger from my boot. Taking several deep breaths, I center myself, knowing I'll have to tap into the darker parts of my soul. I wait for him to give me permission to begin, and when he gives me a single nod, I slice the blade into my palm. I hold my fist out over the hard ground, allowing my blood to pool before placing both hands within it.

The surrounding energy connects with the magic in my blood, and I release the tether holding the shadows at bay. The world is plunged into darkness as the temperature drops dramatically within the shadows. The voices around me rise to a fever pitch of panic. Seconds tick by while I isolate the souls of those not too far gone. Once I have them in my grasp, I alter the curse. Sweat beads along my brow despite the chill. I continue to push, trying to finish before the shadows consume me. Oblivion pulls at me as the last souls slip through my shadowy embrace. I have just enough energy to pull back and lock the shadows away. When the edges of my vision darken, the sweet release of sleep sweeps in.

When I come to, a beautiful man stands before me. His ember skin shimmers purple in the morning light as violet eyes stare at me with interest. Not sexual—more like he wouldn't mind taking me apart to see what makes me tick.

"What are you, little Valore?" the man standing next to him asks. They could be twins. The only difference I see is the alpha's purple coloring, whereas this man's is green.

"Yes... I'm curious as well," the alpha interjects thoughtfully, running his hand over his overgrown beard.

"I'm Valore." Narrowing my eyes on this man for bring to light something I'd rather not look too closely at.

"You are far more than that, but I can see you are not ready to face it just yet." There's an undercurrent of humor lacing his voice.

Rather than deal with that, I turn in a circle, looking at all those now on two legs and very much naked. I look back at him, lifting one brow as if to remind him of what I've just done. Instead of looking contrite, he seems to be enjoying my little display.

"What's your name? If I'm going to see so *much* of you..." I trail off, letting my eyes drift down his body and back to his face, "shouldn't I at least know your name?" I respond primly.

"It's Harken, My Queen." He smiles boldly at me. "Why don't I take you back to your husband before I decide to keep you?" he states like that's even an option and I have no say. Silly male.

"If it's all the same to you, I'd rather fly down myself," I reply, feeling the heavy weight of my wings pull at my shoulders before flaring them out to show their impressive span.

"If you can fly, why didn't you do that to begin with?" The man beside him asks.

"I've spent most of my life hiding what I am. Because of this, it's not second nature to me," I say before driving off the side of the mountain, feeling the wind in my hair. Feeling... Free.

Chapter Thirty-Four

ASHER

It wasn't ever my intention for Devany to find out. Especially not after realizing she had no genuine memory of me... Not that it matters now.

Regardless, I shouldn't have left her like that... But, had I stayed, things would've likely escalated.

So, I walked out and headed for the sparring rings to put Ansel through his paces, in an attempt to clear my head and cool my temper.

Sweat and dirt coat my skin, causing my hair to stick to my face and neck. The air is thick with the scent of the ocean mixed with blood and dirt. Our breath crystallizes in the frigid morning air. Not that I pay the chill any mind with the fire burning in my veins.

This toxic mix of emotion is overwhelming Anger. Irritation. Hurt. I realize my emotions are irrational. Let's be honest, she was a traumatized adolescent who had just seen her father murdered. I'm sure that until that point in her life, she must have been fairly sheltered. But knowing this doesn't stop my heart from breaking just a little.

White-hot pain erupts from my left bicep, slicing through all thoughts.

"Are you going to fight or just stand there and let me use you as target practice?" Ansel asks in a disgruntled and somewhat putout tone. *Asshole.* Can't he see I'm going through something?

My eyes drift up to the windows above the massive door leading into the palace—the windows that lead into the room I left her in.

I have to physically fight the urge to go to her, locking my knees in place. I turn back in time to counter Ansel's strike... Just barely. He slides back two steps, but halts his attack, eyes drifting toward the sky. Mine following suit as a startled breath leaves his lungs.

"What the fuck is going on?" he asks quietly, eyes staying fixed on the sky. The voices around us rise in panic. People running and looking for shelter.

"My sentiments exactly," is my only reply as dragons of all shapes and sizes drive toward us, landing anywhere they can find space.

I move toward the one closest to me, but before I do so much as raise my hand to gesture peace, it lets out a piercing scream that rocks the ground beneath our feet. The others do the same. They seem almost startled by the pain—eyes wild and fearful—their large bodies tumbling to the side. The people within the city proper drop to their hands and knees, screaming in tandem with the dragons.

I drop to my knees as well, covering my ears in an attempt to lessen the damage. I feel what can only be blood leaking from my ears. The sticky fluid dripping into my palms and trickling down my wrists.

Between the sound of my heartbeat and the screams, it's hard for me to focus. The voices vibrate through my mind. It takes a moment for me to realize they're not only screaming aloud—but also telepathically. The noise is so full of pain that it breaks a piece of my soul.

Their bodies convulse—bones breaking—scales receding to reveal fresh, clean, unmarked skin. The gory scene plays out as the screams increase.

My eyes collide with a young dragon a few meters away. The grunts and growls taper off to a more human tone until forty naked men and women stand before me.

"This has Devany written all over it," Ansel says, his eyes on our newest citizens.

"They're going to need homes," I say on a quiet breath as I rotate in a small circle. His head nods absentmindedly, taking in the sheer number of people. This is but a small portion of the dragon shifter population on this island.

Out of the corner of my eye, I see the soft light of our morning sun catch on the iridescent black feathers of my wife's wings. She glides down to us, soaring among the dragons, their large bodies dwarfing her own.

I lean against the fountain in the center of town, watching as she flies closer, gracefully twirling in the sky above. When she lands, there's barely a sound as her small feet touch down and she continues to walk without missing a beat.

The three shifters that flanked her in the sky land beside her. Their transition from beast to man happens quicker and far less painful than what we witnessed down here.

Two of the three shifters drop back to walk behind them. Which means the shifter that walks directly beside her must be the alpha. He stands about a half meter taller than Devany, the reflection of purple scales offsets his warm skin and violet eyes that pulse with strength.

"Wife, I take it you're responsible for this?" I ask her, looking around, taking in the sheer scale of what she's accomplished here today.

"How...? You've broken the curse?" Ansel asks her quietly. My eyes come back to her, watching as she wrings her hands nervously.

What could she possibly have to be nervous about? She just

saved our people from a curse they've suffered through for decades.

She looks around at the shifters we now have on two legs before her eyes land on Harken. He smiles at her, his eyes traveling the length of her body. A hint of pink colors her cheeks and I'm unable to stop the growl that claws its way up my throat. The bastard has the audacity to wink at me. Next thing I know, I'm across the courtyard, pulling Devany into my arms. His smile doubles and he wiggles his eyebrows at me. *Asshole.*

To bring us back to the situation at hand, I repeat the question to Devany.

"I could not break the curse, only alter it. They can shift within our land. But if they wish to leave, it will be on human legs." Her voice is soft, but not without its strength. While this is not an ideal outcome, it's a vast improvement.

I look toward Harken, catching his attention. "You are, of course, welcome to stay in the palace. As well as those who do not have a place to go. Tomorrow we will look into a more permanent solution." He replies with a dip of his head before directing his people.

Devany's body sags in my arms, her eyes closing and her head dropping to my shoulder. Not giving her any time to argue, I swing her up into my embrace.

"Asher, put me down," she whispers harshly, her voice heavy with embarrassment.

Her eyes dart nervously around, but no one pays us any mind as I leave the courtyard, heading straight for the palace.

"Shhh... I'm taking you to bed."

Chapter Thirty-Five

ASHER

Devany has spent the past week avoiding me. She keeps our conversations to that of our people and their needs, doing her damnest to prevent us from talking about all things we've left unsaid. The only time she's vulnerable is in the quiet of the night, while she's wrapped up in my arms.

The only time she speaks more than a few words at a time is when we're discussing our new housing crisis. We are egregiously unprepared for the influx of unexpected denizens. So, we spend our days working to remedy the situation. Our citizens are warm and welcoming, and everyone does their part to help the newest members of our community make our kingdom feel like home.

Those Valore amongst us with a gift for the earth element draw stone from the dirt, creating homes where there had been none. For those who lack the earth element, they carve and stack stones one at a time. But the blood, sweat, and tears are worth it just to witness the joy they feel when stepping into their new homes.

Devany and Bellicent toil near the ocean's edge, working on the lower row houses. While Ansel, Harken, and I build a home for a family of five. But my eyes continue to wonder in her direction, taking in every smile she gives freely. The way her eyes light up when someone engages with her. The look of concentration on her face as she builds a home for one of our own.

It makes my heart hurt. I miss her smart mouth.

The day ends when our pale sun sets, finally giving way to nightfall. Bringing an end to the day's projects. Tonight, we celebrate the first full moon of spring with a fête of baked goods and succulent meats, cooked over open flame. A break well earned.

We all head back to our homes to clean up for supper and it feels good to be home. I've missed this—the camaraderie—the sense of belonging. If only Devany would speak to me.

It doesn't take long for everyone to gather on the sandy shoreline, migrating toward the fires. The flames stretch and dance casting long shadows into the darkness. The atmosphere is charged with excitement and the elderberry wine is following freely as the space fills with conversation and laughter. Children run from one bonfire to the next while the other youths attempt to keep them out of trouble.

The fires that dot the beach are surrounded by benches and filled with people. The scent of roasted meat assaults my senses, making my mouth water. Those manning the spits remove the meats from the flames. While others load up plates with sides dishes. It doesn't take long before plates are being passed around and the conversation quiets some as we all enjoy our meal. Devany sits next to me quietly, still not fully comfortable with open social interactions. Bellicent helps ease her into the situation, keeping her engaged in the festivities. It brings an unbidden smile to my face every time her face lights with laughter.

I watch the flickering firelight paint her skin orange as it distorts the shadows playing along her face.

With Devany barely saying more than two words to me at a time, we've yet to discuss the revelation of our shared past, and it feels like the calm before the storm... I have no idea how to proceed. I Know I can't continue to allow her to stick her head in the sand. But where do we begin? Too many things are happening around us all at once. So many obstacles are being thrown in our path. There's just not enough time to spend on *us*.

With that thought, I rise to my feet, startling Devany. She looks up at me with those innocent eyes that have seen too much, her lips parting slightly in surprise.

I hold my hand out in front of me. "Join me in bed, wife." The deeper octave in my voice can't be mistaken.

My eyes take in every detail of her face before landing on her mouth as she traps her lip between her teeth, warring with herself on whether she should take my hand. Her cheeks turn a fetching shade of pink, but she puts her hand in mine, nonetheless.

Even with the fire, the icy breeze off the ocean kisses our skin, pulling a shiver from her slender frame. I remove my tunic, holding it out for her. Not one to pass up warmth, she wordlessly steps into it. When she's dressed against the chill, we make our way across the sand. The ocean mist coats my skin and Devany's scent floats on the breeze, ensnaring me as it always does.

With everyone down by the shore eating and drinking, the walk back to the palace is quiet. The glowing stream cutting through the city proper, leading to the equally empty palace.

I move aside, allowing her to step over the threshold in front of me. She leads the way up the stairs with me close behind. Not that I mind, it's a beautiful view.

Devany walks to the middle of our room with her back to me. My tunic slides from her shoulders and along her arms, catching on her fingertips before floating to the floor. I watch the way her sleeveless arms move. My eyes follow the line of her back to the loosely fitted pants that do nothing to hide her perfect ass.

Her shoulders are tense, and without looking back at me she asks, "Should we talk about—" she pauses, taking a deep breath as her shoulders creep up by her ears, "about it..."

Finally, she turns toward me, her eyes finding mine, but she looks so lost. I decide to keep it light, starting much the same way as the last conversation.

"Let me tell you a story about a brave little girl I met in the forest." I smile at her, hoping she'll see the humor in starting this way now that emotions aren't running so high. But when she doesn't return my smile and her eyes mist with tears, I realize I've missed my mark.

"Don't try to appeal to my ego, Asher. I know what I am." Angerly, she bats her tears away.

She drops her hands to her sides, balling them into tight fists as she visibly shakes. Much to my horror, I see the damage I've done with my careless words. I let my emotions get the best of me, and as her words sink in, my own anger rises.

"You really think that's what I'm doing? Appealing to your ego? That couldn't be further from the truth. You're one of the bravest people I know." What starts as an angry statement ends in a whisper. Because I finally realize how little she truly thinks of herself.

"I ran, Asher! My mother was being raped and murdered, and I ran!" she screams at the top of her lungs, falling to her knees before me. Without a second thought, I kneel with her, taking her hands in my own and bring them to my lips. I place a kiss on each of her fingers, staring into her eyes, refusing to let her hide. Not from me... Not in this.

"You were thirteen, Devany. You did what you needed to do to survive. What your mother wanted you to do..." I pause for a moment to let my words penetrate her mind. "I don't mind slaying your dragons when you can't." She opens her mouth to argue, but I can't take the space between us any longer. I slam my mouth onto hers and lift her into my lap. She's still for a moment before her hand tunnels into my hair, deepening the kiss.

By some miracle, I pull back, ending it before we can get carried away. I lay my forehead to hers, waiting for my pounding heart to calm. Devany sits quietly on my lap. Her arms wrapped tightly around my neck.

I draw back, pulling on her hair lightly so I can see her exquisite face, but she refuses to look at me. I release her and close my fist around her throat, tipping her back and forcing her gaze to mine.

"You are more than the sum of your pain... So much more," I tell her softly while my thumb strokes her neck gently. She closes her eyes, shaking her head as if to deny my words.

"Look at me." My voice is quiet but firm. She needs to hear this—to understand. Patiently, I wait for her to work up the courage to open her eyes.

"I mean it, *a stór*... with everything you've lived through, you still manage to be kind and compassionate. Most others would have hardened their hearts to the world, but not you..." I place a light kiss on her quivering lips as she tries to hold back her tears. "You're so very strong, Devany." I lean forward, kissing her tear-stained cheeks tasting their saltiness on my tongue. She breathes in a heavy, shaky breath.

I stand with her in my arms and walk us to the bed. There, I place her on her feet and step back from her. My eyes take in every inch of my wife—her beauty is truly remarkable, there's no question about that. But it's her inner strength and that spine of steel that draws people in.

She stands perfectly still as I take hold of her shirt, dragging it over her head. Her hair falls around her shoulders in a tangled mass of curls. I reach out, palming the side of her breast, my thumb softly stroking her nipple. The sharp intake of breath followed by a soft moan pulls a smirk from my lips and I drop to my knees before her.

"Asher, what are you doing?" Her tone is sharp enough to draw my eyes to hers.

"Shhh, let me take care of you... Let me show you how you're cared for." I don't know how to tell her what I feel... Not in words. But I can show her.

She gives me a timid nod. Her eyes taking me in while I loosen the ties to her pants.

I lean forward, placing a kiss on her hipbone, just above the band of her pants. Before trailing my lips along the skin to her other hip, with taste of her skin upon my lips. I keep my eyes on hers and slide her pants down her shapely legs. My fingertips skimming the backs of her thighs, trailing after the fabric. When the cloth pools at her feet, she steps out but doesn't pull away. I circle her ankle with my hand and lift it up onto my shoulder, opening her up for me.

Turning my head slightly, I press my lips to the warm skin on the inside of her knee. Her fingers tangle in my hair, pulling gently. I hold her eyes as I drag my nose along her inner thigh. My hands sliding up to her ass before pulling her sharply forward. Her gasp is music to my ears.

My tongue slides between her folds, as the sweet taste of her bursts on my tongue. Her fingers tighten in my hair and her head falls back on to her shoulders. I gently suck her clit into my mouth, giving her just enough to drive her crazy. She squirms and moans, grabbing hold of my horns and using them to pull my face closer. It's a good thing I'd gladly suffocate with her taste on my lips.

"Please." Her breathy little plea reaches my ears, and far be it from me to deny her. I slip a finger into her core—curling it forward—finding that sweet spot. I increase the pressure on her clit, sucking it deeper into my mouth. I add a second and feel her flutter around me. She moans my name loudly as she comes so beautifully around my fingers.

I stand and lick my fingers clean before swinging her into my arms and placing her onto the bed. She turns her dreamy eyes on me, looking about ready to pass out. So, I place her beneath the blankets and make quick work of my clothes before joining her and falling fast to sleep.

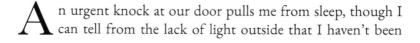

An urgent knock at our door pulls me from sleep, though I can tell from the lack of light outside that I haven't been out for long. I look down to find Devany wrapped around me like a sexy little vine.

She is so beautiful, inside and out. For the life of me, I can't understand how she has a heart as big as she does, having grown up behind those walls. It's a testament to how incredible she truly is.

"Your Majesty, we have news from Narcissa and Kane." She stirs in my arms at the sound of their names.

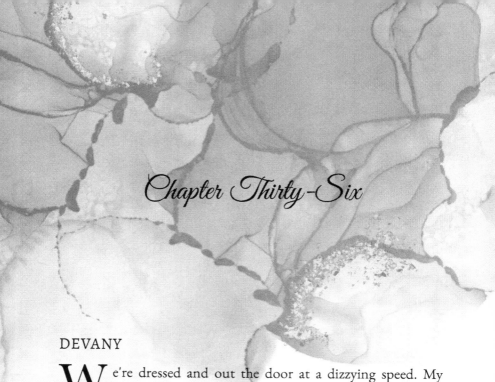

Chapter Thirty-Six

DEVANY

We're dressed and out the door at a dizzying speed. My heart forces its way to my throat, the anxiety constricts my chest and makes it hard to breathe. *What has father done now? I never should have left them.* How can I keep making these mistakes with the people that mean the most?

Asher and I cross the threshold into the receiving room after what feels like a short eternity. The room is an impressive mix of rough honed stone and dark, rich woods. Lofty ceilings stretch several meters high with a wall of windows that stand just as tall. A magnificent fireplace dominates the wall opposite the doorway. Its raging flames illuminating the space.

Candles of all shapes and sizes are spread around the room, flooding the space with pools of light. The mineral deposits in the stone walls glitter in the candlelight, looking very much like the night sky just beyond the windows. Shadows cling to the walls and converge in the corners just beyond the glow's reach.

Perched along the back of a large sofa is Narcissa's familiar Coda, a hawk of prodigious size with beautiful downy feathers in shades of brown, black, and white. He watches the room with keen intelligence, screeching and flapping his glorious wings when anyone gets too close—eyeing them with suspicion. Everyone gives him a wide berth, watching him with trepidation.

Just as I make my way to the lovely creature, a female soldier speaks up. "Your Grace, you shouldn't get too close." She closes her mouth with an audible *click* when Coda comes to me, preening under my attention.

Absently, I answer the question in the soldier's eyes. "He's Narcissa's familiar." She seems amused once she has her answer.

My eyes stray to a dehydrated and winded shifter standing by the refreshment table. I wait patiently as he drinks glass after glass of water, while eyeing me as if he thinks I may kill the messenger. I break eye contact, not wanting to make him any more nervous than he already is. I check Coda for a message, and sure enough, there's a small note attached to his claw with one sentence on it.

He has Luna.

It can't be... It just can't.

I back away from the animal as if it's somehow at fault for this turn of events. Asher is at my side in an instant, catching me before I can crumble to the ground. I close my eyes to calm my heart and hold back my tears. Once I've locked my emotions away, I look at the shifter, who stares nervously at his feet. I know it is not his fault. I really do... *But.*

"What happened?" I demand through gritted teeth, the ground beneath our feet shakes and rumbles with my anger and fear.

"*A stór,*" Is all Asher says to me, but it's enough to get me to take another claiming breath.

"We started receiving news about two weeks ago of people going missing. Some in the light of day, others from their homes in the dead of the night. But we couldn't find the connection, at least... not right away..." He glances at the floor and the scent of his misplaced guilt seeps into the room. He steps forward hesitantly as I stare out the window trying to compose myself. "My Queen, your father's apprehending those who back you and those lucky enough to fall through the cracks are terrified. We're unsure of how he's finding them." I'm willing to bet good money that the revenant has something to do with it. "What we can gather from the spies still in place is that he's got them locked up in some sort of labyrinth within the lower levels of the palace."

I'm going to fucking kill him!

I don't feel my glamour slip or realize that I'm growling until Asher is standing in front of me, cupping my face in his hands. He leans forward, brushing his lips against mine for a fleeting moment. And brings me back from the edge of my control.

"We are going to get them back, *a stór*," Asher whispers the promise to me, his lips ghosting against mine once more before he steps away from me.

He turns toward a guard near the doorway, addressing her directly. "Wake Ansel, then head to the dock. Get our largest ship ready. We're sailing in a few hours." Asher to fulfill his orders.

His eyes swing back to mine. "You need to give us a layout of the pala—"

"I'm going!" I cut him off, looking him directly in the eyes. I'll be damned if I'm denied this. His eyes harden, and he looks ready to argue, but this isn't up to him. "I'm every bit the queen to your king." Squaring my shoulders and going toe to toe with my husband.

"Room, now." He points to the stairs as if he expects me to hop to.

His eyes become cold and sharp like glass, cutting me to the bone. It takes everything I have not to take a step back. To conceal the flinch, that one look stripping me bare. When I make no move to follow his command, he grinds his teeth, the muscle along his jaw ticking.

"Don't talk to me like I'm a child," I growl at him as I cross the space between us.

"You would rather we have this discussion out in the open?" When I again make no move to leave, he makes a frustrated sound in the back of his throat.

"Everyone, out!" he demands, and the few people left exit. His anger was a physical thing in the room with us. But so is mine. The floor quakes and the fire blazes in response to our power.

"This isn't happening, wife." His voice is deceptively soft, the flames once more controlled within him. While he twirls a lock of my hair around his finger.

Chapter Thirty-Seven

ASHER

"I'll have Narcissa and Kane with—"

"There is no way in creation that I'll be allowing you to go!" my sharp words cut her off.

Those beautiful eyes of hers harden even as they seem to turn into molten metal. A flash of hurt clouds her eyes before a look so full of hostility burns all traces of vulnerability away. Devany pulls her shoulders back, raising her chin and straightens to her full height.

"Allow?" she scoffs, tipping her head back, laughing hollowly under her breath.

"Yes, wife, allow." She attempts to speak, but I continue, undeterred by her wrath.

With measured steps, I quickly close the distance between us, circling around her even as she moves with me, refusing to give me her vulnerable back. *Smart girl.*

I clasp my wrists behind me to hide the shaking of my hands in a futile attempt to prevent Devany from spotting just how much this scares the shit out of me. We can't both go right now. We have an entire island full of shifters who are on two legs for the first time in centuries, and she keeps acting as if she is expendable. Nothing could be further from the truth. I finally come to a stop, leaning forward so we're almost nose to nose.

"Neither of us should be going on a fool's mission when it's more than likely a trap. One that you're apparently more than happy to walk straight into." I reach up, cupping her jaw with both hands. My eyes take in every nuance of her face—from the slight twitch of her left eye to the quiver of her lips. "So please, Devany, explain it to me because right now I want to tie you up for safekeeping and send soldiers in your stead."

"I can't leave my people to suffer. I don't know how he's come across the information he has, but he's going after my people. The ones I left behind. And then there's Luna... I can't lose her." The vulnerability seeps back into her captivating eyes.

She takes hold of both my wrists, pulling out of my grasp. Her eyes turn to steel once more as she becomes the queen she truly is.

"So, you see, husband, I'll be going. It's not up for discussion." Her voice is calm... Resolute.

I pace up and down the room, running my hands through my hair, my patience wearing thin. I need to get her to see reason, my gut screams at me not to let her do this.

I come to an abrupt halt when Devany grabs hold of my wrists, pulling them from my hair, causing me to lift my eyes to hers, drawn in by her sincerity.

"Please understand. Trust me in this." My eyes move back and forth between hers, hoping to see some uncertainty where there is none. I don't like this, but short of tying her to the bed, there's not a damn thing I can do about it.

"You'll take Ansel with you as well." She looks fit to argue before she launches herself into my arms, wrapping her arms around my neck.

"Thank you." She buries her face in the crook of my neck, and I drag her closer, burying my face in her hair and breathing her in deep.

I don't know what I would do if I were to lose her.

A nsel and I are overseeing the last of the preparations for their voyage. The soft light of our pale sun has turned the sky a soft purple.

This moment has come far sooner than I'm prepared for.

"This is going to be a rescue mission in close quarters. So, I think it's best to take a small group in with us, keeping the rest as escorts. Are you even listening?" Ansel huffs out, crossing his arms over his large chest.

But I have eyes for only one person, and she's walking my way —dressed for war. Her pants mold to her legs, accentuating her muscular thighs. A corset of the same leather is laced tightly over a long-sleeve linen shirt. A pauldron sits on one shoulder connected to an arm piece that stops at the wrist. The other forearm is covered in a matching brace that encases her hand. Her long hair is braided back from her face.

She greets men and women on her way. When she reaches me, she seems nervous about my reaction. I can't help but find it humorous because, until this moment, I don't think she's ever cared about what I think. And I absolutely love that about her.

"Are we ready to go?" she asks, giving me a timid smile. I pull her toward me, erasing much of the space between us.

"Come back to me," I whisper, the words meant only for her ears.

My hands slide up, locking the clasp of the necklace around her neck once more. *Where it belongs.*

"Always." Her voice is just as soft as my own as the world around us disappears.

When I had to let her go the first time, it was one of the hardest things my adolescent-self had to endure... This is so much worse. I close my eyes, laying my forehead against hers and breathe her in.

"Promise?" I'm surprised my voice doesn't break on the question. My throat closes with an emotion I don't want to look at too closely.

She doesn't speak as a silent tear trail down her face as she nods her head as much as she can with my hand twisted in her hair.

"If you don't, I'll find you and drag you the fuck back. *A stór álainn*, my beautiful treasure." My hand tightens in her hair, pulling her head back.

She slowly opens her eyes, humming softly in the back of her throat.

"I'm counting on it," she says, wrapping her arms around my neck, pulling me to her, and I come all too willingly. Wrapping my arms around her tightly, I haul her body up against mine as urgency beats a steady tempo in my soul. I try to deepen the kiss further, but she steps back, shattering the spell she always seems to put me under.

Without another word, she walks down the pier toward the largest of my five ships. It sits docked at the pier with its weathered wood hull standing out against the turquoise sea. The long planks are broken up by portholes, railings, and weapons. Three large sails, made up of a blue fabric so dark they appear black, stand tall. A small army hustles about, preparing to set sail.

I watch helplessly as they pull away from the dock. The process is made quicker with the aid of the Valore on board.

Even with this storm of emotions running wild in my chest, I sense Harken before he puts his hand on my shoulder.

"She'll come back," he says with his eyes trained on the quickly moving ship.

I take a deep breath before addressing him. "You're damn right she will."

Chapter Thirty-Eight

DEVANY

I watch as the pier gets further away as the ship pushes through the deep ocean water, aided by the elemental users, water and air working in tandem. I stare at the pier until it's no more than open sea.

A stór álainn—Beautiful treasure. I gaze out onto the water, my heart beating frantically in my chest. I'm so lost in thought as I comb through every interaction we've had.

"At this rate, we'll dock in Edling in a week's time and then it's a three days' ride to the border," Ansel states, breaking me out of my thoughts.

"So long?" I ask on a long breath, eager to get to my people... to get to Luna. He gives me a disapproving look, but whatever emotion he sees on my face has him backing down.

"We have quite a few Valore on board. We could probably cut a few days off if we work in shifts around the clock," he says in a very matter-a-fact tone.

"Thank you." It's the only thing I can think of to say. Ansel places his hand on my shoulder, giving it a small squeeze before he walks away, leaving me to my swirling thoughts.

In the end, it took five and a half days to get to Naphal. We rode long and hard, first through the mountain terrain of Edling and then the deserts climate of Naphal. I've been an internal wreck much of the time. All I want to do is see Narcissa and Kane.

This time when I enter Lysia, I'm not paying attention to the stalls in the marketplace, nor the scent of spices that cling to the air. I don't hear the buzzing of voices, and my eyes don't stray to the many people milling about. I head straight through the city proper with Ansel to my left and a soldier to my right.

Kane waits for us in the courtyard when we pass through the palace gates just after nightfall. He moves to help me from my horse, but I'm not here as the pampered princess. Oh no, I'm here as a queen going to war for the safe return of her people. I swing my leg over my horse and push off, landing in a light crouch. Kane doesn't comment, though he does arch a brow at me, a smile playing at his lips. Ansel, on the other hand, snorts loudly, as if he finds me all too funny. *Asshole.*

Narcissa walks out to us with Chloe on her heels. As soon as we make eye contact, all the others disappear. We run to each other, colliding in the center of the courtyard. It's silent around us, like they can see the gaping hole in our chest or feel the sadness and terror that courses through our veins.

"How many?" I don't need to elaborate. She lifts her head from my shoulder and looks me in the eye.

"The exact number is murky, but it's less than we originally thought. We evacuated all the magic users that had remained from within the village. The only allies we have left within your father's kingdom are the human spies working within the palace." Her voice is cold and free of the vulnerability she had displayed only a moment ago.

While her eyes are hard, her skin has lost some of its beautiful glow... Just how long has she been shouldering the responsibility of this without telling me what was going on?

"Well, we have that going for us, at least," I reply, trying to see the silver lining in this fucked-up situation. Her eyes skate away from me as she takes in a long, fortifying breath. The people around us shuffle their feet as they wait with bated breath for her response.

"Not so much," she states almost under her breath before turning back to look at me. "It took far too long for us to realize that the ones that stayed behind were being targeted. As soon as we did, we evacuated all that remained." She lowers her head, staring at her hands. "But not before he got his hands on eight people. Two are children..." She trails off, obviously feeling responsible for all of this. But the responsibility lies solely with me.

I reach forward, grabbing ahold of her hands, squeezing lightly. Her head snaps up—eyes colliding with mine. She schools her features quickly, wiping away the emotions that were etched on her face.

"Luna was taken a little over two weeks ago. But that's not the worst of it." This time, there's not an ounce of emotion in her voice, not even a quiver. What gives her away is the tremor in her hands as she balls them into fists.

"What the fuck could possibly be worse than this?" I ask, knowing from the look on her face I will not like the next thing she says.

"Devany... he's keeping them in cages. From what we've gathered, they're being kept in the sublevel of the palace." Her voice is soft and soothing, putting aside her own trauma and fear to comfort me. Always so ready to put someone else above herself.

With a tone meant only for her ears, I say, "It's alright... to be afraid or angry." My eyes hold hers and I see the pain she hides flash across her features. I pull her closer, putting my arms around her. After a moment, she pulls back and gives me a small shake of her head.

Before she can open her mouth to speak, Ansel cuts in. "It's probably best if the queen rests. We've been riding for two and a half days. I realize there may be a desire to jump into action. But these things are best planned out," he states in that high-handed way of his. With a respectful nod and a mumbled good night, he turns toward the palace, presumably to his room.

"He's right, it's best you get your rest now. Who knows what will happen in the days to come." She loops her arm through mine, leading me to my room.

It's the first time since my marriage that I will sleep alone. I'm not sure when that started to matter, but it does.

I spend so much of my night tossing and turning. That I decide the best way to work out all this nervous energy is physical exertion. It seems Narcissa and Kane have the same idea as I come upon them sparring with each other. They're not going easy on each other in the slightest. It's a mighty strike of steel every time they clash. A violent explosion of grunts and screams. The two of them are a magnificent sight as they move around the ring.

"I sent a messenger off to Asher. I think he needs to be here with us." Ansel's voice startles me out of my observation. If he keeps this shit up, I'll put a bell around his neck. The bastard smirks, like he knows what I'm thinking. Before sobering. "With any luck, he may be here before we leave on our mission." Narcissa and Kane notice us and end their match.

"We might as well get started, since it appears none of us will be getting any sleep. Why don't you get cleaned up and we'll meet in the war room," I reply, turning around and walking back up the mountain pass.

Ivann and Chloe are already in the war room when I arrive. Kane walks in behind me before the door even closes. The four of us gather around the map, talking about possible strategies when the door once again opens. Ansel holds it open for Narcissa and she gives him a sultry smile I've seen her use a time or two. He returns it with a smirk of his own. My eyes automatically jump to Kane to see if he's going to react—and react he does. His knuckles turn white against the tabletop and a nearly audible growl leaves his chest. The slight vibration works its way up his shoulders, like he's just barely holding himself back.

The two of them step back into their roles once they realize they have an audience. Ansel clears his throat aggressively before making eye contact with the rest of the room. Narcissa simply smiles and grabs an apple from the buffet table before taking her place beside me.

"It's going to be a small rescue mission. We'll be taking about six soldiers from the group we brought with us. With the four of us rounding out the group. I went ahead and took the liberty of sending Asher a missive informing him that we have need of his presence." I observe Ansel while he speaks. The way he makes precise points with a clear and purposeful voice. The picture of a commander. It's easy to see why he holds the position he does within Asher's kingdom.

"I understand your reasoning for calling, Asher. But I won't be waiting on him to act. My people are hurting. They're suffering, and I'll be damned if I'm going to allow it to continue. As soon as we figure out how to safely extract them, we'll be moving forward with the rescue. My timeline is not based on when Asher shows up." His only answer is a simple nod as he takes his place beside Kane. I look to Narcissa, with the silent order to continue.

"This is the information as we know it. The sub-level can only be accessed through the palace waterways. We then need to locate the cells holding the cages and release everyone. Then we need to find a way out." I nod my head absently, my mind working to come up with a plan.

But there are too many unknowns to consider.

Chapter Thirty-Nine

DEVANY

It's dark when leave for Erabis, making our way to the battlement my father hides behind. We make it to the palace as the sun barely kisses the sky.

We stick to the skeletal trees. Using their large trucks as cover, we make our way to the sickly-green aqueduct that will lead us into the lower levels. From my viewpoint, I can just make out the iron bars that block our way.

As we creep through the trees, the silence that surrounds us is overwhelming. The air smelling of death and decay. Humidity hangs heavily in the atmosphere and clings to my skin.

"What of the bars?" I ask quietly, being sure not to disturb our surroundings.

Ansel doesn't stop, throwing the answer over his shoulder. "We have enough able-bodied soldiers to pry them open." I guess it's as good a plan as any. Though I hate to admit the *lack* of a plan is making me slightly ill. Being back here—to the epicenter of my pain—has me choking on fear.

We arrive at the waterway without incident. The ten of us tread our way through the placid water, trying to make as little noise as possible. We keep our backs to the plain stone wall of the palace and our eyes on the two-armed guards walking the battlement above us.

Ansel, Kane, and two of our soldiers lift the gate. It's a slow process—stopping every few inches to be sure we haven't been heard. Once they lift the gate enough for us to swim under, Narcissa jams an ax beneath it. The soldiers closest to the gate cross over first, followed by Narcissa and Ansel. Next is Kane, with me bringing up the rear. But as soon as I pass underneath the gate, I feel it. Something so strong it skates across my skin, coming from deep within the ground. I stand to the side, trying to gauge whether anyone notices, but no one does. *It must just be me.*

I only make it a few meters when the strength of the spell hits me in the chest with enough power to stop me in my tracks. *How is it not affecting the others?* Ansel notices I'm no longer keeping up with the group and turns to look back at me—a look of confusion marring his face while I stand among the dirty water and debris.

"What's wrong?" he demands, walking back to me, taking in my no doubt pale face. "Do you sense something?" His voice is full of urgency.

My vision blackens around the edges, and I stagger back, catching myself on the wall. Pressing my fist into my stomach, I try to breathe through the discomfort. I'm lost to the pain when two firm hands grab hold of my shoulders.

"Talk to me. What's happening? Are the wards affecting you?" His tone is a strange mix of anger and anxiety. I think this may be the first time I've ever heard concern in his voice when directed at me.

"It's a spell, I think. It feels like it's... deep beneath our feet." The words come out on a hard breath.

Ansel looks around helplessly, as if he'll find an answer within the forgotten corridor.

"What's wrong?" Narcissa asks, startling me. *When did she move?*

Ansel looks at her. "Can you use your magic?" he asks in a hushed tone.

The soldiers have all stopped to watch us with varying looks of concern. Narcissa doesn't answer him, her eyes bouncing between the two of us before she holds her hand out above the water. When nothing happens, her head snaps in our direction.

"What the fuck?" she breathes, holding her hand out once more.

A look of concentration mars her beautiful face, and her hand trembles as her skin pales. She looks back at us, shaking her head. Ansel swears under his breath, holding his hand out to use his own magic. When nothing happens, I realize just how hard this mission has just become.

"A fucking spell!" he growls under his breath, taking a deep breath to calm himself. "It looks like we have to do this the hard way... are you going to make it?" he asks me while giving me a once over.

"Now that initial shock has passed, I can manage. I've dealt with worse." His brows furrow, his eyes so full of sympathy that I have to look away.

With a sharp nod from me, he turns and walks down the corridor. Narcissa steps closer, looking me over with a far more critical eye than Ansel did.

"Are you sure you're okay?" Her voice is low enough that this exchange stays between us.

"I have little choice in the matter. We both know I can manage pain." Being a woman of few words, she reaches out and gives my shoulder a quick squeeze.

We walk side by side, catching up with the others relatively quickly. Several meters in, we come to a fork in the tunnel system. The path going straight leads deeper into the palace, toward the courtyard. The passage to our left most likely opens in the village, and the corridor to our right ends with a small set of stairs leading to an iron door.

Through the process of elimination, we decide to take the

stairs. The massive door looms at the top of the stairs, and of course, it's locked. Because this couldn't be easy—Goddess forbid. The guys wiggle the knob several times, shoving their shoulders into it, like if they keep doing it, they may get a different result than the previous attempts.

Narcissa works her way to the front of the small convoy, pushing Kane's hand off the knob.

"Move, let the professionals handle this." Her lips curve slightly, and she elbows her way past Kane.

Narcissa pulls a small pouch from her belt and kneels before the door. Removing two small metal picks, she works them into the lock. After a few seconds of moving the picks this way and that way, the lock pops. She stands, giving the males a cocky smirk. Obviously proud of yourself.

We follow her through the door into an empty room with another door at the end. Narcissa once again picks the lock. We get our first sign of life when we walk through the second door as the delicate sound of a woman crying fills the hall.

Slowly, Ansel and two soldiers check the corners and crevices for unseen guards.

"We have more doors at either end of the corridor. Prepare yourselves. They're locked in small cages and cuffed to the floor." He stands there ever stoic, but I can see the way the muscle in his jaw ticks.

Narcissa walks around the corner and starts picking locks. Kane and Ansel work to break apart one of the rust-ridden cages with their bare hands while the others guard the doors.

I've seen enough pain and torment for a lifetime, but this is disgusting. His hatred knows no bounds. I stop at each cage to comfort and assure them that we'll get them out. They're all malnourished, which isn't much of a surprise. Open, festering wounds and dark bruises stand out against their pale sickly skin. The sight is infuriating.

I check each overcrowded cage and cell, hoping for a glimpse of white hair. *She must be here somewhere...* I refuse to leave her behind. The rising panic takes hold when she's nowhere to be found.

Desperately, I feel along the walls, looking for something I may have missed. When my fingers brush an indentation, I feel along the edge of the stone block and a light breeze comes from the seam between the stones. I trace the impression with my fingers before giving it a hard push. There's an audible click, then the sound of stone-on-stone echoes through the hall. It moves just enough for a single person to squeeze through. *It must not be the main entrance.*

"What the fuck are you doing? We have to get out of here, and you're making a shit ton of noise." Ansel's irritated voice breaks through my thoughts.

"Luna isn't out there. I'm checking in here," I state like it's obvious.

"Absolutely not! It's too dangerous!" He holds his hand out, fully expecting me to take it like I'm some sort of child.

"I wasn't asking for permission. I was telling you," I reply, my irritation climbing.

Not waiting for his reaction, I push my way through the last few meters after which it suddenly opens up to a large round room.

The candlelight is low, leaving the room almost black. I glance around the space, adjusting quickly to the limited lighting. The dirty walls are covered in iron and sliver objects meant to break a person. Worktables littered with hammers, clamps, saws, and various other implements are scattered around the room.

There's a faint whimper that comes from a dark corner that draws my attention. I retrieve a nearby candle, moving toward the sound, and I come face to face with my nightmare. Luna is strapped to the wall, hanging from a hook by her cuffs. So high up that the tips of her toes barely touch the ground. Those fuckers broke her fingers. Something a spellcaster can't live without.

The bastards chopped off her lovely white hair. It hangs in jagged layers by her ears and caked with blood. Her warm green eyes are swollen, making it almost impossible to make out their beautiful upward tilt. Blood seeps from her chapped lips. There's a long knife wound between her breast and another on her side that's bleeding through what's left of her shirt. Her legs are covered in an incredible number of lacerations.

"Please tell me you're real?" is the first thing she says to me. Barely lifting her head from the awkward angle it sits in to look at me.

"Yes..." I cup her face, lifting it so she can see me more clearly. "We're getting out of there. I just need to get you out of those cuffs." While I hold her head, my eyes search the room looking for something, anything, to help me.

"There are keys by the door," she breathes softly—eyes drooping.

I place her head down gently and rush toward the hook. On impulse, I rotate through the five keys so I can lock the door. I turn the key slowly until I feel the lock mechanism click into place. With that done, I rush over to Luna, pulling a bench over so I can stand on it. It takes three tries to find the right key. I have to catch her when the cuffs give way to prevent her from hitting the floor.

"Luna, wake up!" I lightly slap her face, trying to get her attention.

She rouses enough to get her feet under her. I placed her arm around my shoulder and walk her back the way I came. Her feet are dragging, but I jostle her slightly, getting a better grip on her waist. Shouts come from the door, followed by banging.

"Ansel, help!" I call, looking back toward the door to be sure it's holding.

"Devany...? Oh shit!" he huffs, reaching into the narrow passage, grabbing her arm and pulling her forward.

I watch him drag her forward while I help where I can. The loud sound of an ax hitting wood draws my attention to the door. When I turn back, she is more than halfway through. I follow behind her, moving as quickly as possible.

"Ansel, hurry, they're coming!" Even I can hear the panic in my voice.

"Shit!" He hauls her out of the narrow passageway, drawing pained whimpers from her. He whispered gentle words and apologies while moving her bloody hair from her face.

Kane reaches in, helping me the rest of the way out. I'm reaching for Luna as soon as I'm free. I scan the room to be sure we've freed all the prisoners, finding that two are barely conscious.

"We need to go, now!" I stress, glancing swiftly at the last two doors that we locked and barred with the iron cages from the cell room.

Narcissa pulls out a curved short sword. "I'm right behind you, Devy."

One of the soldiers stands with a girl that couldn't be over fifteen, unconscious in his arms. She was damn near skin and bones and covered in bruises.

Kane takes Luna from me, freeing up my arms should I need to fight. Narcissa leads the way, and we follow, keeping the prisoners protected between us. Kane and the soldier carrying the young girl are in the center. Two more soldiers are on each side with Ansel and I bringing up the rear. I grab a long iron bar from an old cell and pull out two daggers from my thigh holster.

We make our way out the door to the sound of something heavy banging against one of the cell doors, the guards no doubt going at it with an ax. Ansel and I are the last to step through the door. He slams it shut and I jam the pole across it and into the stone walls.

We round the corner after everyone else. Narcissa directs the first prisoner to follow the soldier who was already on the other side of the iron gate. She takes a deep breath and dives under. We hear the screech of steel against stone, drawing our eyes to the top of the gate in time to see it descend. Narcissa reaches for the woman, but there's no time to pull her back.

The soldier uses a speed most lack and drags her through before it connects with the ground. I walk forward to check her for further injury and when I find none, my eyes move to the shifter behind her.

"Head back to the Naphal border. Be sure to keep to the trees. They're on high alert, so stay vigilant." My eyes drift back to the woman, taking her in.

She's unnaturally slim with her skin taking on a gray appearance. Ansel steps forward, making eye contact with me as he takes off the thick outer jacket to his leathers and wordlessly passes it to her through the bars. Then turns away as if it were a nothing thing to do for a group of people who have experienced very little in the way of compassion.

We backtrack to the fork in the tunnel to pick a different route. Not that it's much of a choice, two ways are already closed off to us. One goes to the courtyard further into the palace, which leaves us the village pass.

"To the left it is, then," Kane says when we make it back to the fork.

Narcissa silently leads us down the tunnel, wading through the dirty water. Surrounded by slimy walls and the smell of decay. We're halfway to the exit when the sound of crushing metal meets our ears. I can still see the door from here. They couldn't break it down completely, but it's enough for several guards to squeeze through.

"Fuck!" Kane breathes, eyes trained on the approaching group, and I'm inclined to agree with him.

We shuffle the prisoners behind us toward the door. A soldier steps up and takes Luna from Kane, allowing him to fight.

It all happens so fast, the small space hindering the battle. The first man engages with Ansel. The second comes at me but is intercepted by Kane. Two more slipped past them, and this time they make it to me. I block the first's sword with both of my daggers while kicking out at the other. My knee comes up and connects with the one in front of me.

A feminine grunt comes from my right, telling me that Narcissa has entered the fray. The second guard has recovered and is heading toward me. Luckily, Kane is currently dealing with the sword wielding asshole. I block his first strike easily, but the second comes too fast. Thank the Goddess for my fighting leather. He's not so lucky when I shove my dagger into his chest—walking him back against the wall—pushing harder to get through the bone. His hand comes up, slicing my arm along my bicep. But I don't stop—I simply push harder.

"Kane!" I hear Narcissa scream, and I look in her direction.

She runs to the end of the corridor, slicing through two more guards on her way before she leaps off the back of one of the downed men, getting enough height to kick off from the wall. Her sword severs the head of the guard coming up behind Kane. The two of them turn back-to-back, taking on three guards.

Ansel has just finished taking down who knows how many. I have two more to deal with. Grabbing two discarded swords, I meet my next opponents head on. I strike true, putting them on the defense quickly. I come at the larger one hard, carving a sizable chunk out of his dominant arm. I spin in time to block the attack from the other and sending my other sword slashing through the back of his leg, bringing him to his knees, where I promptly removed his head.

The larger guard makes a sound of frustration as he advances on me. I don't feel the wound on my arm, but the blood pouring from it has my hand slick. I can't get purchase on the weapon, so I drop it, deciding it's safer to fight with one weapon. He's moves quicker than I had expected for a man his size.

We strike and counterstrike, each of us inflicting small wounds. Frustrated, I throw my weapon and grab another dagger and run at him, ducking under his strike to grasp his collar. I place my foot on his knee, propelling myself over his shoulder, latching onto his throat, burying my dagger in his thick neck.

I look up to see that all's quiet. We're a little worse for wear but still intact. It's then that I realize Luna has roused. Narcissa and I rush to her side, but she has so many wounds that I'm afraid to touch her. Unsure where to place my hands, we carefully help her to her feet, positioning each one of her arms over our shoulders.

Kane now leads us through the door that opens to the village with Ansel and the other soldiers protecting our backs.

With so many wounded, to say it is slow going would be an understatement. We stick to the alleys full of debris and waste, moving from one to the other. Each one takes us closer to the forest gate. But we come to a dead stop as we face the full might of my father's most elite. There's no way we can win, much less get out alive.

Chapter Forty

DEVANY

Father sits so smugly upon his horse with his little-bitch revenant gleefully waiting for the next order. She betrayed her own kind, not because she thinks we're unworthy of loyalty, but because she wants wherever it is he promised her more. I have news for her—he'll double-cross her just as he's done to those that came before.

"Come along, daughter dear," he says in a tone meant to coax me into doing what he wants as he beckons me forward with a motion of his hand.

Hearing him call me *daughter* causes a sour pit in my stomach. The bastard allowed me to get these people this far because he enjoys crushing their hope, watching it die in their eyes.

"There's nowhere for you to go. Now, come along before you make it worse on yourself," his gaze slides to the people cowering behind me, "and on them." He smiles at me, his eyes bright with anticipation of the pain he plans to cause.

Not that I'm going to give him the chance. I look back at Narcissa as she holds up a barely conscious Luna. The flow of blood coming from Kane's wound has increased. I will do anything to keep these three people alive, even if it means walking back in my father's palace knowing I won't walk back out. I turn and meet Ansel's stare, and from the look on his face he knows exactly what I'm going to do.

"Don't you dare," he whispers angrily, his amber eyes flashing.

"Let them go, and I'll come along without a fight." The lie leaves my lips easily.

"Why would I do that?" he queries snidely.

"Simple, father, I'll kill you." I smile sweetly at him, but my eyes have a dangerous glint in them. If he were smart, he would heed the warning.

"We'll run you over before you have a chance, daughter." He spits the word *daughter* at me as if the word itself tastes foul on his tongue.

"Possibly... but not before I kill you." I allow him to see the truth in my words. I can see him swallowing his fear from here. "Who's to say they would even avenge your death? It's more than likely they'll run with their tails between their legs like the cowards they are." They all sneer at me, but I only smirk at them in return.

"Alright, I'll make a deal with you. If they can get past us, they're free to go. What say you, daughter?" It's a shit deal, which is why he offered it. He just doesn't have all the facts.

"Alright, Father," I respond quietly. Confusion clouding his eyes, an indent appearing between thick, unkempt brows. Which causes me to slip up and smile.

I turn to Ansel once more, but he's already shaking his head at me. His refusal is on the tip of his tongue. "Do it."

"Don't make me do this, Devany," he pleads, his eyes bright, almost like he'd shed tears for me.

"I am your queen. Now, do it," I reply with authority, my tone unyielding. This is the only way.

"Devy?" The sound of Luna's weak voice has me looking over my shoulder at her. Tears fall unchecked from her pretty green eyes, making them shine like colored glass.

I look between her and Narcissa, allowing them to see how much I love them and working hard to keep my own tears at bay. I refuse to give my father the satisfaction.

"Take care of each other," I whisper before my eyes flick to Kane, imploring him to stand down. He practically shakes with the effort to stay where he is, even as blood drips from the large gash in his side.

"Don't you fucking dare say goodbye! Do you hear me, Devany?" Narcissa's voice is full of steel, like the clank of two swords.

I turn away, unable to look at them without losing my composure. Not taking my eyes from my father, I reach down and remove the silver dagger from my hip holster and cut my palm deeply. After all, there's power in blood. The scent of it fills the air around us, flooding the space with power, overriding the wards the reverent has placed.

I feel the change in the atmosphere as the portal shifts and opens. I can see how nervous the guards are to see this level of magic at work. It's truly magnificent. I turned my back on my father and his men. To watch my people—my family—make their way to safety.

Ansel must've opened the portal directly into the courtyard because I watch as Asher turns around, his gaze moving from one person to the next as he searches for me. When he doesn't see me, he looks directly into the portal, his gaze colliding with mine just as my arms are forcibly wretched behind my back. He runs for the portal, but Ansel intercepts him, and all I can think to do is mouth the words *I'm sorry* before that portal snaps shut.

They turn me to face father. He's dismounted but comes no further—and he won't until they have me collared, ensuring that I'm cut off from my magic completely. A soldier I know well steps forward with an apology in his eyes. I give an imperceptible nod of my head to let him know that it's okay. The deafening click of the metal lets me know that my next nightmare has begun.

Epilogue

ASHER

Ansel's and I collide with enough force that we gouge the earth beneath our feet. I move him closer to the portal—closer to Devany—before I feel the impact of a second body pushing me back several meters.

"Don't you fucking dare, not after what she just sacrificed." Kane's voice breaks in over the loud sound of my labored breath.

When I look away from the now-closed portal, I realize he was the other person holding me back. But I'm too angry and heartbroken to see reason. I quickly turn and punch Ansel in the jaw, his head snapping to the side, causing him to step back a few steps.

"That was my wife you left behind." My nostrils flare as I bare my teeth at him. My jaw clenches so tightly that it aches. I tunnel my hands into my hair, pulling at the strands violently. "Open it back up right fucking now!" Swinging my hand out at the now empty space.

"No... I can't do that." His response is resigned. There's so much pity in his voice that I find myself advancing on him once again.

"What do you mean, no?" My voice becomes deceptively soft and in no way represents the turmoil going on within me.

"She's my queen, and she gave me an order!" he shouts at me, eyes darkening and becoming hard as stone with both of his hands now fisted at his sides.

Ansel is like a brother to me, but he left my wife behind. How do I forgive that? Unable to look at him a second more, I turn away.

"What do you want me to do?" He pleads, though there's an undercurrent of desperate anger.

"You've done enough, don't you think?" I call over my shoulder without looking at him.

There's no knowing what I'm liable to do if I continue to face off with him. I scan the courtyard, looking out over our people. It seems I have Ivann's undivided attention, but I ignore the look in his questioning eyes and scan the area for a bird shifter.

"You." I point at a woman with plain red hair that's stuck to the side of her face from the Naphal heat.

I'm far too angry to be polite. Worry claws its way up my throat, making it hard to swallow. I feel as if I'm choking on it as I try. Will there be anything left of her by the time I get there?

"Leave for Draic. Tell Bellicent that Devany has been taken. Tell her to load three ships' worth of soldiers. If Kól wants war, then he's fucking got one."

Glossary

Pronunciations
   <u>Names:</u>
   Asher: a-Shr
   Ansel: an-sl
   Bellicant: BEL-ih-sent
   Devany: DEV-a-nee
   Kól: Kol
   Tempest: tem-puhst
   Lela: Lee-luh
   Narcissa: Narr-si-sah
   Luna: LOO-NUH
   Kane: Key-in
   Ivann: ee-VAHN
   Eva: ee-vuh
   Chloe: klow-ee
   Nyra: Nai-rah
   Nalin: Na-lyn
   Cyrus: sai-ruhs
   Ryun: ree-ooh
   Minas: mi-nas

Neve: NEEV

Kingdoms:
Erabis: ERR-ah-BUHS
Draic: DREY-EH-K
Naphal: naw-fal
Hepha: hee-fa
Froslien: fro-s-leen
Aiteall: AT-ell
Narci: Nar-si
Brynhild: brin-hild
Mageia: ma-GEE-ah
Majondir: ma-jon-dier
Gali: Gal-lee
Nysar: nai-sar
Edling: ed-ling
Sólalis: so-les
Kannon: ka-nuhn

Landmarks:
Tartin Woods: tart-tan
Sadeen River: sah-d-EE-n
Neveen Mountains: nev-vee-in
Covenia River: co-vee-nah
Jamshid Palace: Jam-Sh-ei-D

Misc.:
Hestra: heh-struh
Hadeon: Hay-DEE-on
Synder Berries: sin-der
Valore: vah-lor
Alanus: a-la-nus

Term of endearment:

A Stór: uh-stohr

Milis: mil-is

Álainn: aw-len

Acknowledgments

I'd like to give a special thanks to my daughter, a.k.a my ideas woman. She has this way of walking into my office, reading two lines and then giving me some profound idea before walking out as if she was never there. Leaving me to wonder if it was all some sort of fever-dream. I'd also like to thank Samantha Swart for making the editing process painless and productive. Thank you for helping make my book the best it could be.

About the Author

T.A. Benton Is A First Time Author Taking The Leap Into The Literary World With Debut Book, Crown Of My Enemy. The First Book In Her Lovely Enemies Series. She's Writes Spicy Fantasy Romance, Breathing Life Into The Stories That Live In Her Mind. T.A. Is A Mother Of Three And Avid Reader Of All Things Romance. When Not Out With Her Kids, She's Wrapped Up In A Good Story. Whether Reading One Or Writing One, Shares A Love For The Written Word. She Currently Resides In Georgia With Her Family.

Throne Of My Blood

EXCERPT FROM SECOND BOOK IN THE LOVELY ENEMIES SERIES

Chapter One
Asher

The sound of snapping bones greets me as I descend the steps to the lower cells, each step taken without conscious thought, the path burnt within my memory. The individual flights are barely visible in the wavering light coming off the evenly spaced torches. The snap and crackle of the flames loud in the silence between screams.

My life has become much like this corridor, dark with only fleeting bouts of light.

Ansel's methodical voice reaches my ears just as I step off the final step. "Now, shall we get back to the issue at hand and let's bear in mind that if you don't start answering my questions, I'm going to stop being so nice... Where is she?"

I stop and hover in the doorway, leaning against the metal frame as I wait for his answer.

"Fuck you! That cunt got what she deserved!"

The word *"Got"*, past tense, rings in my ears. *It can't be... if she were no longer among the living, I would know.* I can hardly breathe past the blinding anger and fear that now clogs my throat.

I'm across the threshold before it even registers that I've moved. My hands wrap around his fat neck. It's another few precious seconds before the scent of burning fresh has me blinking down to see the skin around his throat charred and blistered. His lifeless eyes staring at me, mouth hanging open on a silent scream.

My heart pounds in my chest as my shoulders heave with each short, ragged breath I take. The room around me wavers, nothing more than a blur of color. His blank face is the only thing in focus.

I close my eyes to block out the site, forcing my hands to release what's left of his mangled throat.

By the Goddess, don't let her be dead.

Dropping the corpse, I let it fall to the floor and step over him, motioning a soldier over to drag the body away. The more time that passes, the harder it is to recognize the man I've become.

I take a handkerchief from my pocket, wiping the ash from my hands. *One. Two. Three. Inhale. One. Two. Three. Exhale.* I countdown each breath like a mantra, glancing around the room while my breathing evens out. The act itself meant to buy me time to bring my erratic heartbeat and reckless anger back under control. My eyes touch on each person before they eventually land on Ansel.

He stares at me for a moment, his gaze raking over me. No doubt trying to gage my mental state. Which hasn't differed from the day she was taken. I swimming in guilt and anger every day. He doesn't say a word, just stares at me, the low groans of the prisoners background noise to our silent conversation. After a few tense moments, he nods his head, apparently having decided that I'm stable enough to proceed. With his eyes on me, he motions for two more guards to be hung up.

After the soldiers make quick work of hang these two up, I step forward and ask them the only question that matters. "Where is she?"

They don't even so much as acknowledge I've spoken. Staring

stoically ahead. Though there is fear hiding in their eyes. I tilt my head to the side, the corner of my mouth curling up at the prospect of spilling more blood. "So let it begin."

My fist meets the first guard's ribs with a satisfying crunch. Next, his nose gives way in a gosh of blood, and his cheekbone is soon to follow. I work him over, only stopping to asking the same question in between each circuit to no avail. Each time he refuses to answer I begin the process a new. Time becomes nothing more than a construct, passing both quickly and slowly, my mind finding a stillness it only gets in these moments of repetition and exertion.

He goes limp far too soon, escaping into the veil of death and into the arms of its God. where he will receive his punishments for the life he's led. I find it funny. He probably embraced the sweet release of death, only to experience something much worse. *Karma's a bitch,* after all.

I move on to the next guard, but the bastard stares past me at the wall. This act of rebellion and dismissal cracks something inside of me. I grab hold of his throat, dragging his face forward so it's an inch from mine.

"Where the fuck is she?!" I scream into his face, the word torn from my chest, raw and ragged.

He remains silent, even as fear shines bright in his eyes. This time I take a large piece of wood to the outer edge of his left thigh, the bones cracking audibly. I carry on from there, giving him much the same treatment as the one before. He fairs a little better than his comrade, but his body gives out just the same.

My muscles scream, and blood covers my hands, staining my skin. I have two lifeless bodies and zero fucking answers.

Death and pain have become a common occurrence since Devany's capture two months ago.

Two fucking months.

Two months of her enduring the Gods only know how much pain and torture at the hands of the man that calls himself her father. Two months of me going out of my mother-fucking-mind — possessed with the need to get her back... To bring her home.

How broken will she be by the time I get to her? Will there be any of her left? I never should have let her go without me.

The pain in the chest cuts so deep I have to breathe through the agony, pushing the emotions back down, blinking away the sting in the back of my eyes.

It's gotten to where I spent more time in this windowless cell beneath the Jamshid Palace of Naphal than I do in my own rooms, much less my kingdom. Which I'm currently ruling by proxy. Terrified to leave the border Erabis shares with Naphal.

With nothing else to do, I take my anguish out on Erabis' guards, needing to hurt them until they feel even a tenth of what I do. To drown them in fear, like she no doubt is. I don't know how much longer things can go on like this.

I force myself to take one step and then another, away from the prisoners. Turning my back to them in a feeble attempt to my tame my already volatile temper.

I concentrate on the space around me. The sound of each deep breath I take. The creaks and groans of the metal cell doors. The constant sound of water dripping from the stones like a broken harmony, echoing off the roughly honed walls. The cold moisture that hangs in the air, clinging to my skin and hair, cooling my hot flesh.

My body wound so tight, it's weighted down in agitation. I bounce from foot to foot on the balls of my feet, shaking my hands out and rolling my neck to release the tension in my shoulders. Flexing my blood caked hands, reopening the wounds on my knuckles, preventing them from healing.

They remove the corpses and pile their mutilated bodies in the corner with the others—bones broken—burned and beaten, each one reeking of corruption.

I stare at the jagged slaty-grey wall, silently counting the dust mites that float just above the surface, working to calm my emotions. Listening as they bring the last two prisoners forward.

Their heavy chains rattling loudly against the hooks in the ceiling as the soldiers lock them into place.

It's not long before Kane beings striking one guard repeatedly. The sound of skin striking skin followed by grunts, groans, and heavy breathing fills the room—bouncing off the thick stone walls.

"Enough!" Ansel barks, leaning back against the wall.

Kane stops his assault abruptly, taking several steps back from the prisoner. His shoulders heaving as he draws in deep breaths of air, reining in his temper with each inhalation until he once again becomes that calm killer everyone underestimates. This has been hard on Devany's people, but none more than him. He spent his life protecting her and now she's all alone and it's taking its toll on him.

Out of the corner of my eye, I see Ansel push off the wall and walk toward the prisoner Kane had just finished working over. He passes me and I hear the chains rattle just out of sight.

"Do you wish to change your stance on holding your tongue?" Ansel queries, his voice monotone, sounding as if he's well and truly bored with being here.

I keep my back to the scene, slanting my head in the prisoner's direction, listening for his answer. Thank the Goddess he doesn't keep me waiting. Too bad he's still being difficult. Good thing I had already planned on killing him.

"Fuck. You." His head turns toward Ansel as he pants out his reply.

Not that he can see him with both his eyes swollen shut—the skin around his eyes black and blue. Blood pouring from his many wounds, soaking through what's left of his garments.

I turn around in time to see the dumb fuck pull his head back and spit blood in Ansel's direction. The bright red wad landing on his boot. Ansel makes a sound of disgust from low in his throat and he bares his teeth at the fool. His jaw ticking as he visibly works to hold himself back. Ansel looks from the blood and then up to the guard's disfigured face, taking a threatening step toward him, finally losing the fight with his control.

Bellicent steps up behind the beaten, pulling his head back violently. "Since he doesn't want to talk, maybe I could play with him a little, possibly take his tongue instead." Her claws protract with her remark, dragging one down his throat, and he visibly shivers at the contact.

"Get your filthy hands off me, shifter bitch!"

Much to his dismay, she remains unaffected by his outburst, merely laughing. To some, she may seem to enjoy herself—the taunting and the pain. However, her dark onyx eyes show you what she hides so well. Fear. Regret... Guilt.

I've had enough of this one's mouth. I would rather round up a new set of prisoners to take my anger out on.

Stepping forward, I invade his personal space, roughly grabbing hold of his chin. His eyes narrow... *well, at least I'm sure they would if his face still had the ability to move, that is.*

The guard to our left finally rouses enough to remember where he is. *Though I have no idea how the dumb fuck could forget.* He jerks his chains as if to get away. I slant my eyes in his direction and he simmers down, a whimper leaving his lips.

"I think I've had enough of your mouth, being that what I want to know hasn't come out of it." My eyes roll back to the asshole dangling in front of me. The dispassionate words leaving my lips devoid of emotion.

"You can fuck right the fuc__" his eye bug-out as I cut off his words, forcing fire down his throat slowly, being sure to control the flame. To make it hurt and when he takes his last breath, it's my face he sees.

My focus shifts to the last guard suspended from the ceiling, his injuries minimal compared to the others. He looks up at me, His shifty eyes brimming with fear. His toes shuffle along the dirt floor, trying to find purchase to relieve the pressure on his wrist. Wherever he finds in my gaze has him quickly averts his eyes in hope I won't give him my full attention.

In five steps, I'm standing in front of him, my boots becoming the only thing he can see. I reach down, grabbing a hand full of his hair, pulling his head back roughly, forcing him to look at me. When he tries to pull away yet again, I tighten my hold on him, making a show of looking around the room littered with bodies before bringing my eyes back to his.

"I won't lie to you. You're dead either way. But how much pain you experience is entirely up to you..." I trail off, once again looking around the room. This time I feel him follow my gaze, taking in the room. A shaky breath leaves him in a rush.

"What say you? Quick or painful?" I smile broadly, flashing my fangs at him. When he jerks out of my grip, I laugh. Admittedly, somewhat manically. I feel the fight leave him on a heavy breath.

"Is my wife alive?"

The whole room tenses as we all wait on bated breath for the answer that could very well break me. He doesn't answer with words, just nods his head once. After a moment of contemplation, speaks.

"She's being held in one of the diplomatic rooms in the heart of the palace... She's alive, though I'm sure she wishes she wasn't. On the days she displeases the King, she ends up strapped to the whipping post in the center of the courtyard..." The words said so quietly I barely hear them. But hear them I do. "Which is more often than not, it seems. She fights him at every turn. It's been some years since she's been publicly beaten. He claims he can beat the 'tainted blood from her.' Other days, she's expected to act like the princess he raised her to be." A flick of my wrist has a cascade of blood falls from his throat, pooling at my feet. The thin hidden blade returning to the loaded leather wrist-sheath attached to my forearm.

She's alive... This is the first news we've manage to get out of that cursed court. A painful breath leaves my lungs, as a piece of me unwinds with that knowledge.

I've been in a constant state of worry knowing she was back

there reliving her childhood abuse. That it would somehow break her this time around.

But to hear she's fighting... settles something in of me. Though I really shouldn't have expected anything less of my headstrong wife.

My heart says this is a good thing, while my mind is filled with dread. How long can she truly keep that up for before it all becomes too much?

Either way, Kól is a dead man! And when I get my hands on him, his death will be slow and painful.

"She's alive. This is good news, Asher." Ansel points out, laying a heavy hand on my shoulder.

Which I quickly shake off. It's his fault she's there in that fucking place. I don't care that he was following orders.

He never would have left me behind, no matter what I told him. The only reason he left me at the barrier in Naphal was because I forced him out. *So I ask, What I'm I supposed to think?*

"Is it?... How broken will she be when we get to her?" I ask him through clinch teeth, a snarl on my lips.

I watch remorse cloud his features. But I care very little for his guilt. His brown hair hangs listlessly around his face and his skin is too tight for his features, making his cheekbones sharper—almost jagged. Purple crescents mare the skin below his eyes. As Devany would say, *'It's all in the eyes'*, Ansel's copper gaze has lost their shine.

My eyes cut from him to Bellicent, standing near the entrance. "Dump these bodies at the border. Be sure to leave them in a place they'll be found. Then round us up a few more, higher up on the food chain this time. Happy hunting." Her eyes dart between the two of us, worrying her bottom lip like she used to do when we were kids. Likely wanting to say something, but with a solemn nod, she leaves us behind. It truly isn't fair of us to put her in the middle.

That damn drip of water echoing off the stone walls is loud in the sudden silence.

Ansel and Kane stand quietly in the space. Neither of them speaks, awaiting on orders. Or maybe they're just trying to be in the moment with me, to lessen this hallow feeling.

I just can't.

I head for the door, unable to bear one more moment in this cell. The walls feeling like they're closing in.

"Asher." I don't reply. I just keep walking, heading up the stairs. I need a fucking minute to process. Alone.

I've only just closed the door when Narcissa turns the corner, walking down the beautifully carved hall, lanterns tucked into niches along the wall. The floors turning from rough stone to painted tiles. A sharp and bright contrast to the cells below.

She heads my way and if the look on her face is anything to go by, I won't be getting that break anytime soon. I stop a few meters from the door leading to the dungeon, letting her come to me.

With calm, confident strides, she heads straight to me. A plethora of small braids piled high on her head, a few hanging loose, framing her face. The rich umber of her skin darker in the low lighting of the hall. Sam's imposing frame hot on her trail. His eyepatch reflecting the lantern light, the black leather standing out against his lighter skin. His short blonde hair slicked back from his face.

From the look of determination in their eyes, they must have once again made contact with their spy network within Kól's palace. With any luck, they have actionable information.

"They've upped their slave convoys." She states by way of greeting. Her shoulders back and head held high, every ounce the commander she is.

The sound of the dungeon doors opening behind me cuts off what I was about to say. "Asher we need to__" Kane's words stop abruptly and I can practically feel the breath he takes. His body going preternaturally still when he spots Narcissa standing before me.

I don't turn to acknowledge him, simply giving her my full attention. "What do you suggest?"

"I think we should start hitting the convoys. Save these people before they can be sold and lost. It also has the added benefit of hitting him and his traders in the pocketbook." Just one more layer in this fight, but she's not wrong.

"Did you get anything?" Her voice is suddenly soft and hesitant. I don't need her to elaborate.

I ball my fist, reopening the wounds along my knuckles.

"They confirmed she's alive, but you probably knew that before I did if your spy chain has been reestablished."

She shakes her head. "No, they've caught glimpses, but not long enough for them to ascertain her state. Many of them ran after Devany's capture."

I nod my head, realizing they must be terrified now that Kól has Devany under his thumb again.

I should have done a better job protecting her.

"I agree with your assessment. Hit the convoys." I state, needing to concentrate on the things I can control.

A wave of emotion sweeps over me. Sadness. Fear. Anger. My body swaying with the force of it.

I need to get the fuck out of here.

Putting one foot in front of the other, I close the distance between me and Narcissa. "And you'll take Kane." I command as I push past her and Sam.

As I turn the corner, I hear her say. "I don't need a fucking babysitter!" Which almost brings a small smile to my face. For two women who don't share blood, they're an awful lot alike.

Made in the USA
Columbia, SC
17 August 2024

40166009R00217